CW00485222

HEADACHES & HAUNTINGS

An ordinary girl. An extraordinary life

CHRISSIE HERON

In the beginning ....

1965 – 5 years old

When I was little my father asked me 'who I was talking to?'

I was sitting on the steps at the entrance to our tenement building, playing with my dolls and pram. Billy McMeekin would come and sit with me. Billy loved to play football with the bigger boys across the street, but not now. He just sat in silence with me, watching the other lads have fun. He was in my class at primary school, but I hadn't seen him for weeks, his desk in the corner of the classroom lay empty. Billy was the same age as me, a chubby wee boy who always wore his Sunday best clothes when he came to sit beside me, being so young this never struck me as odd. He would sit with me on the outside steps waiting on his father coming back from work. Once he arrived, Billy would just vanish.

My father towered over me. 'I said who are you talking to girl?'

'Just Billy daddy.' I said whilst I looked up at the giant figure of my father standing above me.

'Billy who?' he asked.

'Billy McMeekin daddy.' I replied sheepishly.

Before I knew it, I was being dragged by the arm into the building and slapped not once but twice across the back of my thighs. The first slap caught me by surprise, the second smack was excruciating and stung for the rest of the evening. I was only 5 years old; it wasn't my earliest memory, but it was the first time I had been struck by my father and I never, ever forgot it. It became one of my many life defining memories.

Once inside our second-floor tenement flat I was summoned by my father to the sitting area in the kitchen, I reached out to my mother, she would give me the cuddles I needed. As I whimpered and cried my mother sat on her chair, legs crossed with a cigarette in her hand. She shook her head and said nothing, a look of disappointment etched on her face as my father verbally assaulted me. He stood in front of me with a rolled-up newspaper in his hand, he was a man of little words, the message was simple.

'Stop embarrassing the family and stop looking for attention, do you hear me girl?' I heard him loud and clear. I was to stop talking to the dead.

Billy McMeekin had died from an asthma attack the month before. He lived with his parents and grandparents above us on the third floor of our tenement. A distraught and brokenhearted Mrs. McMeekin had her boy buried in his best Sunday suit. Back then, I had no idea what it meant to be dead.

My name is Catherine Morag Jamieson, but everyone calls me Cat. Ever since I can remember I have been able to see and communicate with the dead.

I want to set the record straight right from the outset as the psychic world can be a little confusing. I can't see into the future; I am not a fortune teller. I don't use a crystal ball, palmistry, or tarot cards to predict your future. I'm not a psychic, like a clairvoyant, they use their abilities to give you an insight into the future. A psychic can read into your future, but a medium communicates with the dead. I am best described as a psychic medium; I speak directly to a spirit who wants to deliver a message to a loved one or pass information onto someone else. I am the conduit between the physical world and the spiritual world, I see and speak to the dead the same way I communicate with the living around me.

During my lifetime, my name and reputation will become synonymous with murder investigations and paranormal television. Before I reach my 30th birthday I will be the biggest celebrity psychic medium in the world, quite a feat for a young lassie from Glasgow who left school at 15 without a single qualification! My life has been one hell of a ride, a roller-coaster of emotions, great heartache and more twist and turns than Lombard Street in San Francisco. The freak show which is my life was to take me on a journey from humble beginnings to unimaginable wealth.

Despite incredible fame and fortune my search for privacy and contentment would become a never-ending journey, a destination I never found although I desperately ached for it. Throughout my life, I was forever on the move, different homes, separate locations, different people. My unique ability, to see and communicate with the dead was once described by scientists as

'Outwith scientific law and explanation.' and 'Outside normal sensory channels.'

I was observed by doctors, scientists, professors, and other eminent professionals who all tried to explain my psychic ability. Despite all the tests, recording and compiling of data no one could answer the one simple question. 'How does she do it ?' I was a phenomenon. Science is powerful and there is very little it can't explain, but when science can't explain what it hears and see's it will try and prove it doesn't exist. I could not be explained.

I was regularly interviewed by the press who called me a freak of nature, beyond explanation, a charlatan, a con artist, a liar, and a trickster and so it goes on. I have been called many names, but I much prefer to be called Cat.

For me, my ability to converse with the dead and see the spirit manifest before my eyes was never odd or the least bit strange. I have never known any other way. I see full body apparitions in the same way I see the living around me. Spirits can appear several times a day or sometimes just a few times a week. It would depend on the circumstances, where I was and who I was with. I am unable to hide from these indiscriminate spirits, they appear randomly and without an invitation and I am never given any warning. Spirits appear anywhere and at any time, some are incredibly vocal, and others are shy but all of them have one thing in common, they have a message to deliver or unfinished business they need me to attend to. My life was dominated by them, twenty-four hours a day, they woke me up, they interrupted conversations and generally disrupted my day with their no filter approach. Like a petulant child, they demanded to be heard. This was no Hollywood movie, this was fact, this was my life, day in and day out. From an early age I had to learn to live and walk with the dead. My ability to communicate and help set a spirit free has taken its toll on me both mentally and physically.

In my experience, most spirits do not want to move on. Normally the spirit of the deceased wants to stay with their family or remain in the property they lived in before death, eternally going through the day-to-day tasks they would normally have done when they were alive. By the time I have contacted them they are normally in a confused state, not realising they can move on, get out of wherever they are trapped and transcend to a higher level.

Over the years I suffered from horrendous headaches and lengthy bouts of anxiety. As a teenager, I was allowed days off school where I stayed in my bedroom with the blinds and curtains drawn, much to the envy of my brother and sister who were shuffled off to school in all weathers. My mother would write a note to the schoolteachers telling them I was ill due to bad period pain; it was never questioned by the teaching staff even though my absences would occur several times a month. I was an easy target for those who liked to gossip. Locals spoke about me from an early age and once my reputation in the area increased so did the bullying. I had just a few friends, not everyone wanted to play or associate with me, mainly because no one knew what to expect. My behaviour was erratic as spirits would come and join me and I would start to communicate with them. Strange conduct at the best of times and I do appreciate some people were frightened by this. I was so conscious of everything that was going on around me forever waiting on the dead joining me for a conversation, much to the dismay of friends I may have been with at the time. I found it almost impossible to ignore their presence. One minute I was chatting with friends and the next minute I looked like I was talking to myself. I would strike up a conversation with wayward spirits despite no one else being able to see or hear them, except me. I was aware of their presence, and I was not prepared to ignore them. I can't tell you how many parents had come to our family home over the years to complain to my parents about me terrifying their child because I had spoken to a loved one who had died in their family. It freaked people out, it wasn't something I was aware I was doing. People are terrified of the paranormal. I can recall being accosted in the street by individuals I never knew telling me what they thought of me, calling me all sorts of names, and generally making life quite miserable for me. Freak, witch, weirdo, evil, I've heard it all. Sometimes I am more fearful of the living than I am of the dead!

I have messages to deliver, I am the conduit between the dead and the living but not everyone wants to hear what I have to say. I convey the messages, good and bad. Many people have suggested what I have to say is just a figment of my imagination, I am attention seeking, or simply a fraudster. When it suited the community, I was gifted and praised by everyone, but disappoint them and I was fodder for their side stabbing remarks. It made no difference what I had to say, I was dammed if I said it and I was dammed if I didn't!

When I was nine years old, I was given a diary as a birthday gift, it had a little lock and key and a picture of a horse on the hard-front cover, I adored my diary. It became my confidante; I could record my spiritual encounters and experiences in private and without any interruptions. I devotedly wrote about my life every day, recording my emotions and feelings. I would sit in bed at night and write, lost deep in the enjoyment of recording my daily adventures. When finished I closed the cover over and secured the lock with the tiny key. Locking away my secret world from prying eyes. Later in life, I wrote my diary whenever I felt the need, in the morning, throughout the day, in bed at night. Simply putting pen to paper was my guilty pleasure. I loved my secret companion, my little book of personal and precious thoughts. From that very first diary, over the years I moved on and enjoyed writing a daily journal. I wrote every day of my life. I recorded my ideas, my thoughts, my feelings. It was my friend when I had no one else to talk to and a companion when nobody was around. I would vent my anger and frustrations, page after page. Afterwards, I loved to look back at my work and reflect on events or encounters. As I grew older and found myself alone and thoughtful, I would flick through the pages of old journals, popping in and out of my life, enjoying the written snap shots from the past. Basking in page upon page of written memories, my penned photographs.

At my lowest point, my writing was therapeutic, it helped reduce my anxiety and stress levels. I enjoyed writing to myself, recording the good and the bad and being honest. My diary became my best friend and more importantly, I was able to recall and document the many conversations I had over the years with the spirits who introduced themselves to me. These lost souls, many of whom had no idea they were dead, possessed so much energy and character, I felt the need to document our conversations. There was to be no unfilled white pages in my diaries as I had so much to say. Later in my life, there was to be no privacy. My diaries would be exposed and disclosed for all to see. If I feared my privacy, I would never have committed so much to my journals, but you can't live life in fear of what may or may not happen. Ironically, for someone who sought privacy, I became an open book for all to see and analyze.

Based on my many, personal, and frank journals over the years, this is my story.

CHAPTER ONE
THE BEGINNING

1960 – 1969

We all have memories of our childhood, they carve out the path towards who we are, they mould your character and personality. Our memories should evoke moments of fondness, happier times, growing up surrounded by family and friends, little girls playing with their dolls and prams and boys playing football in the back yard or in the street, knees covered in mud. Boys using their sweaters for goal posts, rolling in the grass oblivious to how their mother would remove the grass stains from their trousers. Back in the 'good old days' when the summer school break seemed to last forever, and it felt like the sun shone every day. Childhood is a time when lasting memories are formed, the time you went on family holidays or when your baby brother or sister was born and suddenly you were no longer the youngest member of the family, or simply pleasant recollections from the street you were brought up on.

In the early sixties everyone knew each other in our street. We looked out for one another just like one big family, neighbours looking after neighbours and siblings looking after each other. Our tenement building was like one big house, four storeys high with three families living on each landing. The families of the tenement shared two outside toilets between them, sometimes there was over fifty people in each building. Despite the cramped living conditions, the women of the tenement kept the internal building and toilets clean and tidy. A large wooden thread bobbin was passed through your letter box when it was your turn to clean the outhouse and stairs, once done you then passed the bobbin onto the other neighbours and so it went on. I remember spending time at night cutting squares out of newspaper and piercing them on a hook to be used as toilet paper. Soft toilet roll was a luxury we never experienced.

My mother use to hide in our neighbours' house when the rent man came calling. He would bang on the door and shout through the letter box. Dad got paid on a Thursday and sometimes there was no more money left by the time the rent man came calling after the weekend. I can see my mother now, hiding behind the heavy front door, in silence, waiting for the rent man to go away. The door would remain firmly closed until he left the building and was out of sight along the street. A wee Jewish man came round every week giving out 'tic' money to those who needed it. The women hid this from their husbands as the repayment rate was incredibly high and the last thing these families needed was more debt. The 'tic man' frightened me as he was accompanied by the spirit of a man who terrified me. I would hide behind my mother when he came to the door to collect his money. Thankfully, dad put an end to him loaning money to my mother. He paid him off one night when the horrible little man turned up at our house to collect and dad answered the door. He wasn't expecting the mouthful he got from my father and was sent on his way with his tail between his legs. He never came back to our door again, but he was a regular in the street. Most families relied on him to get through the week.

My father was the patriarch of the household, and my mother was the homemaker. Despite the faults in the building, and the state of disrepair, my mother kept a lovely home. Unlike other flats in the tenement, mum kept our home spick and span, rarely anything was out of place. Even the rat traps were hidden behind furniture as my mother was so house proud. If they were out of sight they were out of mind. It was dad's job to empty the traps in the back-alley bins, mother refused to even look at the dead rodents. I can still hear the noise of the traps snap shut and the rat scurrying to release itself late at night when we were in bed. I kept my arms under the covers for fear one might climb up the side of the bed and bite me. They never did.

Religion, well, it never existed in our home! I don't think it existed in our street. The only god we had was the new God of Housing, the newly developed housing corporation who had promised social housing for everyone. My mother prayed to him on a regular basis and regularly visited his office.

My mother and father were just an ordinary working-class couple, childhood sweethearts who like many others came from the same town, went to the same school, knew the same people, and had the same dreams. Bill and Maureen Jamieson both came from solid, traditional families. Loved as babies and brought up saying please and thank you. Mother had never dated anyone else except my dad. They would have had less problems in their marriage if she had not married the first guy she met. My dad, was an engineer at Thomson Pumps, following in the footsteps of his father. Back then, it was a natural progression to leave school and start an apprenticeship with the same employer as your father. Thomson Pumps employed a lot of men locally and the salary was decent. Jobs were abundant and apprenticeships for young school leavers were plentiful. It left little to the imagination and no real effort to find employment. You finished school, you started an apprenticeship, you met a local girl, you started courting and you got married and had children. The cycle continued. My mother and father got engaged in the summer and were married by the winter of the same year.

I was born on 12th November 1960, the fourth child of Bill and Maureen Jamieson. According to my mother I was a month early and took everyone by surprised when I decided to make an appearance. Mum would often regale us all with stories about how small I was when I was born, 5lbs 11 ounces, and yet I could scream loud enough to waken the whole house when I wanted fed. Those who met me would comment on my striking blue eyes, piercing and hypnotic. My brother and sisters had hazel eyes and dark brown hair as did my father, my mothers were green, and her hair was peroxide blond. With my thick red hair and blue eyes, I stood out from everyone, I was different even then. For many years I was led to believe I was born in the sitting room of my grandmother's house as my mother's labor was short and swift. The midwife had been called but there was a heavy fog that evening, and she was unable to find the house in time to help with my delivery, so I was born under the watchful eye of my gran who cut my umbilical cord and wrapped me in a white crocheted shawl. My makeshift cot was a large wooden bottom drawer, it had been pulled out and lined with towels and a shawl. I slept in this for a week until dad acquired a cot. Neighbours rallied round with bits and pieces for the newborn. Gran was given hand me down baby clothing. She knitted cardigans and booties and crocheted a pram cover and shawls. In time these too would be handed down to another newborn. Nothing was disposed of back then; it was used until it fell apart or it was passed from family to family in the tenement.

Often, the culture that existed within the tenement building was one of generosity and hope. Families lived so near each other it was almost like living in the same house. We all shared the common entrance and stairway access up to the fourth floor. Despite the thickness of the sandstone, you could hear much of what went on in the building. Every argument echoed throughout, babies crying, and alarms going off, you heard it all. These sounds were part of the very framework of the tenement, there was rarely complete silence. The tenement was one big living organism, each family inexplicably related simply by being part of the infrastructure and architecture.

My gran on my father's side, who everyone knew as Granny D. was an avid knitter and was able to knit small newborn cardigans in less than an hour, followed by mittens, woollen booties and hats, any spare wool was used for pom-poms to adorn knitted hats. She lived directly across the cobbled street in another tenement building, had done most of her wedded life. She was a hard woman and even in her fifties was no one's fool. She was as tough as old boots and had lived a dreadful life with her husband, Grandpa Tam. He was a drinker, a gambler, and a womaniser. She had once beat up my grandfather's mistress in the street after he had taken his wages and spent some of it on a bottle of perfume for his lady friend. When gran found out he was with her, she was livid. She dragged all five of her children, three of them in a massive silver cross pram, down to the local pub. As the children waited outside (this wasn't an uncommon site outside a Glasgow pub in the 50's), she stormed into the bar area, slapped my grandfather's face, and dragged his lady friend from her chair out into the street. She assaulted the woman by slapping her repeatedly on the face and pulled out clumps of her hair. Granny D was a formidable character and not to be messed with. She lived with us at one point when grandpa died. She hated him so much she left him to die in bed after a suspected heart attack.

'Those fags will kill you some day, hopefully soon.' Gran would shout when he would go into coughing fits and spit green phloem into her shiny clean Belfast sink.

The sixty cigarettes a day most certainly did help kill him but to be sure Granny D left him alone in his bedroom and ignored his cries for help as he slowly and painfully died in his bed. To drown out his moaning she had played her Bush radio throughout the day and late at night. When the house went silent, she kept his bedroom door closed for two days. On the third day, my father had called in on his way home from work and discovered grandpa dead in his bed. Granny D showed no remorse or any emotion at the loss of her husband, in fact she seemed relieved. When the funeral director arrived, he insisted the police were called, 'just to eliminate any suspicious circumstances.' The arrival of the police in the street had all the neighbours desperate to know what was going on. Granny D told a bemused police constable.

'He smoked 60 fags a day and drank whisky like a fish and still thought he could shag every slapper in the town, it was more like suicide than murder, don't you think?' Gran told the police she knew he was dead when she could smell the distinct odor of his decomposing body coming from the bedroom. She was taken to the police station; gave her version of events and was released without charge. After the postmortem, a death certificate was issued. It confirmed he died from pulmonary embolus due to acute myocardial infarction. Gran let it be known to all and sundry he had died from syphilis. She had a wicked sense of humor and giggled at the thought of his many lovers hearing the news!

Being the youngest my brother and sisters kept an eye out for me. Margaret was 14 years my senior, Mary, 8 years, and Billy 5 years. Despite the age differences we were close knit and had each other's back. From an early age I was drawn to Margaret more than my mother. My instinct was to run to Margaret if I needed to be consoled or cuddled. She in turn was the first to see to my needs before my parents. Margaret never questioned my ability to speak to the dead, she was open minded and allowed me to participate in the many conversations I had at night with Agnes, an old woman who had died in the flat many years before it became our home. Old Agnes died from TB. Margaret, Mary, and Billy, would lie in bed at night and listen to me converse with her. Often, she would have the energy to move items in the room, this terrified Billy, but confirmed Agnes's existence to the others. All four of us siblings shared a bedroom in the tenement flat whilst mum and dad had the recess bed next door in the kitchenette. At night, Margaret, Mary, and I would snuggle up in our double bed whilst Billy had a small single bed underneath the large sash window. His bed was pulled out from the inside wall to avoid the damp getting on his bedding. I have wonderful memories of my sisters reading to me in bed, the small headboard light gave the cold bedroom a little glow of warmth. Mum would come in at night and tuck the bed covers tight under Billy's mattress before kissing him good night. Margaret, Mary, and I were blown a kiss by mum before the bedroom door was closed for the night.

One evening Mary had me provoke the spirit of a man I had seen in the stairwell, I tried to summon him many times, my relentless attempts to reach him concluded when a loud growl was heard in the bedroom. Margaret shut down the conversation right away and we went to sleep with the bedside light on.

Margaret protected me from the outside world, she got to know my friends and allowed only those with good intent into my circle. She only wanted me to experience genuine friendship and not be damaged by those who wanted to befriend me for the wrong reasons. As far as Margaret was concerned, I was to be nobody's stooge; I was no-one's entertainment. Margaret was there for me when my parents were not. Being the youngest, it was often thought I was spoilt but nothing was further from the truth, more love and attention was given to the other siblings, I got what was left. I found out later in life why this was. I was never happier unless I was the center of attention and this is where Margaret indulged me,listening intently as I 'blethered' and rambled on relentlessly with exaggerated stories wrapped in silly harmless lies, mainly about discovering fairies at the bottom of the garden, or being followed home from school by puppy dogs and of course the many dead people I would talk to. All innocent and believable to a 6-year-old, after all Billy McMeekin was my witness!

As a family we made our own entertainment. At home,

In the evening, normally on dad's night off, I would put on mini displays for the family. Perfecting dance routines as I pretended to be a ballerina, twirling around on my toes with one of my mother's scarves as a prop. Margaret would clear a space in the center of the parlor which designated my stage. I would perform imaginary magic tricks to my thrilled captive audience. I just loved this family time, all of us together, laughing and singing to Nancy Sinatra, 'Those Boots Are Made for Walkin,' The Beach Boys, 'Barbara Ann' Petula Clark and Dusty Springfield, to name but a few. These were the good times, dad, mum, Margaret, Mary, Billy, and I making memories that would last a lifetime or so I thought.

I missed Margaret dreadfully when she left home in 1967 to study nursing. She stayed in the nurse's home which was only a few miles away but to me it was like she had moved to the other end of the country. I missed her so very much. At first, she would come by the flat several times a week when her shifts and studies allowed it. She would always go out her way to cuddle me and bring us all a bag of sherbet lemons or sour plooms. Just having her back in the flat, made me incredibly content. I missed her so much. It was about this time I started suffering from separation anxiety. With Margaret gone from the house, I struggled to sleep at night, I would cry in bed and Mary would try and console me, but it never felt quite the same. Margaret spoke to me in private about the apparitions and my conversations with the spirits of the dead. Mum and Dad would have been furious if they heard us, it was a taboo subject around the house. Margaret never questioned my authenticity or implied I was lying. Instead, she encouraged me and reminded me that I should use my gift wisely and never abuse it. She insisted I was discreet and warned me what others would do if they found out. For now, I had to learn to be careful.

When I told my mother, I had seen 'ghosts' she would simply shake her head and change the conversation.

'Stop being silly Catherine, just stop it, you'll frighten Billy.' Mum would say.

God help me if dad heard my stories. He was less sympathetic and forbid anyone talking about my 'gift'.

Both mum and dad were having none of it, but Granny D was more open to my revelations and the detailed conversations I could have with the dead. She was further convinced of my psychic ability when we were alone one afternoon, and I had a visit from her dead sister. We were sitting in her scullery kitchen and a Robin appeared at the open window, and just then her younger sister, Betty appeared. She was standing by the window, dressed in a white communion dress with a lace veil that covered her face.

'Betty is here.' I said with much excitement about a woman who died before I had been born. I described the young girl who was standing in front of me, and I recalled the horrific events that led up to her death, the candle, the curtains catching fire, the smoke, the door was locked, the flames, the choking, her dying. Her appearance was both disturbing and emotional. It was the one and only time I saw Granny D cry.

I only encountered a few malevolent spirits as a child, these angry entities frightened me. One, was a little boy called Henry, about 12 years old. His family had died in a fire, many years ago, on the top floor. He was from a family of five originally from Ireland who all lost their lives from smoke inhalation and were found huddled together in the bedroom. A portable paraffin heater they had in the hallway had toppled over and set fire to a rug. They were unable to get out of the front door due to the intense heat and the flames forced them back into the bedroom to certain death. Someone smashed the window, but the fall alone would have killed you. The broken window was engulfed with flames and their desperate screams for help could be heard by everyone. Nothing could be done to save them, not even the men from the street who raced to help, the heat was savage, and the flames scorched the body, all attempts to rescue the family were doomed to fail. The fire services could not save them. The burnt-out apartment was never renovated but stood as a warning to all, never leave a paraffin fire unattended or in an area it can topple over. Their top floor flat was boarded up and remained empty.

When Henry, the young son appeared to me, he was terribly thin with black smoke rings around his mouth and nose. He locked me in the outside toilet, my cries for help went unheard for some time. Another time he bit me on the arm and pushed me down some stairs. He was a nasty piece of work, always up to no good. I knew he was the cause of several falls by neighbours on the stairs and noises in the night. I knew he was around when I could smell burning.

'Can you smell smoke and burning Billy?' I asked one wet afternoon when we had been confined to the flat. Without taking his eyes off the images in his comic Billy sniffed the air and looked up.

'Yes!' he said, running through to the parlor to be with the other family members. Even he was frightened from Henry.

It was confirmation I wasn't going insane. Later, in my life, when the flats were being prepared for demolition, I wondered if Henry, remained imbedded in the groundwork of the land, causing havoc, haunting the new tenants because he was unwilling or unable to cross over. I hoped not as he deserved to find a forever resting place rather than continuing his miserable search for a home he would never find.

Our tenement building was due to be demolished and we had been promised a brand-new home in one of the new towns being built on the outskirts of town. My father's engineering company was relocating to New Weston, one of the townships that had been created to accommodate the overspill of thousands of people from the city. A new house had been allocated for the family. The money the company was saving by relocating to a rent-free factory had afforded dad a pay rise, enough to invest in a family car. In the summer of 1969, two days after man landed on the moon, dad picked up his new car, an Austin 1100 . It was secondhand but looked brand new to us. Mother was over the moon with the introduction of a car into the household.

She did not like travelling on public transport and saw a car as something of a status symbol, which it was back then.

Dad was hoping the fresh start would settle my mother. She was forever restless and would regularly scream at my father in resentment. She blamed him for our life, our accommodation, venting her frustrations at him for her miserable life stuck in a damp, cramped flat. A dwelling place which was not fit for purpose, where rats were commonplace, and dampness was everywhere. There were no amenities or safe areas for the children to play, just condemned flats and wasteland. Gossip was a pastime amongst the woman in the street. Mother hated idle chit chat, and never joined the other wives outside the local corner shop or out on the street. Her delusions of grandeur irritated the other woman and often mum became the subject of the conversations. Her demand for a better life put my father under a great deal of pressure. Mother craved a twin tub washing machine, but there was not enough water pressure coming into the building to have one, so mother and Granny D washed the family's clothes by hand in the 2 massive Belfast sinks in the parlor. Pulling the soaking wet clothes though the ACME mangle positioned between the sinks then hanging the clothes out to dry at the rear of the building. Tenement life was tough, sharing a toilet, no bath, no hot running water, or central heating. The only upside of tenement life was the great sense of community and the fact everyone was in the same predicament. Now we knew we were moving house; it couldn't come fast enough.

October 1969 – Four weeks before we moved house.

Granny D did not get on with my mother, she just tolerated her. Mother reminded gran of my grandfather's many mistresses. My mother had a thing for the men, she would disappear for weeks on end and Granny D and Margaret would look after the family, prepare the meals, and complete the daily chores. Mary, Billy, and I accepted dad's explanation about mum going to visit a sick family member in Ireland, that is until I overheard Granny D and dad talking about mum one night in the parlor when I should have been tucked up in bed. The parlor door had been left ajar and I could see gran pulling on her jacket and adjusting her head scarf. Dad was sitting bent over the dinner table, he had his hands on his head and a Players cigarette burning away between his fingers. He looked upset. They were both talking about mum and the married man she was with. Gran was speaking as if this was a regular occurrence. Mum had 'gone to Ireland' maybe once, twice before but I had no idea this was code for her running off with men!

Mother had been gone for some time, perhaps a month, it might have been longer. We were due to move house shortly, our new life, our fresh start. Beyond the door, dad was confiding in gran, blaming himself for her leaving, but gran was having none of it.

'It's my fault she's gone off with another man, I'm never here!' Dad blamed himself.

'Don't be so stupid Bill! She doesn't know how bloody lucky she is, she's a selfish cow!' Gran would have been happy if mother never came back, it would have given her control of the house and possibly the opportunity to move in and take care of the family. She continued to remind dad, he was a good, hardworking man, a good father, a good husband, it was his wife who had to change and not him. Dad was defending our mother, he wanted her back where she belonged, with her husband and family. His revelation irritated gran, but she knew it was pointless to go on. Bill would always side with Maureen

He had a plan to get mum back home, he was coming off the night shift and was going to be around the home more, it was the best way to raise the kids and keep an eye on mum. I could see by my father's face he had been worn down by grans relentless criticism of my mother. Grans tough upbringing meant she took no prisoners even when it came to her daughter in law, but even Gran knew when to give up.

Dad was a chain smoker and had lit another cigarette before the last one had burnt down. He sucked the smoke deep into his lungs before releasing it into the smoked filled room.

'She blames herself for what happened to Margaret!' spurted Dad. Gran finished the conversation abruptly.

'No one must ever know, except you me, Margaret and that bitch, you call a wife, understand me, now drop it, Bill!'

What did she mean? What didn't we know ? What were they hiding? At that moment I heard the front door open, it was Margaret. I snuck back into the bedroom and quickly got under the covers. It took me a while to get to sleep as grans words kept going around my head.

'No one must ever know! – know what?' I was going to ask Margaret in the morning. When did my mother have the time to start an affair, arranging illicit meetings and between them form a plan to disappear, run off like love struck teenagers? She a married woman and her lover a married man? Dad was too soft with my mother she could get away with almost anything with him. He didn't stand up to her despite gran telling him to be 'tougher with her!' but this was not in my dads' character. To him my mother was fragile, complicated, and beautiful and did not know what she was doing. She had the ability to humiliate my father in a few sentences. Despite his tough demeanor and his six-foot two frame, dad was not strong enough to tell her to STOP! He was too afraid of the consequences. Apparently, my mother's philandering had been a major issue in their marriage, and she had always managed to deflect the problem back to dad. Rightly or wrongly, he loved our mother and would forgive her many infidelities. It was a long running scenario, mum got bored, dad worked long and unsocial hours. She would turn to other men to fill the physical and emotional void. The affairs never lasted long, my mother was high maintenance and extremely demanding. A narcissist, it was all about her. Once the man's money ran out, or she had lost interest, she came home, and dad welcomed her back with open arms and a sympathetic ear.

Woman cheat on their husbands more than we think it's not exclusively a male dominated sport. Mother used the excuse that she felt neglected and was bored, she grumbled dad wasn't about a lot, he was working or sleeping. The fact is she cheated on my father because she got away with it. He took her back every time! Dad loved her unconditionally. Despite the screaming and the fighting and the threats deep down she must have cared for him at some point. It wasn't so easy in the sixties to get up and walk out on your marriage with four children, you made your bed, you lay in it. Plus, my mother was work shy. She only ever had one job, working in a chemist as a counter assistant, hardly taxing, until she married my father and she never worked again.

My father had the patience of a saint, he probably could have had any number of women as a wife but had chosen my self-absorbed, egotistical mother.

Dad had one goal, to keep the family together and gain my mother's approval. He was working long hours so he could provide a better life for his family away from the appalling living conditions in the tenement, which through no fault of our own we had found ourselves in. Our brand-new home was on the horizon. New opportunities beckoned. The question was,

was mum coming with us?

The atmosphere of our home was defined by how my mother was feeling. If she were down, we all got to know about it, and we would walk eggshells around her until she decided we had all been punished enough, especially dad. Nothing would get done and she would spend the day in bed, demanding silence in the house. She would take codeine and drink cheap tonic wine which left her comatose or aggressive. Margaret and dad tried to intervene and offer help, but she would not seek any medical treatment. Over the years, we all learned to stay away from her when she was in one of her moods. Later in life she was diagnosed with a bipolar disorder.

During her manic episodes mum was either on a high, the life and soul of the party. Laughing, singing, and smiling she would be reckless and impulsive, craving attention and confirmation that she was still beautiful and desirable. But when she was low, it was best to stay well away from her as her tongue was so sharp, she would have cut you in two.

CHAPTER 2

My 9th Birthday.

My nineth birthday was memorable for several reasons. Margaret gave me a diary as a birthday gift, this was to be the start of my obsession with documenting my life, every day without exception.

First diary entry - Wednesday 12th November 1969

I don't know whether to be happy or sad, one minute I am happy because Margaret has bought me this fantastic gift , my very first diary and I love it so much and the next minute I am sad because mum has come back and everything in the house has changed because she is here. I enjoyed it more when she wasn't here, I prefer having Margaret and gran looking after us. Why did she need to come back? It's all about her, it's my birthday but she wants to be the one who is the center of attention.

My mother returned on my ninth birthday; she was in the flat when I got home from school. I immediately felt overwhelmed with disappointment, she was playing the dutiful mother and wife, taking the credit for the small buffet of sandwiches and sausage rolls gran prepared and laid out on the dining table. She lit the candles on the cake Margaret had bought and began singing 'Happy Birthday to you …'. Prompting the others to follow. It all seemed surreal. She had been gone over two months and now she was back, parading around the room like nothing had happened. No explanations or apology. Looking immaculate in her capri pants and gingham shirt. The room stunk of Je Reviens perfume, which was ironic as the name in French translates as 'I will return'! My mother was attracted to shiny things, a bit like a magpie. Being spoilt she didn't have to put too much effort into doing anything that did not benefit her directly. So, once her lovers' money had been used up and the lust and novelty had been replaced by reality it was time for my mother to leave and come back home to her family. Billy and Mary hung on her every word and Granny D and Margaret raised their eyes to the ceiling each time mother fabricated another lie about her whereabouts over the last eight weeks. Father looked like the cat that got the cream, he asked everyone to quiet down as he had an announcement. He placed his cigarette in the ashtray and stood up from his chair.

'The housing agreement has been signed for the new house, and we can move in next week.'

We all cheered with delight. For one moment I wondered if Billy McMeekin would be coming with me!

The family was back together, and we celebrated my birthday by exchanging gifts and cards, eating snacks and cake, knowing it would be the last time the flat would be the venue for another family get-together.

No one heard the front door being knocked at first, but the thumping became louder and louder, dad shuffled in his chair and wondered what all the ruckus was about. The pounding on the door vibrated in the small hallway. Mother had turned off the record player and dad jumped up to see who was there.

'What the hell….' he raged .

The heavy wooden entrance door looked as if it was pulsing with each thump, it looked like it was about to be kicked in! My father was wrenching at the brass handle as he tried to twist the doorknob and force the door to open. It wasn't budging. The thumping continued and became more rapid. Billy put his hands over his ears and Margaret put her arm over my shoulder.

'Stop banging arsehole, I'm trying to open the door!' yelled Dad. The thumping on the door got louder and faster as dad pulled and twisted the doorknob with no impact. It was as if the door had been welded shut. Suddenly, the banging stopped, and the door blew open. Dad was thrown back with such force he landed on the hall floor, without hesitating he got up and raced down the stairs. I have never seen him so angry. We all stood transfixed as we could hear him sprint between floors, searching the front and rear of the building. Within a few minutes he was back.

'What happened?' mum asked.

'I don't know!' said dad, who was clearly totally bemused at what had just occurred.

'That was terrifying, there was no one about! Not a soul!'

Roy Caldwell, our neighbour opened his door after being disturbed by the racket. He offered to help my dad. His wife Jenny appeared with their baby son James over her shoulder and mum invited her into the flat. Granny D made her excuse and left as did Margaret, who had to get to work. Mary, Billy, and I stayed in the parlor trying to get our heads around what just took place.

It was then I saw it. Halfway through placing my birthday cards on the mantelpiece, I saw it out the side of my eye. It was in the corner of the room on the ceiling. I could feel my body tremble and hoped no one would notice.

'I have come for your mother.' it said over and over. I had no idea what it meant but I wanted it to disappear, it didn't. I felt nervous and vulnerable because it knew I could see it. I could feel the power it possessed. It slid down the wall and came right up to my face, I was petrified. It was a male, odious and threatening ,I froze and then screamed out.

'Leave us alone, you are not wanted here, you're dead!' The room fell silent. Mum broke the silence by nervously giggling.

'I think someone has had a sneaky glass of sherry, what do you say Catherine?' said mum nervously. How was I going to explain my way out of this without Margaret being here? The figure vanished but it was only a matter of time before he would be back! For now, the malevolent entity had left the room.

When the neighbors had gone mum poured herself another gin and settled onto the sofa, dad lit another cigarette. Mary, Billy, and I had been allowed to watch some television. I was anxiously waiting on my mother saying something about my outburst, but nothing was mentioned. Maybe, tonight was not the right time, after all she was just back, and it was my birthday.

My dad was a logical thinker he based everything on facts and would methodically go over a problem and come up with a solution. Everything had to have a rational explanation for him. His theory was plausible, he had put the door episode down to pranksters in the building. Teenagers with nothing better to do. Banging on the door and then running off perhaps to hide in one of the empty flats. The heavy front door was warped with age and damp, it probably just jammed in position. What he couldn't work out was the force he encountered when he was thrown across the hall. It had been a crazy, long day and everyone was tired. During my father's explanation to the family, my mum never took her eyes off me. I knew then the telling off was coming the next day, she would wait till I was on my own. She always did.

The same entity appeared several times that night whilst we were in bed. Even in death it was still fighting for my mother's attention. Tormented and trapped, his extreme energy and pain was too much for a nine-year-old child to understand. A negative spirit like this sucks the life out of the home, it will search out the vulnerable and try and attach itself to them. It can be draining and exhausting to continually fight off their energy I repeatedly told him to move on, his presence was not wanted, he was dead and as such he had no business to be in our home. Mary could feel the coldness as his spirit came and went into our bedroom throughout the night. The light on the nightstand would flicker and the room would feel heavy with negative energy. Although never discussed much, Mary was aware I was sensitive to the spirits of the dead. She never saw any of the apparitions, but she told me she did feel their presence.

Mothers mental state changed in the final days we stayed in the flat, she seemed more content, settled and looking forward to the imminent house move, even Granny D mentioned she and mum were getting along a lot better than before. Dad believed the move was going to be the fresh start we all needed, especially my mother.

We started clearing out cupboards and putting belongings into wooden boxes ready for the upcoming move. The pictures were removed from the walls, leaving stains on the wallpaper where they had once hung. Mum wanted to pack her beloved 'artwork' for fear we would damage it. The Mona Lisa would have required less packaging. It was all meticulously packed away in newspaper. The mass-produced print of the Chinese girl, Green Lady and my mother's pride and joy, her print of Tina, the lady by the tree and Lalinda, the Gipsy, mysterious and exotic, sultry and sexy, Tahitian beauties.

Mum dyed her hair back to its natural brunette colour as she thought she looked like the ladies in the paintings. She didn't. Only the golden sunburst wall clock remained in the hallway, mum was going to sit this on her lap in the car when we finally left the flat. The apartment looked bare without all the clutter.

My father was promoted to factory manager at work.

His new position and salary guaranteed the family a comfortable lifestyle. Money had been tight before but now he was able to start saving money every week. My mother was not aware of this, she was not a saver, Granny D said she spent money fasten than water went through a colander. By controlling the money, he could control my mother. Working daytime regular hours allowed dad to monitor exactly what everyone in the family was up to. Especially mother. Up till now, my father lived a nocturnal lifestyle, but our lives were just about to take a dramatic change for the better. New town, new house, new life here we come!

A mental war of attrition was about to commence with my parents, who was going to break first?

Meanwhile, as gran and mother packed up the flat in preparation of the move, I had been in bother at primary school. I was sent home with a letter from my teacher for the attention of my parents, I decided to give it to Margaret to read. I did not need my father to know I had been in trouble at school, he had enough going on in his life, anyway it was a lot of fuss over nothing.

My primary school was built in 1881, it was the primary school for all the children in the area. The original sandstone brick was dirty after years of exposure to the elements. I was always creeped out by the marble busts of Shakespeare and Byron which sat in the windows of the stairwell and the black cast iron banister of the stairs. There were no internal toilets. Both the boys' and girls' toilets were outside in a separate building. Sensible pupils would use the facilities during the comfort breaks and at lunchtime, if you were excused during class, and nobody wanted this, you had to run across the playground and into the long damp, dark, narrow, toilet building. This building was haunted. A fact that was acknowledged long before I saw what I can only describe as a black shadow person many times. Even I found the place eerie. Back then I had no idea who it was, he was just an angry spirit who liked to bang the doors and set off the taps. I told him I could see him, but he never answered me. Like most of the pupils, I just went in, did what I had to do and got out as quickly as possible. I told the girls about the shadow man and in turn they told the teacher. The girls were frightened to go and use the facilities alone. The school bully, Lesley Campbell, who frequently used the end toilet to smoke her cigarettes claimed I had held her door shut and turned on the taps when she was using the facilities. Mr. Lyndsay, the janitor was livid having to mop the area up again as the water never drained away on its own. Mrs. MacFarlane the head mistress summoned both Lesley and I to her office. I stuck with my truth.

'The toilets are haunted Mrs. MacFarlane, I have seen the shadow man, it was him who must have turned the taps on and held the door!' I said with all the confidence in the world, after all it was the truth. Mrs. MacFarlane was having none of it. I stuck to my story and for good measure reported Lesley's cigarette lair to the head teacher in the hope this would deflect any blame from me. It was the wrong tactic to use, it made me look desperate and Lesley was coming out of this as the victim and I as a bully and a liar. Despite my pleas of innocence, I felt there was nothing I could say to convince her I was not involved in the incident.

'I have been watching you Jamieson, and I do not like what I see, I will not tolerate liars in my school!'

I felt Mrs. MacFarlane had already pre-judged me and I was not being given a chance. Lesley Campbell said nothing, she simply stood with her eyes to the ground and hands behind her back. I was the one digging the hole. 'I am not a liar!' I screamed!

I could feel the situation escalating out of control, I was not helping the situation by screaming back at a senior member of staff. Forever the disciplinarian, Mrs. MacFarlane revealed my punishment was two strikes of the leather strap across my outstretched hands and a request for my parents to come to the school to discuss my behaviour. The pain of the leather belt across my bare palms was overshadowed by the sheer agony of being called a liar. Lesley got a good telling off for smoking in the toilets despite her pleas of innocence. I was furious, I could not control my anger and roared out at Mrs. MacFarlane.

'Your daughter is behind you, and she isn't happy with you, she says you should be home resting!' I had no filter; it was out my mouth before I could stop it.

The room went ghostly cold and silent. Both Lesley and Mrs. MacFarlane stared at me in utter shock, unable to speak. I knew at that moment I was in serious trouble. I had said way too much. Lesley Campbell wasted little time in spreading the news throughout the school. She added a little creative spin to the story by suggesting I was going mad; I was talking to myself and pretending there were ghosts in the room. Apparently, I was screaming and behaving like a woman possessed, unable to be controlled. Lesley continued to dine out on this story when she moved to New Weston and attended the same secondary school as me. I think that day affected her mentally as she became obsessed with me, determined to humiliate, and demean me at every opportunity. I loathed her and avoided her at all costs in secondary school. I wished she were dead. I was probably the only person from school who did not attend her memorial service after she was killed by a drunk driver. She was only 14 years old.

I didn't know Mrs. MacFarlane's daughter had died until that fateful afternoon when she appeared to me, nor did I know our head teacher was ill. Mrs. MacFarlane died from breast cancer three months later.

The following day, Margaret attended the school

without my parents' knowledge. Mrs. MacFarlane had taken time off due to illness, so we met the deputy head teacher, Mr. Park. He was short in stature and to the point. Margaret, forever the diplomat listened to his suggestions on how I should be disciplined both at home and in school. She apologised for my behaviour and put it down to my mother leaving the family home and only recently coming home. Margaret passed off my vivid imagination as simply attention seeking, she agreed with Mr. Park mainly to pacify him and put an end to the meeting. Margaret listened but had no intension in implementing any of his strict disciplinarian ideas. With just a few days to go before we were due to move away from the area Margaret felt the best course of action was to agree and keep a low profile.

On the day we move house, I could hear my mother crying in the parlor. Dad was consoling her. The news had come by letter, posted through the door by hand. Joe Mullen the man my mother had ran off with had killed himself, he had jumped from a bridge. It happened on the same day I saw the malevolent spirit in the parlor. Could this have been the spirit of the man I saw in our house at my ninth birthday party making his final journey into the afterlife. He clearly had a message he wanted to pass on to my mother before he crossed over, but I was too young to understand why he was in our home or what he was trying to say. Much like his mental state at that moment in time he jumped from the bridge, it was erratic and incomprehensible, tortured, and angry.

His wife had forbidden my mother attending his funeral even though she had no intention of going. It was the first time I had heard about someone committing suicide and the thought of it stuck with me for some time. Communicating with spirits who had taken their own lifes were to become familiar visitors to me over the coming years.

Gran had come in to help with the move, dad handed her the letter to read, but she did not acknowledge my mother who sat smoking and whimpering on the sofa. I had never known my gran to show any emotion, she never hugged us or said she loved us. She was strict and lacked any passion. But to be fair she was there whenever we needed her and today was no exception. A man had died, and a family had lost a father and husband, but my mother wanted to make this about her grief. She was a selfish woman, seeking her own pleasure with no regards for others. She had little consideration of our needs as a mother but maybe this was because she had no maternal instinct as opposed to just being a bad mother. She was a skilled manipulator, and my father was unable to say no to her. I could see why so many men were attracted to her. Mother was an attractive looking woman who took a lot of pride in her appearance. I never saw her without her red lipstick and make up on, today was no exception.

CHAPTER 3

A new life in New Weston

Diary entry - Friday 21st November 1969

Really excited as we moved to our new house today, the house is enormous, it's like a mansion with lots of fields round about. We have a separate toilet and bathroom, indoors!!!!!!! Dad allowed Billy and I the day off school, so I said goodbye to all my friends yesterday. Margaret did not turn up I have not seen her for two days when she came to the school meeting with me, I am not happy with her, she wants to spend her time with this guy and not us anymore. It was Mary's last day at work as her office job in Paisley is going to be too far for her to travel to each day from New Weston. She starts a new job in a few days. Mary came home with flowers and chocolates. We ate the chocolates after a chip shop dinner, it was delicious!

By the end of 1969, most of the families had moved out of the tenement block. Once a flat was vacated, the landlord would quickly cover up the windows and entrance doors with metal boards which were bolted onto the walls. This kept the undesirables and vandals out, not that there was anything to steal, it was a deterrent for hooligans who enjoyed setting fire to empty buildings. Most of the empty flats had been stripped back to the floorboards and the copper piping removed, as families moved on to their new council homes.

With just three families remaining, the building felt deserted and lifeless. Despite the cramp conditions I will always remember the tenement being alive and bustling with the noise of the families, dogs barking and pungent cooking smells, now, it had gone silent. Once, every window had been dressed in lace and displayed oversized vases of artificial flowers, now they were empty, each window now looked like a sad tearful eye, expressionless and lifeless. Some windows were boarded up and others had been smashed, shards of glass remained in the wooden pane. A voile curtain that had been left behind was blowing in the wind waiting to face the wrecking ball and cranes. As we left in my father's car for the very last time, I looked out the rear back window for a final glimpse of the street. Billy McMeekin stood on the corner and waved as we drove by. I waved back knowing this was the last time I would see him.

Demolition was a certainty, progression and upgrading of the area was all part of the urban regeneration plans by the local authority. A new cycle was about to start, new homes for new families as a new decade was about to begin.

***

Number 10 Queens Drive was as palatial as the name implied. It was our palace, and my mother was the queen bee. The four-bedroom end terrace house was everything we could have dreamed off. Generous size rooms, back and front garden with an area for growing vegetables. Billy had his own bedroom as did our mother and father. Mary and I would share the biggest bedroom overlooking the back garden. Granny D secured the dining room/bedroom downstairs until her one-bedroom pensioner house became available in the next phase of construction. I was in complete awe of the toilet and separate bathroom. I stood and stared at the flushing toilet, knowing there would be no more running out into the landing, wrapped in a coat and slippers, brandishing a huge key and a torch to use an outdoor toilet. I would no longer have the indignity of using a basin we kept under the bed should we get caught short in the night. We also had a separate bathroom where we all enjoyed the privacy and luxury of a warm bath and not just on a Sunday night. We had a heating system throughout the house, so we no longer had to huddle around a coal fire or wear extra clothes and socks when we were cold. Our fortunes had changed along with the other families who had moved to New Weston. What was once a small village surrounded by fields had been transformed. The newly acquired greenbelt land was now a desirable new town with its own local council, plenty of new homes, a couple of primary and secondary schools and in the heart of the town, a new shopping center.

Mother settled very quickly and became obsessively house proud. She took to her old Singer sewing machine and made curtains and accessories for the house. Matching arm covers were made for the sofa and chairs along with scatter cushion covers. If it could be made with a straight line of stitching, my mother would make it.

Father became a workaholic spending long hours at works. He was trusted and respected by the directors of the family-owned business. The staff also liked Bill, he was fair and respected by everyone. Having worked his way up through the company he understood the problems and how best to overcome them without upsetting production, the employees, and the hierarchy. His natural ability to pacify and manage everyone, even the trade union representative made him an ideal candidate for promotion. The company was growing rapidly, and new orders were coming in each month, suppliers needed reassurance that delivery dates would be met. My father was a man of his word. If he said an order would be on time, it would be on time. This promise often kept him at the factory late into the night.

Father's pride and joy was his car. It had transformed our lives, as we were all driven to the shops, work, and school. The odd time we went to the beach but only in the summer when dad was not working, which was rare.

At home, he showered my mother with enough money

to buy whatever she desired to create her dream home. A new black and white rented television arrived and took pride of place in the corner of the lounge in time for Christmas and a twin tub washing machine made the laundry a less arduous task. Granny D still washed her clothes by hand, refusing to give up old habits, however when the pain of arthritis claimed her hands, she gave in. She religiously hung her clothes out on the washing line, even in the winter. When there was a good wind in the air, she wouldn't waste it. Even on Christmas Day Granny D had her small washing out to dry. Old habits die hard I suppose.

Diary entry - Christmas Day 1969 , Thursday 25th December.

First Christmas in our castle. Margaret came on her own for dinner as Joe her boyfriend was working. She gave me a beautiful pink diary with a gold lock. She also gave me a silver necklace to keep the key on. Mary and I were given bubble bath, I have never had this before, never having had a bath before we moved here. I am going to pour it in my bath tonight before I go to bed. Margaret is staying the night, I am soooooo happy. Billy loves Led Zeppelin, Margaret got him the single Whole Lotta Love. He must have played it about ten times on the new record player before Dad took it off. It's been a good day, wish Margaret still lived with us ......

On Boxing Day, I was awoken at 6.30am by someone crying. It was coming from downstairs. I looked over at Mary and Margaret and they were fast asleep. I put on my dressing jacket and slippers and went down to see if it was gran. As I entered the lounge, I turned on the ceiling light and the bulb blew, shattering glass fragments all over the new carpet. I had to rely on the light from the kitchen pouring into the lounge. The crying stopped. I jumped as I saw Isabella Pacini standing by the fire. She lived next door with her husband and daughter, they were a beautiful Italian family and wonderful neighbours. Isabella had been ill for some time and had come out of hospital to spend Christmas with her family at home.

'Catherine, little one, do not be frightened.' I wasn't frightened just puzzled. I shook my head and listened intently to what she had to say. Isabella spoke in Italian at first, I had no idea what she was saying.

'Catherine, I have a message for Guido.' Her thick Italian accent was difficult to understand.

'Tell Guido, I love him, and I am sorry I could not stay longer, I heard what he said when my eyes were closed, I could hear everything.'

She spoke in Italian once again and then said very softly.

'Tell him he is braver than he thinks. I will walk beside him until we are together again'

I could feel the energy in the room, there was a force at work, a force stronger than death, it was called love. Isabella looked beautiful, younger looking than I remembered, her black hair was swept back from her face, and she appeared pain free.

'You will pass my words to Carlo, molte grazie?' I nodded unable to speak, the energy in the room was overwhelming. I was not afraid, instead I felt honored she had come to me.

Isabella understood she was dead, she had unfinished business which had stopped her from moving on, the afterlife could wait. She had a message for her soul mate, and I was to deliver it. Her final words which she could not express to Guido in life came after her death. I would deliver the message. Knowing this she smiled and disappeared. The gentleness she conveyed was touching, she confirmed my belief, a person that is pleasant and caring in life is the same in death. In life, I had spoken to Isabella many times and she had been nothing but pleasant. She never passed anyone in the street without saying hello. Both she and her husband Guido, were always together, they were dedicated to each other and were still very much in love after 40 years of marriage. Their older daughter, Carla stayed at home and worked in the café they owned in the village area of the town.

I gave Isabella my word to deliver her message and bid her farewell. At that moment, gran entered the lounge. She wanted to know what was going on and 'who I was talking to' I turned to gran and burst into tears.

'Oh Gran, Mrs. Pacini, Isabella, is dead.'

Gran never asked how I knew, nor did she try to hug me despite my distress, it was just her way of dealing with things, she simply said.

'How sad, Isabella will be at peace now, poor Guido' It was at that moment I realised; she knew!

Gran knew all along. She wasn't shocked when I told her Isabella was dead, she never asked any questions. I followed gran out of the lounge and into her bedroom.

'Gran you know I can speak to the dead.' I nervously asked.

'Catherine, there are many things I know about you! You have a rare and special gift! You must learn how to embrace and use this, respect it.' Gran made it clear she had said enough.

For the first time I could ever remember, she put her arms around me and pulled me into her chest. Gran was never one to show any emotion or public affection, she never had. I could feel her embrace was full of genuine love and warmth. It felt emotional and caring. We made a special connection that night a bond that we would share for the rest of our lives.

I told her about the message I had to deliver to Guido.

'We will go over and speak to Guido together; I will come with you.' Gran said.

Gran cuddled me tightly as the sun began to rise, its rays defused through the hallway net curtains and across the floor of the small room. It had just gone 8.00am before I climbed the stairs back to the warmth of my bed. Gran and I would visit Guido later and deliver the message together.

July 1970

Diary entry - Saturday 25th July 1970

Dads got a new car, a beige Vauxhall Viva. He keeps looking out the lounge window at it. Mum is so house proud. She got a fridge today, she stood outside as the delivery men brought it in ensuring everyone in the street saw it. Having cold milk is wonderful. She has an eye watering array of colours in the kitchen and throughout the house. Orange and green and browns a real assault on the senses. Pampas Grass has been added to the front garden as mum says it's very trendy. She truly is becoming more of a snob every day.

Everything in New Weston was new, the schools, the shops, the roads, the park, the people, the apparitions! There was even a swimming pool and sports facility something that had been unimaginable at our previous home.

Dad, Billy, and Mary were all working and bringing money into the house and for the first time we had a family holiday to the Island of Millport where we stayed in a static caravan that had a lethal cocktail of paraffin lamps and a bucket as a toilet. It rained for most of the time we were there. Typical Scottish weather. Mary chose to stay at grans for the week. Billy and I fought the whole time and mum and dad spent most of the week in the George Hotel drinking and arguing when they returned to the caravan site at night. The best thing about the time away from home was mum refused to cook in the tiny caravan so we had fish and chips most nights for dinner and in the morning, I was introduced to a full Scottish Breakfast in the shore front café. It was like nothing I had ever eaten before. Sausage, bacon, black pudding, egg, potato scone, beans and toast all washed down with a pot of tea. Delicious.

Billy made friends easily. By the summer of 1970 he was playing for the local amateur football team and was an extremely popular teenager. He always had friends over at the house or friends dropping by looking for him. His future had been secured when dad confirmed he would be working with him at Thomson's as an apprentice engineer when he reached sixteen in August. He would not need to return to school or worry about finding a job. Dad was also on hand to drive Billy back and forth to work. Everything just seemed to fall into Billy's lap. Friends, girls, jobs. He came and went, did little about the house, had his own room and could do no wrong. Billy was the golden child.

Mary was happy working for a firm of lawyers based in the town center. She had no aspirations in life except to have a job, meet someone nice, fall in love, get married and have a family. All in that order. She had met a lad whom I never took to, his name was Michael Spiers. Billy told us, he had knocked a dog down with his motorbike and never thought anything of stopping his bike and going back to jump on the squealing dogs head several times till it was dead. Whenever he came to the house to pick Mary up, I would feel uneasy. I thought he was intimidating and aggressive. He worked in the local abattoir about a quarter mile from our house. They supplied bacon, beef, and lamb to many of the well-known hotels, restaurants, and supermarkets in the country. Sometimes the poor cows would escape and run down our street, the terrified beasts would be round up by the slaughterhouse men and dragged back to face their execution. It broke my heart when I saw the trucks filled with cows, pigs, and sheep driving towards the slaughterhouse. I just knew those poor trapped and cramped animals were on their way to die a horrible death, I believe these poor animals instinctively knew their fate, it was to be the main reason I became a vegetarian.

Michael Speirs worked there; he would brag about assaulting and clubbing the animals as they came in to be slaughtered. Teasing and kicking them. Laughing as they squealed in pain. He described the killing of the animals in such a glorified way, he obviously enjoyed his job, or did he just enjoy torturing and killing poor defenseless animals. He came to our house one night with a cow's tongue for my Gran. She loved him for it. In my view you had to be completely insane to want to work in an environment where all you ever saw day in day out was death and blood, squealing and pain. Coming home each night smelling of death. At what point do you achieve job satisfaction? With so many jobs available in the area why did Michael Speirs choose this one? I thought he was a psychopath; I could never understand what Mary saw in him.

I know Michael did not treat my sister Mary the way she would have liked. She came home one night and as she removed her clothes for bed and slid into her nightdress, I noticed her upper arm was covered in bruises. Mary said Michael and she had been play-fighting. I suspected there was something she was not telling me or anyone else. My worst fears about him were about to come true!

Diary entry: Saturday 31st October 1970

Margaret came over this weekend, she was not working a shift. I always get the biggest hug when she sees me. I miss her dreadfully, for me a weekly visit is not enough. My greatest wish is for her to come and live in New Weston, but I think her partner Joe has other plans. He was hinting about moving to a bigger house, near the beach, sounds lovely. Maybe a house by the sea or in the countryside,

super excited, I hope she has a spare room so I can stay over during the school holidays……

On my 10th birthday in 1970. Mum tried to make a real effort by preparing a small buffet of cocktail onions, cheese and pineapple skewers, vol-au-vents, and tinned sausage rolls. She was at home in her orange and brown kitchen. New fitted cupboards replaced the old pantry that was in the tenement.

Margaret and Joe came to the house with my gift and dropped a bombshell. They would be following in the footsteps of his sister and emigrating to Australia. Margaret by now, was a qualified RGN nurse and Joe an electrician, exactly the type of skilled professionals Australia wanted. With his parents and sisters already resident in Melbourne, they had a family sponsor and jobs waiting. What did Scotland have to offer? Disillusioned with life here, they saw their future in Australia. Both drawn by the dream, the weather, and the outdoor living the country had to offer. They planned to emigrate in March (1971) but first they had decided to get married in the New Weston Register office on Christmas Eve, just a small ceremony with only a few family members and friends. Margaret asked if I would like to be a bridesmaid and I said yes.

When Margaret said she was emigrating I was stunned, my first reaction was numbness, I was unable to talk. I stared at Margaret; her lips were moving but I did not hear anything else she said. I simply nodded to her questions. How could she leave me? From that day, I hated Joe. If it weren't for him Margaret would never have gone to live thousands of miles away from her family and those who loved her. It was Joe who wanted to move and be with his family. It was Joe who was going to be behind the wheel driving the car. It was Joe who would be over the alcohol limited. It was Joe who would kill Margaret! In the coming weeks I became extremely emotional. I was miserable and struggled to sleep. I cried and cried. I did not want Margaret to leave or marry that man. Looking back ,the only feelings I had were of doom and disaster, it was then the terrible headaches started. The throbbing, aching pain. The days were passing too quickly, and I seemed to be in a permanently depressive state. Margaret had tried to reach out to me, but I was unable to accept her decision to move to Australia. I tried to stop her, but it was no use.

Diary entry - Christmas Eve 1970. The Wedding

I hated everything about today, I especially hate Joe. Mum and Dad are not upset Margaret is leaving us, she is going to the other end of the world. I wish he were dead, and Margaret could come and stay near us. There were two spirits at the Castle Hotel tonight. They just drifted about the main reception area. I was not in the mood to talk with them despite the old man trying to communicate in a dialect I did not recognise. He followed me back into the function room and finally disappeared after I continued to ignore him. This is going to be the worse Christmas ever!

I wrote so much in my diary I used up both Christmas and Boxing day's pages. My rantings were mainly about how much I hated Joe.

The wedding on Christmas Eve was short and sweet. The bride did not wear white, but a pink trouser suit. Both Mary and I had matching floor length pink dresses and lavender floral headbands and hand posies. Mother had managed to run the dresses up on her Singer sewing machine, most of the stitching involved straight lines, exactly what my mother specialised in. When the fifteen-minute ceremony was over, we stood outside in the bleak December weather to have the official wedding photographs taken. Bride and groom, bride and groom with best man and bridesmaids, father of the bride and mother of the bride with bride and groom. The rotation went on and on and I was unable to smile despite my father's request to 'cheer my face up.'

About thirty close family and friends attended a wedding dinner at the Colquhoun Castle hotel. It had been an eighteenth-century mansion which had fallen into a state of dilapidation after the second world war, latterly it had been a nursing home for the old and infirm. It had closed due to bad management and escalating costs. By 1960 in lay empty and fell into a state of disrepair. A developer bought the building and rebuilt and refurbished the house back to its former glory. Despite having never been a castle, the new owners rebranded the building as Colquhoun Castle to attract the lucrative wedding business. It worked. With a sweeping staircase and a massive crystal chandelier as you came through the entrance, the venue was fit for a king. As father of the bride, my dad paid for the wedding reception. It was his wedding gift to Margaret and Joe. During the speeches, The Best Man read out telegrams from Australia and Joe moaned about the Scottish weather, repeating how much he was 'looking forward to the sunshine and beaches 'down under'.

I simply hated the man.

CHAPTER 4
1971

By the summer of 1971 I was coming to terms with living without Margaret. My mother and father offered no help with my grief.

'You need to let it go Catherine.' Were my Grans words of advice? 'You just need to accept she has gone.' Gran could be so hard at times.

My only consolation was Margaret wrote to me on a regular basis. She would put separate letters in her envelope to the family, one for each of us. She regularly sent photographs, in every picture she would be smiling and looked happy. Most of the images were taking on a beach or beside a swimming pool or barbecue. Life looked great, full of sunshine and smiles. Here at home everything was grey and miserable.Mary and I celebrated getting our own bedrooms the day before my birthday on 11th November 1971. Gran had been offered a single bedroom pensioner cottage less than a ten-minute walk from our house. She was thrilled as were we. I loved my Gran, but she was a stern, cold woman who rarely showed any emotion or love. We had grown close since Mrs. Pacini's death and we had both gone to see her husband to pass on his late wife's message.

Gran was my go-to person when I needed to talk. My mother had grown distant and unapproachable, and dad was never about, he spent most of his day at the factory.

Mother was delighted when gran moved out.

'She has outstayed her welcome and the time has come for her to have her own home.'

Dad and Billy arranged for all her belongings to be moved and set up in her new house. She seemed to adapt to anything you put in front of her, nothing really fazed her.

In February 1971, when the country adopted a decimal currency, gran took to it like a duck to water. The old money of pounds, shillings and pence was replaced with a new system. There was one hundred pennies in the pound and no shillings to be seen. Gran had no issues converting to the new coins. For a few months, the shops still showed old money and new money prices as some people were still struggling to understand. Gran said.

'You need to move with the times, get with it.'

Mum has said it was gran who created the tension in the house, now gran had moved into her own home the tension was still there. Mum was the instigator. She initiated every argument and picked fault in everything we all did. Nothing was good enough for her exacting standards. Mum, who was still living in her Good Housekeeping and Peoples Friend mode, no longer wanted old hand me down furniture, everything had to be new.

She brought out the singer sewing machine and made pink curtains for my bedroom and pink cushion covers for my single bed. Having my own bedroom, I felt liberated and free. My sense of independence was overwhelming because I could now close my bedroom door and lock the world outside. More importantly, I no longer had to listen to my mother and father quibble and verbally spar with each other night after night. I could just retire to my own bedroom and write up my diary, listen to the radio or talk to Mrs. Pacini when she cared to visit me. I had seen and spoken to her so many times Mr. Pacini welcomed my messages from his dead wife without hesitation. I was the conduit between her, and Guido and I was happy to do so.

Diary entry - Friday 12th November 1971 - My 11th Birthday.

Margaret sent mum the money to buy me a new diary. I will go to Woolworths on Saturday and buy one and spend the rest of the money on a Pic and Mix. Mary has split with Michael Speirs, she has met another guy at work. Mum hates Michael as he told her 'Your peroxide white hair makes you look like Myra Hindley'. My mother was furious as she thinks Hindley is probably the evilest woman alive and possibly the ugliest. She had gone back to platinum blonde recently and has now dyed her hair back to its natural brown colour. Gran said 'why lie when the truth will do' don't really know what she means but I don't think it was a compliment about mum. Dad had a telephone installed so we can call Margaret and Joe in Australia. He says it's expensive to call that distance so we will limit it to only once a month and only for a few minutes at a time. The telephone has taken pride of place on a new telephone table in the hallway and dad has instructed us not to use it. It is for emergencies and Margaret only.

It wasn't the same celebrating a birthday without Margaret at home with the family, I was not looking forward to Christmas without her. Our connection went beyond just being sisters, I would have loved for her to have been my mother, I would have been with her now. I became obsessed with writing in my diary and filled pages will the smallest written text so I could cram as much as possible into each page. I dreamed of being in Australia and wished my life away until the day I could travel over to be with her and Joe.

Mum and dad were fighting a lot. Just silly things at first, mainly about dad not being at home. He worked long hours and mother would nag and nag him the minute he came through the front door. Dad couldn't win. I used to think he worked long hours to make life better for us, but I soon learned there was more tempting offerings in the office which demanded his attention.

Diary entry - Thursday 10ᵗʰ February 1972

The power cuts have brought us together as a family. I don't know much about the miners' strike, but I know we have no electricity in the evenings. Mum has been cooking our food in the morning before the power goes off. Thankfully, we have a coal fire where mum has been heating up the food at night in pots, a bit like camping. We have candles stuck on saucers all over the house so we can see what we are doing. We have all been playing cards and board games in the dark, huddled in the lounge with just the coal fire and candles for lights. The evenings are cozy with us all together, but I miss Margaret. You can't leave the house at night as there are no street-lights. I need a lit candle in my room at night as the darkness is just too much for me, the strain on my eyes makes me feel sick, some nights I panic, when I open my eyes it's just total blackness, it feels like I have gone blind!

    1972 brought power cuts, puberty, misery, spots, cramp, and migraines into my life. I became extra sensitive to spiritual energy and would react instantly if I were to enter an emotionally charged room or property. Trapped spirits were drawn to me. They manifest without warning and demand my attention. Often it took me a few minutes to differentiate between the living and the dead as they looked so similar. I was often surrounded by the shadowy presence of spirits; I'd forget myself and start communicating with them if they approached me and tried to speak, I would answer them back. I did this wherever I was and whoever I was with. I was rarely afraid of the apparitions but understood it could be frightening for others who were with me. Looking back, I must have been quite an oddity. In our community everyone talks, it's like a hobby, some are better than others, it was how messages were circulated and gossip was created. Like Chinese whispers once the chatter moved down the line the message became contorted and had no baring to the original communication. Some of the things I heard about myself were truly outrageous and so far from the truth. I was just an ordinary girl with an extraordinary talent.

I quickly gained a reputation as someone who could communicate with the dead. People began to refer to me as a mystic, but this was a simplistic description which was incorrect. The older women called me a 'spey-wife' a Scottish term for a fortune telling woman, this was not correct, I was unable to predict the future. I was a mystery because no one understood me, I could not be pigeonholed. Some people just thought I was odd, maybe if they had taken the time to get to know me, they would have felt differently towards me. As a child I was precautious, it was a sign of things to come as I never truly trusted anyone. I wasn't popular at school and didn't make friends easily. Who wanted to hang around with someone who claimed she could communicate with your dead granny! I frightened people but that's only because they fear the unknown, they fear death. I bridge the gap between the dead and the living. I talk to the dead, I never question why, this is me, this is my life and I had to live with it. I do not believe that death is our last destination in the way most people perceive it. I know we can store residual energy even after the heart stops beating. We remain conscious outwith our body until we are accepting of our death and choose to finally move on. Some spirits are unaware they are dead, they can appear confused and stay trapped and tormented, attached to a person or a property. Some fear they will be judged for their sins. Other spirits have unfinished business and will not move on until they have delivered a message or resolved a problem. Some fear they will be judged for their sins, others are worried about how their families will cope without them. I can communicate with them in death exactly as I would have done in life.

Is this a gift or is this a hindrance? It was certainly not deception; Demonstrating my ability and continually being judged was commonplace as I was constantly having to prove myself to the skeptics, supplying evidence revealing names and genuine information the living could verify. I recognised at an early age I possessed something which could give me real power and I was determine I was going to use this gift wisely. I was determined to be someone who did good in their life and use my power to make something of myself.

CHAPTER 5

1972

Diary entry - Saturday 1st July 1972

It was all over the news today, the radio and the television, it is terrifying, a young girl was murdered just a few minutes from our house. Gran was here at our house today; she was out talking to all the neighbours to get as much information as she could about what had happened. The young girl had been out at night walking her dog and was reported missing by her family when the dog returned to the house without her. So many different stories, Chinese whispers, and gossip but the truth will come out as the girl's father works with my dad.

When news of the murder broke, the whole town fell into a deep sense of shock. How could a crime like this have happened right on our doorstep and no one had seen anything suspicious? The media descended, television crews interviewed people on the street and newspaper journalists were relentlessly looking for a story.

Not only did the community struggle to deal with the horrific murder of a young girl but they had to deal with the possible betrayal that it may have been one of their own who had committed this heinous crime. Every man in the town was under suspicion and every parent was extra vigilant. Men were viewed as potential murderers; mothers escorted their children to and from school and there was a strict curfew with children playing outside in the street. Parents did not allow their children especially their daughters out alone day or night. Those who did choose to go out, went in pairs or groups of three or four. Safety in numbers. There were more police patrolling the town, there presence was reassuring. Curtains twitched and chains were put on entrance doors before they were opened. Someone was hiding a murderer, and no one would rest until he was found.

The girl's mutilated body had been stuffed into an old suitcase and dumped in the undergrowth next to an underpass near our house. The victim's father worked with my dad and had done so for many years. He was a good man, a single father of two teenage girls. Like us, the family had moved to New Weston at the same time and looked forward to a clean slate and a bright future. The police officer in charge informed the directors of Thomson Pumps about the murder and discussed with my dad about interviewing all the staff on their whereabouts on the night the girl was killed. As a show of support and sympathy, the management and workforce clubbed together for the devastated family. My father was nominated to visit the murdered girl's family home. He had reservations about going, what the hell did you say to a man and his family after his daughter has been brutally murdered. Flowers just didn't do it and was a signed card by all the staff really going to distract the pain that had been inflicted on his family. Flowers and condolences, it just wasn't enough. My dad organised for Jim Shaw to stay home with his family on full pay for however long it took for him to return to work. It was unprecedented but then again so were the circumstances. The police had a reason to believe the man who murdered his daughter may well have worked in the factory. There was no evidence to suggest this yet, but they had to start their investigation somewhere. An enquiry room was set up and all the male staff members were interviewed one by one. Thomson Pumps employed fifty-two men.

The town was shaken and stunned. A seventeen-year-old girl had been strangled, mutilated, and dumped in a suitcase and a killer was potentially living in the area. The person had to be found, before he struck again.

The young victim was called Linda Shaw, destined to be referred to as Linda 'that poor wee lassie that was murdered'. Maybe by not saying her name she may still be alive. By using her name, we were giving her an identity, and yet trying to identify her had been difficult as she had been mutilated and battered beyond recognition. Police tape cordoned off the area where the body had been dumped and two policemen stood guard and warded off the ghouls who came down to see the murder scene. What had once been just an ordinary underpass linking the town center with the pathway towards the railway station had now become a no-go area, a place of terror and violence, forever to be known as the underpass where the girl was murdered. The killer would have been caught sooner as his DNA would have been all over the body and the murder scene, his skin, hair, blood, and other body fluids would have been everywhere, but DNA evidence was not available in 1972 and the painstaking search for the murderer would take the police more time, more questions, more paperwork, and more legwork. Detective Chief Inspector Colin Smith was overseeing the investigation. I met him when he came to our house to speak with my father.

The minute DCI Smith came through the doorway to our home I had the most overwhelming feeling of fear. I physically felt nauseous as he walked into the house, and this stayed long after he left. My mother was fawning all over him, offering cups of tea, best China cups, the biscuits with the foil on them were all brought out for his visit. My father was handed his usual ceramic mug. I listened intently at the lounge door.

'We need the names and addresses of all the staff who work at Thomson Pumps can you get me them to me as soon as possible?' DCI Smith demanded as he stirred his tea and unwrapped the foil from his first mint biscuit.

His questioning seemed random, but they were cleverly delivered, very matter of fact.

'Did anyone of the men call in sick over the weekend or the Monday?'

'Did Mr. Shaw mention anything to you which may help us with our enquiries?'

'Has Mr. Shaw seemed off or odd at work recently?'

'Is your son Billy about today I would be keen to know if he knew the victim, I think they were a similar age, am I right Mr. Jamieson?'

Every one of his questions was loaded and suspicion was on everybody and anybody. He sneaked the question in about Billy subtly, but my father was quick to dispel any suggestion that his son had been involved in such a heinous crime.

'My son has either been with me, at work or with his football team friends over the weekend, I can verify his movements!' Dad was livid at the insinuation and instantly put up his guard. My mother thought she added value to the conversation by telling DCI Smith.

'Billy would never hurt a fly let alone murder a woman on his very own doorstep!'

'Or anywhere else for that matter!' Dad quickly interjected.

Conversation over, he knew that DCI Smith picked up on every word and dad had no intention of tripping up or bringing any attention to his own family. He was willing to help with the investigation, but he wasn't willing to be investigated.

When DCI Smith left the house, I took to my bed with an awful headache. I had closed my bedroom window blinds and curtains to keep out the light, but I was unable to keep out the sound of my parents arguing as their raised voices penetrated up through the ceiling and into my bedroom. I lay down on my bed, my head was in freefall as I felt sure DCI Smith had brought something into the house. I could sense a strange energy in the room. Suddenly, I felt someone beside me. I sat up, bolt right, there was someone in the bedroom. I switched on my bedside light and looked around the room. I could hear a faint whimpering. I closed my eyes and tried to focus. The room was colder than normal, and I could smell a sweet floral smell. I was unable to place the scent, but I had smelt it before. I sat for a moment or two on the side of the bed.

'Who is here, show yourself!' I bravely called out. My fingertips were freezing cold. The smell returned but I still could not place it. Someone was in the bedroom with me.

'Linda is that you?' I asked as the name kept coming into my head.

I could hear my heart pumping in my chest. There was no response, nothing. But I knew it was her. I was unsettled and began to fidget and felt uneasy. I was having flash backs, it looked like the underpass, my cheek was throbbing where he had bitten into Linda's face and spat her torn flesh onto the wet ground. My head was being thrust back as the killer grabbed at my hair and forced me to the ground. I heard Linda's jaw break as the monster jumped on her face. I needed to get out, I needed to get out of the room. I could not un-see the violence, Linda was being beaten, choked and sexually assaulted, the vicious frenzy was relentless and unforgiving. She did not have the breath or strength to call out for help. Death was her only escape and it wasn't coming soon enough.

I went downstairs simply to get out of the bedroom, but I had an overwhelming need to get out of the house. There was only one place I wanted to go. I had to go to the underpass, I had to see where she died. I had to see his face. The face of a murderer.

Mum and dad were still bickering when I put my anorak and shoes on and slipped out the back door and down onto the street. Mr. Pacini was in his back garden tending to his rhubarb, it had been raining, typical Scottish summer weather so I pulled up my hood and walked quickly to the underpass which was only minutes away. The police barricade was in place but there were no policemen in attendance. There was no one around, no police and no people. Only the police signage indicated this was a crime scene along with some flowers and a few cuddly toys.

It was about 6.30pm, I climbed over the police barricade and headed into the underpass. The heavy rain clouds above were dark and foreboding and had restricted the amount of light getting into the dark passageway. There were no lights inside the underpass, they had been turned off, but I could see someone had painted RIP Linda on the wall. Whoever did the artwork used an unfortunate colour which looked more like blood than red paint. I slowly walked into the tunnel, looking back a few times to see if anyone was about. I was more nervous than frightened. I could not have been more than a dozen yards into the underpass when I suddenly had a moment of clarity and realised, I was going to be in serious trouble if I was caught here. How the hell was I going to explain this to my parents! I had crossed a police line, walked around a crime scene, I started to get cold feet. I turned to leave, and I immediately sensed she was here, Linda Shaw was here! I could feel her presence.

'Linda is that you, I am here to help!' I stammered.

'Show yourself and tell me who did this to you?'

From nowhere an unseen force slammed me against the damp wall of the underpass, I was almost knocked out. I closed my eyes, and he was there, holding me from behind by my hair. We were leaning over Linda; something had been stuffed in her mouth to suppress her screaming. I was suddenly overcome by a series of stark images from the night of the murder. At first, I could not see his face properly, it was contorted and out of focus. He moved fast, his arms violently smashing against Linda's body. The blade ripping at her flesh. I could see a pool of blood and I wanted to close my eyes, but it was not possible as I had to see his face. It was as if I was inside a horror movie, filming a scene and the actors were oblivious to me. I was a paralyzed onlooker just watching and witnessing this diabolical scene, unable to move or shout. I watched the frenzied attack, the unrelenting punching and kicking. Linda did not stand a chance against this maniac. The fragile seventeen-year-old could only hope to die quickly. He was slowly strangling her, then suddenly let go of her throat and delivered a fatal blow to her stomach, the jagged edge of the knife sliced in and out of her torso. Now close to death he performed his last frenzied attack and jumped on her chest, the impact of his body weight shattering her ribs. For one solitary second, I saw his face and immediately knew who it was!

The roar of a male voice behind me broke the energy in the underpass. I opened my eyes as if awakening from a deep sleep and immediately the images disappeared. A policeman was screaming at me to get out. His voice was echoing through the passageway. I knew instantly I was about to be in serious bother, and not just with the police! A policeman grabbed me by the upper arm and escorted me out into the evening light. A few people saw me being dragged from the underpass and put into a police car; it wouldn't be long before the gossip would start!

Diary entry - Saturday 8th July 1972

My father went berserk tonight when I came home in a police car, all the neighbour's curtains were twitching when I got out of the back seat and went into our house. I must have been the absolute talk of the street. I got a severe telling off from the police but that was nothing compared to my father, he has grounded me for the week......

Back at the house, my mum, dad, gran, and Mary gathered in the lounge. My father would hear nothing about my encounter in the underpass, he just did not want to know and warned me to keep my mouth closed.

'It's all bloody attention seeking, that's what it is!' he screamed at my mother.

'I blame you for bloody encouraging this bullshit.' He continued to shout at my mother despite the abusive comments being aimed at me.

'Did you actually see the killers face Cat?' Mary asked timidly. Dad jumped in right away.

'I won't hear any more of this do you understand me, it's like a bloody freak show.'

And so, it went on and on, my dad only stopping his tirade of abuse to light his cigarette and pour himself a drink. Mum grabbed the bottle from him and poured herself a double measure of gin, filling the glass up with tonic and lit another cigarette. They were preparing for battle. The alcohol would later be used as an excuse to justify their foul mouths and vulgar comments. It was a well-rehearsed pattern. I could sense there was going to be trouble ahead.

I was the owner of a huge secret and the burden of concealing this information was painful. This secret, like all secrets, was going to come out at some point, it's human nature to talk, we are not designed to keep secrets, I would trip up! I knew I could not discuss anything that I had witnessed, but the five people in this house knew what I saw, and it was only a matter of time before I broke my silence. My father's face was ashen with anger as he looked straight through me, I had let him down yet again.

'Never mention to anyone what you think you may or may not have seen, you have been warned lady!' His eyes were filled with hate. He threw back his drink and slammed the empty glass on the sideboard.

I simply nodded my head in agreement knowing now was the wrong time to tell my father who the killer was. We both knew who the murderer was!

Mum continued to be verbally bombarded by my father. The fighting would continue long into the night

'Are you listening to me Maureen?' dad growled.

She knew how to wind him up and just ignored him. Mum wore her deep red lipstick, sucked on a cigarette, and sipped on her gin; she had heard it all so many times I'm certain she simply switched off. A young girl had just been murdered and I knew who killed her, why didn't anyone want to know this? As far as my mother and father were concerned it was business as usual. Smoke and mirrors, my parents were the masters in the art of matrimonial deception. My father played along to project the illusion of a perfect marriage. So long as the house was immaculate and everything was in its place, the narcissistic world my mother lived in could not be disrupted. She simply didn't allow it.

I was sentenced to one week confined to the house, no going out, no visits to the Guides on Wednesday and certainly no Saturday night at the youth club. Alice Cooper was telling us all that 'School's Out Forever', I wished it was. It was the summer school break, and I was stuck at home. But more importantly I had important information that had to be passed to DCI Smith – and quickly before the killer struck again.

During my seven-day confinement, I spent most of my time in my bedroom. I wrote letters to Margaret and crammed my diary full of self-pity. Mum continued her obsessive cleaning routine around the house, cleaning floors again and again. She would religiously hang out washing, every day if the weather allowed, there was always something drying outside, it was an annoying compulsion. If you used a towel to dry your hands it was whisked away for washing and then hung up outside, to dry, dancing in the breeze, pegged to a rope stretched between 4 steel posts. A nine -foot wooden pole hoisted the laundry high into the sky. I would watch my mother from my bedroom window, pinning the clothes up in a particular order to satisfy her OCD. Like me the clothing fought against the elements, desperate to be released. Stuck in my bedroom was a powerful distraction for me as I tried to analyse what I had witnessed. It felt like my head was about to burst as I was unable to erase the horrific details of what took place in the underpass. Billy was avoiding eye contact with me, and I could see he felt uncomfortable in my presence, and dad simply ignored me around the house, it was as if I wasn't in the room.

Something happened that night in the underpass that completely changed me. I became possessed by a greater power. There had been a change in the energy that surrounded me, it was so powerful I knew it would change my life forever. I could see full apparitions and talk with spirits. This was not a burden, it was not sacrilege, it was a gift, and I was going to learn how to put it to good use. I suddenly knew what I had to do, and my father and brother were not going to like it.

CHAPTER 6

Dysfunctional Family

We were a dysfunctional family; everything was based on a lie. My mother and fathers sham marriage was slowly coming apart at the seams. I often thought I was to blame as I would hear them say my name during their frequent arguments. Dad spent most of his time at the office and mother hated him for it. She was incapable of having a conversation with anyone without lying. She told neighbours she came from a middle-class family from the southside of the town and her father was a draughtsman. Neither were true. She lied about the most ridiculous silly things. Mother bragged about being a champion ballroom dancer before she met my father. This was a lie. She lied incessantly, slipping lies into her conversations with so much compassion and confidence you would never have known they were untrue. Even I believed some of them. My father let her away with it in public and then pull her up for it in private.

Their fighting would always start the same way, a series of insults and verbal attacks at each other and one of them would throw in the line, 'they could have done so much better in life if they had not settled for one another!' That would set them off and all hell would break lose. This would always result with the 'why did I marry you?' argument.

My mother had an extremely high sense of entitlement. She saw no reason why she should not possess all the things she envisioned. She wore glass custom jewellery and pretended it was diamonds. She referred to her oversized rings as cocktail rings. When my father was promoted to General Manager of Thomson Pumps, she demanded he buy her a diamond ring and paraded it to all and sundry. Her logic behind this was purely self-obsession, another step-up the social ladder to greatness in her world!

It would be unrealistic to suggest all children are brought up being nurtured by their parent's creating memories based on love and puppy dogs and long hot summer days. Not all parents provide a loving, nurturing foundation for their offspring and subsequently what these children experience in their early year's lives with them forever. I was in this category. In my parent's defense they had no idea what they were dealing with, nor did I as I considered myself normal – whatever normal was! Many of my childhood memories filled me with dread and horror, the kind of memories you cannot blank out or try to forget. The memories that keep you awake at night and follow you day after day and night after night. I saw and heard a lot as a child, some things I should never have seen. Many of the spirits I encountered spoke to me as if I was an adult. I was a child. Mum and dad did their best to bring up four children, but we were subjected to their problems in the marriage and were often caught up in the middle of their fighting.

They would get physical; mother would lash out at my father, and he would retaliate. Our parents fighting became a normal part of our upbringing. It was an everyday occurrence and we learned to live with it. Our family façade was so carefully designed looking in you would have thought we had all the trappings of a normal and enviable family life. This was so far from the truth. Our whole life was based on a lie, and I was soon to learn my parents hadn't yet disclosed the biggest lie of them all!

My father was similar in personality and nature to my gran. Austere and lacking in emotion. I can never remember him cuddling me or showing any real affection. He interacted differently with Margaret, Mary and especially Billy, the Golden Child, whom he had a real father son bond with. Dad always made me feel like I was a hindrance and out of place in the family unit. I was looked upon differently not only by my parents but by my brothers and sisters. My father never seemed to have much time for me. Once I found out why, I understood his reasoning! He was never violent with me or any of his children, but he did keep me at a distance. Often, I felt uncomfortable and uneasy in his presence. Not because I was frightened of him, in fact, it was the opposite, I believed he was frightened from me! I spoke to him just after he died, and he asked me to forgive him. I told him there was nothing to forgive him for. He never appeared to me after that.

By November 1972, I still struggled making friends. I had either been in trouble with the school, or I had been fighting with the kids on the street. I told Joanne Reid, the local bully who lived in the next street and made my life a complete misery in high school, that there was a wee girl in spirit form living in her house. Sally haunted their home and most probably had followed her family from their previous house. Sally was about 9 years old. I exaggerated my description of the little girl mainly to frighten Joanne, a taste of her own medicine shall we say. While she had me against a wall one day after school, with her posse of friends egging her on, I told her about Sally. Their cheering soon stopped when I described Sally's burnt face and limbs in detail.

'Sally says you had better stop being a bully or else you might join her sooner than you think?' I said in my most devilish voice.

Within the hour, Joanne Reid and her mother, Dorothy, were at my house, banging on the front door. Fortunately for me, my mother and father were both out. Unfortunately for the Reid's Granny D answered the door. Mrs. Reid was obviously a woman well versed in doorstep confrontations. A woman with little decorum and a vocabulary like a shipyard welder. She had a disgusting habit of spitting whilst she screamed her obscenities at gran. Joanne stood behind her mother, it was evident where she had inherited her bullying qualities from, not only did they look alike, but they also sounded alike!

Mrs. Reid was a mother on a mission, apparently her daughter, Joanne, had been left terrified after an encounter with me in the street in front of her friends. Mrs. Reid was here not only to give me a public dressing down, but also demanded an apology. Gran was having none of it! She tried to stop the crazed woman from spewing out her spiteful, defamatory allegations. There was no break in her hostility as she continued to scream at the top of her voice, hoping to draw attention to herself.

'She is a freak, a modern-day witch, no one likes her, you need to take control of her ….'

As the abuse continued, gran calmly slapped Mrs. Reid across the face with such force Mohammed Ali would have been knocked over. The shouting stopped, and Mrs. Reid stood silent and in shock!' Gran a woman of little words, small in stature but enormously brave, wanted to speak! Her tone was low-key and slow. She pressed her face up to that of her opponent and said,

'Shut your disgusting, foul mouth and get your rancid breath out of my face before I drag your fat ass into the street and kick the hell out of you!'

Dorothy Reid took a step back. Gran turned to me.

'Any last words Catherine?' she asked.

'Yes Gran.' I composed myself before I opened my mouth to speak.

'Sally says she is disgusted to call you her mother when you behave like this!'

The words were out of my mouth before I could stop them. For a split second I feared Dorothy was about to faint, she lost her footing and only regained her balance by clutching onto a handrail.

'Do you want to continue this conversation inside in a civil manner, Dorothy?' Gran asked.

Mrs. Reid and her daughter sheepishly entered the house, we made our way into the kitchen and sat down at the dinner table. Order of the day was a pot of tea; it solved all life's problems. As gran set out the cups and saucers, Dorothy Reid started to talk, calmly and lovingly about her daughter Sally, Joanne's twin sister. At the age of nine Sally had died a horrific and painful death after pulling a pot of boiling lard over her body. It took three days for her to die from her burns. Ninety percent of her little body had been covered by the boiling liquid. It was a tragic accident but, Dorothy had never forgiven herself, moving to the new house was supposed to be a fresh start but Dorothy felt she had left her dead daughter's memories back in the old house. She began to sob. Joanne put her arms around her mother's neck as she cried. True to form Gran showed no signs of sympathy or emotion, she simply filled the cups with hot tea.

My head was aching, the more Dorothy spoke about Sally the more painful it became. Someone was trying to communicate with me as I sensed a shift in the energy around me. The pressure in the room was intense. A spirit was trying to come through, I focused. The sound of a child giggling could be heard coming from the lounge. There was no reaction from the others, they obviously heard nothing, so I said nothing. Suddenly, I was hit by an invisible force, it wasn't painful, it just took me by surprise. A spirit was trying to get my attention, I knew it was Sally before she spoke to me. The little girl appeared at the kitchen door and beckoned me into the lounge. I followed her. Sally did not possess any of the burnt tissue Dorothy had described earlier. She looked almost angelic, dressed head to toe in a white dress and cardigan. She had several messages she wanted me to relay to her mother and sister. We talked for several minutes before I suggested I brought her mother and sister into the lounge. I wanted to share the energy with them and pass on the love. Spirit communication is about energy, and I had to keep the energy levels high if this was going to work. I called for Dorothy, Joanne, and Gran. I was about to perform my first private session communicating with the dead. I was 12 years old.

'Dorothy, Joanne, Gran, I am just going to talk with Sally, please listen, I need you to be positive not skeptical, open your mind and heart and accept what I am about to do and say.' The room went deadly quiet.

I felt calm and composed. For me, it was the most natural thing in the world. Gran joined us. I needed her emotional support and energy.

'Please remain open and accepting, as it influences the positive energy in the room' The words came to me so naturally. I sounded like someone who had done this before rather than the novice I was. Over the next 30 minutes I spoke to Sally and conveyed messages to her mother and sister. I was able to identify confidential information and delivery accurate proof to Dorothy that I was communicating with her dead daughter. Sally stood in the corner of the room; I spoke on her behalf. Emotions were high and I became exhausted channeling the information. My strength started to decline and drain form my body. I was mentally exhausted, and my audience were visibly stunned.

When everyone left, I knew it was only a matter of time before Dorothy and Joanne would discuss what had gone on with anyone who would listen. I felt like a weight had been lifted from my shoulders. I felt validated.

***

I was in second year of secondary school and hated it.

I spent a great deal of time in the library reading up on topics like psychic ability and extrasensory perception. The librarian teacher was called Miss Campbell. She had a bohemian sense of dress and walked with a real attitude. If Miss. Campbell did not like you were out of the library toot suite. She had quite a following of sixth formers who hung around her in the reading room like a bad smell at lunchtime. It was quite a little clique. Whilst I was researching at the back of the library one afternoon, I was asked to take part in a photography art project. Basically, a team of sixth year pupils were taking random pictures in the library and developing them in the chemistry department. The photographic brief was a set of images which were to be natural and convey the day in the life of the library. I smiled and posed with books and nonchalantly looked pensively into the distance whilst the camera clicked away. Once the session was over, I never thought much more about it. A week or so later Miss Campbell asked me to join her for a 'cup of tea' at lunchtime in the library. Perhaps I was going to be invited into the clique! At our meeting there was no one in the library except her and I, which was strange, normally she had her sixth form followers hanging on her every word floating about making tea and complimenting each other on how fabulous they were. We sat down and after a small amount of chit chat, she laid out the black and white pictures on the desk. At first, I was unsure what I was to look at, but it didn't take much time to spot the white streaks and orbs in every picture in which I was featured. No one else had white glowing balls of light surround them, just me.

'Catherine, do you know what these are?' she asked as she spread the images across her desk pointing at the orbs in the photographs.

'I am not sure exactly what they are, but I see them a lot, normally before a spirit appears.' I replied.

She explained orbs are normally associated with spirts who may be trying to communicate with us. They are thought to represent the energy field of a spiritual being. Miss Campbell appeared sympathetic and comforting so I began to open to her and said more than I intended to say. I talked about my ability to see and speak with the dead and how my family had tried to silence me discussing this for fear of embarrassing them. When the school bell rang to confirm the end of lunch, I realised I had said too much.

'Can I trust you to say nothing about this?' She nodded her head, but I knew she would talk and talk she did - at the first opportunity, she couldn't wait !

Diary Entry - Friday 8th December 1972

There are 23 days left till the end of the year and they have still not caught Linda Shaw's murderer. I am so nervous he will strike again. He has got away with it once. My head hurts knowing who he is and not being able to tell. I do not know how long I can keep this secret ....

In some ways I was beyond my years in how I thought and how I talked but I was not a typical 12-year-old girl. I had few friends, well friends that were alive! I suffered from severe headaches on a weekly basis, my mum and dad did nothing but argue, my mother had OCD and was a compulsive liar, my brother was the Golden Child and could do no wrong, (or so they thought), my sister Mary had just announced she was leaving for France to work in a hotel, my gran was thought to have killed my papa. My father was a workaholic, and my oldest sister, Margaret, who I missed everyday was at the other end of the world. Could life be more extreme!

At home, Billy was in the kitchen making a sandwich, he had the countertop covered in bits of bread, salad cream and tomato. Mum would be furious if she saw the kitchen like this. Her OCD would go into overdrive and her anxiety would hit the roof. There was a letter from the school on the telephone table in the hall. It was addressed to Mr. and Mrs. William Jamieson;

it hadn't been opened. It had to be about me, so I opened it.

Both my parents had been summoned to attend the school to discuss my behaviour? I knew it would be about the situation in the library and the big mouth of Miss Campbell. I disposed of the letter and mentioned nothing to them, they would be none the wiser. There were only a few weeks to the Christmas break. It would all be forgotten in the new year. If the school wrote again, I would ask gran to attend, she would put them in their place.

Diary entry - Saturday 6th January 1973

Spent my pocket money in Woolworths, I bought the single, Jimmy Osmond's Long-Haired Lover from Liverpool. I must have played it twenty times on Billy's record player. Its number one in the charts. Mum bought Carly Simon, You're so Vain. I think this is the perfect song for mum, maybe Miss Simon wrote it about her ...... the police took Billy away tonight for questioning.

DCI Smith and a colleague arrived unannounced at the front door and asked for my father. It had just gone 5.30pm on Saturday evening. Dad took them into the lounge and closed the door behind them. They had come to ask Billy some questions about the murder of Linda Shaw. Billy was in his bedroom, headphones on listening to David Bowie. Gran and mum had just come through the door after spending the day in Glasgow, they were laden with bags of shopping from the sales. My dad had asked Billy to come down to the lounge and help the police with their enquiries. Dad knew it made sense to cooperate with the police, this was a murder enquiry and not a shoplifting offence. If you had nothing to hide, there was no point in antagonising them, the last thing you wanted was to get on the wrong side of the law. I could hear raised voices. Dad and Billy came out the lounge and put on their jackets, DCI Smith was being his usual inquisitive self, fingering the keys on the key holder on the kitchen wall.

'Better take your keys Billy.' Suggested Smith before Dad, Billy and Smith left for the police station. Mum and Gran stayed with me, tensions were high, my mother chain-smoked her way through a twenty pack of cigarettes in three hours, filling the lounge with thick cigarette smoke that clung to your hair and clothing.

Back home, Billy updated mum and Gran on what had happened at the station.

'I was bloody terrified and so naïve. It was just as well dad was with me, or I might have ended up saying the wrong thing.' Said Billy

'You can't say the wrong thing if you're innocent boy!' said Dad as he lit up the first of many cigarettes that night.

The outcome could have been so different as they were determined to arrest someone for Linda Shaw's murder. Billy looked visibly shaken I could sense he was still frightened even though he was back home.

'They asked me if I recognised a key ring, they had with BILLY embossed on it, I told them I don't have a key ring charm and had never seen it before.'

Smith produced a metal key ring charm with BILLY embossed on it. The keyring was found hidden in the mud at the entrance to the underpass. DCI Smith asked for the keys Billy had taken from the house. On the chain one of the metal rings had broken off and part of the keyring was missing. Smith suggested the one they had found had belonged to Billy.

'Thought you didn't use a key-ring Billy?' enquired Smith, the questions were going in a more sinister direction.

Bill Jamieson was quick to jump in and answer.

'That's not your keys Billy, they are my spare set and for your information it was a keyring that belonged to my daughter with a pink dog on it, I pulled it off!' Dad declared.

'Now if you don't mind, I think we have answered all your questions and we would like to go home.' Dad did not like where this interview was going.

DCI Smith was a calculating, manipulative, character. His interrogation methods were intimidating. Being interrogated by the police is not a fair fight, their questions are loaded and designed to trip you up. One minute they were friendly the next you were the target of their investigation.

'It's just routine Billy, just a few more questions than you can go.' Smith was determined to continue with the interview. His colleague said nothing, he just smoked cigarettes and took notes. Dad took control of the situation.

'My son is an innocent man, and he will not be answering any more questions without a lawyer, now if you don't mind.' Bill stood up and gestured to Billy to do the same thing. Just like a crucifix to a vampire Smith and his colleague backed off. Bill and Billy said their goodbyes and got the hell out of there.

The key ring may or may not have been a valuable lead in the murder investigation, it may have been a long shot or even a coincidence, but Smith was going to use every lead he was presented with to make a conviction. Smith wanted everything photographed at the crime scene, every scrap of evidence was catalogued and analysed. He requested dozens of photographs were taken of the victim, most of the images were tough to look at and Smith thought they would sway any jury in a murder case when presented at court.

'No self-respecting member of the jury would let any suspect walk free from court after seeing the pictures of that wee lassies butchered body. They would never let him roam the streets again!' Smith was thinking ahead. He knew how the lawyers could coax a not guilty verdict when there was little evidence to convict. But a picture paints a thousand words.

The clues to finding the accused were in the pictures. Smith was hoping the bite marks on Linda's cheek would lead them to their man. Impressions and photographs were taken of the bite marks, and they had been presented to a dentist. The dentist confirmed the accused would have a slight overbite and strong front incisors as considerable force would have been required to rip and tear the facial flesh.

'Let's just say the bastard would have had a good set of teeth based on the dental impressions that were taken!' Smith imagined the defendants' teeth being kicked in once he was behind bars. If there was one thing inmates hated – it was nonces and child killers. Linda Shaw had only turned 17 the week before her brutal murder.

 The police didn't have much to go on, no weapon had been found and the killer had been meticulous not to leave any clothing or clues at the scene. By all accounts he wore gloves and possibly a balaclava.

Smith made an appeal to the members of the public; someone must have seen something. When Smith was interviewed for the evening news, he asked the public to be vigilant and help find the killer.

'Think about the night she was murdered; did you see anything suspicious? Did someone not turn up for work in the morning? Did someone you know suddenly have scratches or bruises to their face or body about this time? Did you find any blood on clothing? Someone knows who the killer is? Dial 999 and ask for the police. You don't need to give your name.' Smith looked directly into the camera as he delivered his final sentence. 'This could have been your daughter!'

Smith was in the police station HQ after the interview was televised. His team were fielding the incoming telephone calls. Each one would have to be followed up and checked before they would be eliminated from their enquiries. It was like a needle in a haystack, but Smith always got his man.

DCI Smith needed to find and arrest someone soon to close

the case. It had been several months since the murder had taken place and the police were struggling for leads. The public wanted the killer caught and put behind bars. Most of the males, especially teenage boys, in the town had been approached and interviewed. Their whereabouts and alibi had been accounted for on the night. Billy was interviewed again and heard nothing more. On the evening of the murder Billy said he had been at a friend's house, went to the chip shop on his way home, bought some fish and chips and came straight home. My father confirmed he was home about 10.00pm. I knew they both were lying because Margaret telephoned from Australia at 10.15pm and neither my dad nor Billy were home.

Over the course of the week, DCI Smith came to the house several times. Dad was concerned when he turned up at Thomson Pumps, it didn't take much to get the staff gossiping. Smith had finished interviewing the male employees so why did he need to keep coming back to the factory. Smith was hanging about like a nauseating smell, if he was not sitting outside the factory in his car, he was driving passed our house several times a day. Dad said it was police harassment. Money that had been put away for the family to travel to Australia was now being considered for a lawyer.

Linda Shaw had been the focus of my dreams for several nights. She had shown herself to me many times asking for help to bring her killer to justice. I was torn, I knew I had to tell Smith but had been warned off by my dad. I wanted to put an end to her pain and suffering along with that of her families. She had been tortured in life and I did not want to be held responsible for her being continually tortured in death. Her spirit had to be set free and allowed to rest in peace. The truth had to be told, I had to tell the police the truth and reveal who her killer was. I decided, in the morning I would call DCI Smith and request a meeting with him, in private. If need be, I would take gran with me.

***

School was a nightmare, the stories circulating around the school about me were instigated by Miss Campbell the librarian, a despicable spinster who was not to be trusted. She orchestrated the spread of nasty gossip via her naïve posse who were happy to follow her orders. She groomed pupils to divulge personnel information about themselves and then shared the details with other pupils. I was one of her victims. There was no private discussion with her, it had all been well orchestrated with the intent of it being leaked. Campbell was the worst kind of teacher, it became evident why she chose to surround herself with ignorant sixth formers rather than go to the staff room, she simply was not liked by the other teachers. She was a woman in a position of authority, and I trusted her, she abused this trust. My year head teacher, a lovely man called Mr. McGinley asked me to stay away from her. His advice came too late to stop the gossip.

Brian McGinley. Head of Year Teacher, when interviewed about Catherine Mathieson in 1982:

'She was beyond her years, I taught her in my History and Modern Studies class from the time she was 12 years old till she was fifteen. When she walked into the classroom, she had a presence. I could never put my finger on it. It was like she walked into the class and brought another dozen souls with her. She thrived on asking you questions, always curious to know about you and never talked about herself. I had heard what others had to say about Catherine but never thought much about it. During one of my classes, she wasn't paying much attention, dreaming, and fidgeting, scribbling on a piece of paper, generally having no interest in the class, which was unusual. I asked what was up and she said she would tell me later. After class, when the other pupils had left, she came up to my desk and said as calmly as you like, that my father, Jimmy McGinley was immensely proud of me and enjoyed the classical music I played in the car, especially Vivaldi's Four Seasons. While she was talking, I could feel the whole energy in the empty class-

room change. My father had died just a few weeks before, it wasn't common knowledge to the pupils, but Catherine knew his name, she mentioned the music, which was accurate, and she spoke using the same words and mannerisms as my dad. Catherine said he had come into the classroom and sat with her that afternoon while I was teaching and had enjoyed listening to me. It brought me a deep sense of comfort knowing he was still around and looking out for me. She said another few personal things, nothing random but very precise. The energy that was coming off her was powerful, it was one of those moments you never forget. I knew then she was destined to do well in life with such an incredible gift! Brian McGinley

CHAPTER 7

1973

Diary entry - Sunday 11th February 1973

My father has forbidden me to speak to the police, the effect this is having on me emotionally is devastating. I feel I am being guided by the victim Linda Shaw to tell my truth, she visits me most evenings and is a tortured soul. I have dark circles around my eyes, I think this is simply from lack of sleep. My mother has commented on my weight lose but I have little or no appetite. I have spent a great deal of time in my bedroom talking to other spirits, but Linda Shaw desperately needs my help. If I do not disclose the killers name, I will end up going mad. My father has taken to ignoring me and this has caused even more tension around the house. Margaret has not called for two weeks, and Mary is in France. My mother is in denial and my father, well, I have no influence on him. If I speak to Gran, she may tell my dad. I have no one to confide in!

My diary entries were becoming darker and more depressive. Some days I felt like I could not take much more of the voices. My childhood memories revolved around me talking to and seeing people who were dead! There was always a spirit trying to communicate with me. Sometimes I thought it was me that was being haunted.

Diary entry - Tuesday 20th February 1973

Last night I had a nightmare and woke up crying. It was so vivid I had to get out of bed and come downstairs into the lounge. I had the most crippling head pains. I hope I do not live to regret what I did tonight?

I left a telephone message for DCI Smith to contact

me, I said I knew who murdered Linda Shaw. I could identify who the killer was, I provided specific evidence, details only the person that killed her or the coroner would have known. Hopefully, my evidence would put the murderer behind bars. Naively, I thought I could keep this from my father. I was so wrong.

When DCI Smith arrived at our house he was accompanied by a female constable. As expected, dad was furious when he found out why Smith had called round. Reluctantly, they were both invited in and shown into the lounge. Their arrival at the house had one saving grace, they turned up in an unmarked police car. Both mum and dad sat in on the interview as a minor I was unable to be interviewed on my own . Despite my mental maturity I was still a child. I admitted making the telephone call to the police station, I wanted to put an end to the lying. Linda Shaw deserved to rest in peace and her killer put behind bars.

My father was incensed, everything he wanted to repress about my psychic ability was about to be exposed. My mother seemed to be enjoying the attention, the best China was out along with the foil biscuits. Gran stayed out the way in the kitchen but within ear shot.

Smith had so many questions. Everything about my night at the underpass was questioned then questioned again. The more evidence I was able to provide the more he wanted to hear. Smith sat and stared at me, taping his pen on the arm of the chair. I was a mystery to him, he found it difficult to grasp what he was dealing with, a young girl who professed to talking to the dead. There was no rational explanation for everything I knew about Linda Shaw's brutal murder. What I was confessing could not be explained. Smith looked perplexed as he sat forward on the chair. I had his full attention.

'Who did it Catherine?' his stare was intent as he waited for my answer.

'It was Michael Speirs, he killed Linda Shaw!' I said with a great deal of relief.

Smith spoke to the female constable who was dispatched with the name and the instructions to pick up Speirs immediately.

Bill and Maureen sat in disbelief. Gran came into the room and put her arms around me.

'Well done, Catherine, you have done the right thing.' Smith said reaching over to pat my hand.

He stood up and zipped up his anorak. 'We will talk tomorrow.' He made his way to the door and turned then turned back to my mother and father.

'Don't be too tough on the girl, she did well, you should be proud of her!'

Mum and Dad said nothing. Dad gave Smith a look of total disdain. Gran got up to show him out.

'I want you to come to Greenock with me tomorrow, along with your mother. I have something I want you to see.' Smith changed the subject. 'Be ready for about 10am!'

His tone sounded optimistic. In my heart I felt he was starting to believe me. It had gone 10pm before Smith and his colleague left. It was too late for me to accompany them to the police station; it could wait for now. He arranged for my mother and I to be picked up in the morning. As he left Smith turned and smiled.

'I hope you're right little lady, for now let's keep this quiet, the press will have a field day if they found out about you and how we managed to catch a killer.' Smith bid the family goodnight and left under the cover of darkness.

Inside the police car Smith looked at the female constable and spoke.

'Best you forget everything you heard inside that house tonight. If any of this gets out, I will know it was you! I will personally see to it that you are kicked out of the force and back sweeping up hair in your local hairdressers – do you understand?' Smith despised females working in the police force, as far as he was concerned, they should stick to cleaning up the house and having children.

They both drove back to the station in silence.

The thirty-mile journey to Greenock was silent apart from the police radio going off in the background. DCI Smith was not a particularly chatty man. As we drove along the dual carriageway the River Clyde was on our right-hand side. A submarine was propelling through the grey water destined for the nuclear submarine base further up the Clyde. The terrifying black tower hid the mammoth vessel hidden beneath the water. It was the first time I had seen a submarine this close, and it was an incredible site. Mum, Smith, and his colleague smoked throughout the journey with no consideration to my coughing in the back seat. I rolled down the window for some fresh air.

Smith broke the silence to talk.

'I'm taking you to an area where we found a body a few nights ago, tell me what you think?' What did he mean think ? Think about the view, think about the area?

An hour later we turned off the carriageway and pulled up at a remote area of land not seen from the road. I followed DCI Smith as we walked under the railroad bridge and stood in the archway, the ground was littered with old beer cans and wine bottles. I instantly felt tense. My heart was racing, I immediately knew why I was here! Smith wanted to test me, it was his little experiment, could I really talk to the dead!

'Catherine, can you contact the spirit of a man whose life ended tragically under this archway.' goaded Smith.

'I can't do this on command Mr. Smith, I don't just conjure up spirits!' I was uncomfortable and looked towards my mother for help.

'Mum I want to go home now?'

I could see DCI Smith wasn't happy. 'I'm disappointed in you Catherine.' he paused for effect.

'A young man died a brutal death here, perhaps you can help put his spirit to rest.'

I wasn't a freak show, and I didn't appreciate being brought to this odious place. I wasn't here for his entertainment, the show was over, I needed to get away. Mother led the way back to the police car. My head was spinning, and my stomach was knotted. Unable to control myself, I was violently sick in the long grass. Mother took a handkerchief from her bag and handed it to me, one of the more caring things she had done for me in a while. I had a strong feeling something was about to occur, and it wasn't anything pleasant. Feeling uneasy I worried that something had attached itself to me. Not all spirits stay in the area they died, their residual energy can remain, it is this energy that can then attach itself to you and this was the last thing I wanted.

I looked round about me and thought about the addicts who used this area as a drinking den, shooting up heroin into their ruptured veins. It would be a sobering thought if they knew what monstrous act had been committed at the site.

I didn't want to stay, I wanted to get out of there, I caused a scene and we all agreed it was time to go. We headed back along the motorway in silence. DCI Smith, said nothing about what had happened at the arches, his silence could be far more intimidating than his questioning. I was exhausted and just wanted to rest, some spirits could drain me both emotionally and physically.

In the back seat of the car, I became agitated and anxious. I could see Smith watching me in the rearview interior mirror.

My body was itching and burning. My mind drifted back to the arches, I closed my eyes and sat back in the seat. I regressed and was back at the scene on the night of the murder. I could feel my body start to violently shake, I may have looked like I was having a fit, but I was in a deep psychic state. I could see the boy who was murdered at the archway, he looked about 16, he was taken there by two other men with the soul intention of torturing and killing him.

I opened my eyes and I was staring directly at Smith!

'Take me back to the archway, now!' I demanded.

Smith slammed his hand on the dashboard. 'Turn the car around Frank!'

The driver braked suddenly and steered the car across the dual carriageway almost hitting an oncoming car before we raced back to the site. We were all thrown back into our seats such was the speed of the car.

Back at the arches, I made a connection with the human spirit of the deceased boy. I asked for some space and privacy, there was no fear in me just an eagerness to set this tormented spirit free.

My mother wrapped herself in her coat and tightened her head scarf. She watched in disbelief at what was going on.

'Am I speaking to the spirit of Alan Rankin?' I called out.

I repeated the question as I fell into what I can only describe as a half-conscious state. I was not aware of anything around me, my mind was completely focused on speaking to the spirit. In my hypnotic state I felt the air around me grow colder and heavy.

'Alan, show yourself, I am here to help you.'

I pleaded for him to manifest. I could feel his presence, but he was unwilling to show himself at first. I focused on his spirit and remained emotionally calm and mentally clear in what I wanted to achieve – I wanted to see the face of the men who killed him.

When he finally appeared, it was just a haze, an outline of a body. I reached out to him.

'Show yourself Alan, I am not here to harm you just to help you move on and find those who did this to you.' His full apparition appeared to me, and I began to communicate with Alan on a different level to the other spirits I had previously met.

The first thing I noticed about Alan was, he had a beautiful face, angelic. He looked so young, not much older than me. He was sixteen.

Alan Rankin was gay, addicted to codeine and any other opiate he could get his hands on, Marijuana and amphetamines had been replaced with heroin and this habit did not come cheap. It was so much easier to be a male prostitute and feed his habit than a shoplifter. He just did not have the speed or nimbleness to evade the security guards in the stores, nor did he possess a mislaid moral compass. Even when he was stoned and desperate for a fix, he refused to rob the old and frail. He must have been the only heroin addict with a conscience. He knew what was right and what was wrong and tried to act accordingly. Besides, selling his ass was a sure means to make some quick and much needed cash. Alan enjoyed having sex with men but knew if he was caught with another man, he faced a jail sentence.

Same-sex activity among men in Scotland was illegal until 1980.

Alan slowly started to communicate with me, he told me he had gone willingly with the two men to the arches, he knew they would supply him with what he needed plus some much-needed cash. He had been with them several times before but confessed they had been a bit rough with him on previous occasions. This time, they insisted they would take turns having intercourse with him while the other watched, nothing perverted just straight sex. The two men were well known hard men from The Port, if anyone knew of their sexual orientation, they would have been hounded out of their housing scheme. They snorted a gramme or two of cocaine before they left the car. The arches were perfect, it was so well hidden and off the beaten track, no one would have heard you scream, the only noise you could hear was the distant sound of the cars on the dual carriageway. Money was exchanged and Alan was given a small foil wrapper containing heroin. The three men drank some cheap tonic wine and began to masturbate each other before getting out the car.

The situation got violent almost from the outset. Alan was gagged and repeatedly raped. A belt had been placed around his neck and pulled so tightly his airways were restricted as he struggled to breath. His arms were tied around his back. He slowly died from asphyxiation. On his final gasp he thought about his mother, sat at home worrying where her son was and what he was doing. The two men who took his life in such a horrifying, perverse and violent manner were called Jim Slain and Peter Burgoyne.

I explained to Alan it was time to move on, he had to accept he was dead, I promised I would pass a message to his mother, she loved him unconditionally and would understand his deviant nature. No one chooses their sexuality and drugs can visit anyone's door, rich or poor. The depravity and immoral acts inflicted on this innocent boy stayed with me for some time. There needs to be acceptance of your death before you can have peace, you must accept you are dead and move on. When you die, most people pass on and make the transition to the other side freely and instantly, sometimes they decide to stay. A spirit can stay earthbound if they have been taken suddenly and are not ready to move on, they may have a message for someone or they have unfinished business. Sometimes they are confused or concerned about those they are leaving behind. Alan remained earthbound because he had been taken too soon, there was too many things he wanted to say before he moved on.

'Tell my mum I love her and I'm sorry.'

Alan sobbed, he was concerned about his mother, she was fragile and lived for her sons, she wouldn't cope without her beloved son so soon after the death of her husband. Alan asked me to do two things for him. One - visit his mother and explain how much he loved her, he wanted her to know the truth about his death and not what the newspapers had decided to publish. Two – Tell the police everything about his murder and name the men responsible. I promised I would do both.

'I'm frightened to go!' I told Alan there was no need to be frightened any more, the time had come for him to cross over, and I was going to be here to assist with the transition. I closed my eyes and focused on the energy surrounding us. I blocked out all that was happening and focused on the transition. It was as if I had been transported to another dimension , an out of body experience which allowed me to walk Alan to the doorway of eternal peace. I persuaded Alan it was safe and time to cross over and asked him to visualise his father who was waiting on his son. His father was holding the door open and inviting Alan to go to him. It was beautiful, calm, and loving. Alan walked towards the doorway to be with his beloved father. The door closed. I knew Alan had crossed over when the energy levels changed, and I began to come back to reality.

I was so traumatized by the violence surrounding Alan's death my body was trembling. Mentally I was drained and needed support emotionally. Smith took me under his wing and placed his hand on my shoulder as we headed back to the waiting car.

The journey back to town seemed to last forever. Smith turned to look at me. 'Let's get you back young lady, you've done an excellent job today.' He saw I was trembling and placed his corduroy jacket over me. It felt like a big hug.

My mum moaned about catching her stockings on some nettles and how she would have to buy a new pair. She never once asked how I was. I just don't think she had the capacity to share any empathy with me.

At the police station, I was supported by a female police officer; she held my hand and was sympathetic, offering support and kindness as I recalled all the details of my psychic encounter with Alan Rankin. My mother asked to make a telephone call and returned to the interview room with freshly applied lipstick. The female officer reminded me of my sister Margaret, she oozed genuine concern and understanding, she cuddled me and placed a blanket around my shoulders. My mother watched on as another woman consoled her child.

DCI Smith had me recall every detail of my conversation with Alan. We went over again and again every minute details until I physically broke down and asked to go home. Smith agreed and immediately terminated the interview. I had seen and done enough for one day, I wanted to be home. It had all gotten too much for me and I broke down crying.

'Please, let me go home, I am exhausted!' I begged.

Smith immediately organised for a driver to drop mum and I off at the house.

At home, my head was aching. Mother gave me paracetamol and one of her sleeping pills and ushered me up to bed, my whole body was drained. Once I was in the sanctuary of my own bed; I settled under the covers and allowed the medication to take effect, I quickly fell asleep. I slept for 15 hours straight.

Several days later, DCI Smith organised for a female police office to come to the house. She let me talk to Alan Rankin's mother on the telephone. I was neither allowed nor was I capable of meeting his mother in person. I think that was for the best. I had laid his spirit to rest and could deal with no more anguish. My part in this investigation was over. Several months later, thanks to the evidence I provided, Jim Slain and Peter Burgoyne were found guilty of Alan Rankins murder. They both received fifteen years each in jail.

A few years later, Slain was found hung in his cell, it was believed to be suicide and Burgoyne engaged in a fight in the exercise yard that resulted in his death after a pencil was plunged into his neck and he bled to death. On 1st March 1973 DCI Smith arrested Michael Speirs and charged him with murdering Linda Shaw. In December 1973 he was sentenced to life in prison. He laughed as he was taken away to start his sentence. He showed no remorse for his crime.

Michael Speirs when presented with irrefutable facts and undeniable evidence in the form of pictures of the murdered girl's body revealed himself to be one of the most cowardly killers imaginable, destined to spend the rest of his life behind bars. He had no conscience and turned out to be an extremely violent man. His ex-girlfriends had all confirmed the brutal side to his nature. Three of his partners had confessed to being assaulted by him during their relationships. He had bitten into an ex- girlfriend's breast and left puncture wounds. A similar attack had been made on Linda Shaw. His alibis were so unbelievable they were contested immediately by Smith and were proven to be fabricated. During interviews Speirs talked excessively to distract and deflect the attention from him and nowhere in his testimony did his story match. His well-rehearsed script was full of flaws. He was the chief suspect and all the evidence pointed towards him. His statements were false and inconsistent. Speirs was shocked at being caught, he really did think he was going to get away with murder, thinking he was smarter than anyone else, especially the police. He eventually confessed but never showed any signs of remorse. Dental reports confirmed the teeth marks on Linda Shaws chest had matched the bite marks to Speirs. We may never know his motive for the murder, but we do know Speirs was a man who liked to control women. He had selected to end the life of a random young girl who was in the wrong place at the wrong time with the wrong man.

His history of violent behaviour was undeniable and with credible witnesses, mainly ex-girlfriends and female co-workers who were willing to take the stand against him, his chances of getting away with murder were slim. Speirs was cold and calculating. The murder was premeditated, he probably planned the scenario repeatedly in his head and acting out his extreme fantasy. A monster in the making, Linda Shaw was an easy target, a vulnerable, young girl. Speirs was a manipulative predator who deserved his punishment. He had been smart enough to cover most of his tracks, but he never anticipated one thing - me!

Every man in the area had been a suspect, every woman knew there was a killer on the loose, now, the town could relax, an evil monster had been caught.

I was never mentioned in the court proceedings and never had to take the stand.

The only question I had was - how long were they going to keep my identity a secret!

CHAPTER 8

Bonjour Sacha

Diary entry - Thursday 1ˢᵗ March 1973

Mary is coming home next week to visit the family and bringing her French boyfriend. Everyone is excited about meeting him, especially gran as she has never met a Frenchman before! Dad called Margaret last night and was unable to speak to her, Joe said she was out, but dad had planned to call her tonight and Margaret said she would be home. Something isn't right! I am almost a teenager and I feel like I have never really had a childhood. I have seen and heard things that no person let alone a child should see or hear. The school have decided I should speak with a child psychologist, Further disappointment for my dad! I suppose the good thing about seeing a specialist is I will get a half day on a Friday from school as the clinic is not in New Weston.

Mary came back from Paris for the week with Sacha, she was in love and wanted the family to meet him. Mum and dad were still fighting over the most ridiculous things and because of this mum had been sleeping in Mary's old bedroom. Deception reigned at the Jamieson residence, so mum had to move back in with dad while Mary was home. This was not going down too well with mum. Playing happy families never lasted long in our house, it was a volatile environment, anything could spark an argument, combined with copious amounts of alcohol, it was a lethal concoction. Over the years, mum had threatened to leave on numerous occasions but changed her mind when dad would offer her a present or brought her home chocolates. She was easily swayed. Their relentless arguing resulted in the most hateful things being said. Unforgiveable, nasty, vile comments,

'They are just words said in the heat of the moment, they don't mean anything.' she would say.

If that was the case – why say them. I can tell you, their screaming and shouting over the years had a negative mental effect - on Margaret, Mary, Billy and I. Forever worrying when the fighting would break out and walking eggshells around mum. We never knew what state of mind she would be in at any time of the day. I was always anxious just waiting for things to blow up.

Billy had been dating a young girl from the factory, her name was Debbie, she had incredible fashion sense considering the 70's was classed as 'the decade style forgot'. She would come to the house wearing the most amazing platform shoes and flared trousers.

Billy was into David Bowie and dyed his hair bright red to emulate his hero, the colour was almost the same as mine. For the first time in my life, my red hair was trendy! Dad wasn't happy with Billy and Debbie going out together as he thought relationships within the workplace never worked and inevitably ended in someone being heartbroken, normally the women. Staff dating was frowned upon, but the golden child ignored protocol and went ahead with the relationship, Billy always did what he wanted, and dad turned a blind eye to it.

My father picked Mary and Sacha up from Glasgow Central train station. Sacha spoke perfect English and my dad took to him right away. As they came through the front door of the house, they both brought sunshine and sophistication on a damp wet winter's night. Mary was tanned and toned. She spoke fluent French and smelt of Guerlain Shalimar. The scent was wonderful, it was feminine with bergamot, mandarin orange, lemon, and citrus. The whole house smelt like a spicy floral garden. Sasha was like a bronzed god with massive brown eyes and long black eyelashes. He was gorgeous, perfect in every way, his wavy brown hair sat perfectly on his shoulders, he even shocked everyone when he came down to breakfast one morning with it pulled back in a ponytail! It was official, Sacha was the sexiest man alive as far as I was concerned and when he spoke, oh la la!

I literally could not take my eyes off him and found myself blushing when he spoke to me. Mary noticed and giggled at my reaction. They both seemed so content and happy together. I was extremely envious of them. Mary had changed so much, she presented herself with so little effort, her style was simple and yet so chic, a pair of flared jeans and crisp white shirt with a blue head scarf tied over her head and under her hair, it was so random and yet so stylish.

Mum said she looked just like Lauren Hutton. Mary even managed to persuade dad to buy a pair of denim jeans and shed the dated look he had. Suit trousers, shirt, and cardigan. His suit trousers were banished to the wardrobe after work. Dad took to this new relaxed style of dressing right away. It suited him. It made him look more relaxed.

Mary and I found time to talk in private, she came into my room and sat on the bed.

'This is for you.' she said, handing me a brown paper bag with 'Pour petite Cat' written on the front. Inside there was a clear lip gloss and a blue eyeshadow, a T-Shirt with 'Paris' embossed on the front, an assortment of mini-French perfume samples and a belated diary for 1973.

'It's a diary from Paris, I thought you would like it for your collection.' she smiled. It was perfect, Mary had put so much thought into the gift.

'So how have you and all your dead friends been?' Mary giggled as she tickled me on my side.

'Oh, you know Mary, when you can talk to the dead

you're never alone!' We both laughed.

The conversation became more somber as we discussed Michael Speirs.

'You know he would hit me and force me to do some horrible things.' Mary confessed.

'I was so frightened from him, France was the only way to escape his bullying, it was the best decision I made, what he did to Linda Shaw could easily have been me.'

Mary shuddered as she thought about her ex-boyfriend.

I confided in Mary about the murders. I told her what my connection had been in finding the killers. She shivered as I described some of the gruesome details.

'You have an incredibly special talent Cat, be sure and use it wisely and to your advantage.'

The telephone ringing interrupted our morbid conversation. My mother answered it with screams of delight. It was Margaret. It was customary for her to call and let my mum and dad know she was home, and we would ring her back. The cost to telephone Australia was so expensive every second was accounted for. Tonight, the call went on a minute or so longer to allow Mary and Gran to speak with Margaret. I was only ever allowed to say a few words, no more than a few seconds.

Billy, Debbie, and Sacha burst through the doorway laden down with take away food. It was a treat for everyone, fish, and chips wrapped in newspaper. We made our way into the lounge, fingers as cutlery and kitchen roll for napkins. Only my mother and Sacha used a knife and fork. It was Sacha's first-time eating chips from newspaper and drinking our nations favourite fizzy drink - Irn Bru.

Tonight, all French cuisine was off the menu.

It was Sacha and Mary's last night before they returned to France so after a late dinner mum wanted to party and insisted, we all had a drink. She got out the vodka and prompted Billy to get Sacha a can of lager from the fridge. She assumed the role of DJ and lined up several singles for the stereo. Rod Stewart, David Cassidy and The Osmonds.

Dad was not willing to go along with her plans; he was content to settle down for the night and watch Parkinson, his favourite chat show. It was turning into a typical Saturday night with alcohol and arguments. We all knew where this was going. Gran was the first to make her apologies and asked Billy to walk her back to her house. She would be back in the morning to say her goodbyes to Sacha and Mary.

The more vodka my mother consumed the louder she became. She persistently goaded my father.

'Don't be such a bloody bore Bill, you will do anything to ruin my happiness!' Her fake well spoken, accent was quickly dropped and replaced with her colloquial Scottish drawl. The slurring drunk had entered the room, hell bent on causing chaos. This led to one almighty argument between her and my father. The facade of a happy family she had tried to keep up all week abruptly came to an end. Her flawless plans for the final evening would not be going ahead. Another great night ruined by alcohol and self-regard, welcome to the Jamieson family, Sacha.

One thing for sure, he wouldn't have understood what my mother was yelling, thankfully!

Saturday morning, Gran as usual was at our house. She enjoyed watching the wrestling on World of Sport on a Saturday, mainly because we had a large rented colour television, the only one in the street. Gran's television was a small portable black and white set. She loved to watch the wrestling. especially the wrestlers, Mick McManus and Kendo Nagassaki When they appeared in the ring, they drove the audience wild, Gran became another woman, she yelled and cursed at the television like a woman possessed. She was unrecognisable when she was drawn into their ridiculous theatrical performance.

'HOLD HIM DOWN! SIT ON HIM! KICK HIM OUT THE RING!'

She shrieked at the television oblivious to anything else that may have been going on in the room. Today of all days I needed Gran at the house, her screaming and yelling at the wrestling was exactly what I needed to hear. She was my distraction; her yelling gave the house a life, today I didn't want to be alone. Feeling mentally depressed and being bombarded by several spirits who were pushing me to acknowledge their presence was exhausting me. I was fighting to ignore them. Sacha and Mary were leaving today, and I was going to miss them both so very much. When I waved them off, I felt emotionally drained, my depleted body appeared to be crashing at an incredible rate. I was needing space, I needed to escape, I needed to recharge. And then it happened!

Diary entry - Saturday 17th March 1973.

Sacha and Mary are travelling back to France today. Dad drove them to Glasgow Central Station late afternoon. They both start new jobs in Monaco next week. Monaco sounds wonderful. As Mary and Sacha left, they both gave me a warm hug. As I embraced Sacha, I had a horrific sense of dread, something I had never experienced before. I had a very unusual and disturbing feeling. This was more than a bad sensation. I immediately felt that this would be the last time I would meet him. I knew he would be dead within the year. I wanted to pull Mary back and warn her, but she seemed so happy, smiling, and looking forward to Monaco and I had no right to end her happiness. I waved goodbye and held onto my fake smile until the car disappeared out of the street. This is the first time I have had a premonition, an acute gut feeling, I am frightened. I didn't feel good about the whole experience, I was terrified. I cannot influence destiny and Sacha's fate was certain, I was sure. I wasn't going to change it. What is happening to me? My head was throbbing, and I had to spend the rest of the day in my bed with the blinds closed. I could hear Gran downstairs in the lounge, knowing she was at home comforted me and I felt less afraid. I listened to my radio and pulled the covers up over my head. I tried to focus on anything except what was going on in my mind. I didn't want to face the world. Margaret, where are you when I need you?

Winter - Saturday 13th October 1973

Mary rang the house telephone this evening to break the devastating news that Sacha had been in a car accident. He had been driving from France to Monaco when his Renault was involved in a fatal accident. The other car was on the wrong side of the road and collided with Sacha. He was rushed to hospital, but Sacha was pronounced dead on arrival. He was only 25 years old. The other driver died at the scene. It was thought that the male driver had been under the influence of alcohol. Mary was devastated and decided to remain in Monaco and continue to work. Little did we know she would never come home again.

'I consider Monaco to be my home now.' Mary declared.

August 1974

By now my reputation as a psychic medium was gaining momentum, despite me being so young. Most of the stories I had heard about myself were grossly exaggerated. My father was not comfortable with any of it mainly because he could not understand what was going on. He liked a quiet life, and I was only bringing attention to the family. I felt I wanted to set the record straight and had the opportunity to do just that when I was approached by a journalist who wanted to write a feature about my life for the local newspaper. The interview would allow me to get my point across to their readers. Dad was not pleased, but my mother loved the idea. Mum was thrilled when Billy had his picture in the local newspaper, a group picture of him celebrating his football team winning the regional football league. She bought several copies of the newspaper and showed it to everyone who came into the house. The newspaper picture was cut out and pinned to the factory noticeboard at Thomson Pumps for months until someone had defaced it and it was hastily removed by management.

Mum organised for the reporter to come to the house during the day. Gran sat in the lounge, knitting, she was here for extra support. The reporter was called Paul Jackson. Mother took to him right away, mainly because he was young and a bit of a flirt, I didn't like him, he was overfamiliar and stank of cigarette smoke. The reporter had come with a photographer who took a few photos before the interview started. Mum managed to squeeze into a few of the pictures, she was desperate to be in the image that would appear in the newspaper.

'I really think I should be in the picture with my daughter, will it be printed in colour or black and white?' It was always about her.

She wrapped her arms around me, grinning like she had just won the football pools. I was embarrassed by her antics and could feel my face turn bright red. Paul had brought a prop with him and asked me to pose with it, a crystal ball. I refused immediately; the production seemed like a lot of effort for a local newspaper.

From the outset, I started to regret the interview; things didn't feel right. Sitting at the kitchen table, Paul pulled out a shorthand notebook and began to scribble on a blank page. He lit up a cigarette and made himself comfortable. Mum pulled out the best China cups and saucers and put a plate of biscuits on the table. She reached for her cigarettes and joined us.

Jackson confirmed, the feature was only going to be published in the local newspaper, so I was happy with that. I was almost fourteen years, but I looked and spoke like an eighteen-year-old woman. At first the interview was generic. I was nervous and my head was throbbing. As expected, my mother stayed with me in the kitchen. As a minor she had to be with me. There was a heaviness in the room, it was bitterly cold despite the mild weather outdoors. I was anxious and unable to focus on everything that was going on. The photographer said his goodbyes, packed up his camera equipment and left. Jackson and I continued to talk about my life and what the future held. It was all very civil, but I was irritated, I was unable to fully concentrate on the task at hand. Jacksons mother had dominated my emotions as she was desperate to speak to her son.

'Excuse me, Paul.' I said as I put my hand up to his face to stop him talking. I spoke to the spirit, a woman who was determined to get my attention.

'Please let me finish what I am doing and then we can talk, I know you are here, and I will speak to you shortly.' I insisted.

To the skeptic I was talking to myself or perhaps putting on a show. It's impossible to continue with an interview when spirits continually hassling me to get my attention. It's like being in a busy, noisy room and everyone is trying to talk to you at the one time. It's an impossible and frustrating task.

Paul looked perplexed.

'Who are you talking to?' he asked.

'Oh, she does this from time to time when she is being bothered by her dead friends!' My mother cut in before I had the chance to answer.

'Let's just concentrate please.' I said as I gave my mother a look that said, 'Shut up!'

There was a rise in my anxiety, something didn't feel right, the energy in the room had shifted, this was never a good sign!

His initial questions were straightforward, and relatively easy to answer.

'When did I discover I could speak to the dead?'

'How often do I see dead people?'

'What do they say to me?'

'Why do they appear to me?'

I answered all his questions despite my mother trying to take the floor. I sensed his irritation with her interfering but there was little I could do.

'Cat can you show me evidence? For example, can you see any spirits around me I know lots of people who are died.' he claimed.

Jackson was pushing me hard for a reaction and I wasn't happy. Goading was never a clever way to get my attention. I can't just perform on command.

I had answered all his questions and despite putting my side of the story across to him, I feared he already had a hidden agenda on how the feature would be written. The interview was over for me.

'You have plenty to write about, considering it's just a short writeup!' I came across as petulant.

'Just a few more questions Catherine!' He had no intentions of stopping just yet.

'How do you know DCI Smith and why was your name kept out of the Linda Shaw murder, it was you who identified Michael Speirs as the killer was it not?'

I felt trapped, tricked, deceived! There was something sinister going on here and it wasn't a dead malevolent spirit. It was Jackson. I wanted him out of the house.

Paul Jackson was a journalist with aspirations of working for a national tabloid. He specialised in investigative journalism and wanted to make his name in exposing stories that secured him the front page or a double page spread. Jackson imagined moving up the corporate ladder of success, by creating controversial headlines. Eventually he would move down south and work for a Sunday newspaper, exposing love rat husbands and kiss and tell wannabes. His investigative prowess was excellent. He had been very clever. I wanted my story out there but not like this. This was not why I had agreed to the interview. I asked my mother to leave the room, just for a few minutes, she wasn't happy but did as I asked. Jackson wanted proof, so I was going to give him it.

I looked Jackson in the eyes. ' The nature of what is going on here is really dark, I can sense it, you are dangerous!' I would give Jackson what he wanted. I was going to give him the evidence he craved, proof of my power.

'Why did your mother take her own life?' I didn't hesitate to ask him.

He sat up bolt upright and looked me straight in the eye.

Jackson was uncomfortable as his smug expression had gone from his face and I felt totally in control of the situation. I asked him to be prepared as I was about to conduct my own interview.

'She is here, your mother is here!' I looked for his reaction.

'She was the one I silenced, so I could answer your questions, your mother wants to talk to you?' Jackson was stunned.

His mother, Sadie, wanted to communicate with her son. She had been pushing me all night and now it was her turn to command our attention.

Sadie Jackson, in death had found a voice and was prepared to speak about her suicide.

I blacked out at the table, once I came to, I was transferred back into the Jackson family home. Sadie was alone in a gloomy, damp room, she was sobbing, her life was about to end. I stood beside her as she placed a noose around her neck and stood on a small wooden stool which she instantly toppled over. His mother's last gasps of air were taken at 3.20am in the back bedroom of a council flat in Glasgow. With her last breath she thought about her son, Paul, the journalist, the lad who loved to write, the boy with the imagination, the wordsmith. Her despicable son who had disowned her in her moment of need.

Paul Jackson had a dream. He wanted to escape the poverty and be someone. His ability to write with creative flare and influence others was his way out. Paul was the son who never came to visit anymore, the boy who told his mother, he never wanted to see her again as she was 'an embarrassment' The minute her heart stopped beating, her last thought was about her son. There was no pain, no struggle, death had been welcomed into her flat on that cold, wet evening.

Sadie Jackson had imagined ending her own life for months and now the time had come. No more torment, no more anguish. She hung herself and her lifeless body swung for several moments, in an empty bedroom cupboard. She was home alone. Council workers found her body a week later. Her life was over, suicide is never an easy way out, especially for the family left behind, but Sadie had had no support, and no one really cared. The children had grown up and left, they had families and lives of their own. Her husband had long left the family home. Back then her depression had gone undiagnosed, there were no help groups or support. It was day to day survival like many other families.

Back in the 70's, depression was a stigma, it was not seen as a tolerable mental illness.

'Pull yersel together wuman!' is the last thing you want to hear when you are in a deep, dark, depressive state, but that was the suggested remedy.

But the long miserable days and the feeling of despair, the insomnia and the feeling of worthlessness made every day a long painful day.

'Somedays I just couldn't get out of bed.' Sadie confessed.

'None of my children showed any sign of sympathy or helped me, every day was agony, overwhelming and painful, they only ever came to visit me when they needed money.' As the time went on, Sadie's deep depression turned to thoughts of suicide.

'My husband left when Paul was little and no one came near the house, I was all alone.' Sadie sobbed.

No one knows why someone chooses suicide, one dominant reason is, they are suffering mentally so badly they can see no way out other than death. Paul's mother loved her children but hated life. For her, every day was an effort just to exist. She spent each evening deciding how her life would end and would tonight be the night.

A great deal of effort and planning was put into her suicide. She organized everything; from the clothes she would be wearing to the letters she would be writing. Jacksons mother wanted to die, for her what was the point continuing with a life that caused her so much personal agony. Things had been difficult since her husband had moved in with another woman. He said her depression and gloom was the main reason he had an affair and moved out. The shame on the family was awful.

Sadie worked three cleaning jobs and once the kids had moved out, she spent the evenings in her empty council house feeling lost and lonely. Her sad life offered no sense of joy. Her job was done, she had produced three sons to continue the family name and now she was exhausted. No desire to continue, life was not what she had anticipated, it was a struggle, devoid of love and appreciation. A war of attrition every day. But not today.

Over the next hour I was the voice between Paul and his mother. His selfish determination and narcissism forging his career had broken down the relationship he had with his mother and siblings. He showed no sign of guilt about his lack of affection for his mother. He forfeited attending his mother's funeral to attend a job interview in London and had lied to the family, citing illness as his excuse. Paul Jackson was a self-absorbed, egotistical man. A trait required if you were destined to go places in the world of investigative tabloid journalism.

As we said our pretentious goodbyes at the doorway, I could see the cynic who came into my life to try and expose me as a fraud was now walking away with his tail between his legs. It was he who was exposed as the fraud. He did not merit the title of son!

Sunday 25th, August 1974

Diary entry. HEADLINE – World Exclusive! PSYCHIC HELPS PO-LICE CATCH KILLER!

A fourteen-year-old psychic medium is behind the recent arrest of the killer of teenager Linda Shaw. Police Detectives recruited sleuth psychic medium Catherine Jamieson for an undisclosed fee after they struggled to find any clues to the grisly murder.

OMG! I am all over the Sunday national newspaper, not only is there a two-page spread but pictures of Linda Shaw's murder scene, and images of me walking along the street oblivious to having my picture taken. I look terrible, Dad is mortified, and mum is furious, mainly because they did not print her picture..............

Touché Paul Jackson, he managed to get his revenge by writing the most offensive and untruthful feature about me. It didn't appear in the local press, but it did appear in a Sunday National tabloid newspaper. Much of the copy was inaccurate, he focused on a non-existent arrangement I apparently had with the police to identify and catch criminals. The whole write-up was a series of lies and misquotes. What was supposed to be a human-interest story for the local press was now breakfast fodder for the masses. I had been exposed in the most despicable manner. Jackson never held back his libelous comments.

'A neighbour who did not want to be named.' and 'a family friend commented.' there was no neighbour or family friend, it was all lies and there was nothing I could do about it. I would be the talk of the town.

'Can we sue them for lying?' mum threatened.

'Don't be so stupid women! Where the hell would we get the money to fight a national newspaper, it would cost ME thousands of pounds!' Dad barked.

He was right, I was to learn later in life that the tabloid newspapers got away with printing whatever the hell they liked. Why? because it's not worth the trouble taking legal action. Mitigation is never achieved; the only winners are the lawyers. The story was out there now and there was nothing I could do about it.

The flood gates were well and truly open. Over two million households bought an edition of the paper and would have seen my picture. I was not prepared for what was about to happen, my life was about to change beyond all recognition.

Diary entry - Monday 26th August 1974

I did not go to school today; mum called the headmaster and he agreed I should stay off for a few days or until the gossip calmed down. I wrote Margaret a long letter and asked mum to send it to her address in Australia. I poured my heart out and begged her to let me come to stay with her and Joe. I miss her and Mary so much. I just cannot live here anymore!

The telephone must have rung fifty times whilst I was home. The minute I finished one call; it would ring again. Most of the callers were frantic parents asking if I could find their child who had gone missing, others asked if I could contact a dead loved one. English accents, Welsh accents, Irish accents, the calls were coming from all over the country. The relentless ringing resulted in me taking the phone off the hook. Strangers came unannounced to the front door. They knocked and rang the bell, banged on the glass, and shouted through the letterbox. I locked the door and hid in the lounge. A few people unashamedly looked through the lounge window and asked if I would open the door.

'Go away, I have called the police!' I shrieked as I pulled over the curtains.

In desperation I called my father at work, and he arranged for Billy to come home to support me. Mother had done one of her disappearing acts and was nowhere to be seen. Gran arrived at the house at the same time as Billy, and she was not short in verbally assaulting the ghouls who were hanging outside our house. It was a terrifying experience. A police car arrived, and DCI Smith got out and came up to the front door, Billy let him into the house.

'Can you do something about this madness?' Billy pleaded.

'I will organise for a policeman to attend outside' said DCI Smith as he picked up the telephone to call the station.

Gran made a pot of tea and DCI Smith pulled a chair out at the table and sat down beside me.

'How are you?' he asked. 'I'm terrified if you must know.' Smith was the only person to ask how I was coping with all the chaos that had come about from the newspaper article.

Smith was a handsome man, probably in his early thirties who displayed control and intelligence. I liked him. He spoke to me like I was an adult and recognized my capability.

'I need to speak with your parents, we need your help

again!' I stared at him in despair. Not again, I thought!

As tough as the murder scenes had been to visit and the gruesome images I had witnessed, I wanted to work with Smith again. I liked him, a lot. He seemed to understand me.

Saturday 30th August 1974

A Royal Mail van arrived today, and the postman delivered a sack of letters addressed to me. Some of the envelopes simply had my name and New Weston on the front and others merely said Catherine Jamieson Psychic. There were over five hundred letters. We took turns opening them, Billy, Mum, Dad, Gran and I. Very few of the letters I opened were worthy of a reply. Gran and Billy enjoyed going through them, taking turns to read some of them out aloud.

'It's like the Bay City Rollers fan club.' laughed Billy.

They all sat around the dining table ripping the letters open and reading some of them aloud. It was all one big game. Gran found three five-pound notes and hastily the search was on for more money. Eventually my father scrunched together all the paper, postcards and opened envelopes, headed into the back garden, and burnt them in the garden in a metal bin. Another sack arrived on the Monday. Gran opened every card and letter. Her excuse was.

'Just in case someone has sent you money, cheques, or postal orders, you wouldn't want to just throw them out, would you?' She secretly enjoyed reading the letters and cards, it was a thrill and a bonus if one or two of them had some money inside. I allowed her to indulge in opening the mail addressed to me. I certainly had no intention of dealing with the begging letters and reading the horrible comments others had written about me. None of it was good for my mental health. I realised from an early age; the haters will always hate. There was an element of society who enjoyed writing vile offense letters, twisted, disturbed human beings who just had to let you know how they felt about you. Thankfully I never had to read too many of them, I suppose Gran was my first official assistant!

Paul Jackson interviewed after his radio show in October 1979: When asked about Cat Jamieson.

Cat Jamieson, now there is a name! An amazing public figure and businesswoman as we all know, I think her alleged psychic ability is questionable. If it truly exists it, is an unbelievable gift. Cat is incredibly convincing. She scared the life out of me when I first met her she told me a few home truths, but from a professional perspective, she was possibly one of the more fascinating characters I have had the pleasure to interview. Do I think she speaks to the dead? No! I think she thinks she does! Cat is a very clever woman, she is entirely transparent, her gullible persona is what you are drawn to. Cat has a remarkable ability to communicate with people on a highly emotional level. She reads your emotions, when she talks to you, she has an instinctive ability to interpret your facial expressions and body language and from this she can determine if you are depressed, sick, happy, sad. I think Cat is a magician, her mysterious skill is not consciously learned, she is the David Copperfield of her profession. The master illusionist, her naivety, and her belief in what she thinks she is seeing, and hearing are real to her. The Cat Jamieson phenomenon is a business, she is no more a psychic or able to talk to the dead any more than you or me! Paul Jackson

CHAPTER 9

1975

I kept a low profile in 1975, the previous year had been horrific, it had mentally and physically drained me, and I found it difficult to trust anyone. My family had also suffered, my father was simply embarrassed about the whole situation. My relationship with my father had been affected by the newspaper exposure and all the publicity that followed its publication. Emotionally, my father was deeply hurt. He immersed himself in his work, staying at the factory until late at night. One of the Thomson brothers died, and my father assumed his role by being voted onto the Board of Directors at Thomson Pumps. The whole family attended Peter Thomson's funeral; out of respect my father had suggested I stayed home.

> 'It's mainly for adults, family and business acquaintances.' he lied.

I knew my attendance would have caused a stir and my father was concerned I would make a scene. His many years of dedication and loyalty to the Thomson family had been recognised. He took on the role of Managing Director. The promotion came with a young German he fell in love with, her name was Mercedes Benz. She was bronze and sexy and had an 8-track cassette player that my dad just adored. He listened to Patsy Cline and his favourite Tammy Wynette tracks over and over. His glove compartment was crammed full of eight track cassettes. It was a beautiful car which took pride of place in her own private parking space in the company car park.

> 'Isn't she beautiful, German engineering at its best.' He

was smitten

My mother basked in the glory of her mini celebrity status as 'the mother of the girl who could speak to the dead'. The newspaper scandal was no longer her preferred topic of conversation, it was all about the new Mercedes. When she got out of the passenger side, she always stopped to check out who was looking at her before she closed the passenger door. She would pose just long enough for the neighbour's in the street to notice her.

Billy, my brother was neither impressed or ashamed of my mini celebrity status and would not stand for any malicious chat or badmouthing about his little sister. His friends, when they came to the house, would treat me with the utmost respect but you could tell there was an elephant in the room. The subject was never raised such was their respect for me and my family. Billy was a protective blanket. If someone made a comment, Billy set the record straight, professionally, and courteously. But Gran, now she was a different story, if someone made a comment in the street, she was right in there. She would verbally lash back at onlookers; God help you if she saw you staring at me. Her verbal arsenal stopped you in your tracks, her tongue took no prisoners.

'Take a picture why don't you, you piece of shit?' she once called out to two women in the street.

'Did your parents never tell you it's rude to stare?' was her favourite line of choice.

'Staring like a dick won't make yours any bigger, so trot on idiot!' was my personal favourite.

I watched her one night when two Bible thumping ladies came straight up to our front door, they asked for me and Gran told them I was not available. 'The child should talk to God, only he can save her.' one said. Gran closed the door over and lead the two ladies back down the path onto the pavement. She had her back to me, but I could see the faces of the two churchgoers.

One reacted as if she had just had a conversation with Satan himself, she looked like a quivering wreck and fell to her knees, her two hands in front of her mouth, the other just stood and stared at my gran as if she were the anti- Christ, her mouth wide open. On the way back up the path, gran looked pleased with herself and winked at me at the window. I never did get to hear what she said to the ladies!

'Oh, I just told them you were unavailable for comment.' she chuckled.

The public can be very cruel and thoughtless, and Gran liked to remind them of this when they stepped out of line. Outside in the big wide world, Gran would masquerade as my minder. She could construct a one-line answer that would decimate a grown man into an apologetic imbecile. I never heard anyone challenge her for more than a few sentences. She specialised in verbal annihilation, had no filter, and didn't care who she offended or put in their place. She may have been small in stature, but she had a heart of a lion and protected me from the human hyena's who were just waiting to pounce on me.

'I'll knock anyone into next week that tries to mess with you when I'm about!' she would say.

After the newspaper expose, I rarely left the house alone, I felt safer only socializing with the family at home for fear of being hurt or exploited again. I had no real desire to go out of the house once I came home from school. I made a conscious decision to concentrate on my exams, I knew if I left school without any qualification's life would be extremely difficult for me. My dad pressed the point almost every week, 'Get qualifications and get a decent job'. I never heard him say this to Billy, it was just assumed he would follow in dad's footsteps, join Thomson Pumps, complete his engineering apprenticeship and work in the factory until he retired and walk away with a handsome company pension. In less than a year Billy was in a supervisory role at Thomson Pumps, fast-tracked because he was the son of the Managing Director. Life was so easy for Billy; it was all handed to him on a plate

**

The reality was, I just was not cut out for school, I was not academic, I hated homework and being told what to do? I could not concentrate for prolonged periods of time without being interrupted by a wayward spirit trying to get my attention to pass on a message to another pupil or teacher in the class. I called it spiritual tinnitus. Their voices were constantly in my ear, in my head, in my space. For me to sit any exam would have been difficult. I was unlike the other students who came into the assembly hall or classroom prepared to sit down for two hours in silence, psyched up and ready to take their exam. They would be in the zone, able to concentrate in the perfectly muted conditions the school assembly hall offered. Exam conditions presented limited interference, the sound of the odd student coughing, the slow-paced walk of the headmaster around the desks, the pages being turned as students progressed through their exam papers. For me, I would come into the hall, followed by several spirits all baying for my attention. It was like being followed by the London Symphony Orchestra. I am sure you can see this did not bode well for ideal exam conditions.

My life became monotonous and predicable for a while. In school I was treated like a freak. I spent most of my break times in the library up at the back of the room with the other outcasts just to avoid some of the verbal bullying. Gran spoke with my father, and it was agreed I should see a child psychologist privately. Mum and dad never discussed this with me, only gran.

It was decided once dad found the right psychologist, I would be going along with gran to be assessed. My father was determined to find out what was wrong with me, but I simply could not be fixed, there was no remedy, dad was not willing to concede.

By the Winter of 1975, the few friends I had, would come calling at the weekend and for a while I ventured out with them to the local youth club on a Saturday night. My hormones were going crazy, and my body was developing quickly. I was getting wolf whistles on my way home from school, the lads on the construction sites would shout out from the scaffolding. I secretly enjoyed it despite turning bright red as I walked past them. I spent hours styling and brushing my long hair. I hated the colour as I was only one of a handful of people in school with red hair. I started wearing mascara to accentuate my almond shaped blue eyes, a bit of face powder hid my freckles. Looking back, I was very pretty but at 15 years old you are never happy with your appearance. At school, I loved running or playing hockey, often the older lads would come over to the hockey pitches during P.E., I enjoyed the attention, it was a peculiar distraction.

Their comments always ended in ridicule. 'Hey Jamieson, are you ginger all over?'

The best form of defense was to ignore them, the skeptics and all the bullies but not all the boys.

I met a lad who was three years older than me. His name was Jim McGowan. He delivered the milk in the morning and came round to collect the money on a Friday night. I always made sure I answered the door to him each week. One of my friends knew his brother and with a bit of hinting and some intervention from another friend, he got the message that I fancied him and before long he asked me out.

'I heard you fancied me, want to go to the pictures on Saturday night, if not I'll take my girlfriend? and with that one liner I was hooked. My heart absolutely melted each time I saw him, Jim was to become my first love.

I told my parents I was going to the youth club on a Saturday night and would arrange to meet Jim outside. He was too old to get in, so we just walked about the streets, talking rubbish and giggling. My friend, Carol, chaperoned me as I was so shy. She was keen on Jim's best friend so all four of us went about together. I found it awkward to talk to Jim, what does a fifteen-year-old girl and an eighteen-year-old boy have in common? Whatever it was, we just clicked, he made me laugh and introduced me to so many new things. He never asked me for anything or pushed me into doing anything I didn't want to do. I would sneak out of the house to meet him and tell my parents I was going to visit friends. As I walked down the street, I would apply my strawberry lip gloss. It was Jim's favourite.

'Hey Cat, you're my strawberry girl, right?' Yes, I was.

I had to be home no later than 10pm if I had school in the morning. One night we just got carried away, kissing under a bus shelter as the rain battered off the corrugated roof. It was almost 10pm,

I had to get home. If I was late my dad would read me the riot act and ground me for the week. Platforms shoes are not designed for running in, so I pulled them off and ran back, my feet were soaking wet and cold in the rain, but I was exhilarated and buzzing. I was feeling on top of the world.

Diary entry Sunday 23rd November 1975

*** OMG, Jim McGowan he is so gorgeous xxx best night ever xx He *has the most gorgeous eyes xx I just love, love, love, him to bits xx ***I must let Margaret and Mary know all about him, I will write to them both in the morning.*

Jim McGowan and I became two souls in the one body, our relationship was meant to be and we saw each other most days. We just connected and I felt blessed to have him in my life. Jim came to the school gates if he finished work early and drove me home in his works van. He was the guy the other girls wanted but he was exclusively mine. Our relationship wasn't complicated, it was like mother earth, natural and loving. He became instrumental in everything I did in my life, even as a teenager I couldn't imagine his energy not being around me. He had a free spirit and marched to his own drum, and I loved him for it.

Initially, Maureen and Bill were not impressed when they found out I was dating Jim and refused to let him come into the house, God forbid let us be on our own. As far as they were concerned, he was too old for me and too forward! His parents were more liberal and allowed us to sit in his bedroom listening to records and cassettes. He introduced me to groups that defined my youth as he had such great taste in music which he inherited from his parents. They regularly had records playing on a weekend when I was at their house.

Jim's parents were real party people, they even had a mock bar located in the corner of their lounge. His dad was a self-employed joiner and Jim followed in his footsteps, working in the family business. His milk round gave him additional funds as his apprenticeship wage was so little. Their family dynamics were based on love and respect. His parents oozed tenderness and warmth towards each other, they were a cool, fun couple. I wasn't surprised to find out they were not married as neither of them conformed to how society expected them to live. They lived life to their own rules.

'My mum and dad don't need to be married, they are committed to each other spiritually, what difference will a bit of paper make?' I had never thought about it like that before, but it made sense.

The McGowan's were the complete opposite to my family. Jim's parents welcomed me into their family with open arms, his brother and sister became good friends, and I loved their company. It was such a wonderful time in my life, and I remember it with fond memories.

Jim and I would sit in the darkness of his bedroom and listen to iconic albums like Tubular Bells by Mike Oldfield and The Dark Side of the Moon by Pink Floyd, Fleetwood Mac. and Roxy Music, whilst my friends were listening to glam rockers The Bay City Rollers and Swedish, pop supergroup, ABBA.

Jim's home was positively charged with so much energy and laughter. It smelt of incense, sage, sandalwood, and lavender, just being there helped reduce my headaches. I was never bothered or pestered by any spirits while I was in their home. It was as if any lost souls who were with me never came across their front door. His family home offered me a secure base to enjoy respite from the many spirits who demanded my attention throughout the day.

Jamie and Sue McGowan could be described as hippies, they lived by the slogan 'if it feels good, do it'. Jim said they lived to love, who they wanted, when they wanted. There were no taboos to their sexual practices. They welcomed similar friends to their home and indulged in orgies, smoked marijuana, took mushrooms and LSD.

By the end of 1975, I was in a good place, I had a lovely boyfriend I was keen for Margaret to meet. My sister confirmed by letter she would be back in the Springtime and would be staying for several months. Her marriage to Joe was on the rocks. Living eleven thousand miles from your family, friends, and everything you ever knew was extremely difficult for her. Australia was not the dream life she had expected, barbeques and outdoor living is only fun is you're sharing it with someone you love and members of your family.

I was unashamedly delighted, I missed her so much. From a selfish point of view, I was pleased the marriage was over, Margaret was coming home and that's all that mattered to me.

Margaret wrote to my parents 'I have a difficult decision to make, it's been tough especially being here on my own, I will never accomplish anything if I stay with this man, I need just a few more months and I will be home'.

She had planned to give her employer three months' notice and was secretly saving for her flights back to Scotland. Dad had said he would pay for her to return home, but Margaret was determined to do things her way. With her covert plan in place, Joe was oblivious, if he were to find out about her escape plan back to Scotland everything would be jeopardised.

Living with Joe had been like 'treading around eggshells' she penned. Margaret had gone on to describe how Joe had become withdrawn and spent his evenings smoking marihuana and drinking bottled beer. If he wasn't working, he would be with the lads or gambling on the horses. Any love they had for each other had now gone, the drugs and gambling had seen to that. Margaret was feeling trapped and lonely, but she had to wait till the time was right before she could leave. Financially things were so bad they moved in with his family. Joe lost his job and self-esteem and Margaret had become the scapegoat for his agitation. Her solitary wage was not enough to pay all the bills and pay rental on a house, so in the short term they had decided to accept his sisters offer and move into her spare room. The original short-term plan to stay at his sister's home while they got back on their feet, was now becoming a more permanent solution. Joe had just given up, happy to rely on others for support. The great dream was over, living out of carboard boxes piled high in your single room was not the answer. Living in the sunshine and searing heat was not always pleasant, temperatures in summer sored, it was impossible to stay outdoors for lengthy periods of time and air conditioning was a costly necessity. Joe had no intention of moving back to Scotland, he had left the country of his birth owing thousands of pounds in unpaid debts. Australia had been his security blanket as no one would chase his debts over there. Returning to Scotland would change that, he would no longer be protected.

Margaret never went into detail about the troubles in her marriage, but Gran suspected Joe had been involved with other women.

December 1975.

We crossed off the days on the calendar as we awaited Margaret's safe return home. We lost touch with her for some weeks, no telephone calls, and no letters. I never received a Birthday card or diary for my birthday, something of a tradition now with Margaret and me. When we still heard nothing by Christmas Eve 1975, my mother, father, and gran started to worry. Father had spoken about flying out to Australia to find out what was going on. To our great relief, Margaret called on Christmas Day, she confirmed she had left Joe and was staying alone in a shared flat somewhere on the Gold Coast. I only got to speak with her for a minute, but I sensed she was frightened and troubled. Dad took the phone from me and wrote down her address and contact details. He gestured for me to leave the room while he spoke in private to Margaret.

I joined mum and gran in the lounge, but not before I heard dad confirm he would pay for Margaret's flight home immediately. Mum paced the room sucking on her cigarette, she was delighted Margaret had called but worried something was very wrong. I feared for Margaret's safety and looked forward to her coming home to the security of her family. I had an overwhelming feeling something awful was going to happen and I couldn't shake the feeling off.

Dad stayed on the telephone much longer than usual.

When he came back into the lounge mum was annoyed, she had not had the chance to speak with her eldest daughter, as way of an apology, dad assured mum she would be home in a few days, and they would have as much time as they needed to chat.

Now, Margaret had been in touch, the atmosphere in the house had completely changed, there was an air of excitement. It was the best possible Christmas gift; Margaret was coming home. Merry Christmas everyone.

CHAPTER 10

1976

2nd January 1976

I woke up at 4.00am and knew Margaret was dying. She reached her hand out to me and I held tightly onto it.

'I love you, my beautiful baby girl' she sobbed.

Margaret was going in and out of consciousness. Her car had been crushed between two trucks in a road traffic accident on the Princes Highway near Sydney whilst she had been heading to the airport. Her suitcase had burst, and her clothes were strewn all over the motorway. Joe had been chasing her in another vehicle, he was drunk, angry and hell bent on stopping her getting on a plane. The smash happened in an instant, the force of the collision caused Margaret to sustain major internal injuries and the devastating impact on her chest had led to her lungs filling with blood and slowly ending her life. She was pinned behind the steering wheel, cold and frightened with only minutes to live. Blue lights and a siren could be heard in the distance, but it was futile. Margaret would be dead by the time the paramedics arrived.

I was transported to beside the driver's window of the car. Margaret was in shock; she had a few cuts to her head and her chest was crushed by the steering wheel. I held her hand, it was shaking and felt cold. There was not much time to talk.

'Listen to me, I am your mother, Catherine!'

Margaret paused to catch her breath.

'You are my daughter!' Margaret exhaled and blood

sprayed over the dashboard of the car.

Her breathing was short and sporadic, only a few more intakes of air and Margaret and her unborn baby would be dead.

'I wanted to keep you; I could never have given you up.' Margaret knew death was approaching, her breathing and heart rate were shallow.

'Jon-Jon is your father.... a showman.... a traveler.... too young.... too young.... gran.... mum.... My baby girl......'

As the life poured out of her, she was no longer able to speak, her grip weakened, and her breathing finally stopped. Blood ran from her nose and mouth. Her broken body had been forced so far forward neither her arms nor head could be moved. The paramedics arrived at the scene, but it was too late Margaret was dead. Her lifeless body would need to be cut out of the wreckage.

Her eyes were wide open, fixed, and vacant. I closed mine, but the image of her dead body would not go away. I let out a piercing scream that brought mum, dad, and Billy racing into my bedroom.

'What's happened, were you having a nightmare?' Billy asked as he tied his dressing jacket around his body

'Margaret! *My* mother is dead!' I screamed out before I realised what I had said.

The room went deadly silent. Maureen put her hands over her face. Bill stepped back from me. I crawled off the bed and lay on the floor. I was in extreme pain, despite having no physical injuries, mentally I was in agony. I cried for the woman I was told was my sister only to discover she was my mother. I cried for the mother I loved and had now lost. The woman I thought was my mother, whom I had called mother all my life was stunned, she knelt on the floor beside me and shook me like a doll, I was delirious, incoherent. I was the witness to my own mothers' death. I didn't know who I was or why I was seeing this horrific accident.

'Why do I see things, why am I different, I just want a normal life!' I begged for an answer that would never come.

'Don't cry Cat, it'll be all right; you'll always be my baby sister!' Billy sobbed. He put his arms around me and pulled me to my feet.

'Let's go downstairs and we can go over everything you have seen and heard.' said Billy as he took my arm and we headed down the stairs into the kitchen. Dad dealt with the situation exactly as I thought he would. He passed the buck to Gran. 'Billy get your clothes on and go get Gran.'

Dad left the house. This was more than he could comprehend, he had to get out, he had to leave the commotion that was going on inside the house , he had to breakdown and fall apart on his own, out of sight of the family. He made his way along the street, tears rolling down his face, no one was about, the dawn chorus was the only sound. He had no idea where he was going, he just walked and walked. There was a red telephone box at the corner of the main street, he opened the door and stood inside. His heart was breaking, his beautiful Margaret was she really gone? He told me many years later just before he died, that he felt such a huge loss, his uncontrollable grief was overwhelming. He never questioned my vision; knowing in his heart Margaret was dead.

Emotions were running high, Maureen was stunned, she was convinced I was wrong, and it was all a horrific night-mare. As far as she was concerned Margaret was on her way home, she would be here with her family in two days' time. Her flight was due to leave Australia in a few hours. Margaret could not be dead, it must be a huge misunderstanding, surely this time I was wrong!

Gran and Billy arrived back. Gran, put the kettle on as if making a pot of tea would magically made the situation easier.

I looked at the woman I had called mother for the last fifteen years, she came towards me. I was expecting her to take me in her arms, hold me, show some emotion, but instead she slapped me across the face with such force I could taste blood in my mouth. Her hatred was real, I felt it. She struck me as if I had caused the accident, I wasn't the one who killed Margaret, I loved her. My body went onto shock.

Minutes before, I had stood in the darkness, watching the woman who confessed to being my mother dying. Her body had been crushed and severed below the waist, it was a horrific scene, one I will never forget. Gran and Billy pulled Maureen away from me. The atmosphere in the room changed. Maureen's reaction said it all, the great secret was out. I sat on the floor, broken, my back against the lounge wall in total shock and emotionally shattered.

From that night on I never called Maureen, mum again.

My whole life changed the night Margaret died. I questioned exactly who I was, and why my life had been kept such a mystery. I needed to know the truth, and this could only come from Margaret. I had to reach out to her. The whole family was in shock over Margaret's death, as I lay in bed that night, unable to think straight, I could hear Maureen crying, we were all hurting. There were so many questions but not tonight. My head was throbbing, how could I comprehend what had just happened, it had all been a lie, the only surprise to the family was that I knew. Gran was unable to look at me, she knew, they all knew. 'Oh! Margaret why was I never told you were my real mother.' I was 15 years old and had no idea who I was. Despite my grief I knew my anguish had to take a back seat. Margaret was dead, she was gone, she had forgotten to tell my heart how to go on without her. It was all about Margaret and I accepted this. Within a few hours my life had been turned upside down, I resented everyone. No one would fill the void Margaret had left. No one was ever as interested in the things I did than Margaret, she was so proud of me. Our bond was a special one, a true mother and child bond, I just didn't know it. One thing I did know was true, I knew I would never come to terms with the grief and loss. Everything I had ever known was going to change. My world had literally turned on its head , everything I thought was real was false, hopes and aspirations for the future were gone in a heartbeat. My brother Billy was now my uncle and my sister Mary, my aunt. My mother and father as I had known them were now my gran mother and grandad. The dead baby Margaret was carrying would have been my little brother or sister. Now wasn't the time to ask questions, I had to respect everyone's grief. I would ask the questions when the time was right.

Over the next twenty-four hours Bill and Maureen scrambled for any news about Margaret's whereabouts. Bill called the telephone numbers Margaret had given him and got no reply. Joe could not be contacted. The airline after much persuasion, finally released details that Margaret had not checked in for her flight. The twelve-hour time difference hindered our progress. Bill was unrelenting, he was desperate for news, he called Margaret's previous employer, St Vincent's Hospital in Sydney. By chance, the nurse who answered the telephone knew Margaret and gave Bill the contact details he needed for the police and another hospital in Sydney. The police questioned him on the whereabout of the accident, I had no idea, I could only confirm the colour of the car and that there were the two trucks involved in the crash. Bill spent, what felt like, hours on the telephone, repeating the same information over and over. I had to find a way to help Bill, there was only one thing I could think of doing.

I took out a crushed business card I had in my purse and called the telephone number on it. Three rings later and I heard the familiar voice.

"It's Cat, it's my turn to ask for your help!"

It took just two hours for DCI Smith and two colleagues to turn up at our house. Standing in the doorway was Smith and two police officers. Smith's face confirmed what we already knew. Margaret was dead. He confirmed this and told us everything he knew about the accident. He produced a folded fax document, he carefully read out the details of the crash. He tried to protect us and our feelings and tentatively only read what we needed to know. Margaret was dead and Joe had identified her body at the police morgue.

'Margaret would have felt no pain and most probably died on impact.' Smith lied. His words brought solace to the family during our time of sadness. Bill, Maureen, Gran, and Billy sat in silence, listening intently to every word Smith had to say. Each one of us heartbroken with grief.

My description of the scene was far more horrifying than the version given by Smith. After all I was there. Margaret did not die alone; I was there to provide words of comfort and ease her distress. My mother, Margaret, was in great pain, pinned to her seat, virtually impaled on the steering wheel, she clung to life for several minutes after impact. However traumatic and frightening the scene may have been, her last moments were filled with love and dignity.

'Why do I need to die?' Margaret exhaled for the last time. There was a sense of relief when she died, she no longer had to suffer any more pain or constraint. Her spirit was free to move on.

'Good-bye mother, I love you' I whispered, hoping it was only a matter of time before we were together again.

Diary Entry - Friday 9th January 1976

I am broken, I am so very broken. If this is living, and being alive, I do not want to live anymore! I am in so much pain, my body is hurting. I have lost a part of me, my greatest advocate.

Grief had taken over all our lives. I have no idea how we will get over Margaret's death. She has gone and so has part of my life.

Gran had asked the Doctor to visit the house, she thought I needed medication to deal with the shock, I heard her on the telephone telling the doctors receptionist my sister had died. Even after Margaret's death the lies continued. The doctor came to the house and diagnosed shock and exhaustion. He prescribed sleeping pills and tablets that made me feel disorientated. He knew who I was, much like everyone else in the town.

The severe emotional and mental impact of what I had witnessed had a massive effect on me. I was having flash backs, nightmares, and anxiety attacks. I was unable to perform day to day tasks, having to face episodes of severe depression, tearfulness, and deep sadness. My depression magnified knowing Margaret's body was being transported home, we had no idea where she was on any given day, I felt guilty she was travelling alone; Joe was a useless piece of shit! He never kept us up to date despite instruction from Bill. Joe never contacted the family for three days after Margaret died. Bill despised him but kept control of his emotions, he was unwilling to risk anything going wrong with his daughter coming home to her final resting place.

My boyfriend, Jim's parents were extremely sympathetic, his mother wrote a beautiful and touching letter and sent flowers to Bill and Maureen, their kind words fell on death ears as neither of them had the mental capacity or good manners to react to their kind gesture. Bill and Maureen's response was simply to ignore them. Jim's mother offered me emotional support and became the savior of my sanity. She was a beautiful person, inside and out.

I was not ready to talk, to anyone, grief stricken I took each day at a time and Jim gave me space. I loved him for it. Daily, I focused on trying to reach Margaret. I so wanted to speak to her. It would take over five weeks before Margaret's body would be back in Scotland, but I reached out to her spirit. I needed to speak to her.

Bill organised the funeral, there was a lot of documentation involved in getting Margaret's body home. It was an incredibly challenging time for everyone. Joe delayed the process by asking for Margaret to be buried in Australia. He essentially held my father to ransom and settled for a cash payment to release her body. Billy persuaded Joe to fly home and attend the funeral and offered him a further cash enticement to do so. Joe agreed, but he refused to travel on the same flight as Margaret.

It took a lot of patience and negotiation to get Joe on side. He proved to be incredibly difficult and disingenuous, having to be in control. Joe was calling the shots for the moment and my father was going along with it despite his utter contempt for him, Bill kept up the act, he had to, he wanted his daughter Margaret home at any cost! One evening as we waited on Margaret's body coming home, I sat down with the family and described in detail what I had seen. I told them Margaret's final words. Her fear of Joe and her love for me. I was unwilling to hide anything from them, why should I. I told Bill and the family, that Joe was indirectly responsible for Margaret's death. It was him who pursued her along the motorway at speed.

'Joe tried to force her off the road by ramming the side of her car with his and pulling out in front of her vehicle in the hope she would stop her car.' I explained.

I could see Bill's face go red with anger. I continued. 'He was willing to do whatever it took to stop her reaching the airport, even if it meant imminent death.'

Margaret wasn't a confident driver, she was forced to make sudden and erratic judgments in controlling the car, terrified and in a state of panic this was only going to end one way, one of them was going to die.

Joe had discovered her plans earlier that day; Margaret was travelling back to Scotland. He knew, if she got out of the country, their relationship, and his control over her would end. Earlier that day during their last telephone conversation, he had screamed down the phone to her

'You will leave Australia over my dead body!' little did we know how true his words would be, but it was to be Margaret's body and sadly, not his. His final humiliating telephone conversation had left her fearing for her life. Bill was incensed but remained calm. He had to get Joe back to Scotland at any cost. He thought about how he was going to expose Joe for what he was. He reluctantly agreed to Joe's terms until the funeral was over, but once Joe was here and Margaret was laid to rest, Bill was going to deal with him, once and for all. As far as Bill was concerned, Joe was not going to be travelling back to Australia, he was not going to be travelling anywhere ever again! No more Mr. Nice guy. Bill Jamieson was a man seeking revenge. As far as Bill was concerned, Joe was the man who killed his cherished daughter, a murderer, a jealous, misogynist who had made his daughters life hell. Joe had chased Margaret along a notoriously dangerous stretch of road at speed, he had deliberately caused Margaret's death. Bill Jamieson had decided, he was going to kill him!

Joe was nothing but trash, a man who could not be trusted. His allegiance was to himself and no one else. Joe Paterson didn't know it yet, but Bill Jamieson was about to make him face the consequences of his actions.

Grief is an individual experience, as a family our levels of grief was beyond anything any one of us could ever have imagined. I wanted to reach out to Bill and Maureen, but they had both become withdrawn and distant. They avoided my questions and eye contact but promised we would talk about my birth mother when Mary came home, and all the family could be together. I had to accept this, there was nothing I could do, right now all the energy and focus was on Margaret and bringing her back where she belonged.

Mary came back home from Monaco to be with the family. She walked through the door and instantly put her arms around me. Her love was real. Bill would not allow her to drive into France to Charles De Gaulle airport and insisted she depart from the nearest airport to her home in Nice; Nice Cote d'Azur Airport was only an hour's drive by bus. Bill would not take the chance of losing another child especially on the treacherous coastal roads of Monaco with its many twists and bends and tourists driving about as if they were racing in the Monaco Grand Prix.

We all loved Mary being in the house, especially me. She brought a great energy with her which reminded us of happier times.

I was a complete wreck; my health was in such a bad state I decided to look after myself and no longer attend doctors or attend appointments with psychiatrists. Both professions were unable to help me or correctly diagnose any mental problems. I was an enigma. I decided to go and research an alternative way of life, I was in search of the truth. I became obsessed about the future and finding my real father. The only way for me to predict the future was to create it. I needed to be connected to something, I needed to find my family. I wanted to be close to a man I had never met, my father. Finding him would allow me to leave the darkness behind and find a light in my life. Now, the search was on to find my real father. Perhaps he didn't know I existed, but I had to know. He would want to know I was alive. I had to find out if my psychic ability was something I had inherited from my biological father or his family. My fabulous mane of red hair and blue eyes which had been so alien to the rest of the family, was this something my father had passed onto me through his genes. I had so many questions. My urge to find my genetic family would become an obsession. I had to find my father. But it was like finding a needle in a haystack, the showmen community were a close-knit group, finding the information I needed would elude me for years to come.

At home, the situation was tense, I was picking up negative vibes coming from Bill and Maureen. Things had falling into place; I now knew why Bill had been so distant and indifferent towards me throughout my life, I had always felt it. He never showed me any real love despite being his grandchild. I was the dirty secret he kept silent about. The pressure to do this over the years must have been enormous. Were they ever going to tell me who my real mother was? Were they ever going to tell me who my real father was? Did they think their daughter had given birth to a child who had been cursed ? Why didn't they adopt me? I had so many questions but no answers.

Bill never wanted me. I was not wanted; I was not his daughter. I was not responsible for Margaret's death, but I was beginning to feel like I was. I chose to be free from this guilt and the overwhelming lack of sympathy I was receiving from Bill and Maureen. I understood they were mourning the loss of their daughter, we all were in mourning, did they also want to lose their granddaughter. I had to find my own way in life. I reached out to Gran.

'You are not my Gran; I no longer feel the family love me.' I confessed.

I was in pain saying the words, but her reply was reassuring 'I will always be your Granny D.' she must have felt my pain because she continued.

'You have always been loved, you were born from love, Margaret loved you, but you were born in a time where it was almost impossible to be an unmarried, underage mother.'

Gran did not hold back; her honesty was brutal; it was what I needed to hear.

'In order for you to stay with us, protect Margaret's reputation and be part of the family we had to lie, it was the only way.'

Gran was unsympathetically honest. She came from a place of brutal reality; romance did not come into it. Despite her coldness she had rare moments of pure affection.

'My heart is broken!' I told gran, but her reply was harsh as usual,

'You should start loving somebody and your heart will get better. Where is that nice lad, Jim?' I took her advice seriously, right now I didn't even love myself. Jim was waiting in the side wings, patient and silent. He deserved to be loved.

As we awaited Margaret's body, the tension in the house was unbearable, I felt like a stranger in my own family, the family were distant, the dynamics had changed. I had a knot in the pit of my stomach which wouldn't go away. Bill would come home, and I would never know what mood he would be in. He increased my feeling of disconnection, guilt, shame. Nothing can prepare you for the death of your mother, the pain was crippling. One minute I was fine and the next, I am crumpled up in a fetal position on my bed in unbearable pain. Margaret would not want to see me like this, she would want me to support the others, be the better person. Why have such a wonderful gift and not share it. After much thought, I decided, I wanted to make my mother proud, and reach out and meet my biological father, find out about my family, the showman community and understand their culture, my heritage. I was grieving not only for the death of my mother but the death of my whole family. I wanted to be part of a family who cared. I needed to get out of the stale atmosphere of the house, away from the deception and lying. It was time, I started to look after me. I picked up the telephone and called Jim's number. He came and picked me up. Inside his van, Jim threw his arms around me, his hug was filled with love, he held me tightly and I cried.

Back at his house he suggested once I turned sixteen, we fled, moved away to create a new life together. Our very own personal journey to find my family. Escapism was going to be survival for me, and I couldn't think of anyone else but Jim to accompany me.

The family may have been a mess, but I can only control my life and keep learning from it, I cannot control the world. I had found the strength inside me to do something better with my life. I was slowly becoming a more balanced person, I knew I had to start all over again and build a new life, regardless of what my 'parents' thought. I had to find an inner strength to move on but first I had to get through the funeral.

Thursday, 12th February 1976

It was just over five weeks since Margaret's death. When the coffin arrived at Glasgow Airport, Bill was waiting, he had arranged a private hearse to take Margaret to the undertakers where the mortician began preparing her body for the family to view. Margaret stayed in the funeral chapel for several days and we all took turns to stay with her. I struggled with her appearance. Her face was blotted, and her skin tone was wrong, the cosmetic restoration made her look like a wax work dummy, it didn't look like Margaret.

Monday, 16th February 1976 - Margaret's Funeral

Margaret's funeral was well attended, the church was crammed full after gran had put a funeral notice in the local paper. The family was supported by those who knew Margaret, friends, distant family, cousins we had not seen for years, school friends, neighbours, even dads company turned out in force to support him. Joe turned up with a girl on his arm, some of Bills friends had to physically hold him back when he saw Joe come in the church.

'Could he be any more disrespectful.' Scowled Bill.

Despite this we celebrated Margaret's life in church, singing and recalling stories of her life, Bill stood up and said the most beautiful eulogy. Afterwards Joe made no attempt to talk to guests or family members. The money Bill loaned him to buy a black suit and tie had been spent elsewhere as he arrived in black jeans and a new black leather jacket.

Margaret was laid to rest in the New Weston cemetery in a corner plot. It rained all day, but it never discouraged over one hundred people attending the graveside and then onto the local hotel for the funeral reception.

I looked around the function suite, so many people, some were smiling, and others were laughing, how could they, today of all days. I felt numb, I was going through the motions, shaking hands, and telling people I was fine, but I was not feeling anything, there was nothing left inside. I was in the depths of depression and feeling incredibly lonesome. Someone suggested after the funeral things would go back to normal! Life would never be normal again. How could it be when the voice of reason, our darling Margaret, was gone.

Maureen was drunk, she had been hitting the bottle harder than usual over the last five weeks, surviving on a diet of vodka and cigarettes. How could you blame her, she had lost two of her children? Dressed in black she looked gaunt and emaciated; the alcohol had ravaged her once good looks. Even at their own daughter's funeral Bill and Maureen continued to argue. Bill asked Maureen to stop drinking but his request fell on deaf ears. He tried to keep it together, losing his daughter, Margaret had been one of the hardest things he had ever had to face. He watched Joe mingle with others in the room, Bill was so
riled with rage he thought about killing Joe there and then, but he had to be patient, he had to wait till the time was right. There had to be no witnesses.

Billy came over and asked if I was all right, he told me he was moving out to set up home with his girlfriend. I congratulated him but secretly I envied him.
Mary went through the motions, talking to everyone and reminiscing about Margaret with many of the mourners. She stood out with her French chic style and Monaco tan. Many of the men watched her as she crossed the room, Mary had a wonder-

ful ability to make everything about her, even at her sister's funeral.

The funeral purvey was held at the Belmont Hotel, the oldest building in the old village, it dated back to 1760. Once an important coach house and inn, used by weary travelers in days gone by, the building dominates the Main Street. This magnificent sandstone building stood on the original route between Glasgow and Edinburgh. Over the years thousands of people had passed through the building, the good, the bad and the evil. Three lost souls remained in the building refusing to move on. During the funeral meal one of them came and stood by me in the function room. Death may have taken the body, but the spirit was still present.

This male spirit introduced himself as William, he had worked in the stables and loved horses. His earthbound spirit refused to move on as he feared what would happen to him. He was afraid of both heaven and hell so sought sanctuary in the hotel. He told me the inn was his home, but he missed the stables and the horses which were now long gone. William had never lived anywhere else, the inn offered him security, and shelter. His mother had left him as a child working at the inn and promised to come back when she had the means to look after him. She never did. William was fourteen years old and died from Tuberculosis, he was buried in a pauper's grave in the grounds of the West Kirk Church in the village.

William was aware he was dead, he rejoiced in the company of the people who come and went at the hotel but kept far away from the other dominant entities who lived at the other end of the building. When he finally appeared, I could see he was just a young lad who looked younger than his fourteen years. He asked if I knew his mother and I said no. He was full of mischief, dashing in and out of the tables looking for coins to steal. I had no reason to show him how to move on, he seemed to be happy enough and certainly was not bothering anyone. Our conversation was basic, he had little vocabulary and told me he did not attend school. When William got up and walked away, I watched him look in a lady's handbag at another table before he disappeared and was gone. I came back to reality and realised everyone at the table was looking at me!

'That was all very Randall and Hopkirk!' cracked Tony Mathieson.

A distant cousin who had no filter with a few drinks in him. By now, my reputation preceded me. I realised I had been talking to William out loud and had attracted some attention. Sometimes I found some spirits difficult to differentiate from real people and I get caught up in the communication, it confused people as it looked like I was talking with myself. Quiet odd.

My father was not pleased, and I did not want to upset him any further, today of all days.

'Best not to cause a scene Catherine' he said as he handed me the house key and suggested I got a taxi back home. I grabbed my coat, said my goodbyes, and left for home. Jim was outside, we hugged, and I asked for some space, he understood. Today, I wanted to be alone.

Back at the house, I knew I was not alone. I often felt a presence around me, I had learned to live with this, but today it felt different. I stood in the kitchen in the silence for several moments, the house was still and cold. The kitchen wall clock had stopped working the day Margaret had died, perhaps it reacted to the overwhelming sense of sadness that engulfed the house. I was drawn to the lounge. I tentatively opened the door and walked into the room. My heart was pounding, as I slowly turned round, Margaret was standing by the back window!

I was not afraid, it was a profound moment, a relief. My heart was racing as we both stood and stared at each other. It was the Margaret I knew and not the empty shell that I had seen in the coffin.

There she was, Margaret, my mother, she smiled, and I smiled back, words for now were not required. She appeared just as she looked in life. She was dressed in her denim jeans, and a gingham shirt. Her black hair was swept back in a pony-tail. Despite all the darkness I had been through since Margaret had died, there was now a glimmer of hope. Margaret had come back; she had come home. For one shining bright moment I felt happy. The energy in the room was overwhelming, it rushed around me, engulfing my body. I wanted to cry out, say something profound but there was no room for words. Just being here said so much.

It was a deeply emotional moment I will treasure. Welcome home Margaret.

CHAPTER 11

Revenge

Joe Paterson had a few days left before he was due to fly back to Australia. He had forgotten how cold a Scottish winter could be and had the audacity to ask Bill Jamieson for some money to buy a jumper and gloves. Bill had said yes and agreed to meet him near the entrance to Glen Drummond Park and not to come by the house.

The snow had already started to fall when Bill arrived in the company van and asked Joe to jump into the passenger seat. Once inside the car Joe had signed his own death certificate. It was warm inside the van, but the atmosphere was icy cold. The conversation was limited, as far as Bill was concerned there was nothing to discuss, small talk was not an option.

'I presume you had Margaret insured then Bill?' no reply. 'Don't suppose you want to cut me in on the insurance Bill, Margaret left a lot of debt back home?' no reply.

Joe Paterson's sense of humour was so dry, Bill had no idea whether he was joking or just being a prick. Bill focused on the road as the snow became heavier.

'So where is the money Bill, I need to get some gear before I fly back?' no reply.

'Did you tell anyone you were meeting me tonight?' Bill asked casually

'No' Joe lied.

Bill slammed on the brakes and Joe went flying forward and smashed his head off the windscreen with such force he was knocked unconscious and cracked the glass. His body slumped forward. This was going to be far easier than Bill had envisaged. No struggle, no fighting. Bill got out and raced to the passenger door, he secured Joes hands and ankles with cable ties he had brought from the factory, he dragged Joe out and forced him into the back of the transit van. Joe regained consciousness as the last tie was pulled tightly into position around his ankles. The steel claws nipping at his skin. He began screaming, shouting, and cursing, rolling about the back of the van in a sheer panic. Bill drove the van further into the darkness. It had just gone 4pm and The Four Seasons were singing 'December 63' on the radio. Bill turned the volume up to drown out the screaming. Undeterred by the heavy snow landing on the windshield Bill cautiously headed out onto the back roads and farmland of Auldlands, eventually turning left onto a single-track road he pulled up beside what was now a dilapidated farmhouse. There was no one about. Bill turned off the engine and pulled on his leather gloves. The only light came from the torch he produced from the glove compartment. The snow continued to fall.

Joe struggled but was unable to break free from the restraints as Bill opened the back door and dragged him out of the van by his feet. Joe bounced his head off the frozen ground. Bill reached into the back of the van and pulled out a thick twine rope already shaped into a noose. Joe continued to yell for help, Bill stuffed a dirty rag into his mouth to muffle his screams, holding his nose as he did so to avoid being bitten. He bound his mouth with gaffer tape, fortunately he could breathe through his nose. The noose was tightened around Joe's neck, and he was dragged along the ground into the derelict building. The whining had stopped, had Joe given up so easily. Bill threw the rope over the exposed ground floor ceiling joist before lifting Joe up onto his shoulders, he tied the rope to the post and took the strain, Joe, close to exhaustion, was tiring quickly. He fought for his life, but he was no match for the superior strength Bill possessed that evening.

'This is for Margaret, you bastard!' Bill threw the rope over the joist and dropped Joe from his grasp, Bill pulled the rope with all his strength and raised Joe off his feet. It took several minutes for Joe to exhale his final breath; his feet were only several inches off the ground, the action had been a victory. Joe swung from the joist; he struggled as his hands and ankles were tied. The twine rope strained under the weight. Within a minute he was dead, and his lifeless body stopped moving. The restraints, tape and rag were removed, and the ground was surveyed around the body to be sure nothing had been left behind. The snow was getting deeper. It would take some effort to get the van out of the snow but if he drove slowly and kept to the left of the field, he would be home within the hour, the falling snow would cover up the tracks made by the van. Two hours later, Bill was back at Thomson Pumps. He hosed down the van and wiped the windshield inside and out. The crack on the glass could be explained by saying a stone had hit it. A chamois was used to wipe clean and buff up the chrome handles. Bill checked and checked again for any clues inside the van which hinted at what had just taken place. When he was satisfied, he replaced the keys in the wall locker and turned off the garage lights. In the morning Joe would organise for the young apprentice to valet the vehicle thoroughly inside and out, just to be sure there was no signs of Joe Paterson. It was remarkably straightforward ending a human life. It was over and Bill Jamieson had no remorse. He would pour a large whisky when he got home and sit by the television. Maureen would be drunk and most probably sleeping on the sofa. If he needed an alibi, she would be it. It would probably not come to that. He hoped.

Susan Smith was expecting Joe home. She had only been seeing him for a few weeks, but he seemed keen, and her biological clock was ticking. He should have been back hours ago. Joe had told her he was meeting Bill Jamieson to pick up some cash and he would return with some fish and chips and a couple of bottles of cider. The football was on, and he wanted to see it on her new rented colour television. At midnight, she gave up waiting for him, locked her front door and went to bed. It had been a long time before she had been stood up by a guy and she wasn't at all happy about it. Why had she been so gullible, Joe had borrowed a five-pound note, her last before payday and promised to repay it when he got back that night. Story of Susan's life, what a rat!

It took almost a month for Joes body to be discovered. He was found by the local farmer who was left in a state of shock after finding the rotten corpse which had been half eaten by the foxes, rats, and birds. Joe could only be identified by a pinky ring found on the ground; it had fallen off after the rats had gnawed at his fingers. Exposure to the elements had quickly decomposed his body. His mother had reported him missing when he did not get on his flight back to Australia. His death was a mystery. The police had suggested suicide, but when interviewed by the police, Susan Smith had confirmed Joe was in a good frame of mind when he left her flat, saying he would be back in a few hours. She told the police Joe had gone to meet Bill Jamieson as he had promised him some cash. His final words to Susan were, 'He was coming back to the house with take away food and alcohol.' Susan had no reason to think he wouldn't come back. She confirmed he wasn't unhappy or feeling gloomy when he left her home at 4pm. Could he really have committed suicide? Was it possible? Even a narcissist was known to take their own life every so often.

The police called at Thomson Pumps in an unmarked car, but the boys in the warehouse knew right away it was 'the polis' Bill brought them into his office right away. When asked about Joe Paterson, Bill denied meeting him, claiming he never turned up at his home as arranged. Bill said Joe called to say something had come up and he would get back to him in a few days. When he never turned up Bill assumed he had returned to Australia. 'We had already said our goodbyes and parted on good terms.' Bill lied

'Maureen can confirm I was here all night.' The police never contacted Bill again re Joe's death. Had Bill literally got away with murder?

***

The days following the funeral, I could feel Margaret's presence around me at the house, there would be a dramatic shift in energy when she came into the room, a lightness in the air and a pleasant familiar smell I began to recognise as her natural fragrance. The scent was reassuring and soothing. Knowing Margaret was around me was comforting.

Before Mary left for Monaco, I invited her into my bedroom. We lay on my bed watching a vibrant bright orb light which danced above the room at tremendous speed like a real-life Tinkerbelle. I told Mary it was Margaret and each time we said her name the orb would dart from one corner of the room to another. It was a fabulous and powerful experience which brought a sense of overwhelming affection and warmth into our lives that night. I would often talk out loud to Margaret and she would respond by filling the room with positive energy or gently moving an object. Margaret would only appear to me at home, it was here where I felt her protective energy surround me. Her human like physical appearance would manifest without warning, when Margaret chose to appear, she normally had something she wanted to communicate to me. It felt like her apparition took a lot of effort and energy to manifest, her body looked fragmented. Often, I was unable to see her feet or her legs below her knees. She would disappear mid-sentence, which was upsetting as we would be in the middle of a conversation or sharing a special memory.

I was incredibly blessed to have had a mother who loved me so much, she refused to give me up as a baby and decided to watch me grow up hidden behind the guise of a devoted sister. I had an incredible closeness with Margaret and felt we shared a stronger maternal bond than I ever did with Maureen, who brought me up as her own child. Having her in my life again completed me. Margaret told me, not being able to love me the way she wanted to love me was like a wound. I can only imagine her pain, handing your baby over and trying to move on in life must have been extremely hard for her, she was nothing more than a child herself. Every day she watched another woman nurture her child. Margaret told me she tried to find a substitute for losing her baby, she had to occupy herself outside of the house to keep her mind off being with me. This was the first time she had ever been allowed to talk about her grief, with me, her child. We comforted each other over our loss.

Margaret recalled, 'My heart was broken, I had lost my baby and the boy I loved and had no support, I had to learn to live with the pain.'

Margaret was never able to talk about the anguish she felt with anyone, it had been forbidden. It was a secret only a few people new about and they were sworn to secrecy.

I wanted to know about my father. I remember the conversation Margaret, and I had the night she died about who my father was.

'Tell me about Jon-Jon, my father?' I asked hesitantly. Margaret closed her eyes and smiled. Her whole face lit up as she thought about her lost love. Margaret spoke about my father with such love and affection. There was genuine tenderness in her voice. She described the way they first met.

'He was beautiful, it was meant to be'

Margaret recalled how they first met and reminisced about that fateful Summer of 1959 when the showmen came to town. I listened intently; it was a beautiful but sad love story.

CHAPTER 12

The Showmen are coming to town.

It was late August 1959 when O'Malley's travelling fairground arrived and set up in their usual spot on the outskirts of Paisley. When the convoy of trucks, trailers and living vans arrived, they brought the High Street to a standstill, what better way was there to proclaim to the good people of the town, the showmen were here. The message was loud and clear, O'Malley's had arrived. Let the show commence.

Not everyone enjoyed the funfair being around, but, for the working-class folks of Paisley it was a time of excitement and entertainment. The showmen brought life to the town; it took one's mind off the monotonous day to day lifestyle many of the local folk lead. The same Irish showmen, The O'Malley's and their families had been coming to the town for over twenty years. They travelled from Northern Ireland and went from town to town all over Central Scotland. For six glorious weeks they brought to the area a sense of drama, theatre and entertainment, loud pulsating music, a fabulous kaleidoscope lightshow, an array of stalls and stands designed to thrill those who dared to visit them.

The show people stood out with their thick Irish accents, tanned faces, and self-assertive personalities. Fathers of teenage girls would spend the next six weeks worrying about their daughters as the Irish lad's charm and striking good looks were destined to break many a girl's heart. It was the same story every year. This year it was going to be Margaret Jamieson's heart that would be broken. When the showmen inevitably dismantled their rides and pack up their candy cotton food stands, they would leave a catalogue of destruction and heartbroken girls in their wake. It wasn't just the young girls who hung around the fairground attracted to the lads, some of the married women were unable to resist their Irish charm!

Jon-Jon O'Malley senior led the convoy of trucks. When they arrived at the playing fields on the outskirts of town he jumped down from his lorry and pulled down a banner attached to the entrance fence. 'Gypsies Out!' It wasn't the first time he came across ignorance and racism; he'd dealt with it all his life.

'Bloody fools!' mocked Jon-Jon senior in his strong Irish accent,

'We're no feckin gypsies, we're showmen, we work for a living, we are businessmen, we put on a show and entertain people, gypsies don't!' He pitched up his trailer and immediately everybody pulled together to erect the fairground, the stalls, and the stands, whilst the women unpacked the trailers, strapped the babies into their prams and set up home.

There was always a few of the flatties (showmen's name for town people) who didn't want them in town, but for most of the town folk the travelling funfair was a wonderful distraction that brought the community together.

The O'Malley's spent six months of the year travelling with their family, bringing much needed entertainment and excitement to the central belt of Scotland. Jon-Jon senior had tried to settle in the one place, but he could never put down roots, the ground kept shifting and he was drawn back out onto the road. It was in his blood, a way of life. He came from a dynasty of showmen. His wife Roisin was from a circus background and knew no other life but on the road. Their marriage was a perfect merger and seven children later they still worked and lived together as a close-knit unit. Their children led quite different lives from other children, the five boys and two girls were expected to contribute to the family business and help run the home. Family was everything and schooling took a back seat for the travelling families. Jon-Jon senior did not come from a literacy rich background and could neither read nor write. He never had the opportunity as a child to learn to hold a pencil properly, but his numeracy skills were exceptional. He could accurately calculate how much revenue had been generated at the end of each evening based on the amount of people who visited the travelling fair. The six months the O'Malley's spent travelling in the spring and summer normally set them up financially for the winter. In the winter months Jon-Jon senior and his family moved back home to Northern Ireland where they owned a farm and several acres of land. The stables were used for livery and housed many thoroughbred racehorses. Stable hands, mainly from the O'Malley family would muck out and prepare the bedding and food for all the horses. It was a lucrative business, much of the fees were paid in cash, just how Jon-Jon senior liked it. The winter brought a mountain of maintenance to be conducted on the trucks and amusement rides. Jon-Jon senior's father was an excellent sign writer and would spend hours painting much of the equipment. His sign writing ability was well known within the showman community, his vibrant colours and decorative handwritten lettering was legendary. His sign writing was in such high demand clients had to book months in advance.

The winter was set aside for a continual maintenance programme and every piece of equipment whilst dismantled was check thoroughly, cleaned, and lubricated, painted, and packed away.

Jon-Jon O'Malley, was seventeen, a fifth-generation showman who worked on his father's Waltzer ride. Much like the circus, the fairgrounds were a magnet for runaways and lads who were attracted to the excitement of being part of the showmen travelling community. Keeping the show on the road required a substantial amount of manpower, the funfair would not exist without the many dozens of lads that joined O'Malley's Amusements each year. The bright lights and freedom beckoned those who wished to escape their hum drum lives or the predictability of a nine to five job. Touring with the showmen community seemed like a glamorous life but nothing could be further from the truth.

It involved hard manual labour and long hours, working in all conditions, and never finishing until the job was done. It was hard physical work, often dismantling and erecting rides on the same day. Many a loner had turned up at Jon-Jon Seniors trailer looking for work and the chance to escape from their tedious lives. Some of the lads were wanted by the police and chose to keep a low profile, it was easy to slink into the background and hide in one of the many trailers and living vans within the travelling convoy. When the police came calling, Jon-Jon senior would assure them his team of boys were family, he never dropped anyone in the shit. The police were normally looking for a scallywag who had run away from trouble, or a disgruntled father searching for the lad who had left his daughter pregnant. Jon-Jon senior never condoned their lifestyles, the mavericks and reprobates that joined his crew were some of the best men on the showmen's circuit. Like his own sons they were tough, hardworking, and loyal.

Jon-Jon senior treated all his lads like family. He and his wife Roisin had brought up seven kids on the road in their trailer and every one of them was engaged in the family business. Jon-Jon junior had rarely gone to school and spent most of his time shadowing his father and uncles, learning firsthand how the business operated, the traditional showmen way. Jon-Jon junior had inherited a love of the fair, dismantling, and erecting the rides, maintaining, and repairing the equipment and most of all acquiring the skills required to make money, which was called 'the gift of the gab!'

Every member of a showman's family knows how to make money and never feared a hard day's work. It's a tough, hard life for everyone, the women knew their place. They were expected to be home makers and mothers who could juggle working long hours on the stands and stalls, caring for the children, and combining the role as mother and wife with a full-time job. Show people are tremendous sales folk with an in bred work ethic that goes back many generations.

Everyone who knew her referred to Roisin O'Malley as 'Mammy'. She had fabulous flaming red hair as did her children. It made them stand out in the crowd, Jon-Jon junior had grown his hair and it sat on his shoulders, rich red curls an incredibly unique style for its time. The O'Malley's were a beautiful looking family. Roisin was never seen without her make up and gold jewellery, day, or night. Her flaming red hair piled up high on her head, hooped earrings and dramatic black eyeliner was more theatrical than the traditional day to day effect, after all she was from a circus family. The whole family worked together to a strict routine. The older girls took turns in looking after the younger children whilst Roisin performed her daily cleaning duties and kept the living vans spotlessly clean. The men dealt with the mechanical and operational side of the fairground and the women organised all the domestic and home related duties. Roisin hand washed all their clothing daily and no matter what the weather was like she would hang the sodden washing out to dry under a tarpaulin sheet. It was a finely oiled machine and when the fairground was operating everyone had a job to do.

There were no childcare facilities, she housed the baby and toddlers in the large coach built silver cross pram which she positions beside the coconut shy she operated when the fairground was open. The children learned to entertain themselves whilst 'mammy' worked.

Roisin was a master saleswoman tempting crowds of teenagers and lads to face the challenge and win a prize. Her coconut shy side stall, was popular with everyone, winning a prize couldn't have been easier, throw three wooden balls at a coconut and try to knock two down to win a coconut, it was amazing how many people could not achieve this. Or take aim at the Shooting Gallery, one of the most popular stalls with the lads, try your hand at the Tin Can alley side stall, each player has three beanbags to throw at a pyramid of cans, the goal was to knock the pyramid of cans down to be a winner. It was a thrill to win a prize, a candy apple on a stick, a coconut, or a small ceramic figurine or cuddly toy.

Margella O'Malley, the oldest daughter spent the day making toffee apples and candy cotton. Strawberries dipped in chocolate and hot chestnuts and sold them each evening. She would pick up the discarded candy apple sticks from around the ground in the morning and wash them thoroughly before re-using them in a fresh batch. Nothing was wasted, lost property was rarely claimed and anything worth keeping was handed out to the operators, jumpers, coats, scarves, gloves. It was a self-sustaining environment. The days leading up to the opening night attracted groups of girls who would congregate to watch the lads build the rides, slowly bringing the amusements to life. Many of the teenage girls would openly flirt with the boys who worked the rides and relationships were struck up. The funfair boys were gregarious and playful, some took bets on how many girls they could bed bragging about their conquests. Many of the girls fell for their charm and banter, captivated by their good looks and sexual attraction. The lads were hard to resist as their confident demeanor and incredible pulling power made them difficult to fend off. Jon-Jon Senior did not condone the behavior of the male operators who were not family, but he did come down hard on his sons when they mistreated any of the girls. He expected his own boys to show a bit of respect and self-control. Jon-Jon senior expected his own boys to marry a girl from the showman community, only the daughter of a showman could understand the traditions, the heritage and the arduous work associated with living and working with a travelling fair family. Much of the year was spent living in a small trailer with limited resources, living on top of one another.

Show people worked long hours in tough conditions, both Jon-Jon senior and junior were focused on the money, they both had eyes like an eagle and watched the operators intently to make sure all the money was collected and handed in. The money they collected from the public had to be accounted for. The theft of a couple of shillings a night soon mounted up. You had to have eyes in the back of your head. It was important to get as much money out of the public as possible and at the same time eliminate the amount of theft from the lads working the rides. Jon-Jon junior had the ability to watch all ten Waltzer cars and calculate how much money was due for collection on every ride. Not bad for a lad who rarely attended a school.

The Waltzer's attracted the biggest crowds and thrill seekers. Some people could afford to go to the theatre, the funfair was the working classes theatre. At night, you were guaranteed full capacity every ride. Jon-Jon junior and five other lads worked the cars, The Waltzer was the favorite ride, the centerpiece of the funfair it epitomised the term 'All the fun of the fair'. Groups of girls and boys congregated around the perimeter of the ride, inches from the moving cabs. Jon-Jon senior controlled the ride, and the lads collected the money from those seated in the cars. Jon-Jon senior recruited several lads who would ride the Waltzer platform and spin the cars by hand to the delighted screams of the boys and girls inside each car. Five people could ride in each car, the car spun separately on platforms as it raised and fell on the undulating floor. The faster the cars would spin the louder the screams, the spinning intensified the G-Force within the car. 'Scream if you wanna go faster ladies!' was a familiar line the operators would shout out. The boys took full advantage of the screaming packs of girls that would hang about the ride. The Waltzer provided the ultimate pick-up point for the lads to meet a girl and they took full advantage of it.

Margaret Jamieson had not planned on visiting the fun-fair that night, as fate would have it, she had been in the town center in the morning with friends and was approached by two lads handing out flyers.

The boy with the flaming red hair thrust a flyer into her friends' hand and began flirting with Margaret.

'Hello there, I'm Jon-Jon' his thick Irish accent, tanned face and beautiful smile was something Margaret had never encountered before. He was confident and knew just the right things to say. He grabbed her attention by making her laugh. 'Here, take these ladies, tell them Jon-Jon gave them to you' The flyer was for unlimited rides on the Waltzer for her and two friends, that night only. It was Saturday, the perfect night to visit the funfair.

***

The Waltzer ride was crowded, Eddie Cochran was singing 'C'Mon Everybody' so loudly Margaret could not hear Jon-Jon junior ask for her money. She showed him the flyer and he smiled and pulled the safety bar tight up against her body.

"We'll hello beautiful, glad you could make it." Jon-Jon flashed his incredible smile and spun the car Margaret, and her friends were riding, they screamed enjoying the moment. The music was loud and the attention from the two male operators was constant. Jon-Jon caught her eye and they flirted at the end of the ride.

'What's your name?' asked Jon-Jon. 'Margaret' she smiled.

'I'm glad you came, I remember you from today, can you hang about till the end of the night?' Jon-Jon did not have much time to speak, he only had a few minutes between rides. Margaret was immediately smitten, no one had ever spoken to her like this before, he was confident, outgoing, and incredibly handsome. He did not wait for her answer he just grabbed her by the arms and placed a kiss right on her mouth. It felt like an electric shock.

It was not the most glamorous of starts but for Margaret, this guy was something else, she stood by the barrier with the others and watched Jon-Jon work the ride. She was mesmerized, he commanded his stage and unknowingly performed to the audience at the barrier, most of which were young ladies looking for a little romance.

The final ride was at nine o'clock, Cliff Richards and the Shadows played Living Doll.

'You are my living doll.' Jon-Jon smiled. 'Can you hang around till I finish?' he presumed, 'No, I must get home.' Margaret knew there was no way round it, she wanted to stay, of course she did, but her father would be waiting, curfew was 10pm, no later. It was almost 9pm.

'Meet me tomorrow at 1pm at the Cross in the town center.' Jon-Jon pulled Margaret to him and kissed her. Margaret naturally responded, it was her first real passionate kiss with a boy, and it felt good. Her friends were talking to some lads at the entrance gate. They called out to her to hurry up. Jon-Jon watched as Margaret walked away. She was frightened to turn around, the thought of Jon-Jon watching her made her nervous. Within minutes she caught up with her friends stunned at what had just happened and already looking forward to meeting Jon-Jon tomorrow!

It was ironic, Just the year before Margaret was too old for the teacup ride and not old enough for the big wheel. It was as if she had grown up that night, just a few months before she had been playing skipping ropes with friends, now, she was meeting a guy, on a date.

Little did she know, Jon-Jon was going to completely change her life. The next few months would be like a rollercoaster ride of every emotion a woman could experience.

CHAPTER 13

My first job - Summer 1976

The summer of 1976 was the hottest summer I ever remember. The heatwave went on for weeks and weeks. The government imposed a hosepipe ban because of the drought. No more watering the garden plants or cleaning the car. In New Weston the water supply was regularly turned off to conserve water, dad would fill bottles of cold water in the morning and put them in the fridge. With the mains supply of water turned off you had to stand in a queue to collect water from a standpipe at the bottom of the street. A bucket of water was glamorously left beside the toilet in the morning 'just in case we really had to flush'. The temperature was so hot, the tarmac on the street started to melt. Dogs and cats stayed indoors, and you were considered wealthy and extremely fortunate if you had an electric fan in your home. Dad brought his table fan from the office home at night, and we took turns standing in front of it to cool down. It was a wonderful summer; I don't think we saw a cloud in the sky for weeks. Everyone was walking around with a healthy tan.

Gran said. 'It's the first time I've seen you with a bit of colour around your face'.

I was a few months short of my sixteenth birthday and like every other sixteen-year-old who was still at school, I had a Saturday job. I worked for a fashion retailer based in the shopping center in Paisley. The shop owner picked me up and dropped me back home every Saturday. I was happy enough to do this as the part time roles in New Weston were either in a chip shop or delivering milk. To get into Woolworth's, you had to know a man who knew a man who knew the manager just to get an interview. I was given the opportunity to work throughout the summer break as the owner, Jill and I got on extremely well. She was a lovely person, similar age to my mother but with a completely different outlook on life. Jill was an entrepreneur, forever opening shops or trying out new ideas. She was forward thinking and charismatic, always thinking about business and how to improve it. I really looked up to her, she inspired me to think about what I could achieve in life. Jill would say motivational lines like 'It never occurred to me that I could never achieve my ambitions.' She demonstrated to me it was possible for a woman to be independent and run her own business.

'Not all women were designed to be housewives and mothers' she insisted. I had to agree. I always felt Jill had a strong aura around her. Nothing ever appeared to penetrate her confidence, she was driven and not afraid of hard work. I found myself hanging on her every word and even starting to sound like her. She had the ability to make everyone feel relaxed and bring the best out in you. Jill was exactly what I needed at this point in my life. She offered me the full-time sales assistant role in her Paisley store, and I accepted. Now I had a reason not to return to school! When I told Bill he just shook his head, he was not impressed.

'A bloody sales assistant, that's some career choice!' he moaned.

If I had come home and told Bill I had been accepted for Harvard University, he would still have scoffed. I wasn't considered the Golden child, that title had been afforded to Billy.

I knew the Paisley store was haunted but said nothing. I has seen several apparition's whist I had been inside and outside the shop. One of the girls, Sally, who worked along with me on a Saturday only lasted a few weeks. She had gone into the back-staff room to have her tea break and fifteen minutes later came rushing out screaming into the front shop, throwing staff and customers into a state of panic.

'What's wrong, what's happened?' Jill snapped.

Sally, the sales assistant, was mumbling as she recalled her back-room encounter.

'There's was a man in the corner, he tried, he tried to touch me (sobbing) touch me, I want to leave, need to go now, get my bag, my purse!' and with that she was gone. She was clearly terrified of what had just happened. Jill had no luck settling her down, customers were staring and some of them left the store. I knew exactly who she was talking about and went into the staff room to confront him.

Paisley jail housed many of the reprobates, murderers, and rapists from all over Central Scotland.

Most of the condemned men either died in the jail or were hung at the rear of the prison and buried in anonymous graves, most definitely beneath the new shopping center. Prisoners were unable to communicate with the outside world and those who attempted to escape found the only way out was over a wall impregnated with broken glass. Guards patrolled the wall. To escape, you would have to sidestep the soldiers, scale the wall, and jump fifty feet into the shallow rat-infested river below. Escape was not an option. Often, those who died were homeless men, transients, and outsiders with no family, no one would have reported them missing or would have claimed their bodies. The dead would be buried on the prison grounds in unmarked graves.

In 1969 The Plaza Shopping Centre was built on the grounds of what was once the grounds of the jail.

George McMillan was born in Dumfries into a farming family. Despite professing his innocence after a coroner's inquest and witness testimonies, he was found guilty of the 'rape, mauling and murder' of a young girl in Dumfries and sentenced to death. On the 15th of May 1836 he was hanged along with two other men in front of 5,000 spectators in the County square. George was only 28 years old when he swung from the gallows. He was a nasty, evil man, who drank a lot, swore a lot, and loved to start a fight. He preyed on the vulnerable, especially women. He fled to Paisley to avoid being arrested by the police, changing his name, and living anywhere he could. With no permanent abode he survived day to day on a diet of petty crime, theft, alcohol, bread, and gruel. He trusted no man. He was finally arrested for battering a woman outside a bar in the town and was imprisoned in Paisley jail, where his real identity was discovered. The trial judge decided on the death penalty rather than transporting George to Australia. His family had long since disowned him. His body was buried in an unmarked grave on the prison grounds. No headstone, no name, no one cared. Now 140 years on George had found other vulnerable women to torment and taunt.

It was presumed the dozens of bodies that were buried in the grounds had been exhumed before any buildings were erected after the old jail was demolished. This was never confirmed. It was unlikely it took place.

George McMillan was the first malevolent spirit I had encountered. He was disgusting, his language was foul, he would go into the female changing rooms and ladies toilet to watch the girls. If I confronted him, he would release a tirade of filth. It was hard to imagine anyone would speak like he did, every other word was vulgar. He had absolutely no respect for women. I knew he was about when there was an overpowering putrid body odor stench.

I handed Sally her bag and jacket, she grabbed them from me and hastily ran out of the shop. She never came back.

On the way home in the car, I explained to Jill about George McMillan.

'Can you help me Cat, I know all about your psychic

ability, can you cleanse the shop for me and get rid of any negative spirits which have decided to mess with my staff and business?' This was the first time I ever heard Jill sound so gloomy.

I took the Monday morning off work with Jills permission and went to Paisley Library to do a bit of research. Jill had recruited the services of a professional psychic medium and shamanic energy practitioner called Maggie McCallum, apparently, she was well known in the area. We met and she took an instant dislike to me. Perhaps she used her psychic power and sensed I did not like her!

Maggie suggested the malevolent spirit was a male who died on the land the shopping center was built on, possibly the prison, she was correct, but she was unable to tell me his name or communicate with him. I was.

With Maggie on board, Jill, Maggie, and I started the cleanse the shop after it closed on 'half day Monday.' Apparently, there had been disturbances all day in the building, cups falling over, staff feeling like they had been touched, lights flickering in the ladies toilet. Jill had even had to come to the store prior to opening to reset the burglar alarm.

Jill, Maggie, and I were in the staffroom, as Maggie prepared her potions and bragged about her various cleansing conquests, I could sense George was in the room. I called out his name, I could smell his nasty odor.

'George McMillan, I am speaking to you, the male spirit who comes into this shop, show yourself?'

'What are you doing?' whined Maggie as she prepared herself for the cleansing. 'You have no idea what you need to do to get rid of a malevolent spirit, please take my lead, the practice of burning sage is sacred and deserves our respect, I will summon the spirits, NOT YOU!' Maggie looked at Jill and shook her head. I was aware burning sage is thought to ward off negativity and toxicity, clearing the badness out and allowing more positivity to enter your space. I would never disrespect this ancient ritual and was insulted Maggie would suggest this.

'What is that rotten smell?' Jill complained. 'He's here.' I said waiting for Maggie to interrupt me.

'Fuck you!' raged George, he was here and had brought his rancid smell and vile dialogue with him.

I thought Maggie would have seen the apparition, but she gave no sign any spirits were about. Both Maggie and Jill were oblivious to George being in the room. I was frightened but felt best not to show it.

I confronted him. 'George, you don't need to stay here anymore, you no longer need to feel trapped.' He circled the group, looking at what we were all doing.

'George, you need to move on, you *are* dead.' I was pretending not to be frightened, but I was. George was not going to go easily. Maggie had already said some horrible things about him, and he was angry at her. Maggie was ready to start her sage cleanse and confront George. She moved around the room fanning the lit sage in the air. Maggie ordered all trapped spirits to move on, chanting and mumbling as she moved about. She recited the Lord's Prayer and other Psalms.

'By the light of my soul, in love, I release all negative influences in this area, mind, body and spirit.' She repeated these words as she walked around the store. Dowsing holy water and waving the lit sage throughout the shop.

'Jill please open some of the windows so we can let the smoke out along with this vile, evil spirit.' Maggie continued to walk around and recite her mantra over and over.

'A simple cleansing will sometimes clear any unwanted spirits from the area, it's just like erasing a cassette tape, we can wipe clean this room and ask the evil spirits to leave.' Maggie asked me to summon George.

Maggie lit another huge sage bundle, she let it burn for a few seconds before blowing it out. Maggie went from corner to corner of the shop reciting her mantra and wafting the sage smoke with her fan.

George was standing by the changing room mirror; he did not want to leave. He was a man who was going to stand his ground.

'Get out whores!' he screamed, knocking over the waste bin, and spilling the contents onto the floor. A person that is nasty and evil in life is the same in death and George was in a rage. He pulled at the ceramic bust on the console table and it crashed to the ground. Maggie and Jill turned round to see what was going on. I continued my verbal bashing with George. I picked up one of the sage bundles and began to wave the smoke in his face. He pulled back.

'You don't like this do you George!' I had found my confidence. 'You don't like a woman standing up to you, do you George.'

In life, George was not ready to die, he did not want to depart this earth. He was told his death sentence may possibly be reprieved and he could be sent to Australia, another prisoner had already been transported to the port for his removal. George waited in hope, he felt sure the news would come. The day of his hanging came as a complete surprise, as the guards stormed into his cell, he was dragged up onto his feet and taken straight to the gallows, gripped with fear he walked into the unknown, a priest stood at the base of the gallows delivering the last rites to another prisoner, the guards did not stop long enough for George to ask for forgiveness.

'No! No! Stop! I'm going to Australia, No!' He spat and cursed to no avail.

The horror was real, no one listened, their grip on his arms was too much for him to break free, he struggled and fought for his life, but he was outnumbered. He would not win. His hands were tied behind his back and a hood placed over his head. The noose was placed around his neck, and he plunged through the trap door all within a matter of seconds. His screams could not be heard above the baying crowd. There was to be no mercy, his hanging was their entertainment. He died fearing purgatory and facing his demons in hell.

Because of his sudden terrifying death his earth-bound spirit was in limbo and struggled to move on and cross over.

'George it's time to go, the good people who work on this land do not want you here, you have no right to torment them, go now!' I waited for a response. I wanted George to get closure and move on.

I could hear, Maggie reciting her chant. She was demanding the evil spirits left the building.

'Evil spirit be gone from this building.'

'I don't care for her lady.' George was referring to Maggie

'She is not you're judge and jury George, God is.' I wanted him to listen to me.

'She says I'm evil; she be a fusty strumpet.' George could be hard to understand but I understood one thing. He did not like Maggie. In his rage he pushed over the glass flower vase, it shattered on the hard-tiled floor.

'George, is there a reason you are here?' If I knew why he was here I could perhaps use this to move him on. Was he being mischief and looking for help to cross over?

'I shall give thee what thou shalt want.' said George, but I had no idea what he wanted.

Maggie was still smudging the room with sage and reciting her verses. Jill was following her around looking terrified and clasping her hands as if she were praying.

'Shhh, can you hear that?' Maggie stopped smudging and stood in silence.

'George McMillan, I command you to leave this building now, your presence is not wanted here, leave now!' demanded

Maggie.

George stood beside me. He was an earthbound spirit; he had attached himself to the ground around where he had died and was attached to the women inside the shop. He was a spirit who had died suddenly on the gallows, and for this reason had not crossed over. A young man with his whole life in front of him who had feared death but could not avoid it. George was a confused soul; he was dead but did not want or know how to move on. He was probably brought up in a god-fearing Christian household and feared being judged for his sins, so had stayed earthbound for fear of going to hell and not heaven. He never intentionally wanted to cause fear or disruption, he just enjoyed the energy the girls and the female clientele brought to the building, but his energy was just too frightening and overwhelming for staff and customers. They could not co-exist.

George was weakening, I could feel his energy diminishing, I knew how I could get him to move on.

'George, you will not be judged, I will show you how to cross over, you can be reunited with your family, they are waiting for you, go to them.' I called out to George.

The war of attrition between Maggie and I was slowly breaking George, Maggie was wearing him down. He had been cornered; his only escape was to move on.

I was overcome with emotion and physically drained, the door next to me opened suddenly and the whole doorway was illuminated by an incredible white light. The echoes of the past were calling. I sensed George McMillan's energy being dragged towards the light, something was there waiting for him. I could not see who was beyond the light, but I could feel them. There was a greater power beyond the doorway. It was overpowering and could not be resisted. It pulled George forward. I knew, there would be no more pain, he would not be alone, he would be surrounded by an incredible surge of love. The experience was beautiful, it was filled with affection and optimism. I had made a real connection and thanked the spirits, this was an incredible moment, I felt elated and exhilarated instinctively knowing George was destined to rest in eternal peace and have closure despite the many sins he committed when he was alive.

'George you are free to go, go towards the light through the doorway, go and be free, you no longer need to walk this earth in fear, you will not be judged, God or no man will ever judge you again.' I was speaking from the heart, I had a strong connection to the spirits, and could feel them all around me. Their combined strength was enabling me to move George forward and complete the cross over. I had no idea what I was doing I was simply following the flow of energy and the magnetic pull beyond the door. I watched George cross the entrance and immediately felt the atmosphere in the area change. The light went out and George was gone. The store went silent.

Maggie and Jill stood beside me in amazement.

I fell to the floor in exhaustion, I was emotionally drained and cried tears of absolute joy.

'I don't know what I just saw, what did I just see!' Jill was frantic.

Maggie extinguished the sage bundles by smothering them into sand to be used another time. She came to my assistance and put her arms around me.

'He has crossed over.' Maggie declared 'Any tainted spirits have gone from this building.'

The atmosphere felt peaceful and clear. The air felt lighter and less oppressive.

The three of us sat huddled together on the floor and contemplated what we had just achieved. The sun was going down, and as its final rays poured in through the window onto the floor beside us, we held each other, the warmth was real. It was over. George McMillan had finally crossed over.

Maggie Smith claimed another successful cleanse, she gave an interview about the haunting to a national newspaper and used artistic license to dress up the narrative about George's removal. I was not mentioned by name in the feature, it was all about Maggie and how she removed the malevolent spirit. Jill and I read the story, her total disregard to the truth appalled us; our recollection of the event was hugely different, we both knew the real story, we both knew the truth.

Margaret and Jon-Jon's First Date – Spring 1960

Margaret was running late for her first date with Jon-Jon. It had already gone way passed the time they agreed to meet, and she worried he would not wait for her. The bus took so long to get to their planned meeting place she literally would have been quicker walking. She jumped off the bus at Goldberg's department store at the Cross in Paisley and checked herself out in the massive display windows. She was looking good. Most courting couples met here, underneath the town hall clock.

Jon-Jon was patiently waiting. He wore jeans and an oversized leather jacket. His blazing red hair sat on his shoulders, and his skin was beautifully tanned making his green eyes look even more dangerous than she had remembered. As he leaned against the wall, hands in his pockets, he looked just as attractive as he did the night before. He was exciting, different.

'Hello Margaret, you look grand.' He planted a kiss on her cheek as if it were the most natural thing in the world. Margaret thought to herself, Jon-Jon was like a feral animal. He was uncontrollable and lacked any manners; body language said a lot about you and Jon-Jon's body was screaming danger. It made him more exciting.

'Hi Jon-Jon.' Margaret smiled nervously.

'You look delicious.' He smiled as he pulled her towards him.

Margaret could feel her face go bright red as Jon-Jon slid his arm around her waist and started kissing her on the lips. He was a cheeky, confident lad, it was impossible to dislike him. Margaret loved his thick Irish accent; she could listen to him for hours.

They made their way to Coia's Café, where Jon-Jon bought ice cream drinks and told Margaret she could have anything she wanted. She ordered a strawberry milk shake. Jon-Jon spoke to the proprietor like he had known him all his life, that's how Jon-Jon was, he made everyone feel relaxed. They spent the afternoon talking and laughing getting to know each other. Late afternoon, he walked Margaret home. They stood in a shop doorway and kissed for the last hour before Jon-Jon made his apologies and raced back to the fairground. He could never miss the start of the fair. As a showman his work ethic was so strict, he would never let the family down such was his loyalty and respect for his father.

For the next few weeks they met up every day, sometimes only for a few minutes as Jon-Jon's daily tasks did not allow any time away from the fairground. Margaret was besotted by him. She made her way to the fairground most nights and hung about the Waltzer's where Jon-Jon worked the family ride. There was lots of eye contact between them, and he would often sneak over for a quick cuddle or kiss.

Jon-Jon led a nocturnal lifestyle, he and the other ride operators went from trailer to trailer after the funfair closed and enjoyed each other's company. His mother, Roisin would make big pots of home-made soup and Irish stew for everyone to share. Her home-made bread was legendary and was served with every meal. Jon-Jon had introduced Margaret to some of his extended operator family, she met Rosin and Jon-Jon senior briefly, they did not approve. Margaret believed given time they would grow to like her, just as they adored everyone else in their extended family circle. The other operators and their partners welcomed Margaret, but knew it was a passing phase, all relationships on the road only ever lasted for the duration the fair was in town.

Margaret had not only fallen in love with Jon-Jon but with the whole showman way of life. She had a romantic notion of travelling with a family who looked out for each other. For an hour or so they met during the day and Margaret would make her way to the fairground for a few hours in the evening. All this was done in secrecy and hidden from her parents, she simply told them she was visiting a friend or going to the youth club. It didn't take much to persuade Margaret to slip out of her home each night after the family had gone to bed. Jon-Jon would be waiting at the entrance to the tenement, and they would cycle back to his trailer. Margaret would perch herself on the back seat of the bike and cling onto Jon-Jon's body. Their nighttime activities were never noticed, and Margaret became very skillful at unlocking the front door of the family's home and sneaking out of the building undetected returning only as the sun came up in the morning. Margaret had taken to going to her bed later in the afternoon for a rest, she put it down to not sleeping well at night Gran and Maureen never questioned her cat naps.

Bill and Maureen were unaware of Margaret's illicit affair and the catalogue of lies she had told them to be with Jon-Jon. They were too engrossed in arguing and drinking each other under the table to take notice of what was going in their own home. Margaret saw no comparison between her mother and Roisin. Roisin was nurturing and looked out for everyone, her children, her husband, the other operators, and their partners all fell under her remit as a care provider. Maureen did not. Roisin treated every one of her seven children the same way, there was no favourites, just different personalities. Margaret had never met a more caring woman; she would miss her terribly.

Margaret feigned being ill and was rewarded with several days off school, she spent the time with Jon-Jon. Burning the candle at both ends was taking its toll on them and it was only a matter of time before Margaret would be caught. They became complacent and forgetful as time was running out.

Jon-Jon and Margaret were inseparable, the six-week run in Paisley was almost over, there was only two days to go before the fairground rides would be dismantled and the funfair would move onto the next town twenty miles away in Hamilton. Having to say goodbye to girls was always difficult. Many of them became inconsolable, crying and causing a scene. Over the years Jon-Jon junior had seen many of the guys go through it. Rarely did any of the boys give up their job for a girl. Jon-Jon junior had been in this position before, it went with the territory, with so many girls hanging about the funfair at night looking for romance it was unavoidable. He had learned to let go of other relationships at the end of the run, but there was something about Margaret, he was going to miss her, for the first time he was not looking forward to saying goodbye. Margaret was going to be difficult to get over.

Margaret tried to avoid the deadline, the thought of not seeing Jon-Jon was unbearable, not having him in her life was unthinkable. She looked at Jon-Jon as he slept, she had an idea, an urge, maybe a whimsical idea, but an impulse non the less and it was not going away!

Bill Jamieson was woken by cats fighting in the bin shed, it was just after 4am. He got out of bed for a cigarette and looked in on the children 'Where is Margaret, she's not in bed?' he alerted Maureen.

Bill Jamieson was raging. Where the hell was she. His 14-year-old daughter was missing. He lit up a cigarette and threw on some clothes.

'Where the bloody hell is she?' he said out loud as he pulled on his shoes ready to hit the streets.

Instinctively he knew a boy was involved. Had to be. She had not been taken from the house, wherever she was, she had gone of her own free will. Bill noticed the door was not locked, but on the latch. Margaret had let herself out of the house. Lately Bill thought Margaret had been secretive and impossible to live with. She had been caught wearing lip gloss and Bill had demanded she wiped it off her face. Maureen had suggested their daughter's mood swings were down to hormones and Bill accepted this. But in his heart, he knew she was hiding something, and he was going to find out exactly what it was, if it was a lad, he was going to get a right bloody hiding.

Having no idea what to do Bill headed out onto the street. Should he call the police, should he stay home and wait for her? Mary mentioned her sister had been going to the fairground a lot and thought she had met a boy who worked there. 'Might be worth a start' he said to Maureen as he pulled on his jacket.

Maureen stayed up and made tea and lit a cigarette. Outside, the town hall clock chimed five times as Bill Jamieson turned the corner and headed along the street. He recalled a story one of the lads in work had told him about his brother's lass falling for one of the boys in the funfair, it seemed like a starting point, so he headed for the show grounds.

The final days were passing too quickly, at first, Margaret thought it was a crazy notion, but the closer the deadline got for the fair to up sticks and move to the next town, the more serious she was about joining Jon-Jon and his family. Margaret had already started to compose the letter she was going to leave for her parents. It was straight to the point and as heart-less and unemotional as her relationship had become with both her mum and dad. Margaret had once been her father's favourite child but since the birth of Billy, she had taken a back seat to his affection. Jon-Jon provided all the love and attention she needed.

Margaret had decided, she was going with Jon-Jon. He had declared his love for her and she for him, nothing was going to stop them being together. In just over a year, she was going to be sixteen and could be married with the consent of her parents, until then she would work, travel, and live with Jon-Jon junior.

She would talk to Jon-Jon later that night and they could make plans. Like her, she presumed her parents would fall in love with Jon-Jon and consent to their relationship. She wrote her letter.

Dear Mum and Dad

Please forgive me, I have decided to take some time away from my family, friends, and school. Do not worry about me I am safe and with good friends who will look after me. I will write when I am settled in the next town. I am looking forward to this adventure, I am happy, very much in love and living with good people. Talk soon Lots of Love, Your daughter Margaret

It was time to get home before someone noticed she was not in her bed. Margaret put the letter in her bag, she would leave it in a place where her parents would find it after she had gone. She had to get home and pack up the clothes she would be wearing, she planned on travelling light and taking as little as possible. Margaret had learned from the other girls living in the trailers that space was limited, and clothing was limited to essentials only and a small luxury item. Her plan was a max-imum of three different pieces of clothing, one being worn, one for washing and another hanging up. That was how Jon-Jon junior lived and it seemed to work for him.

Margaret looked at Jon-Jon as he slept, he was incredibly handsome, his red hair tumbled onto the pillow, his tanned skin was even and perfect. Every inch of his body was magnificent. Yes, she was making the right decision, she wanted to be with him, tomorrow night she would be travelling with the family to the next site and so the wonderful journey would begin. The very thought had the adrenalin rushing through her body.

She could not wait to tell him when he woke up. It had just gone four thirty a.m., and for the last time, she was about to be escorted home by Jon-Jon.

'Waken up Jon-Jon, I need to get home!'

It was a peaceful morning; the only noise came from the milkman and the dawn chorus. The local Bobby was walking along the street, Bill Jamieson approached him.

***

Their relationship had started on a lie. Margaret had told Jon-Jon she was sixteen, she lied. Mature mentally and physically developed beyond her fourteen years, Jon-Jon had no reason to think she was younger. He would have loved for the relationship to continue but it was not possible, in his heart he knew his father and mother would never allow it. Tonight, would be their last night. He would tell Margaret when he took her home. This was going to be a difficult one, none of the other girls had stolen his heart as much as Margaret had. Jon-Jon accepted he would marry a showman's daughter; it was tradition, it was his culture, and this could not be changed.

Margaret looked around the living van, the bed where she had lost her virginity to the man she loved, was it possible she could travel with Jon-Jon. She could work nights in the fairground, and they could be together, other women did it, she had met a few of them. The living van next door to Jon-Jon's housed Joe and Mary, they were both young, maybe nineteen, both had left home and joined O'Malley's travelling fairground. Their life was simple, they had each other, a job, and a roof over their heads. Margaret envied them; their lives seemed so perfect. Margaret knew most of the operators were runaways or had left home because of violence. Margaret did not know where she was in her life, emotionally she was a mess. The only thing that made sense was her love for this man. It had been a wonderful journey, for them both, six wonderful weeks and Margaret was not prepared to let it end.

Jon-Jon knew Margaret was going to be heartbroken , she was frightened at the thought of telling her their relation-ship was over. He rehearsed over and over in his head what he was going to say.

The silence was cut short as Jon-Jon senior banged on the trailer door.

'Get up, the police are looking for a lass, is she here?'

Jon-Jon junior jumped up and answered the door, he nodded to his father. He would never have disrespected his father by lying to him.

'Right, both of you get dressed and get out, be at my truck in 5 minutes!' Jon-Jon seniors voice was full of rage.

The police had been to Jon-Jon seniors trailer asking about a young girl who was missing, could he check with the lads and if she was here to get her back home as soon as possible if not sooner! Her description fitted that of Margaret's. Jon-Jon senior failed to mention she was fourteen years of age.

The police were aware that the lads from the fairground would take girls back to their trailers after the fairground closed at night. Most of those reported missing often turned up in some lads' bed. Safe, well, and de-flowered!

Bill Jamieson made his way back home after the police

suggested he was better off there, should his daughter return. They would send a patrol car round to the fairground owner and ask about Margaret's whereabouts. The police knew Jon-Jon senior well, he didn't want any trouble around his business, if the girl was on site, he would see to it personally she was dropped off immediately.

Margaret climbed into the front of the truck expecting Jon-Jon junior to join her.

'Jon-Jon, you wait here boy.' Jon-Jon senior started up the truck and made his way out of the park. Margaret sat stunned in the passenger seat. This wasn't how she had planned it.

'Where do you live?' Jon-Jon senior asked.

They travelled in silence until they reached the bottom of her street.

'Best you get home wee girl, I will tell Jon-Jon to visit you after close tonight, don't come to the fairground tonight, Jon-Jon will be too busy.'

'I'm coming with you tonight!' Margaret blurted.

'Jon-Jon wants to be with me.' she sounded pathetic, like the lovesick child she had become.

'Aye, aye, he will get you at your house at midnight. Now go, get indoors, I will send Jon-Jon for you tonight, he will come for you, don't come to the park, now go!' He lied. How stupid had his son been, he would deal with his next!

Margaret crept back into the flat, the door had been on the latch, she secured the door and tiptoed alone the hallway before the pantry door was flung open.

'Where the hell have you been!' Bill Mathieson wanted answers.

'Start talking Margaret!'

Jon-Jon senior stormed into his son's trailer.

'What the feck are you doing boy?' Jon-Jon senior was furious, he had raced back to site to have it out with his son.

I forbid you from seeing that lass again, she's just turned fourteen years old you stupid bastard!'

Jon -Jon senior grabbed his son by the neck and forced him against the wall. 'Don't feck with me boy!'

'You won't be operating today, get packed up, you're leaving site.'

By the time the town hall clock chimed 9 a.m. a devastated Jon-Jon junior was being shipped off to the new site with a few of the guys to start the ground works for the next fairground arrival. As far as Jon-Jon senior was concerned, the relationship was over. He would talk to his son later about keeping his cock in his trousers and having more respect for the family name.

Bill Jamieson accepted Margaret's excuse for being out of the house in the middle of the night.

She had assuredly explained to her father how she had awoken with a severe headache and menstrual cramp; the room was terribly hot, unable to get back to sleep she decided to get some air just at the front of the close but had seen a family of foxes at play and followed them, she ended up walking further than she had anticipated. It would have explained her disheveled appearance and bed hair. Her excuse seemed plausible, she was home, and she was well. Margaret apologised over and over and asked to go back to bed. Bill accepted her explanation despite some reservations. He let it go.

Maureen found her daughters explanation bizarre, but she was home, and no actual harm was done, no point in reading more into it than there was. As a serial cheater Maureen recognised the signs.

Reveling in her performance, Margaret undressed next to her bed, she was astonished at her ability to convince her father she had simply slipped out for air. Best get some sleep, there was a lot to do before she was to meet Jon-Jon at midnight. Things were going to plan, so much easier than she had thought.

Sleep came easily despite the adrenalin rushing through her body. She smiled as she closed her eyes and thought to herself, this would be the last time she would sleep in this crowded bedroom, it was a great feeling.

Jon-Jon had no way to contact Margaret. He didn't even know her address, Travelling had stopped him attending school and he never learned how to read or write properly so writing a letter to Margaret was out of the question. Before Jon-Jon left the site his father came into his trailer and explained to him. 'Move on to the new site today, or return to Ireland, if you decide to go to Ireland, you'll stay there and have nothing more to do with the fairs, understand boy?' One thing you never did was disobey Jon-Jon senior.

Travelling with the fairground and being propositioned by so many girls was an occupational hazard. Jon-Jon senior knew all about the town girls staying overnight with some of the lads, it was one of the perks of the job. The fairground operators brought an air of excitement with them as they sauntered into town. The boys had charm, the looks, and the banter which the girls loved and could not resist. Jon-Jon senior turned a blind eye to most of the girls who would sneak into a lad's trailer at night. If they were gone in the morning and the girls didn't bring trouble to his fairground, Jon-Jon would let it go. Furtively, he had no time for the town girls, they had no scruples. A showman's daughter had more respect and would never be seen inside a lad's living van on her own, but the girls from the towns, now they were different, they would throw themselves at the boys. 'No self-respect' he would say, not like the girls from the showmen community. He had warned his sons to stay away from the girls from the town. 'No good will come from being with any girls outwith our community.' he warned his sons.

Jon-Jon senior and Roisin ran a strict home and business, no matter what town they set up in the O'Malley's would be sure to find a chapel for all the family to attend mass at least once a week. The locals were friendly and welcomed them each year, offering to fill their many containers with fresh water before they had access to mains water from the street. Just like his father before him Jon-Jon senior had a reputation to uphold. Back then the showmen were close knit and a hard-to-reach community, they relied on each other and not outsiders. His father, William O'Malley had been a well-respected showman who ran a successful fairground. It was mainly a menagerie of attractions, including freak shows, the tattooed man, dancing dogs and horses, entertaining illusion tricks and food stalls, the public loved it. It was on these fairgrounds where Jon-Jon senior learned his craft.

Jon-Jon senior was much like his father, William O'Malley had the gift of the gab and could create believable and gripping stories at the drop of a hat. When he was introducing the performers, he created an atmosphere of horror and excitement, it sold more tickets. He would often recite these stories prior to bringing on his acts, his anecdotes and wild imagery caused chaos and fear with the women and children in the audience.

William's wife Rosie, Jon-Jon seniors' mother, was gifted with the ability to talk to the dead, she predicted her father's death and would often speak out loud to him in her living van. She claimed to be able to see and speak to spirits and would often terrify others with her impromptu and abrupt conversations with a spirit. Her reputation was legendary within the showmen community. She had wealthy clients in every town and performed table séances, at private sessions and at the fairground, communicating messages between the spirits of the dead and the living. At the turn of the century these kinds of events were a source of entertainment with the rich and famous and after the first world war Rosie O'Malley was much sought after. After one difficult séance, Rosie fell into a deep trance after contacting a malevolent spirit. It was said the spirit manifested and those in attendance ran terrified from the building. Rosie was used as a source of power for the spirit as it took over her body and then refused to leave. The séance was cut short, and Rosie was taken back home to her trailer by concerned family members who had witnessed the terrifying act play out. Rosie never recovered, her accent and tone changed, and her behaviour became erratic. She frightened the children and over time she became unpredictable often violent. A decision was made by the family that Rosie O'Malley was kept locked inside her trailer day and night. Her husband, William, said it was for the best. She was taken out for walks by William who tied one of his hands to hers, so she was unable to get away. Rosie's confinement had been a difficult decision to make as the showmen community are family orientated and look after each other forsaking anyone else, family always comes first. Jon-Jon senior believed his mother was insane and that a demon had invader and taken over her body, she had become possessed. The family made the difficult decision to hide her from the public mainly to protect her and not them.

William O'Malley was with a lover when Rosie took her own life. She set her trailer alight. Rosie turned the gas mantels on full and left them to fill the small trailer with fumes. Once she ignited the match, instantly the trailer became a ball of flames. The wooden frame quickly ignited. No one was able to open the door of the van, the tiny windows once broken created a backdraft that only fed the fire. Rosie could be heard laughing and then screaming as the fire consumed her body. Those who tried to put out the flames had to retreat due to the intense heat from the fire, one of the lads said he heard Rosie muttering and calling upon a mysterious force as she placed a spell on William, and the fairground, minutes before she perished. For much of the family Rosie's death had come as a relief, she was deeply loved. However, her ramblings to the unseen spirits embarrassed the family, especially her son, the up-and-coming entrepreneur showman Jon-Jon senior. Jon-Jon had forbidden anyone to talk about the circumstances of his mother's death. As far as Jon-Jon was concerned, his mother had accidently killed herself by unintentionally leaving the gas mantel on. Officially her death was recorded as an accident. Unofficially it was suicide. The hex started the day she died. For many years after his wife Rosie's death, William was racked with pain and misfortune. His lover was killed in a freak horse-riding accident, he lost his brother in a tragic fairground incident, his beloved dancing dogs and horses were found dead in their stables, cause of death, unknown. The fairground was ravaged by fire, and it took many years for William and the family to bring it back to its former glory and popularity. The hex lasted 13 years and almost destroyed the business. The stress was the probable cause of William's stroke which left him paralysed down the right-hand side of his body. He became reliant on walking aids to get him about. In a tormented moment of complete resentment, he begged for his wife's forgiveness and to stop the hex before the whole family were left without a home and income. The curse suddenly stopped, and life slowly returned to normal. It was the first time William O'Malley ever begged for something in his life and he was humiliated having to do so.

When his father died in 1949, Jon-Jon senior took over the business and swore he would make the travelling fairground a success again. He and his brothers worked their fingers to the bone and brought the excitement back out onto the road. Slowly the fairground evolved, and new rides replaced the human attractions, the post war public needed some fun in their lives and a reason to visit the travelling fairgrounds. Over the years Jon-Jon senior learned how to gain the public's attention and flirt with their imagination. He understood their mind set, only curiosity and the need for excitement brought the town people through the fairground gates. He invested money on lighting and mechanical rides. Jon-Jon senior had two rules he adhered to: knowing what acts the public would pay to see and keeping the showground entrance exciting enough for the public to want to come in and spend money being entertained. It was a winning formula.

***

Jon-Jon junior would get over this lass and everything would be back to normal. His father and mother had no hesitation in severing his ties with Margaret, she was just a child. It was for the best. Whilst travelling from town to town, it happened, the flatties, the name the showmen gave to the local people, were attracted to the fairground lads, especially the ladies, they often fell in love with the male operators. It was common for an assortment of broken-hearted girls to be seen at the fairground gates sobbing and crying, saying goodbye to the lads on their final night. It was the decent thing to do, let the girls down gently. Jon-Jon juniors' path had been chosen for him, long before he was born. He would marry, but it would be to a girl from the showman community, it's just the way it was.

Midnight came and went; Margaret had her small bag packed and was ready to be picked up. It had gone one a.m. and there was still no sign of Jon-Jon in the street. Shaking with nerves, she slipped out the house and made her way to the site of the fairground. Something must have gone wrong she just knew Jon-Jon would never have let her down. As she approached the playing fields where the fairground had been, it was desolate. All that was left was the marks and damage on the ground where the rides and stalls had stood. The smell of diesel and the sound of the generators had gone. The silence was broken by a fox who was rummaging over by the bins for scraps of food. Everything had gone, the trucks, the living vans, the rides, the horses, The O'Malley's. The air was still, there was no bright lights, no accordions playing and the family sitting by the fire, sharing food and conversation, no kettles hanging over the fires or clothing on makeshift clotheslines blowing in the gentle wind. It was as if no one had been on the land. Now all there was, was silence. Margaret stood in the darkness, she could hear her heart beating furiously inside her chest, it was surely going to burst or perhaps just break. He was gone, what would she do now, how could she go on without Jon-Jon , all the things they had said and done all the plans they had made, surely these were not lies, what happened to the fairytale, their fairy tale. It was Jon-Jon who spoke about the future and how they would be together! It was him! He made the promises, he said he loved her, it was him! Maybe, this fairy tale had a dark side to it and there was no happy ending, just tears. Margaret was numb. She stood alone, broken, and feeling foolish, what had she done? She had to get back home before her father found the letter!

Bill Mathieson got out of bed, it had just gone two o'clock, he could never get through the night without a nicotine fix. In the parlour, Margaret had left the letter under his cigarette packet. Bill instantly recognised Margaret's handwriting, he lit up a cigarette and opened the letter.

The police patrol car rolled up beside Margaret, she was so gripped by grief and shock she did not hear the vehicle just a few yards behind her. The officer got out and approached her.

'What are you doing here Miss, it's very late, shouldn't you be at home?' 'Yes officer, I want to go home!' sobbed Margaret.

The policeman took Margaret home, once inside the flat the officer spoke privately with Bill and Maureen. It had just gone 3 a.m., despite the time, curtains had been twitching in the street, neighbours stretched their necks to see what was going on in the tenement building. The police car sat outside for almost twenty minutes. Those who traded in gossip were going to have a field day in the morning.

Once the officer had gone, Margaret was sent to bed and the front door was securely locked, Bill Mathieson took the key to bed with him, it had gone four o'clock and Bill had been looking forward to a relaxing day off, now he was going to have to spend it reprimanding his oldest child and deal with the contents of her letter. He was not prepared for the confrontation and had already decided to delegate it to someone else. His mother!

CHAPTER 14

Sweet Sixteen

Diary Entry - Friday 12th November 1976.

It's my sixteenth birthday. I was sent a beautiful diary by Mary. It meant a lot to me. Emotionally, it meant the end of a longstanding tradition, Margaret, my mother had always been the one to buy me my diary. She would write in the inside cover a little paragraph about the year ahead and how she hoped my dreams would come true. I confide in my diary and write my deepest thoughts and fears, my diary never judges me. I can be expressive without fear of criticism. It is more than just a means of reporting what happens on any given day, for me it's a way to release tension and record the many conversations I have with those lost and lonely souls who for one reason or another, choose to remain with us the living ,despite themselves being dead.

My estranged boyfriend Jim had sent me flowers. It was the first bouquet of flowers I had ever received; they were delivered to my house and were beautiful. A small card tucked inside them read,

'To Cat, Happy Birthday, Love Jim'. A birthday card had been hand posted through my letterbox early doors; It read *'To My beautiful Girlfriend'*. The joke was lost on me as we had taken a break from one another. Jim told me he had got some girl pregnant and was being forced to marry her by her parents. His parents were against the marriage but said they would help support the child. Such a waste of life, for both.

Early afternoon, Jim called at the house, he wanted to meet me, set the record straight. I was going for dinner with the family to celebrate my birthday but agreed to meet him the following night.

We met at the railway station as agreed, he looked handsome as ever. We made our way into Glasgow on a crowded train, I had missed him so much and hoped we could work things out. He had bought two tickets for the theatre.

'I want to show you something, this woman is a psychic medium, apparently her show is impressive' Jim said in such a matter-of-fact manner.

'I want you to tell me if she is the real thing or a fraudster?'

Jim was never phased by my inexplicable outbursts when I was confronted by lost spirits. I once told him his grandfather was sitting at the kitchen table beside him. I went on to hold a whole conversation with him about his love for his greyhounds, I even mentioned them by name. He died when Jim was just fourteen years old. Both were incredibly close, and Jim missed him terribly. Jim never flinched when I spoke to the dead, he adored me communicating with his grandfather. His mother complimented me on my ability to comfort people by speaking with their loved ones who were now gone. She was the one who suggested I ran with my 'gift' and made a career out of helping people. His parents were so free spirited and open minded nothing ever fazed them, even the possibility of their son becoming a father was greeted with love and not anger.

'New life is always good news, a wee baby in the house would be sweet.' Jamie McGowan was open to the prospect of becoming a grandfather. Deep down we all hoped Jim was not the father.

It was the first time I had been to a theatre, and I was

loving every minute of it. The inside of the building was ostentatious with ornate gold leaf designs dressed in deep red velvet curtains with massive chandeliers hanging from the ceiling. It oozed character and I could feel the building housed a great deal of residual energy. I was petrified when the lights went down, and the massive curtain was raised. The music was overpowering, filling the theatre and the senses in preparation for the start of the show. The compare introduced the psychic to the audience. I have no idea what to expect but it certainly was not the old, grey-haired lady who came onto the stage to rousing applause. Her list of achievements was impressive, she told us who she had worked with and how she had predicted this, that, and the next thing. She was a self-proclaimed medium and had a massive following in the UK. She spoke about her new book, and how she had the ability to talk to the dead. The audience was mainly women who cheered and hung on her every word. Her name was Dorothy Swanson. From the moment Dorothy introduced herself I was mesmerized. I was captivated by her ability to hold the attention of the audience who were bewitched by her. She had my complete attention. I literally could not take my eyes off her. Dorothy appeared to randomly speak to spirits and matched them with people in the audience. She accurately described the deceased person and passed on messages of love and support to family members. The start of her show was fast paced as she screamed out names of the dead and matched them to people sitting in the audience. The theatregoers showed their approval by clapping furiously or letting out gasps after Dorothy spoke. Everyone she contacted from the spirit world had described how happy they were, those 'who had passed over to the other side' were now with their loved ones. Dorothy was very convincing, but something wasn't quite right. Her questioning techniques came across as simplistic and obvious. I looked at Jim.

'Is she a fake Cat?' he asked. I watched intently.

Dorothy continued cold reading the audience with random requests, 'I have a gentleman here; his name is James who has recently gone to the other side.' We live in Scotland; everyone knows someone called Jim who is dead!

'I have a man here, an older man, his name starts with a M or is it an N and he passed from (holding her heart) a heart attack?' Dorothy was putting out a huge amount of general information to the audience. Vague statements, which could relate to almost anyone.

'He had an accident as a child and fell into some water' Dorothy would observe a particular area of the theatre 'He had a problem with his back.' She would then focus in on one person. 'Was this someone you knew? He says it is you dear!'

By this point the person is so convinced it is them they believe the spirit of their dead grandfather is in the theatre. It was all smoking mirrors, clever rhetoric, before you knew it the audience member is giving out clues by their body language and facial expressions. 'Do you have a grandparent in the spirit world, yes, he wants you to know he loves you and is so proud of you!'

It was beautifully done, slick and seamless. Moving from one side of the stage to another. She was delivering no message just random statements and the audience was enthralled!

It was easy to obtain an audience members name. Row C, seat numbers six and seven. Booking under the name Paterson!

'I'm looking for someone in this area of the theatre with the surname name starting with a P, Palmer, Paterson, yes Paterson!' She was using cold calling techniques to convince the audience she was talking to the dead.

I was not picking up on any of her energy. I saw several apparitions, standing beside their families who were unaware of their presence. I had a woman spirit stand at the end of my row; she was trying to get a message to her daughter. I waved frantically to Dorothy in the hope of attracting her attention. She finally pointed to me. 'Yes dear, how can I help you?' said Dorothy.

'There's a lady here who needs to talk to you' I shouted. Dorothy asked her runner to get the microphone passed along the aisle to me.

'Dorothy, there is a woman here who is trying to get a message to her daughter Carol McGibbon.' Jim was impressed with my confidence.

I felt like everyone in the theatre was looking at me, but I was so determined to get my message out there. The young man who passed the microphone to me asked me to speak up.

'Is there a Carol McGibbon in the theater tonight?' Dorothy asked.

I was getting caught up in the hype and excitement of the show. A voice called out from the back of the theatre. 'I'm over here!'.

I continued with my message. 'Your mother, Peggy is extremely proud of you and all you have done; your three beautiful girls are a credit to you. Your mother is telling me she is no longer in pain and wants you to know you are better off without John your husband, he is no use. Peggy says you have the strength just like she did to get up and go, you must find the strength to do this, do you understand?'

By now a theatre aid had given Carol a microphone.

'Yes! Yes! I understand, thank you!' Carol said between sobs.

I felt I had so much to say but the microphone was quickly taken from my hand. The female spirit to my left was smiling,

I felt she had so much more to say before she moved on. Peggy had died so young. I had delivered her message, but she wanted more.

'Tell my daughter, I have an important message for her which will save her life.' I agreed to get this message to her. I sat down and Jim gently patted my leg.

'Well done girl, I'm proud of you' Jim had the biggest smile on his face. I could tell by his voice, he really meant it. He squeezed my hand.

A quick-thinking Dorothy was like a magpie, stealing my comments and passing them off as her own. Pacifying Carol and repeating the message I had just passed on. The audience gave Dorothy a massive round of applause and she lapped it up.

As the lights came down for the interval, I got out of my chair to find Carol further back in the theatre. Before I could find her, I was approached by a stage technician who said he was with Team Dorothy. He wore one of her 'On Tour with Dorothy Swanson' T shirts just like the ones on sale at the official souvenir stand in the foyer. 'Miss Swanson would like to meet you , please follow me.'

Back stage Dorothy Swanson was smoking a cigarette and sitting in her dressing room in front of a brightly lit mirror. She introduced herself and asked me all about myself. I was amazed at the lack of energy around her, I was confused, was she not the biggest psychic medium in the UK. She claimed to be in touch with the spirits of the dead and was able to communicate between the dead and the living. I immediately knew the woman who sat in front of me was a charlatan, a confidence trickster and a bloody good one at that. Carol McGibbon's mother agreed with me. She had followed me backstage and stood less than a meter from Dorothy.

'Dorothy, can you see the lady sitting in the seat opposite you?' I looked Dorothy straight in the eyes and with her best poker face she turned to me and spoke. 'Yes, ofcourse I can!'

Dorothy was a fraud. Carol's mother was standing by the doorway and not on the chair. I described her as a heavy-set woman about fifty years old, Dorothy agreed. The fact was Carol's mother was slim and blond. I felt terribly disappointed, just how was she able to pull this off. Dorothy Swanson was an imposter, the great pretender. Her agent came into the room. He introduced himself as Danny Lavine and asked me to go on stage with Dorothy for the second performance. Both Jim and I looked at each other and I saw him ever so slightly nod his head. I didn't have much time to think about it before I was escorted out of the room and along the corridor. On the way to the stage Jim pulled me aside and whispered in my ear.

'This is your time to shine kid, let them have it!'

The curtains went up to rapturous applause as Dorothy and I walked out onto the stage. It was a surreal moment. I stood on the stage with Dorothy Swanson in front of three thousand people, we invited Carol McGibbon to come down and join us. To a house full of cheers and applause Carol made her way down towards the stage.

My conversation with Carol was spontaneous and live, there had been no time for a rehearsal and there was no script to work from, we were going to have to adlib. I was unable to see into the audience as the bright lights punished my eyes and I could only see the front few rows beyond the band pit. Once on stage, Carol stood beside Dorothy and me. Dorothy faced the audience and talked about Carol's mother. She repeated the private details I had divulged whilst we had been backstage. Dorothy took ownership of the facts and passed them off as her own. I had told her this information in confidence and within minutes she was repeating it to a full theatre. The audience were deadly silent.

I prepared to communicate with Carol's mother and pass on the honest and truthful messages from mother to daughter. I began by proving to Carol her mother was here.

'Your mother is here; her name is Peggy' Carol gasped and reached out for my hands.

'She died on the way to hospital after being struck by a car. She was only forty-eight years old. Peggy says she misses her grandchildren but comes to the house regularly and watches the children play and run around.'

Peggy described the children in detail, and I repeated her word for word. The facts that were divulged came as a shock to Carol who stood, silent and shaking on the stage, she nodded and agreed to everything that I said.

'Carol, your mother has a message for you and its loud and clear, get out, get out tonight, take the children and leave the house!' The audience were deadly silent as was Carol.

'Go back to your father's house until you find another place for you and the children.' The energy changed in the theatre and around me on the stage.

You could have heard a pin drop in the theatre.

'You and your children are in danger.' The audience were stunned into complete silence.

'If you stay one more night you risk losing everything!'

Dorothy stopped the tension by asking the audience to applaud. She was manipulating the audience to think she was controlling what was happening on the stage.

Whilst Dorothy spoke to the audience, I pulled Carol towards me and whispered to her.

'Your husband is abusing your daughter, Karen, get out of the house!' Carol looked terrified but not surprised. I held her hand as she stood on the stage with me. I could feel the energy in her grasp.

Away from the microphone I spoke over Dorothy directly with Carol.

'Your mother says, there is a key under the padding of your husbands watch box, it will open his safe in the office. It contains some photographs and enough money for you and the children to get a fresh start, but you must do it tonight, go home, when your husband leaves tonight for work take what you can and get out!'

Under the bright lights Carol looked shocking white, she mouthed 'thank you' .

We embraced and it was full of affection and hope. Carol exited the stage and left the theatre. Her mother, Peggy, smiled and disappeared to be with her daughter.

I never saw either of them again, but I knew my work was complete. Carol wrote me many years later to say she and her children were together and in a safe place, she divorced her abusive husband and moved out of the area.

Jim and I decided to leave, I had seen enough. Dorothy Swanson's manager followed us into the foyer. 'That was clever, quite a performance out on that stage, I would love to find out how you did it?'

He was sucking on a cigarillo and had a massive handlebar moustache. He looked like Salvador Dali in a Paisley pattern shirt; I took an instant dislike to him.

On our way home Jim and I decided to rekindle our relationship. We talked about our future together and for once life felt good. He told me about the girl who claimed to be pregnant, he said she meant nothing to him. 'I made a mistake, and I might have to pay for it, but I never meant to hurt anyone, you, her, my parents.' He agreed he would support the child but would not marry her. His parents supported his decision and so did I.

The following year, Dorothy Swanson was headline news. A Sunday tabloid newspaper exposed her as a fraud. She had planted people in her audience throughout her tour. An investigative reporter had witnessed and confronted some of them after being tipped off. He threatened to print their pictures unless they admitted to Swanson's scam. The fake audience members confessed to working with Swanson as she claimed to contact dead relatives during live performances. The planted audience member would go along with Dorothy's poignant details to the amazement of the unsuspecting members of the public that came along to her shows. When interviewed each of them knew Swanson personally and were routinely invited by her to attend performances at her expense. Swanson was born and bred in Manchester, England in 1935, she claimed to have helped the police solve several murders but there was no evidence of this, when asked, no police constabulary in England came forward to substantiate her claims. The murders she alleged to have personally solved remained unsolved. Swanson's sleazy manager denied any knowledge of her wrongdoing. When questioned about their split he insisted they had already severed ties because of 'artistic differences' and nothing else. His press office team issued a statement saying they no longer represented Miss Swanson and had parted company long before the accusation appeared in the tabloids. Dorothy took her own life a few weeks before she was due to appear in court. Her reputation was tarnished by allegations of cheating and deception. The publics opinion of other mediums and psychic performers was now under scrutiny. Most mediums found their reputation was tarnished by Swanson's downfall. Several high-profile theatres refused to book similar artists fearing demand for seats would be low. Hypnotist shows became more popular and replaced the psychic nights for several years thanks to Swanson. Dorothy Swanson single handedly changed the public perception of psychic mediums. Laterly, Dorothy was reduced to doing private psychic readings before her death to pay her bills. I often wondered if she predicted her own downfall and subsequent death. I don't think she did, why, because she was a fraud!

***

Diary Entry - Wednesday 1ˢᵗ December 1976

'If you leave me now' by Chicago was blasting from the radio in the kitchen, I love this song, it evokes so much emotion in me. Jim bought me the 7-inch single and wrote on the label. "Baby, please don't go" Jim must be the sweetest person I know. He is strong and yet I saw him cry once when he talked about his grandfather. He is intelligent, he is my go-to person when I need the answer to a question. He seems to know the answer to the most obscure questions, I put it down to his father, they talk about history and general knowledge all the time. I call him my very own, walking, talking Encyclopedia Britannica! He is romantic, he says 'I love you babe' even when other people are around. He just comes away with it. His mum and dad are the same, forever holding hands and generally acting like they had just met. Jim said his parents met at school; both were hippies, teenagers of the 60's. Their relationship would appear to be based on love, family, and marijuana.

Chicago, the America rock group had written, one of those songs that would forever remind me of Jim. Even to this day, when I hear it on the radio, I immediately think about him. They say you never quite get over your first love and in part I believe there is a certain amount of truth in this. If you only ever get one great love in life Jim was to be mine, I just didn't realise this when I was sixteen years old. Naively, I believed falling in love would always be blissful. Many women desperately search for Mr. Right, but only every find Mr. Wrong. Often, I thought to myself 'thank god that isn't me!' I have Jim. I will always have Jim. He was my best friend, my rock, my Jim. You don't find love it finds you and we were so lucky to have found each other. It was only later in life I realised how much I missed him. I felt comfortable in the presence of Jim's family, they never judged or questioned me about my psychic skill. Their home offered a safe house despite my often-unpredictable behavior. Spirits would call upon me at all hours, unannounced and I was expected to respond. Being a party couple, his parents often had friends come to the house, especially of a weekend. One couple, Roseanne, and Mick came with what I can only describe as the most extraordinary dog. His name was Humphrey, and he was a great big Old English Sheepdog. He was out of control and would bound about the lounge and jump up on the sofa to be petted, he had a lot of energy. It was my earliest encounter of a spirit dog. Humphrey was grey and white; his eyes were hidden beneath his thick coat and his tail was docked. Humphrey was looking for his master, a chap called Tony who had taken his own life after being told his wife had been killed in an accident in Spain. His story was both tragic and incredibly cruel. Tony did not travel to Spain to identify his wife Jeans body. Due to the facial injuries sustained in the accident he had asked not to see her. He wanted to remember his wife as the beautiful woman he knew and loved. His wife's sister identified the body. Tony was devastated when he was told she was dead, inconsolable, and terrified of being alone, he took his own life and that of his dog Humphrey, hours after hearing the news. Oddly, Jean was not dead; it was not her body that lay in the mortuary but that of another woman. Tony and Humphrey were both dead. Three years on, Humphrey had attached himself to Roseanne and Mick, who now lived in Tony's house. I watched as Humphrey lay down next to Roseanne's feet and followed Mick as he went into the kitchen for a beer. Once he calmed down and settled, he was like any other dog. Jim's dog, an old mongrel called Sheba, would never come into the lounge when Humphrey was about, Sheba was too old for Humphreys boisterous carry on and chose to retreat to Jim's bedroom and lie under the bed.

Sheba's absence was only ever noticed once I explained what was going on. Jim's parents were fascinated by my explanation of who Humphrey was. A typical dog, even in spirit, he would come over to me and I would pet him. To me, his presence was like any other dog. I was able to show him the attention and love he so desperately missed. Humphrey would forever be with Roseanne and Mick, even when they moved home after the birth of their daughter. I once saw Humphrey sleep beside their baby daughter whilst she was in her rocker chair. A hugely protective dog, enjoying his family and new baby. Humphrey was content and living in his forever home, each time I saw him he made me smile.

Diary Entry - Friday 24th December 1976. Christmas Eve

My brother Billy has announced his girlfriend is pregnant and they will be getting married in the Register office in January. Bill is furious and Maureen is excited. I'm happy for them. Jim has become a father, a wee girl. No name yet.

On the same day Billy has announced his girlfriend is pregnant, Jim has announced the birth of his child, a baby girl. His new age parents have welcomed the little girl but have put a stop to Jim marrying the mother. Neither Jim or Sherie the baby's mother, love or even know each other. It would be a marriage destined to fail. There may be no future for the couple, but they are parents none the less. Jim has accepted he is a father and will support and pay for the child. It was an expensive price to pay for a one-night stand, now both Sherie and Jim will have to pay for their hour of pleasure for the rest of their lives. A child had been brought into the world, a beautiful baby girl. Part of me is jealous, the other part of me is delighted I still have my Jim. I am going to have to accept sharing my boyfriend with another woman – his brand-new daughter who has yet to be named.

CHAPTER 15

1977

Diary Entry – Friday, 7th January 1977

My headaches have been dreadful. I stayed in bed today until late afternoon. Margaret sat at the bottom of my bed looking over me. I was content knowing she was beside me...

The start of 1977 brought a new job and a telephone call which would change my life. Bill had decided I needed a full-time job which was secure and offered long-term prospects. Maureen wanted me to follow a career in the council or a bank, all she could talk about was the pension and how it would be 'a job for life'. All I could think about was boredom and bureaucracy. In those days someone like myself, with no qualifications or ambitions never really expected to climb up the corporate ladder but I knew there was more to life than pushing a pen and filing documents. The words 'decent job' and 'lifetime' sounded like a prison sentence. My working life was just beginning, and Bill and Maureen were talking about pension pots. Thomson Pumps had an opening for a junior Office Administrator in the buying department. Bill interviewed me over the dinner table as Maureen repeatedly interrupted the conversation by mouthing answers and adding additional words as I replied to Bill. The thought of working with both Bill and Billy did not inspire me but for now it would be the easy option.

Friday 16th September 1977

Billy's son was born on the day glam rocker Marc Bolan passed away. Bolan died after smashing his Mini car into a tree, his girlfriend was driving the car at the time and survived, Marc died instantly. Billy had been a big fan. In memory of his life, we welcomed to the world Marc William Jamieson. He was beautiful, and all 7lbs of him was perfect. Billy had used a full roll of Kodak film capturing the moment the family got to meet baby Marc for the first time. The nurse handed Marc to Maureen,

'Mrs. Jamieson is this your first grandchild?' the nurse asked.

'Yes.' Maureen replied not taking her eyes off Marc.

I said nothing and tried not to think too much about Maureen's response. I was her first grandchild, had she forgotten or did she still think of me as her daughter. It may have been the latter.

Marc slept through the whole introduction, he slept undisturbed as he was passed from one member of the family to the other. The little boy was kissed and held close by all the family, the love and affection towards the new addition was plentiful. As I held him in my arms for the first time, I had an overwhelming sense of tragedy. As I looked at the child, I knew he was not going to live much longer than a few weeks. I hoped I was wrong and quickly passed him to Gran hoping no one saw the look of sheer panic on my face. Billy looked so happy, I nodded in agreement as the proud parents spoke about their dreams and plans for their new family. It was one of the few times in my life I was able to predict the future, it frightened me and added to my anxiety. To think about it was so awful, I kept my prophecy to myself. I was convinced there was nothing to gain from discussing this immense burden with anyone. Jim sensed there was something wrong with me, but I declined to answer any of his questions. There was no dateline for my prediction, but I knew it was imminent. A problem shared is a problem halved, not in this instance. Marc died four weeks later, Marie had gone to check on him as he slept in his cot, he was cold, and his lips were blue. The doctor said the probable cause was cot death. As a family we were devastated. No one fully understood exactly what cot death was and how it could have happened. Little Marc showed no signs of illness to alert his parents, they had followed the midwife's instructions placing him in his cot. He was to be placed either on his side or his front. At bedtime he wore a towel nappy, vest, body sleepsuit and knitted wool matinee cardigan, swaddled in a blue wool shawl. Is there any wonder why he would often be covered in sweat when he was being changed? The midwife had stressed not to place him on his back just in case he should vomit. As new parents they followed the advice they had been given and now with Marc dead Marie and Billy felt tortured, they blamed themselves and felt judged by others outwith the family. I, felt incredibly guilty, should I have said something, would it have saved little Marc's life, probably not but we will never know. I hung my head in shame at Marcs tragic death and regretted not talking to someone. It was something that would traumatise me for many years. Baby Marc never appeared to me, however, at Marie and Billy's flat I would often see orbs flying around the lounge above Marie's head and around her shoulders. It was baby Marc, the feeling I got was one of contentment and innocence. I never told them I could sense their baby's presence, their pain was so deep from the loss I could never express the right words to them, so I remained silent.

***

Working with Bill and Billy wasn't so difficult. I never had to worry about making my way to work each morning as Bill took me in the comfort of his company car. Billy would drop me off at home after work as Bill preferred to stay in his office till all hours. His working life was different from his home life. At work he ran the company with an iron fist, he was looked up to and respected by the workforce, but at home, he and Maureen were forever at each other's throats. Maureen gave him no respect. Screaming and fighting, never a night passed without raised voices coming from the lounge. Each argument was instigated by alcohol and Maureen's increasing paranoia that Bill's late nights were nothing to do with boardroom meetings and additional paperwork but more to do with his extremely attractive secretary Samantha Horn. Samantha was half Bills age, I suspected there was something going on but chose to ignore it. If they were having an affair both kept it beautifully hidden. Turns out they were. With almost one hundred employees at Thomson Pumps, it was only a matter of time someone would see them together. Secrets never stay secret for long, no matter how discreet you are. Ironically, they were caught in Bills Mercedes at the traffic lights on a Saturday morning by two staff members on their way to work. Bill was kissing Samantha's hand, and both only had eyes for each other. Their sighting confirmed what everyone already knew, Bill and Samantha were having an affair. One of the worse things about working in a factory with over forty women on site is the gossip. Once the story broke it moved through the factory like hot lava, moving across all departments, the assembly line, and the transport department within hours. The pervasive nature of the gossip was going to cost innocent people their jobs. The details morphing each time it was passed from person to person. Repugnant Chinese whispers. Donald McKay, the transport manager, had his tongue so far up Bills arse it was embarrassing. McKay could not wait to tell Bill what everyone was talking about, he was such a traitor, Judas, a weasel of a man who enjoyed the prospect of confronting the boss. First thing Monday morning McKay was on site earlier than usual, he lit a cigarette before he chapped on Bill Mathieson's office door. Once inside he shut the door and closed the venetian blind so the team of secretaries could not see what was going on. They could only be talking about one thing. When McKay left Bills office, he looked like the cat that got the cream with his chest blown out and his status as main sweetie wife in the building firmly intact. Many times, over the years Bill had intervened when Donald McKay had been implicated as gossip mongering. Bill had defended him. McKay in the past had denied being involved in any workplace gossip and thought nothing of throwing one of his junior staff members under the bus to clear his own name. McKay would blame others for rumours he would instigate. Bill Mathieson detested gossip, now he was the subject of it.

Diary Entry - Saturday 12th November 1977

It's been quite a birthday; Mary sent a birthday card with a generous twenty-pound note inside it. She is living in Monaco with some guy who owns a computer company and by the sounds of it was having fun. Mary also sent me the most beautiful diary; it had a decorative picture of Monaco on the front.

Inside she wrote, to my darling sister, Have the most fabulous 17th Birthday, Come, and visit me soon in Monaco, where dreams do come true. Love Mary xx

Bill and Maureen had the most awful argument tonight. As I left with Jim about seven o'clock, I could hear them yelling at each other, when I got back home about eleven, they were still at it. Fueled by alcohol, the kitchen resembled a pub bar, filled with empty glasses and bottles of vodka scattered across the worktop. The house stunk of stale cigarette smoke. An ashtray was overflowing with half smoked cigarettes on the kitchen table, I was sure it was empty when I left. From the lounge I could hear Maureen crying, it was a typical scenario, they fought, Maureen cried, they drank some more, Maureen passed out on the sofa and Bill went to bed.

They didn't hear me come home, not that this would have stopped them arguing. The mood indoors was one of extreme emotion. One-minute Maureen was screaming for Bill to get out and the next she was begging him to stay. The place went silent after I heard a plate being thrown at the wall. Bill stayed. In the morning I discovered he had slept in Billy's old room. The plate that was thrown had my birthday cake on it. The kitchen wall was wearing most of the frosting, I cleaned up the mess and put the unlit candles back in their box.

Jim's mum had made me some chocolate muffins, she had seasoned them with Moroccan hash. I thanked her but declined her kind gift!

Diary Entry - Thursday 1st December 1977

Gran has moved in. Like me she is worried about Maureen who spends her life permanently drunk. Bill spends a lot of time away from the house, I can only assume he is with Samantha. Billy and Marie are not in a good place and Mary is behaving like she is a member of the royal family and wants nothing to do with any of us. What has happened to this family? Thank God for the voice of reason named Jim!

The phone rang about six o'clock in the evening, I answered it. I had just sat down to enjoy a bowl of grans homemade lentil soup.

'Hello Cat.' I recognized the voice right away.

'What do you want ?' I asked already knowing the answer.

'I need your help!' Strangely enough I was expecting the call.

'It's been a while' he said. I agreed.

My heart was pounding. I don't know if I was nervous or frightened. I hung up the telephone after agreeing we should meet; how could I say no!

CHAPTER 16

Diary Entry - Monday 5th December 1977

Is this really what is ahead of me, I despise working at Thomson Pumps but where do I go from here? The last thing I want is to be stuck in this town for the rest of my days married with a whole load of kids running around my ankles. Forever struggling to make ends meet from one wage to another. Eternally being known as the 'woman that speaks to the dead'. A girl at work says I should go down to the council office and register for a council house! I really think there is more to life!

The short drive to the office with Bill was silent apart from Paul McCartney and Wings rattling out Mull of Kintyre on the car radio. What was once a beautiful song with an uplifting message had now become so irritating, I began to switch radio stations just to avoid it, much to Bills annoyance.

The atmosphere in the office was strained. It was common knowledge that Bill, and Samantha were having an affair. Maureen knew and so did all the staff. Unlike Billy, I decided not to take sides, Bill had decided to stay at home as Maureen had threatened all sorts if he left the family home. He had been honest and upfront about his affair with Samantha, and he seemed to be happy. Maureen had given up trying to win him back, it was a ridiculous situation, but it seemed to be working, both were living under the same roof and simply tolerating each other. Their marriage was over years ago but neither of them had the guts to get up and leave. Maureen had no idea how to live beyond the doorstep, she had been a kept woman all her life and had never really worked for any length of time, granted she brought up four children and kept a clean house, a housewife was a full-time job after all, working all hours and with no trade union behind her. Now, with just me living at home she relied on Bill, Gran, and Mr. Smirnoff to get her through the day.

As Maureen sat at home drinking and smoking, Bill was with his mistress, Thomson Pumps. He spent more time in the factory than he did at home. He knew every facet of the business, every employee by name, every supplier, and every customer. Nothing got passed him. He treated the cleaner with as much respect as the engineers. Hard work had paid off, working his way up the corporate ladder at Thomson Pumps, Bill had been rewarded with the position of Chairman when Charles Thomson retired. Bill was loyal and was treated like a brother by the Thomson family. His position within the company was secure. Charles Thomson had total faith and trust in Bill, he knew his company was in safe hands with him at the helm. The position came with a handsome salary, company pension, parking space, company Mercedes and Charles Thomson's ex-mistress! Billy had sided with his father about his association with Samantha, much to Maureen's disapproval. Samantha Horn (such an ironic surname) was discreet and confidential, she was a forty something long legged blond spinster who loved travelling and the theatre. She adored Bill and never discussed their relationship with anyone. She was discreet, sophisticated, and cultured. Although she came from the East End of Glasgow, she had perfected a posh Morningside, Edinburgh accent. Samantha oozed fashion and culture. She had been founder Charles Thomson's personal secretary and on off lover for over fifteen years. When he retired and handed the reigns to Bill, she continued in her role. Loyal and trustworthy, Samantha kept her distance from the other ladies in the workplace. She never used the canteen or went on staff nights out. She had sworn allegiance to the Board of Directors, her devotion and dedication had landed her the superior position as personal secretary to the Managing Director/Chairman and as the boss's bit on the side. Not once but twice.

Samantha was always professional when I was around. We worked in different departments. One of her main tasks was safeguarding Bills office, she had no problem stopping anyone trying to get passed her. No one got into his office without her consent, even me!

'Sorry, Mr. Mathieson is not available at present, I will tell him you called!' she was good.

I worked in the sales department and hated every minute of it, I was never accepted and never included in any chit chat or gossip. Perhaps it was because Bill was my 'father' or were they simply gossiping about me. Any chatter would suddenly stop when either myself or Samantha entered any of the offices, I soon learned to ignore it. Regarding Samantha, I neither liked her or disliked her, she was an enigma and kept her cards close to her chest. In the workplace she was proficient and aloof, she made Bill happy so who was I to dislike her. This woman had not split up a family , it was already in tatters. Bill and Maureen's children had grown up and apart from me, moved on. Where had it all gone wrong, I asked myself, I blamed the alcohol. Maybe Samantha gave Bill a sense of purpose, a second chance at love. She ticked all the boxes, attractive, intelligent, independent, and devoted to the job. A dating agency could not have matched a better couple. We all deserve a second chance, even Bill.

January 1978.

By the start of 1978, I had been discreetly talking with DCI Smith. He contacted me at the start of December, and I agreed to meet him for coffee and discuss a case on which he was working. I recognised his voice right away on the telephone. I could hear the frustration in his tone, he was reluctant to discuss anything specific on the phone. 'It would be easier to meet in person' he said. So, we did.

Jim picked me up in his van and I met DCI Smith on the outskirts of the town in a café normally used by council workmen and long-distance lorry drivers. Today it was empty apart from him and I, it was good to see Smith again.

'Thanks for coming Cat.' Smith smiled. I noticed he wore a wedding ring but had never mentioned a wife before. He was married all right, to the job! Smith looked older than I remembered but he was still handsome, he had experienced more in life than most and it was written all over his face. He wasn't alone, his colleague stayed outside in the car. Smith placed his cigarettes and lighter on the table and began to talk.

'Cat, I need your help, you may have seen this on the news or read about it in the newspaper.' He handed me a photograph of a young girl. 'A fourteen-year-old girl was murdered at a caravan park in Loch Lomond last week, a man walking his dog found the body.'

He passed a national newspaper across the table for me to read. Smith went on to tell me about the girl and the circumstances surrounding her death. The crime scene and surrounding area had been thoroughly searched and not one piece of evidence had been found.

'What do you want me to do this time?' I asked knowing the answer.

'How do you fancy a wee trip to Loch Lomond?' Smith stood up and I followed.

Jim and I got into the back seat of the unmarked police car and all four of us made our way to the picturesque village in Loch Lomond. In the car Smith told me more about the case. They had absolutely no leads. No one had seen the young girl leave the site, no one had spoken to her, and no one noticed she had gone until her body was found. Her parents had both been in the caravan park bar with friends all afternoon, their whereabouts had been confirmed by several site users and other reliable sources who saw and spoke to them at the bar. Further investigation confirmed, social work had not one single thing on the family, background checks produced nothing to suggest the mother or father hid anything sinister from their past. The caravan park staff, all seemed to have an alibi which had checked out with other staff members as to their whereabouts on the night of the murder. An appeal broadcast on local television had drawn a blank and no leads came from its airing.

Smith, his silent colleague, Jim, and I pulled up at the caravan park. Smith and I got out of the vehicle and walked the fifty yards or so into the forest. The site was quiet, there were very few people about. A killer was on the loose and the stigma associated with the murder had kept visitors away. We went straight to the crime scene where the girl's body had been dumped. If it weren't for the police tape at the scene you would never have thought a murder had taken place. The scenery was beautiful, contrasted by a dark and foreboding Loch. The killer had selected a serene spot in the forest for his macabre murder, now it was desecrated, forever to be remembered as the spot where a young girl was murdered.

The police presence had now gone. The campsite manager had requested the police moved on, there attendance was terrifying the families who were staying on site and was not good for business. Eventually, the police did as he asked. Smith had been assigned to the case, he requested his team kept a low profile and insisted only plain clothes police constables went door to door questioning the locals about the dead girl. DCI Smith was now overseeing the investigation, and he would not be taking orders from a caravan site manager on how he should manage a murder investigation. A child was dead, and Smith was determined to find the killer.

As we walked around the murder scene, Smith removed photographs from inside his overcoat and passed them to me. He was nonchalant, he displayed no emotion at all, I suppose it went with the job. I, however, was not so comfortable viewing images of a lifeless child and found the experience disturbing. The pictures were of the dead girl, Lynn Ross slumped on the ground, fully clothed, no injuries or marks appeared on her face. She lay on her front, her head turned to the side. Her eyes were open, despite there being no blood or disturbance around the body, she looked dead. Her eyes looked vacant, empty, and fixed. She wore a polo neck jumper which hid the rope marks around her neck. Little was said, the photographs spoke for themselves. Smith lit a cigarette and watched me as I walked around the area where the girl's body had been found.

'Help me Cat, help me find the bastard, who did this to an innocent child?' pleaded Smith

I felt under pressure. I looked at the pictures of the little girl and tried to make connect with her, I could feel nothing. I looked at the pictures again, her eyes were so full of pain and distress, but I was unable to summon her. I called out her name and asked if she was here. Emotionally I directed my attention to the night she was murdered and tried to focus on reconstructing how the attack could have happened, but no, I was unable to pick up anything. I called out for Lynn to appear to me but, she did not.

I could sense Smith was disappointed, I didn't want to let him down.

'Give it time Cat, there's no rush.' I could hear the despair in Smiths voice. The one man who had believed in me and held me in great esteem was disheartened with my lack of communication. 'Give me space' I said as I walked away from the scene.

It was no use. 'I am so sorry Smith, I am picking up absolutely nothing, I can't help you!' Smith lit up another cigarette, 'No need to worry, let's go, have a coffee and come back later, yes?' Smith was patient and tried to persuade me to come back later in the day.

'NO!, I can't help you, take me home now please.' I had had enough. My time here was over.

Smith escorted me back to the car. He lit another cigarette and motioned to the quiet man in the driver's seat. Smith indicated to his colleague to open the car door, but the quiet man looked perplexed. What followed was a comedy of errors in a surreal location between two senior ranking police officers. The quiet man signed back and forth like a racetrack bookie, refusing to get out the car. Smith verbally put him in his place.

'The man is a buffoon, he is so immature he probably still writes with crayons, no wonder he was taken off the case, ignore him.' said Smith.

Their immature antics knocked my concentration and my trail of thought. Just as the rear door opened and I was about to step inside, I was violently struck from behind, I felt something pull tight around my neck, in an instant, I was on the hard ground and then pulled to my feet by the ligature around my neck. Unable to turn around I could not see who was behind me. I pulled at the tight binding around my neck. In desperation I kicked out behind me as I struggled to grip the binding with my fingers, the grip was tightening, I was losing consciousness, I fought back but it was no use, the attacker was stronger, substantial in size to me. The intensity of the grip grew stronger, and I was swinging , my head was spinning, there was no oxygen, I had no memory, I was pulled up by the neck and off the ground hanging in midair. With one almighty thrust I was thrown back on the ground. I felt the rope being whipped off my neck. I lay disabled on the ground awaiting death. My breathing was strained and labored, each breath was shallow and short. And then it happened. I saw his face as he picked up the rope. I saw who it was!

Smith had never seen anything like it! He confessed to being completely 'paralyzed with fear' as I writhed in agony and hovered unaided inches off the ground. When I came to, Smith, Jim and the quiet man were kneeling over me, they all looked concerned. Smith had a cigarette butt hanging out his mouth which had burned out long ago. His face was ashen white, like he had just seen a ghost, perhaps he had. Jim lifted my head off the ground and asked if I was all right.

'What the fuck did I just witness?' Smith was stunned.

'I saw him Smith! I saw him, I saw his face! Lynn knew who he was!' Jim picked me up and carried me back to the car.

February 1978

I always had the radio on in my office, the American songwriter, Bill Withers was singing, Lovely Day, I loved the song, but I could never sustain the eighteen second note he held towards the end of the track, I always had to come up for air to finish singing the final chorus and the word 'Day' It became an obsession for me to complete the note every time it played on the radio, but it was a lost cause. I never ever achieved it. I always had to come up for breath.

At the top of the hour, DCI Smith featured in the news headlines. He had arrested and charged teenager Lynn Ross's murderer. The campsite caretaker, Hugh McNeil, had crumbled under interrogation and had eventually confessed. Smith never mentioned me in his interview, why would he? It would have taken the shine off his arrest.

McNeil had been interviewed twice, but his mother had supplied his alibi, she said they had been together all afternoon working in the site tavern. When the beer stopped flowing McNeil used the excuse to change the beer barrels and slipped down and then out of the cellar to meet Lynn. While the customers concentrated on the bingo and the rollover cash prize, McNeil met Lynn in the site park, she was waiting on him. She was such a tease; it was a game she had perfected and so many men had fallen for it. McNeil and Ross had sex the night before in the cellar, it was quick and awkward and meant nothing to Miss Ross. Afterwards Lynn asked Hugh for money to buy fish and chips from the local take away, Hugh loaned her a five-pound note and she promised to return the money the following night. When Lynn asked to meet him in the park, he thought it was because she wanted to return his money but no, Miss Ross had other ideas. She was about to inflict on Hugh her tried and tested bribery technique she had used on several other men.

Lynn attempted to blackmail McNeil. He was shocked, and she was in her element. She loved the hold and control she could have over men. Her wicked use of vocabulary was more fitting coming from the mouth of an older lady, but Miss Ross was no lady. She demanded McNeil gave her twenty pounds if he wasn't willing to give her the money, she would tell her father he had raped her. The bitch knew exactly what she was doing, she had kept her pants from the night before as evidence, if he didn't give her money she threatened to go to her father and then the police. She had no intention of telling anyone as she was sure McNeil would cough up the cash. This well-rehearsed scenario had worked every time on other guys. To buy her silence, he agreed to pay her a one-off payment and then he wanted nothing more to do with her. Her stay was almost up, and she would be leaving the caravan site to travel back home in the next few days, and it would all be forgotten about. I listened to her confront McNeil, I was disgusted at the way she spoke to him, he was out his depth and was nothing more than a naïve simpleton taken in by a good-looking but highly manipulative young girl.

Linda wanted to inflict one last blow and it was a stunner. 'Oh! and by the way I'm not sixteen, I'm fourteen, peado!'

A frightened McNeil was about to give her £20.00 when she upped her demands to £40.00. McNeil realising what was now going on, refused to pay any more money. Lynn was riled, a scuffle ensued after Lynn said she was going to tell her father, expose him to everyone, concoct a story about him touching her up and then raping her. It was a remarkably well constructed extortion gambit for a girl so young.

'Give me the money!' Lynn was not going to be silenced.

McNeil put his hands over her mouth, but when she kicked and screamed 'rape' he panicked, he had no intentions of raping her, he simply wanted to silence her, stop this madness, she was a blackmailer, pure and simple. Little Miss Ross was a calculating little extortionist who knew exactly how to extract money from men. McNeil removed his hand and put his index finger to his lips in the hope she would calm down and he could think about the best way to end this situation amicably, but Lynn continued to kick out and scream obscenities.

'I want my money NOW!'

What happened next was out of character and changed the destiny of two people. It was madness but McNeil was unable to silence her. Panic stricken he grabbed Lynn's bag and wrapped the rope handle around her neck, his intention was not to kill her but to silence her, he pulled on the rope, maybe this would calm her, let her see he was not going to back down. Lynn continued to struggle, she pulled at the rope around her neck as she fought to breath. She kicked and struggled but McNeil was stronger than her. He tried to make her see sense, stop battling, he wanted her to go away, but it was no use. Perhaps he lifted her body off the ground with the rope, he could not remember, all he wanted was for her to stop, for her to be gone. He wanted it all to go away and be back to normal, his mother would be waiting inside. Her grip loosened and her fight for life stopped. Within seconds her body went silent and limp. She was dead. Confusion and fear reigned. McNeil dragged her body into the undergrowth beyond the park, removed the rope from around her neck and headed back to the bar just as the full house winning bingo numbers were drawn. He hadn't taken in what had just happened, perhaps she would waken up and realise she couldn't just go about threatening men. He had been gone no more than fifteen minutes. As he entered the main hall, he placed the rope bag in the bin, the bin collection was due in the morning if Lynn wanted it back, she had better be quick. Morag, his mother waved to him, pointing at the empty glasses on the tables. He immediately went from table to table clearing and wiping the tabletops. Hugh casually congratulated the lady who won the bingo, kissing her on the cheek. Ironically, tonight's winning full house was for £40.00!

McNeil poured a drink for himself behind the bar as the bingo caller checked the numbers. He threw back his whisky and nervously considered his options. Anxious, he thought about calling an ambulance but what would he say, if he confessed to the police they would not understand, if he stayed silent what was his chances of being caught? Perhaps it was best to keep quiet and say nothing. His disappearance from the club bar had not been noticed. By all accounts he *had* been on site the whole time. Everyone that was interviewed said they saw McNeil in the bar at the time of the murder. When questioned, not one of the eighty people had noticed Hugh had left the bar, they were so engrossed in their game of bingo. Sometime later, Smith and I met for coffee and discussed the case. McNeil had been arrested and a confession was beaten out of him. Smith described McNeil as a child molesting murderer. In the press, Ross had been described as an angelic daughter who enjoyed going to the Girl Guides. I had a different viewpoint, I believed McNeil was a man in the wrong place at the wrong time, a gullible silly man who had been taken advantage of by a dangerous young girl. He had no intentions of murdering Lynn Ross; he was terrified and reacted in the worse conceivable way. Ross was a clever, money motivated individual. Other men must have breathed a sigh of relief when the newspapers published details about her murder. Her name and photograph were all over the television and national press. Smith disclosed to me, once Lynn's bedroom was searched, they uncovered the names and telephone numbers of several men, all of which had been blackmailed by Ross. In her school bag they found bundles of five and ten-pound notes, too much to have been amassed from pocket money or babysitting! Her victim portfolio and stash of money was never mentioned to anyone outside DCI Smiths office and any potential evidence about her promiscuous history was either lost or hidden at the back of a filing cabinet somewhere at the station. Ross made money from extortion; her death put an end to her wicked practice and furthermore, Lynn took her stories to the grave with her. I dread to think what would have become of her if she lived. No one deserves to die, especially one so young. She had her comeuppance, even at such a young age, Lynn Ross was a streetwise, manipulative criminal, capable of squeezing substantial amounts of cash and guilt out of frightened naive men. She played a dangerous game and paid for it with her life. McNeil was a sorrowful pathetic fool, but it could have been any one of those other men who, when pushed could have committed the same heinous crime. McNeil ended up taking his own life before the high court trial commenced. He slashed his wrists in his cell with a razor blade passed to him by another cellmate. There was a rumour he was murdered but I know he took his own life. He told me.

Sadly, what this proves is anyone is capable of murder in the right or even the wrong situation. A few anonymous letters had been sent to DCI Smith, all from men who had been threatened and blackmailed by Ross. These letters were never disclosed in the court or made public. As far as the public knew, McNeil killed an innocent 14-year-old girl. Case closed.

Diary entry Friday 16th June 1978

I got a call from Smith today, the silent man, Jim Allinson, the police driver who drove me to Linda Ross's murder scene has sold his story to a national Sunday newspaper. He has told them every-thing. I need to get out of here! Fast! It's only a matter of time be-fore journalists and the tv news teams camp outside my front door.

I didn't have much time to react, I got the call on the Friday night about the feature coming out on the Sunday. Shortly afterwards a journalist telephoned and then turned up at our door with a photographer looking for some comments. The flash from the camera almost blinded me. I slammed the door closed and called Bill.

Bill suggested I take some time away. Gran recommended we go to Ireland and visit some of the family. Bill arranged the ferry for the Sunday morning and Jim, and I made our way by car to the ferry port. Journalists had been persistently trying to call me and even stopped family members in the street asking about my whereabouts. They wanted to ask me about my side to the story. Jim advised me not to talk with them and this was before the newspaper article came out!

Late Saturday night Jim picked up a copy of the news-paper from a petrol station. The newspaper feature ran across three pages. The headlines on the front page screamed.

'I SPEAK TO THE DEAD; Scottish Police Force use a psy-chic to solve murders!'

Alongside a full colour picture of myself as I left my place of work. I had no idea the picture had been taken. I looked ter-rible. A double page spread in the center pages quoted Jim Al-linson, who had by now left the police, and described how he had witnessed my horrific re-enactment of Lynn's death and observed me levitating off the ground. Much of the article was incorrect or had been grossly exaggerated to make it sound even more sensational. I had been totally exposed, my name, my address, where I worked, my photograph, it was all there in black and white print. There were even quotes from people I knew, some of them from as far back as school. It highlighted to me just how far these journalists would go to support a story and what acquaintances would say and do for money.

I had to escape Scotland and headed over the sea to Ireland. Gran, Jim, and I patiently waited for the first ferry to dock. I was terrified. It felt like I was on the run from the world. We arrived at the seaport at 7am, I thought to myself, by midday millions of people will have seen my face and know my name and all about me and my family. My secret was going to be out there in the public domain and my life was going to be subjected to ridicule and further invasion, it was terrifying. I had no idea how I was going to confront this. Jim said we would face it together with dignity and silence.

'The truth will prevail; this is your chance to take this and make something of your life.' said Jim.

As we waited for the ferry to take us to Ireland, I knew things would have to change. I couldn't keep just running away. I was having to flee my home, and yet I was innocent of any crime. I stood shivering looking out to sea wanting so much to speak to DCI Smith, I knew he would have the right answer.

On the ferry a man was reading The Sunday News. My face was splattered across the front page, I had overtaken Olivia Newton John and John Travolta for the lead story, John Travolta strutted onto the big screen and into my heart. Grease may be the word but today, it was me they were talking about.

'Your hot news today but by tomorrow girlie, they will be eating chips off your face' said Gran as she tried to make light of the situation.

Ireland - Sunday 18th June 1978

On arrival, the Irish contingency did not want me to stay at their house. I was not welcome. Superstition, strong Catholic ideology, and beliefs. Gran stayed with the family and Jim, and I found a traditional hotel far out in the country. Our room was above the bar. I found it difficult to sleep as there was so many lost spirits in the building, they kept me awake most of the night. The structure dated back to 1777 and had a fabulous array of souls roaming the house from various timelines. On our second night, Jim and I sat at the bar with Patrick and Shoran the landlord and landlady. We spoke until the wee hours about their unwelcome guests. Jim had kicked me several times under the table to stop me giving too much away. I let my guard down for the first time and told them more about me than I should have done, including why I was in Ireland. They were both fascinated by my story, and I enjoyed the attention they bestowed on me. I told them,

'There is nothing sinister at play here, I recommend you find a way to co-exist with your visitors and embrace them, learn to live in peace together.'

They both listened intently as I described two of the sprits I had spoken with and told the proprietors who they were. The spirits were going nowhere, they had been around a lot longer than most of the landlords and had no intentions of leaving. Basically, what spirits want they get, to be heard and accepted. My advice was simple, they both had to learn to live with them or move on.

Back in our room, Jim complimented me on how I had managed the question-and-answer session with the hotel owners. He went on to suggest, I should use my gift to bring contentment and closure to those who had lost someone in their life. I liked the idea of working for myself but had no idea how to start.

Late morning, I took to my bed with extreme head pains and Jim snuggled in with me. Downstairs two journalists checked in; they had been invited by the owners, Patrick and Shoran who had been seduced by the cash incentive to talk about me. I had been set up! There was no one I could trust.

Several hours before back in Scotland, Maureen had answered the door to a journalist from another tabloid newspaper, worse for wear with drink from the night before and a tongue desperate to talk, she had inadvertently told them where I had gone and with whom. It did not take the same journalist too long to track Jim and I down. Over the next few days, the press was ruthless in harassing me, I was featured each day in various newspapers, the stalking and deceit were too much, I could not be on the run indefinitely and I decided to return home, face the press, and tell my side of the story. By now, it wasn't just me who was being affected, my family was now being tarnished, their damaging comments were taking their toll on everyone. I returned home with Jim and set up a meeting in a local hotel with the original tabloid newspaper. Several people had made money selling stories about me. I wanted to set the record straight and for the right price I was willing to tell them the real story, straight from the horse's mouth.

CHAPTER 17

July 1978

My expose was a blessing in disguise, I was now a commodity and the media wanted to interview me. Jim set up a meeting with the editor of the Sunday News, the same publication Allinson had used. His willingness to meet me was startling, within hours a meeting point was arranged. Four men turned up to discuss my options, the editor, the chief features journalist and two different lawyers. It was intimidating and frightening but also strangely satisfying all at the same time. The Editor, Jack Neil took off his suit jacket and rolled up his white shirt sleeves. He was a forceful character and got straight to the point.

'We want an exclusive deal, you don't talk to any other newspaper or television station, do you understand?' I nodded in agreement.

Jim was quick to interject. 'We haven't discussed the fee, if it's going to be an exclusive arrangement Cat will need to look at the overall fee and work out if it's worth it before we continue with the meeting?' Jim was managing this like a professional, he had lost his calling in life and should have been an agent. Jim began negotiating with the executives. What I would talk about and what I would not talk about. A woman in a blue dress was furiously taking minutes throughout the meeting. Finally, a price was agreed, Jim took me outside the room to discuss the offer in private.

'Cat, you are looking at six thousand pounds, for an exclusive deal with photographs. A new Ford Capri is about

£4000. You don't need to mention the murder victims or DCI Smith by name. Just answer their questions and agree to some pictures.' I looked at Jim and smiled.

'Yes, let's do it' I said.

And just like that I agreed to sell my story to the biggest national Sunday tabloid in the country. Totally naïve and without the support of any PR or legal representative I entered a contract with the newspaper. Jim was with me every step of the way and I trusted him implicitly. He became my spokesperson and guardian. I was about to enter a new phase in my life and Jim was coming with me on the journey.

Bill and Maureen were disgusted with me, and I was asked to leave home. I stayed with gran for a few weeks, but her rules and regulations became too much to adhere to. I moved in with Jim and his family on a temporary basis, they were more liberal and easier going, nothing seemed to faze them. Bill did not want me in the office, he said I was a distraction, so I handed in my notice and lived off the fee I was given for my interview and the payment I received from the police. The world was my oyster and I had decided I no longer wanted anyone riding on my coat tails. I wanted to oversee my own destiny. Jim suggested I went into the bank and opened a separate business account so I could deposit future cheques. He never asked for any of my money.

'It's your money Cat, I want none of it, I just want you to start thinking about your future and where you want to go with this ?'

The evening before my feature came out, the newspaper put Jim and I up in a luxury hotel in the city of Glasgow. We stayed for several days, I loved the experience, our every need was taken care of. The editor organised for a team to monitored who I spoke to and who I had access to me. The whole thing was very controlled and for the most part I enjoyed it.

My face was featured in the newspaper many times over the coming weeks, and it was agreed I could be interviewed by the television networks, but I had to mention the name of the newspaper , The Sunday News, several times during the interview. I was learning quickly how the media worked.

I was being recognised in the street and strangers would approach me when I was out and about. Not everyone had a good word for me, but I had to take the good with the bad. Jim's mother took a delivery of several sacks of mail from the postman one morning, every letter was a cry for help, people begging for answers, trying to contact long lost family members, reach out to the dead, all of them looking for a reply, hundreds and hundreds of letters were delivered every week to Jim's house or the newspaper. One afternoon I had a call from an agency in London, they wanted to represent me. A long telephone conversation ensued and before I knew what was happening, I was flown to London and stayed several nights in a hotel just off Leicester Square. Jim accompanied me; I was too frightened to travel alone. I had never been on a plane, nor had I been to London. It was everything they said it was bright lights with crowds of people moving quickly at all times of the day and night, no eye contact, no manners and antagonistic. Dupree and Sloane were agents to many of the well know figures of screen and stage including a well know hypnotist. Their executive explained to me they would be interested in looking after my 'future bookings on an exclusive option' I must have missed the part where they mentioned they took 50% of my booking fee but Jim certainly didn't. He negotiated 35% but only if I signed a two-year contract. I went ahead and signed.

I was conscious of my strong Scottish accent, my representative at Dupree and Sloane had suggested I slow down my speech and pronounce all my words in perfect English and not in my native colloquial manner. I quickly learned to change the speed at which I spoke. Talking much slower and articulating my words, so my English counterparts understood what I was saying, most of the time. As a proud Scot there is an irritation in being asked to repeat what you have just said despite speaking the Queens English. I replaced my irritation by simply disguising my strong accent and fitting in with those around me.

Everything was moving so quickly. Jim was continually talking on the telephone or leaving messages for others to call back. I made use of the fax machine at the hotel to communicate with the outside world. The Sunday News had contacted me, their editor in chief, who had a home in London had expressly asked for me to be brought to his home in Holland Park. He was intrigued by my story and wanted to 'discuss one or two things' with me. I was fascinated to hear what he had to say. His name was, Peter Malone, the multimillionaire media mogul. He had recently lost his only son to suicide. He and his wife, Irina, desperately wanted closure. Their family representative told me they wanted me to contact their boy; they wanted answers. The specifically wanted to know why had he taken his own life? The family had no warning or no clues as to their only son's depressive mind set. His death had left his parents with so many unanswered questions. They looked at me for answers.

Jim and I were picked up from our hotel in a chauffeur driven Rolls Royce. It was a tremendous thrill. On arrival at Holland Park, we were met at the doorway by Mr. and Mrs. Malone, I recognised his face from the television. He had recently been involved in the takeover of several commercial radio stations based in the UK, adding another string to his media empire, by branching out into commercial radio. The Malone's town house was magnificent. The hallway of the building was palatial, its breathtaking design was surpassed by the main reception room with spectacular full-length windows, dressed in drapes that flowed with hundreds of meters of sumptuous grey velvet material. The whole place was a visual feast for the eyes. I felt as if my mouth was continually open in amazement.

Jim was more reserved; he certainly had a flare for remaining relaxed and professional in what I considered tense situations. I felt underdressed, Mrs. Malone was dripping in diamonds which sat on her tanned skin. She wore a floating silk Kaftan maxi dress and the most beautiful parfum which followed her about the room. She was the epitome of elegance and good taste. I felt like the 'wee lassie from Glasgow' but Irina welcomed me with open arms and sincerity. Silver frames containing photographs of Max their deceased son dominated the top of the baby grand piano in the corner of the room. There was a large, framed painting of Max on the wall above the fire. The lounge was like a shrine to him.

'Call me Peter and this is my wife Irina, we don't go for that bleedin formal BS in this house.' Peter was refreshingly down to earth with his Eastend accent.

The Malone's were gracious and welcoming. We talked about my 'psychic gift' and the future. We ate finger sandwiches; it was the first time I had eaten a sandwich with no crusts! Two ladies served us tea and offered canapes, a feast of food, the likes of which I had never eaten before, mini crackers with salmon and caviar, vol-au-vents filled with lobster and hand-crafted mini goat cheese tartlets. Every item was a taste sensation.

Once the pleasantries were over Irina handed me several pictures of Max, she described his personality and insatiable love of life. He was much-loved and greatly missed. I interrupted her reminiscing when Max entered the room. I prepared myself.

'Max has a strong energy and has tried to come through to you several times.' I had their attention right away. 'Do you remember being woken up just a few nights ago?' Irina nodded. 'It was Max.'

Jim squeezed my hand and let me take to the floor. It was my time to shine, time to show them what I could do. Max was standing by the piano, he walked across to where his parents were sitting on the sofa.

'Peter, Irina, your son is right beside you.' Max was talking to me, so I began to repeat what he was saying. I soaked up all the positive energy and the emotions in the room, focused on Max and began speaking.

'Max says, he doesn't want to scare you, you may feel him touching your hair whilst I speak to him.' I spoke slowly and clearly.

'He says, you did everything for him, he could never tie his school tie no matter how many times you taught him.' Irina stared at me in silence. Max wanted to share sentimental memories, I was his conduit and repeated everything he said. Peter put his arms around his wife, and both looked at me with such intensity, I felt they could see right through me. Max had a beautiful personality, a teenage boy lost, he looked cold, and his skin was pale, unlike the sun kissed images he portrayed on the silver framed photographs on top of the piano.

'Max why son, why did you take your own life?' Peter called out into the silence of the room.

I looked at Max, 'Do you want me to tell them Max' I waited for his response.

What Max had to say next stopped me in my tracks as I thought about how I would communicate it to his parents. I listened carefully to what Max had to say. Afterwards, Jim told me the tension in the room was extremely stressful as the Malone's hung on my every word.

I took a deep breath and began. 'There is one thing about your sons passing that is negative, there is a reference to an aggressive energy, it comes through with Max, there are no bad spirit's or dark entities in this home, your son is still here, his energy is positive, Max has some unfinished business as he was taken suddenly.' I chose my words wisely. The silence was deafening.

'Max did not commit suicide, he was murdered!' Irina let out a scream and Peter leapt up from the sofa.

'There is a negative energy that follows Max, he is the man who took your son's life, this man has now passed, I cannot see him, but I can feel his negativity.' My mouth was dry, and my head was aching. I asked for water before continuing.

'Your sons perpetrator made money from misery, he sold co-caine, your son owed him a lot of money but refused to pay' There was complete silence.

'It happened here, upstairs in Max room, the house was empty, the bungled threat went wrong, and Max was assaulted, he had his belt put around his neck and was dragged out onto the landing.' I took a breath before continuing. 'The sheer force was enough to break his neck, his final indignity was to be hung from the back of his bedroom door with his trousers and underpants around his ankles. It was made to look like suicide, but it wasn't!' The image of Max's last minutes of life were violent and distressing, there was no way it could be sugar coated. Max looked at his parents, they were stunned. He reached out and put his hand on top of his mothers' shoulder.

'Max says, tell my mother I love her and that I am always here. I am the one who moves her pearl earrings on the dresser' Irina let out a hushed giggle.

Max had accepted he was dead and had chosen to stay close to home with family. He wanted them to know he never took his own life, and his biggest regret was getting involved with drugs. As expected, I had to face a barrage of questions, I felt drained, my head was aching, it was just before midnight when I made my excuses to leave.

Max was dead and his cocaine bill had not been paid, this resulted in his killer being shot through the head, it sent out a message to other dealers. Dead customers do not pay bills!

I had delivered their sons message and tried to answer the multitude of questions that came afterwards. The communication took several hours. It stopped because I had a crippling headache and was no longer able to deliver any further messages. Max left the room and the atmosphere changed. I believe the process brought Peter and Irina some closure and answered many of the questions about the death of their son. Max was still at home; he had no intentions of moving on. His energy would continue to roam throughout their enormous townhouse and remain in their lives. I dispelled the rumours about Max's death resulting from erotic asphyxiation, those dreadful stories were inaccurate, malicious gossip created by people determined to hurt the ones they envied. His body had been dragged and hung up on the back of a door. The humiliating position the body had been left in was designed to embarrass and shame the family. Max Malone was the son of a media mogul, the news of his death inevitably made worldwide news and the mysterious circumstances surrounding his death fed gossip columns of rival publications. The executioner that took their sons life was dead. The mystery was no more, the Malone's wanted answers which I gave them. My job was done and all I wanted was to get back to my hotel room.

Back in our hotel suite I tried to calm myself down. Jim knew to leave me alone, he treated me like a normal human being and gave me space. Talking with the dead and delivering their messages took a lot out of me mentally. I was the channel for the dead to speak to the living, but it wasn't always straightforward. Some days I just didn't know who I was and found it difficult to know whether the pain and emotion I was feeling was truly mine or that of the spirit or their families. I can lose sight of my own thoughts and feelings as I connect with other people's feelings and emotions. It can become confusing as I try to establish how I really feel. Sometimes I just need to be alone to find myself, my feelings, my thoughts. Just me time.

It had gone 3 a.m. before I finally fell asleep. My body was too exhausted to fight my mind which was unwilling to relax. The following morning, Peter Malone sent a package to our hotel. Jim opened the envelope and read aloud a message printed on a compliment slip. 'Thank you. We are on our road to closure. Please stay in touch. Kindest regards. Peter and Irina' the envelope contained £500 in English bank notes. I spent some of the cash on souvenirs in Harrods.

One week later, The Sunday News ran a double page feature about my revelations at the home of the newspaper mogul. I was beginning to realize my name sold papers and so did Peter Malone and Dupree and Sloane. Peter was forever thinking about how to increase circulation and readership and had an unexpected proposal for me. My own weekly column. Not me personally, I would be assigned a journalist to write up the copy. The brief was easy enough, I would meet with a selected group of readers who had requested a private meeting with me. My 'ghost writer' would then creatively write up the copy from my recordings at each meeting. The idea sounded fine on paper and gave me my first introduction working for a national newspaper group. Peter was delighted when I said I would consider his proposal, having me on board was going to boost readership which was already over 3 million readers in the United Kingdom. During negotiations, Peter wanted to bypass my agent and work with me directly, but a legal dispute ensued about my weekly newspaper fee of £500. Dupree and Sloane were determined to have their slice of commission from my new position, so Peter and I came to a private arrangement. The contract was prepared with a weekly fee of £25 per week and another legal contract was prepared to pay me the full fee balance once I was free and no longer contracted to Dupree and Sloane. Jim agreed it was the perfect solution and encouraged me to accept the agreement. I immediately signed on the dotted line.

Promotional pictures were taken, and the newspaper advertised my upcoming column. I even appeared in a television commercial promoting my new feature. Readers were asked to write directly to the newspaper for a private meeting in the hope I could contact someone they knew who had passed away. The response was unbelievable with thousands of letters being delivered to their Fleet Street office. The more bizarre requests were selected to embellish the feature. On paper the idea worked well, but in practice it was a disaster. The feature was cancelled after just six weeks.

CHAPTER 18

A New Beginning

Diary Entry – Friday 5th January 1979

I don't need to be a clairvoyant to tell you 1979 is going to be the start of something wonderful. My move to London is just what I need. The only thing I will miss from back home is gran and square slice sausage! I am soaking everything up about how best to promote myself and oversee my own destiny. The sooner I get rid of my agent the better. Peter seems to think there is a way out of the contract, watch this space.

When I returned to Scotland, I was feeling unsettled. I had been introduced to another lifestyle down south and I longed to return. Dupree and Sloane had flown me down to several business meetings and suggested I relocate to London. Peter agreed and insisted I stayed in London; the newspaper was covering all expenses. There were more opportunities for work down south, so it made sense to make the move. I wasn't going to be missed at home as Bill and Maureen detested the attention I brought to the family and had refused to have me back living at home. I trusted only one person, Jim. Together we made the move down South. Jim refused to live off any of my money and found himself employment with a local builder. He said his priority was me, despite holding down a full-time job he was there for me whenever I needed him. My diary became so busy with appointments and interviews I finally persuaded him to work full time with me. He didn't need to prove anything to me, I trusted him to look after me, no one else had my back like Jim did.

London, despite the millions of people who live there can be a lonely place. I may not have had any real friends, but I was never lonely, not when you have so many spirits to talk to! Margaret was with me, she often kept me company and offered encouragement. She adored Jim and gave us her blessing. I could not have been happier. Jim and I rented a small one-bedroom flat in Gun Street, a grade 2 listed building in the heart of Spitalfields Market. The property was haunted by the spirit of a woman who died during World War two, I saw her several times, but she chose to ignore me. Not all spirits want to talk!

Those first few weeks when Jim was away working only made me realize he was the most important person in my life. Our relationship was never complicated. He understood me and never asked for anything except my love and companionship. Jim put his life on hold to be with me, he told me every day about how much he loved me .When you have someone by your side who is striving for the same goals in life as you are, life is so much easier. He put me on a pedestal and worshipped the ground I walked on. I trusted him with my life. He was my rock; we planned our life together. He tolerated my mood swings and was happy sharing me with the hundreds of lost souls who came into my life. We came from different paths and backgrounds, and it just worked. I felt at ease in his presence and our love grew. Our relationship was easy, we had a profoundly deep connection. Jim was my teacher, a great supporter and long-term companion who gave me unconditional love and accepted everything about me.

'Hey Cat, I love the bones of you girl.' I adored it when he would say this. He dropped the line all the time. Everywhere we went people loved him, he was just so down to earth and honest.

'It's never about me babe, it's all about you, love you

babe.' He was a beautiful man. I would watch other couples smile when he would treat me like a princess in public. Jim proved that being masculine wasn't always about watching football and drinking lager, he would drop everything to be with me or simply talk with me. We were falling, growing, and staying in love. I was the luckiest and happiest girl in the world. Jim was like a big warm protective blanket, comforting and warm. Without his encouragement I would never have made the move to London, it was he who encouraged me to grow wings and fly. I couldn't imagine my life without my one true love being in it.

Jim died on the 14th of February 1979, Valentine Day. He left the flat to go and buy flowers, I asked him not to go, but he was adamant. I watched as he left our small flat, he turned around and looked up at the window and smiled his last smile to me. He had a brain hemorrhage, collapsed, and died in the street only yards from our home. A woman who happened to be a nurse came to his aid as others stood by and stared, but he could not be saved. The blue lights and the noise from the sirens coming up from the street alerted me to the incident. I immediately knew it was for Jim. He had been gone for an hour and I was beginning to worry. I raced down the stairs and ran over to his body. My Jim was dead. This beautiful person that I adored, a gentle soul, loved by everyone who met him. He didn't deserve to die on the wet street as ghouls stood about looking at his dead body. He was no longer by my side, and I was alone. I had no one to grieve with, I was lonesome in a massive city that really didn't care less. Jim was dead, his life had not even started, and his parents were writing his eulogy. He was wrongfully taken from this world at just twenty-three years old. A man wiser than his years and selfless. A loyal and loving partner. My life was the better for knowing and loving him. I never knew it then, but I was never to meet anyone as honorable as Jim. No man could ever compare to him. The Morning News reported on Jim's death and printed a photograph of him and I, we both looked happy and in love.

I could not be consoled. Bill and Maureen asked me to return home and be with them, but I refused. Jim's body was driven back to Scotland to be cremated at his parent's request. They were devastated and reached out to me, speaking to them only reminded me of Jim, I gained no comfort from this and found it easier not to talk to them. Gran came down to London and stayed with me for a few weeks, she made soups and listened to me cry. Margaret still came to visit; her presence was a comfort to me. Peter cancelled my column whilst I came to terms with my lose. It was a concentration of grief; it was overwhelming and all consuming. Peter and Irina insisted I stayed with them while I grieved but I insisted on being alone. I never attended Jim's cremation as I believed my presence would have attracted the paparazzi and the family deserved privacy. We said our goodbyes in private. At home, I waited for Jim to appear to me. I imagined we would talk and laugh as we did in life, but he never showed himself. I often sensed he was around me; I would call out his name and speak to him, but I never received a response. I stayed in shock for over a year, I could not believe he was not here with me. I believe, spiritually, if we hold onto the grief and don't release our emotional bond we have with the dead, their spirit can remain in limbo. Jim came to me in a dream one night and he said I had to let him go. I had to stop grieving and move on with my life. I could only think he had accepted his death and wanted to rest in peace; I knew if he could, Jim would come to me and we would be together, talking, laughing. He was the love of my life, and he would always be in my heart and thoughts. I knew I would never love another man the way I loved him.

When Jim died so did part of me. As I gathered up his clothes and packed them away, I did the same thing with all my own clothing. Anything I had worn whilst being with Jim was disposed of. There was no rational thinking behind this I simply wanted the clothing gone. I had my memories, this was all I needed, for now.

***

The work was pouring in, from police investigations to private sessions with the rich and famous. I was in demand; on radio, press and television. Many of the people I met became clients and I would travel to their homes for private consultations. Television is an incredible medium, the first time I appeared on an early evening talk show I was inundated the following day with mail and requests for appointments. After I appeared on television a few times I was immediately recognised on the street. My celebrity status went through the roof. I enjoyed being on the radio, talking directly with the callers. It gave me a great deal of satisfaction passing on important messages from the dead to their loved ones. I was fast becoming the 'It' person to be seen around town with. Dupree and Sloane were concerned about my 'questionable behaviour in public' and had me attend elocution lessons. I attended one and refused to go back. A representative from the company taught me simple public relations techniques, how to avoid awkward interview questions and how to answer questions in a direct and articulate manner. Despite being horrified at the time, they were right, when I heard myself talking on the tape recorder and play back sessions I was squirming with embarrassment. I didn't need a posh English PR guru to tell me I sounded dreadful; I knew it. I made the decision to alter how I came across and worked even harder disguising my accent. I cleaned up my act and behaved myself when I was out and about in town. My self-confidence was growing , I was only nineteen, but I was unrecognizable as the young girl who came to London just over a year ago.

My main source of income came from private consultations. I regularly visited the Malone's, who became good friends. I never dealt with the monetary side of the business, but I was starting to think that I should. I hated all the administration and answering the telephone. I simply attended the call and my agent dealt with the money. My clients came back to me time and time again. Dupree and Sloane looked after my diary and bookings; they also took care of the rent for my apartment. They paid me an allowance each week of about £600, this to be fair was a lot of money in 1979 but I was working six days a week often 12 hours or more a day. Peter Malone suggested I considered buying my own property. I would have been stupid not to take the advice from a self-made newspaper magnate man who once lived with his mother and four brothers and sisters in a west end one bedroom flat. Property in London was increasing at an incredible rate, and buying a house was a sound financial investment. I have a lot to thank him and Irina for, they looked after me when Jim died. Peter always had my best interest at heart. He was like a father to me and Irina, a very glamorous mother.

Peter's corporate lawyers found loopholes in my agent's contract, and I was soon released from their thieving grasp. My contract was terminated, and I couldn't have been happier. It made sense for myself and Dupree and Sloane to part company, they had too much control over my finances and life.

They fought their corner and threatened legal action. A long dragged-out court case was not what anyone wanted. It was bad for publicity and the balance sheet. I was Dupree and Sloane's Golden Goose, now I was free to move on with my life. I had just over £20,000 in my bank account, a shocking amount considering how hard I had worked. Dupree and Sloane had skimmed a massive amount back in fees and commissions from my earnings, I had learned the hard way, no more agents. I was going to oversee my own destiny from now on. Once the contract had ended, I was going to celebrate, the lawyers assured me it was imminent.

Over the year I had been absorbing the corporate side of the business by sitting in at meetings and listening to discussions on negotiating deals. I learned to say 'no' to bookings or events I didn't want to attend. If I struggled to decide, I would ask myself .'What would Jim do in this situation?' I was starting to think and behave like a businesswoman and before the end of 1979 I had already set the wheels in motion building my own company. I recruited a personal assistant called Jody and a vibrant Public Relations and Marketing consultant called Jemima Coates Smythe. This young lady oozed creative ideas and talked about 'working smarter and not harder, long-term strategies' and 'marketing plans.' As a team, all three of us just clicked and I liked everything about the girls. I could tell we were going to have fun as Jemima's command of the English language and tenacious personality was beyond anything I had ever encountered. Perhaps my life was about to turn a corner.

Diary entry - Monday 12th November 1979.

Happy Birthday to me, all of 19 years. I was mentioned in the Birthdays column in a national newspaper today. I appeared in fourth place after Charles Manson, criminal and cult leader! I suppose I should be happy I appeared on the list. It's been quite a month so far. It's my first birthday without Jim being here. Jemima has insisted I have the day off , so I sat in my lounge and opened the hundred or so birthday cards I received , drank coffee, and listened to Gary Numan with my headphones on, Jemima and Jody are like a breath of fresh air! I had a surprise visitor; you'll never guess who turned up at my door!

I finally severed ties with Dupree and Sloane on Friday 9th November 1979. They had controlled my life for almost sixteen months. It was the best early birthday present a girl could ask for, my destiny was no longer going to be charged at 35% commission. I was free and in control of my future. I called Gran, she was delighted for me, I wanted Bill and Maureen to feel the same way. I called Bill at work and Maureen at home. There was a hole in my heart which could only be filled with love but neither Bill nor Maureen wanted to give any. Both telephone conversations were short and abrupt. The distance between us was just over four hundred miles but, we were a million miles apart. Afterwards, I asked Jody to send flowers to Gran and Maureen. Only Gran called me to say, 'thank you'.

By choice I decided to stay at the flat on my birthday to enjoy some me time. I was meeting a few friends in the evening for drinks. It really wasn't worth celebrating without Jim around. I was expecting a telephone call from Maureen and Bill which never came. Gran had already sent a card. Maureen and Bills card arrived in the second post, it simply read 'Happy Birthday, Best wishes Bill, and Maureen' No sentiments, no kisses.

Early afternoon there was a knock on the door. Despite being warned to check the spy hole before opening the door, I automatically opened it. It took me a minute to recognise the lady standing in front of me. Even when she spoke, I had no idea who it was. Once she dropped the French accent, the penny dropped.

'I thought I would deliver my baby sisters diary in person this year.' it was Mary.

We spent the afternoon together, laughing and talking, mainly about her! She had turned her back on the family. Her new home was based in Monaco where she had married a wealthy restaurateur and night club owner. No one from the family had been invited to the wedding, God forbid we may have embarrassed her or blew her cover in front of all her new wealthy friends. I dread to think the lies she must have told them about her upbringing and family. Her husband, Pierre was much older than Mary, but the relationship seemed to work. She inherited three grown up children from Pierre's two ex-wives, Pierre had no intentions of extending his family and told Mary he had no interest in increasing his brood, Mary was happy with that as she had everything she wanted – money!

Mary's transformation was extraordinary. She looked like a brunette Farrah Fawcett. Luxuriant hair, (or perhaps it was a wig ?) a beach tan, and teeth like an Osmond. The Scottish drawl had been replaced by a convincing French accent. During our conversations Mary never once asked about Gran, Billy, or her parents. The chat was all about her and her fabulous lifestyle. I quickly became aware of her intentions, she hadn't come to London to visit me out of love, she had come to London to see what I could do to enhance her already fabulous lifestyle.

'You must come to Monaco dahling, its simply divine.' she lied.

'I've missed you so much my little Catherine.' she lied again.

Mary handed me a beautiful diary embossed with my name and a personalised message from Mary.

'Pour Cat, Ma petite soeur speciale , Mary x. To Cat , my special little sister.

Mary had never contacted me or the family for over two years. Albeit the odd birthday card and a diary. Today, she was inside my London flat with one simple intention, to increase her own status. The woman who sat on my sofa was not the Mary I grew up with but a woman who craved attention. She said her husband 'worshipped her' and yet she never mentioned him in any endearing context. Every sentence started with 'I' or 'My'. She talked about money and name-dropped French designer labels, whilst intermittently speaking French just to assure me she was a woman of substance and not a commoner. We came from a very humble background, born and bred in a council estate on the outskirts of Glasgow. Throughout our conversation Mary never spoke about family or our upbringing. All references to her childhood and family had been erased, it was as if she had simply blanked out any memories. Each time I mentioned an event from the past she either said she could not recall it or changed the subject. No, no, Mary was not here because she wanted to share her love with her sister, she was here because *my* name was all over the newspapers and magazines. I had what she craved, media fame, I was quickly becoming a household name, I was regularly seen on television, and broadcasting on the radio. Mary knew if she rebuilt our bond and was seen out and about with me, it would open all sorts of doors for her in England. I was going to enjoy her groveling for my friendship and companionship, but not tonight. I was on my way out with a few of my fabulous friends.The telephone rang. It was my Personal Assistant Jody confirming what time a car would be picking me up, I was meeting Peter and Irina plus some media friends for dinner at The Ivy and then onto a record company launch party where I was told I would meet my hero of the moment, Gary Numan. It was a private function, just a few good friends. I had no plans to stay out late. I wasn't shocked when Mary asked if she could join me, but I had to decline her request. Her face was a picture. I made my apologies and suggested we meet up again soon. We air kissed each other at the front door and I sent her on her way. There had been a shift in power, I was no longer the wee girl she had left back home in Glasgow, there had been a coming of age. I was in control and both of us knew it. What she did next questioned my faith in human nature, family, and greed. It was another taste of betrayal and opened my eyes to just how far someone will go for money?

CHAPTER 19

How the other half live.

Diary Entry – Monday 25th February 1980

Met Kenny Everett at Capital Radio in Euston Tower. Discussed the possibility of a collaboration once a week on his radio show, it was just a chat over coffee, I don't think it will work but he was the most charismatic and naturally funny person I have ever met.

My newspaper column had long since stopped as the concept was just not working. I was unable to contact any spirits as the setting was never conducive to invite anyone to come forward. It was so pretentious, and I was never comfortable. Meetings in hotels, clock watching, and I just couldn't summon up spirits on command, the timing and energy had to be right. It ran for six weeks and then I pulled the plug. I had thousands of letters from fans and the publication reported a 3% increase in circulation. Peter called me from his yacht in the mediterranean and I gave him the news, I could almost hear him shrug his shoulders. 'Oh well, we gave it our best shot kid' Peter was forgiving, he didn't sound disappointed, he had bigger fish to fry than me. Instead, he asked me to fly out and join him and Irina.

'There are some people I want you to meet' he said. How could I say no!

***

Jemima had tremendous fun persuading designers to provide clothes for my trip. She had a natural persuasive flare which she used to great effect.

Her motto was, 'I am only three phone calls away from anyone I want to talk to in the World' and she was right.

'Yellow pages or direct enquiries for the telephone number, speak to the PA or secretary and be transferred to the person who makes the decision, jobs done!'

Jemima assembled a suitcase full of beautiful clothes and footwear worth thousands of pounds for me to wear as I lounged about on Peters' yacht. Free of charge, naturally. Afterall I was going to be displaying the designer's clothes. I had no dress sense. Jemima taught me everything I needed to know. What designer names were in vogue and what designers were purely couture. She taught me the difference between a Breitling and a Rolex, Coco and Chanel. Jemima had style and was naturally elegant. She came from money and a boarding school background. Jemima wasn't born with a silver spoon in her mouth, she had a full canteen of gold cutlery! She understood brands and image. I didn't know the difference between Dior and Dorothy Perkins. Jemima's mother spent her afternoons having lunch with the ladies and raising money at charity events in their Chanel suits. Her father was a highly acclaimed barrister in London. Our backgrounds could not have been more diverse, but we worked together beautifully. As part of her marketing approach, she convinced designers and retailers to lend me their clothes. She guaranteed I would be photographed in their designs. Jemima convinced clients that I was a walking advertisement, and they should be paying me to wear their clothing lines. My new celebrity fame and the fascination the public had with me resulted in a high demand for photographs. With Jemima negotiating deals with major fashion houses, I soon learned to wear only clothing I had been paid to wear. Jemima would request designer bags and clothing from a multitude of designers and the products would be sent to my office, it was insane. Paparazzi would follow me in the street, at events and on holiday. The public wanted to know what I was doing and what I was wearing. I was appearing in some of the most popular magazines in the country. A picture of me wearing one of their dresses always resulted in increased sales or their design selling out. Jemima became so good at this, we rarely had to make any phone calls as clients simply sent me items daily by courier or in the post. Over the coming months we had hundreds of deliveries from a multitude of companies and designers all hoping I would be seen wearing or using their products. I rarely bought clothing as so much was sent to me free of charge. I would share everything with both Jemima and Jody. When required we donated items to raffles and charities to raise money. For a while, I never wore the same piece of clothing twice. I knew I was going to be photographed on Peter's yacht or at major events and these images would feature in magazines and newspapers all over the world. I was playing the game; money went to money; it was a crazy but exciting time. Not only was I getting thousands of pounds worth of clothing, shoes, and bags but I was being paid to wear them. It was incredible! I literally had rooms full of designer brands on rails waiting to be worn. Peter's newspapers were renowned for the paparazzi chasing celebrities for that exclusive image. His publications paid handsomely for the right picture. As a close friend, I would feature in many of his publications on a regular basis. If I were wearing a dress or carrying a bag by a particular designer, it would boast their sales and my income. Jemima sold me in column inches, guaranteeing a certain amount each month to each client. It was a win, win situation and Jemima excelled at it, she was a public relation and marketing guru, long before the trend was common practice.

Mary had called for me several times and I had not replied. I asked Jody to invite her to lunch the next time she was in London and coincidently, she was in town. We met in a popular restaurant in Covent Garden. I told her over lunch I was flying by private jet to Peter Monroe's yacht moored in Majorca, she immediately invited him to bring his yacht to Monaco and dine in one of Pierre's restaurants.

'I would love to meet him', ofcourse you would Mary. It was all about her.

Diary Entry - Monday 3rd March 1980

I am on my way to Majorca, Private jet! Yacht! Millionaire Friends! This is the life! I am so selfishly wrapped up in myself, I know I need to change, but not this week. This week I am going to relax and enjoy myself on a yacht in the Mediterranean! How the hell did this happen?

Two days later I was on a private jet, on my way to Majorca. As I sat on the plane and looked out onto the runway, I simply could not understand how my life had changed so significantly. My life was unrecognisable, and I would often sit in disbelief at all that I had acquired in such a short time. I missed Jim dreadfully and wondered what he would have thought of me, sitting on a private jet on my way to spend time on a yacht with a newspaper magnate and his wife who considered me their friend. I believed in destiny and was simply following a path that was already laid out for me. I could feel Margaret's presence but could not see her, this comforted me. Christie, the stewardess offered me a refreshment before the pilot announced we were about to take off. It chilled me to the bone when a middle-aged woman sat in front of me, she introduced herself as Christie's mother, she spoke about her daughter joining her shortly and how much she looked forward to being with her. I could see the monogrammed head rest through her head and realised she was in spirit form. Christie sat at the front of the jet and wrapped the seat belt across her body, her mother smiled at me, looked out the cabin window and then disappeared. For a moment I wanted to stop the flight and get off, but I could not change destiny, nor should I try. I did not fear dying but today was not my time to die nor was it, Christies. I sat back and enjoyed the flight and tried to avoid any further distractions. We landed safely and I was picked up in a chauffeur driven Rolls Royce at the airport and taken to the port. Peter and Irina were waiting for me. I could see they were genuinely delighted to see me. They welcomed me on aboard , the cuddles and kisses were real. The hole in my heart was filled with love just being with them.

A few days into my holiday I read in one of Peter's newspapers about a small private jet that had crashed shortly after taking off from Barcelona. The pilot and the stewardess along with the four Spanish passengers all died. The stewardess was called Christie Henderson. She was 25 years old and had only been on the flight because she had swopped shifts with the other stewardess! We cannot alter fate.

Once on-board Peter's yacht, I drank a glass of champagne with Peter and Irina before I was taken down below to my bedroom where a young lady was already unpacking my bags and putting my clothes into the wardrobe. I was completely overwhelmed by the glamorous design and surroundings. The exquisite, good taste Irina possessed, and the sheer grandeur of the yacht was overwhelming. I pinched myself at my fabulous lifestyle. Despite being multi-millionaires, I found both Peter and Irina down to earth and cordial. Peter would often regale me with stories about being brought up in the Eastend of London and how his family had to survive on little income. His mother worked three cleaning jobs and his father was an illegal immigrant who spoke little English and was illiterate. He worked when he could. Peter helped sell newspapers at a paper stand outside a tube station in London and vowed to own his own newspaper one day, much to the amusement of the other paper boys. His tough upbringing, street wise agility, natural negotiating skills combined with a ferocious desire to move up the corporate ladder was the motivation he needed to accomplish his dream. He owned his first newspaper before he was forty years old. He started as a junior in the mailroom, and quickly moved up the ranks, office junior, junior reporter and news gatherer, senior reporter, chief reporter, news editor, newspaper editor, editor in chief. It took him twenty years working in the same publication to eventually be promoted to the board of directors. With just one person standing in his way towards ownership he organised for him to be killed. A fishing accident, sadly someone else was with the victim that day so both lives were lost. For the other man it was a case of being in the wrong place at the wrong time. It was front page news. Considering both men were experienced fisherman neither had a life jacket on when their bodies were recovered from the still water. Peter denied any involvement, there was allegations and speculation, rumours and gossip about his connection to the crime but they soon dwindled over the years. Back then, in the criminal gangland of London's Eastend, a few hundred pounds bought you anything you wanted if you knew the right people and Peter knew everyone. Peter Malone was not a man to be messed with. Nothing stood in the way of what he wanted, no man and no situation.

Peter and Irina had organised a small dinner party on my behalf and referred to me as their guest of honor. Peter was keen to introduce me to the hierarchy of men who worked in the world of television. The assortment of guests was exciting, many of whom I already recognised. John Purvey, an up-and-coming name in film and TV production based in London was keen to discuss an idea he had for a television series about a team of ghost hunters staying in allegedly haunted locations and reporting their findings. It was a groundbreaking idea. Not something I had ever contemplated as I did not consider myself as a 'ghost hunter psychic'. John sold the concept handsomely, I made no commitment, I considered his proposition and suggested I would have Jody my PA call him and arrange a meeting. We clinked champagne glasses and moved on. Peter took my arm and introduced me to Harvey Winchester, a big name in America for producing investigative journalism programs which were syndicated all over the world. He wanted to introduce me to Ted and Lorraine Warron, famed American paranormal investigators and authors who were linked with thousands of hauntings including the Amityville Horror. They were a controversial couple. He was a self-proclaimed demon-ologist and she claimed to be a psychic medium, they had a massive following.

Winchester predicted this collaboration would be in high de-mand by many of the American television networks. You didn't need to be a clairvoyant to predict this documentary would be a hit! I liked the idea and thought it might be an interesting one-off programme and a terrific way to introduce myself to the American public. I suggested to Harvey we meet up and talk about the project. He shook my hand and held onto it for far too long. He used his thumb to caress my hand and I felt awkward. His breathing was heavy, and his stare was un-comfortable. The young lady who accompanied him was far too young and far too pretty. How could she stand such a vile man touch her? The uneasy silence was interrupted by Peter who apologised for taking me away.

'Stop monopolizing the guest of honour Harvey, hands off she is way too old for you'. Peter obviously knew his guests well. Both men laughed out loud.

Personally, I was more than happy to be rescued, Winchester was not a man I felt comfortable in the presence of, I always went with my instinct, and he frightened me. If I felt like this with twenty people around me, how would I feel in an office or hotel suite with him on my own. Note to self! Never meet Har-vey Winchester on my own – ever!

I was ever so thankful for Jemima filling my case with designer dresses, bags, and shoes because this so-called *small* dinner party was made up of ten couples. Each one wealthier, more glamorous, and more influential than the other. They all oozed money. Diamonds, Rolex, and Cartier adorned both the ladies and men. I wore a white linen designer trouser suit and tied a Hermes scarf around my hair which I had pinned up high on my head. A few red curls escaped my hair clip, but I let them sit around my face. The little bit of sunshine I had caught that day only enhanced my freckles. I did not recognise myself in the mirror, less than a year ago I had never heard of Hermes or many of the other designers, now I was wearing fabulous clothing by up-and-coming fashion designers based in trendy little pockets of London.

Jemima had stuck a bottle of Chanel No 5 in my suitcase. I never liked it and refused to wear it but credited her with thinking of everything. A selection of unopened Dior parfum had been left in my ensuite. I chose Joy Parfum. I was extremely careful not to splash the oil on my suit and simply dabbed the scent on my wrists and neck. Jemima had taught me well. I could hear her in my head as I placed the glass lid back on the bottle.

'Joy, it's a very adult scent, strong and adorable tones on a Summer night, the sweet jasmine will wrap itself around your senses and you will appreciate its creation and history.' That is how Jemima spoke. Her descriptive vocabulary was unlike anything I had ever heard. Creative and rich, just like her.

The dinner guests were gracious and welcoming. As I sat at the dinner table, I was feeling awkward, at times uncomfortable. Jemima had taught me all about table etiquette and good manners, I was fully conversant on what cutlery was used and when. I had perfected the proper placement of glasses at the dining table and could have given a Royal butler a run for his money on table setting rules, however tonight, as I looked around the table I began to feel like an imposter, how the hell had I managed to wangle my way onto this yacht, sit with these beautiful, influential people. Any time now they were going to call me out, point their fingers at me and scream 'fake', 'pretender', 'charlatan'. I made an excuse to leave the table and went to the front of the yacht. The sun had long gone down, and the gentle night breeze helped dry the perspiration from my forehead. My cheeks felt warm, and I had a small stain on my linen trousers from the lobster bisque, this upset me as it exposed my inability to keep my napkin across my lap thus avoiding staining my trouser suit. It was such a simple task and I had failed, been caught out. I sat at the front of the yacht on one of the magnificent sofas out of sight of the guests downstairs in the lounge. Max, Peter, and Irina's dead son, appeared, he sat across from me and smiled. He was dressed in white and had something in his hand. He asked me to pass a message to Irina, his mother.

'Tell my mother I am here and I want her to stop crying'.

He held out his hand. I reached over to him and a small crucifix fell into the palm of my hand. I closed my fist tightly around it.

'Mother gave me this for my First Communion, she placed it around my neck and told me to always wear it' said Max.

'She looked for it everywhere after that night!' he paused and stood up.

'I'm going down below now, I love to listen to the crew laugh and joke' and with that he got up and was gone.

'Who are you talking to?' asked Irina who had come to look for me.

'Max' I said. I opened my hand and showed her the crucifix. 'He wants you to have this'.

We both sat in the moonlight. Irina took the small crucifix from my hand, nothing was said. I could feel the love and emotion envelope us.

I have no filter, never did. I often blurted out things before engaging my brain first.

'I was speaking to Max' I had no reason to pretend . I had been with Irina and Peter several times and Max had made an appearance. He always had a message he wanted me to pass onto his parents. Tonight was different as he had a tangible object he wanted me to give to his mother. It had his name and Communion date engraved on the gold cross. Irina recognised it right away. Tonights encounter with Max had been more poignant than before. Peter confirmed later, the crucifix had been placed in Max's hand just before he had been buried.

'I placed it their myself' said Peter. 'I took it from his neck and placed it around his clasped hands just before his coffin lid was closed'.

I could never have known any of this, I believe it validated my claims that I was communicating with their dead son. It brought Irina and Peter a great deal of solace and our friendship grew from strength to strength. They were like the parents I never had.

My seven days relaxing on the yacht was wonderful. I felt refreshed and spoilt. My every whim had been indulged. Onboard I had enjoyed spa treatments, invigorating massages, and sun tanning on the upper decks. I was surrounded by azure blue sea and the best company I could imagine. Over the week I had been introduced to several influential people who worked in television, and we had arranged to meet up back in London. I wanted to share my good fortune with the family. I decided, I would once again reach out to Bill and Maureen. Invite them to London, enjoy some quality time together. Perhaps Mary would join us. It woud be lovely to see Billy and his family.

I would arrange for Gran to come and stay with me for a few weeks, she was like Switzerland; she never took sides. I knew I could rely on her to organise the gathering; she could persuade the family to join me. I was missing everyone so much and I hoped they would accept my invitation. It was a final chance to have them as part of my life. I was alone in a city that was home to millions of people and making friends was never easy. I sat alone while my family were back in Scotland and it upset me.

I had only just started thinking about finding someone to share my life with, no one would replace Jim but I knew I had to start dating again. I didn't want to be alone, I had so much love to give. I knew Jim would have agreed, I had everything but nothing and longed to be loved again. With Jim I felt protected and wanted, I missed the feeling.

CHAPTER 20

1980 & 1981

Most of 1980 and early 81 was taken up with growing my business and fighting personal and family battles. It took a huge amount of energy and organisation as the demand for my personal consultations seriously outweighed the time, I had available to conduct them. Each session was followed by severe headaches, and I would have to take to my bed for several hours or even a full day after they were over, sometimes I had to stop short during the session due to the pain. There were numerous appointments with doctors who all put it down to emotional stress, no amount of medication alleviated the head pain, and I would be drained of energy after each emotional session. I was so sensitive to psychic activity and was aware that spirits were drawn to me, the deceased could talk through me directly to their loved ones and I felt compelled to deliver their messages, good or bad. It was my calling, my gift. It felt natural and effortless to reach out and connect with these spirits. I was truly communicating on a psychic level and was able to see and talk to the dead. Despite my ability, I had my skeptics, many, many of them. I gave up proving myself time after time to the doubters. To allow them into my life would only have further drained me mentally, so I chose to ignore them. Keep them at a distance. I had proven my ability, time after time, but doubters will always distrust.

One of the biggest challenges I had was trusting people, I was continually being let down and I found it almost impossible to confide in anyone. My sister Mary had used our relationship to get her name and more importantly her face into several newspapers and magazines. She had come to my home, on my birthday and later betrayed me. She basked in our connection and sold a story to one of Peter Malones rival Sunday publications. I was furious as her version of our relationship was quite different to mine, in addition to her lies she had used private photographs of her and I without my permission. Poignant pictures from when we were younger.

To be let down by anyone is upsetting but when it is your family it cuts even deeper. I decided it would be best to keep our relationship at a distance. Mary attempted to contact me several times by telephone, and I had Jody call her back and convey my apologies for not returning her calls. I put it down to being extremely busy with work commitments but, this was a bullshit excuse, I really didn't want to talk to her. We all have a few minutes to pick up a telephone, especially when I could have had Jody dial the number for me! Mary's response to me avoiding her was yet another magazine feature about how I had deserted the family and refused to call her back, apparently, I had delusions of grandeur, was a bully to my staff and only wanted to spend my time talking to the dead! Mary claimed, I had lost touch with reality. Perhaps I had! Fame and money will do that to you, you become detached from the real world and live in your own ivory tower. I was protected from reality by Jemima and Jody. I wanted to retaliate, I was so angry with Mary, I confided in Margaret, like I always did. Jody insisted the best way to deal with this was to ignore it, say nothing, give Mary no reason to strike back. It was difficult, but I did as I was told.

***

Gran came to stay for two months in winter. She made me homemade soup which we ate with fresh baguettes smothered in butter. Every evening meal was served with hand cut chips fried in beef dripping. I had to have the whole flat and the office deep cleaned after Gran left and headed back home to Scotland. The smell of fried food emanated from every room. Jemima was disgusted and refused to stay in my office until it was 'purified and all signs of animal fats are banished from the building', well she was a vegetarian after all.

'I imagine this is what an establishment that offers fast food smells like internally!' Jemima insinuated, having never been in a fish and chip shop! Her flamboyant and colorful language never failed to make me smile. You just had to love her.

My age could often be a hindrance, despite being so young I had lived a deep and full life to date. I had just turned 20 years old and yet I was older and wiser than my years, mainly because I had seen so much. I had steeped myself in my work and was spending so much time making a living I was forgetting to make a life. I had Jody set up meetings with the executives I had met on Peter's yacht. John Purvey, he wanted to create a television show literally looking for ghosts in haunted buildings. I loved the concept and I thought I could work with John; however, it came to nothing as he was unable to raise any financial backing. The idea was also so radical for the terrestrial British television companies it was proving hard to sell to the TV executives. I could not commit to the working schedule John has presented to me and despite several meetings, I pulled the plug on the development plans. John was lovely but he made the mistake of treating me like an industry novice. He had underestimated me and my ability to make decisions regarding my self-worth. I was already running a successful company and making major decisions daily. John had come to the table with a pathetic contract, and I made it known that even double the amount offered would not be enough for me to give up three months of my life to appear on the shows. He was taken aback when I declined the offer and we parted the meeting as friends. He confessed that he was under the impression Peter Malone was steering my career and financially supporting me. Nothing was further from the truth, Peter was advising me on certain aspects of my financial affairs, but he certainly did not manager me or have any major influence over my business decisions. I valued his advice, but I wanted to be in control of my own life.

Harvey Winchester would not take no for an answer, I had no desire to meet him or discuss working on any project he was involved in. I left him in the capable hands of Jemima who not only put him in his place, but his personal secretary was left in tears after a telephone altercation . Jemima truly was a force of nature.

Ted and Lorraine Warron participated in some of the most famous paranormal cases in the 1970's including the Amityville Horror and the possession of a so-called demonic doll named Annie. Ted claimed the last person to mock the doll had died in a motorcycle crash. It had been quite a claim which only enforced the dolls demonic reputation, but as Jemima correctly pointed out, it was simply a claim by Ted himself and was not supported by any evidence whatsoever. Who was the victim and what had the doll got to do with his death? Jemima, Jody, and I went to see The Amityville Horror when it was shown in the cinema in January 1980. All three of us were terrified and held onto each other in our seats. Jody was particularly distressed when Amy, the little girl in the movie has an imaginary friend she called Jody who appeared to be of a malevolent nature. Jody said she slept with the light on for a week after seeing the movie.

I never took the long-distance call from Ted and refused

to speak to Harvey Winchester. Jemima had spoken with a Warron executive, and he had said they were not 100% sold on the idea of working with me. Thousands of people thought the Warrons were frauds and they themselves could not back up some of their stories with actual evidence. After a lot of thought and research into the couple I took the decision not to work with them. I had been having nightmares about meeting them and Winchester. Harvey bombarded Jody with faxes, one even intimated that by not working with him, I would never work in America as he would be warning other studio executives that I was a time waster. I mentioned his antics to Peter, and he simply laughed and said, 'Harvey tends to spit his dummy out of the pram if he doesn't get his own way.'

Winchester may have owned one of the biggest independent studios in Los Angeles but as far as I was concerned, America could wait.

My 20th Birthday came and went, Mary did not send me a diary, deep down I was upset, but I was unable to reach out to her as I feared she could no longer be trusted. Maureen and Bill had little contact with me but did continue to send me rather formal Birthday and Christmas cards. 'Merry Christmas and Best Wishes for the year ahead, Maureen and Bill', no kisses no love, nothing. Grans cards oozed love and affection. I missed her. Jemima and Jody gave me a beautiful A4 diary from Harrods. It had my name embossed in gold leaf on the front and was wrapped beautifully in gold tissue paper. I adored it.

Spring April 1981

My brother Billy, according to Gran, had deserted his wife and child and was staying with a 16-year-old girl who was the daughter of one of their neighbours. Turns out they had been having an intimate affair for almost a year and thought they were safe announcing their relationship on her sixteenth birthday. Wrong! When their illicit affair was announced, her father reported Billy to the police for having underage sex with a minor and barred him from seeing his daughter, of course this only encouraged the love birds to confess their undying love for each other and deny any sexual contact had taken place. She delivered a baby boy two months later; apparently unaware she was pregnant. Billy was charged and faced a custodial sentence, fortunately he was not sent down, but Bill was so disgusted at his antics he sacked him from his management position at Thomson Pumps. Desperate, out of work and short of money Billy thought a quick phone call to a national newspaper and the mere mention of my name would furnish his pockets with a few thousand pounds and a vote of sympathy from the British public. Like Mary, he wanted to get his Andy Warhol 15 minutes of fame. Say what you like about the 'gutter press', but they were not prepared to pay a man who had now confessed to not only having sex with an underage girl, but after further investigation was accused of having a sexual relationship with her fourteen-year-old friend. The young girl who could not be named had confessed they had been intimate in his car on several occasions. The investigative reporter at the newspaper also secured damaging statements from two young female employees at Thomson Pumps. They described how Billy made the females uneasy with his sleazy conduct and comments. The feature was published, I was mentioned fleetingly. Billy was not paid but his intention to make money from his crime was exposed. The headline read,

'Lock up your daughters, Paedo Pest Exposed'

I was made aware of the whole situation as the tabloid newspaper was one of Peters.

Again, I had been let down by those I considered family. Billy is out there, somewhere. I can only hope he is living within the law; I was to find out a few years later he was not.

Diary Entry Tuesday 21ˢᵗ July 1981

I had several people ask for my autograph outside my lawyer's office today. The power of television! I was interviewed last night about the upcoming royal wedding of Prince Charles and Lady Diana Spencer, why they contacted me I will never know. London was looking fabulous. Buildings have been cleaned, the streets look tidy and anything that can be painted was being painted! The sun is out, and life is good. It's the perfect time for a Royal Wedding.

I signed the mortgage documents for my new home with additional space for an office and I could not have been any happier. Jemima had helped me find the perfect property. She had used her impeccable taste and yuppie estate agent contacts to source a magnificent property. It was a unique Mews house within a private cul-de-sac in the heart of Notting Hill, it was perfect.

The property was over three levels and allowed for two bedrooms, a large office area for the girls and a meeting room for clients who chose to visit me at home. It had a private roof terrace and a parking space, although I did not possess a car it would be perfect for clients who wanted to visit me at home. It needed a bit of TLC but nothing that would break the bank. The cobble stone street adjacent to the front door added to the character of this beautiful house. The day I got the keys we celebrated with a bottle of champagne in a wine bar on the Portobello Road , less than five minutes' walk from the house. Jemima described the new property as :-

'It's wonderful, located in the colourful and soon to be cosmopolitan part of Notting Hill'. I had to look in the dictionary for the meaning of 'cosmopolitan', as always Jemima, the Oracle was right. Within a few years the house after renovations had almost doubled in money.

I invited Maureen and Bill to come down to London and see my new home but they both declined. Bill had moved out of the family home and was living with his mistress; Maureen had hit the drink and I was told she was unable to get through the day without a bottle or two of vodka. Gran told me Maureen had struck rock bottom and was dating a fellow alcoholic who was more interested in Maureen's drinks cabinet than her.

'No one drinks themselves happy, most alcoholics end up broke, bitter and alone.' Gran was right.

Maureen was on a road to self-destruction and there was nothing I could do. I was no longer welcome back home and both Bill and Maureen had made it perfectly clear, they wanted no further contact from me.

**

Jody was playing music by up-and-coming new romantic bands Duran Duran and Spandau Ballet in the office and coming into work dressed in her pixie boots and baggie jeans. I blamed Duran Duran for the frilly blouses, it was an ironing nightmare. Jody would come straight to work on a Wednesday morning having been at the infamous Billy's Night Club (Blitz Night club) until after 3am, going back to a friend's squat in Warren Street for breakfast and then headed straight into work, never the worse for wear. She loved to dress up and dye her hair every colour of the rainbow. Jody was predominantly a quiet person but came out of her shell when she was with her new romantic crowd, her newfound focus on her clothing and image made her a talking point. She would say,

'If someone doesn't shout something out at me in the tube or on the street when I am dressed like this, I know I am not doing it right!'

She was doing something creative, outlandish and I loved that about her. She frequented the trendiest clubs in London, sharing the venues with writers, designers, musicians, and other club goers. Many of the people who went to these clubs were soon to become household names through their music or fashion designs. It was 1981. Suddenly you had features in the press on how to copy the makeup of Steve Strange and every shop in the high street was rushing to catch up with the New Romantic look. Jody, this shy, reserved woman was a sensation in the underground nocturnal night clubs of London. She was a party animal by night, frequenting the same establishments as Boy George and Steve Strange. By day (once she had washed the food colouring out of her hair) she was my unassuming de-mure personal secretary who looked and sounded very much like Diana Spencer.

Peter and Irina sent a beautiful Persian rug as a house-warming gift. It came from a carpet showroom in Mayfair, and I can only presume was terribly expensive. Due to tax reasons, Peter and Irina were having to spend much of the year out of the country and I had not seen them for several months. They had invited me to America to celebrate my 21st birthday in November and I had accepted. Until then I had a full diary including several television appearances, private events, and appointments to attend to. The Mews had to be paid for as did Jody and Jemima.

****

The Royal Wedding of Charles and Lady Diane Spencer 29th July 1981.

Over thirty million people in Great Britain watched Charles and Diana's wedding on 29th July 1981 at Saint Paul's Cathedral. Like most people, I watched the wedding on my tele-vision, I was with Nell and Sean, in my fabulous family Mews home. We all sat on the roof terrace, and I drank champagne. It was a beautiful hot day in London, the sun had been out all day, yet Nell and Sean chose to stay in the shade, they both looked so pale, a bit of sun would have done them the world of good, but then again, they had both been dead about 50 years. They were both rotten company but came with the house!

I was settling into my new surroundings and lifestyle; everything was coming together. Peter had told me to enjoy my celebrity status but be on my guard the whole time.

'Not everyone has your best intentions and your back like we do.' I knew he was right.

The amount of hate mail I received would often out-weigh the fan mail. Peter suggested I got a Manager, Jemima was the natural choice, she knew my likes and dislikes, she knew my personality and always wanted what was best for me and not necessarily the client. Jemima had no problem walking away from a business meeting if she was not in control or was not happy with the outcome. Unlike myself, Jemima had no issue with saying 'No!' and she did it beautifully. Jemima was so professional, she had impeccable communication skills. Her creative ability combined with her business acumen made her the perfect Manager. More importantly, I trusted her implicitly.

There was incredible pressure on me to perform and produce results. I found myself going to appointments with more and more demanding clients, whose expectations I was unable to fulfill. Why? I am not an oracle; I do not predict the future I communicate with the dead. I channel what they want to tell the living and not everyone wants to hear what they have to say. Some clients don't fully understand this and become angry or irritated if they don't like what they hear. Spirits don't always have good news to convey. Lately, I have walked out on these meetings as they bring no closure to the client.

There is no revolving door to and from the afterlife. Every spirit I have encountered has not moved on; they have not crossed to the other side and instead remain earthbound. Often, a spirit must learn to communicate with the living, so you need to be patient, it's a two-way conversation, and both must learn to find the best way to talk. If I am stressed, I cannot concentrate, and I will not contact anyone.

My career was moving at an incredible pace, and I worked hard on my reputation. Terms and conditions had to be prepared and signed by clients prior to a consultation to protect me and safeguard any disclosure of our meeting. I always went with my instinct. My client base was growing daily and both Jody and Jemima were effectively running my diary and essentially my life. I looked up to both Peter and Irina and trusted them both. I had gone from self-employed to a private limited company within a few months, I had a hefty mortgage to pay along with two full time staff members, namely Jody and Jemima. Peter had organised an accountant to look after my accounts and reduce my tax returns. I was learning everyday new aspects of business and financial accounting. Once I saw how much money was being generated each day, I kept my eye on the finances. There was only one name required to sign business cheques – mine! Jody wrote out the cheques, attached them to the invoices and I would sign them. I kept my eye on the business, after all it was my livelihood.

***

I had made a conscious decision; America was beckoning, and I had a list of well known celebrities who wanted a private one to one meeting with me. Private consultations generated more than half of the business revenue. They were incredibly lucrative for my company and offered the client complete anonymity. Here at home, clients could drive straight into my private garage which offered a direct entrance straight into my home and office. I would often meet clients in a suite at The Savoy or The Ritz Hotel. These hotels offered exceptional privacy. I could meet my clients in secrecy in a safe, secluded suite away from prying eyes and ears. Prestigious London hotels offered every day meeting places for the rich and famous. I used these hotels so often; I was no longer charged for my room hire as I brought so much business to the hotel. One client, a wealthy American CEO would bring his family and stay for several days at one of the most exclusive hotels in London. Dining and drinking expensive wines in the restaurant spending tens of thousands of pounds in a few days. Another wealthy client booked his daughter's wedding, taking almost half the bedrooms in this iconic hotel not for one but two nights as they celebrated in style. I flitted between several venues in London. Jemima discussed incentives with the General Managers to favour their venue over another. She let Management know my business came with complimentary overnight perks. Jemima wasn't one to beat about the bush. She expected and insisted on free gifts. One General Manager told her, I was an 'extension to their corporate sales team and a VIP guest'

The girls used the complimentary overnight stays, meals, bottles of champagne and spa days. I never felt guilty as I brought so much business to each venue. I knew the concierge and the door men, I looked after them with tips and they looked after me. It was a perfect arrangement for all. Life could not have been better, but I could never enjoy myself totally, I was always waiting on the cards to fall and something to go wrong.

CHAPTER 21

America was calling.

Diary Entry – Sunday 8th November 1981

WOW where has this year gone, just a few days till I turn 21! I leave for America in the morning to spend some quality time with great friends, great food and great weather, America here I come, and I just can't wait ! The Police are sure to be number one this week with Every Little Things she does is magic. Do you think they were singing about me? I do hope so.

Jody and Jemima had organised my flight to New York. It was First Class with British Airways, although it was a fabulous way to travel transatlantic to New York, I was soon to learn, it could not be beaten by Concorde. Flying supersonic and sharing the cabin with so many celebrities was insane. On one occasion Joan Collins was in the seat opposite me and another time I sat beside Ronnie Wood. He slept the entire flight. Oh yes, I had come a long way, a few years ago I was travelling by overnight bus and sleeper train from Glasgow to London. Now I no longer mixed with the hoi polloi.

I handed over my entire business to the girls as I trusted them. I planned to be away for 15 days, so I signed some cheques for Jody in my absence and Jemima, well, no one told Jemima what to do. She knew me better than I knew myself.

I instantly fell in love with New York, and everything American. They adored my accent and made me feel so welcome. I loved the way they looked so intently at my mouth when I was speaking, as if they had never seen another person speak before. Listening to my every word. Once I had spoken their faces lit up, captivated by my refined Scottish accent, and commenting on my pale skin and deep red hair. I was going down a storm. Everyone I was introduced to seemed to adore me. It felt like I was holding court when I spoke everyone listened.

Peter and Irina had the most magnificent penthouse apartment that overlooked Central Park, everything was cream and gold. All that glitters is gold in this apartment, Irina had gold leaf on the intricate details on the doors and ceilings. She had the most superb taste and attention to detail.

The Malones invited guests to my birthday celebrations, and we partied late into the night, drinking champagne cocktails (legally) and dancing to live music on their huge balcony. Peter and Irina gifted me the most beautiful Rolex watch. I loved it; it marked the start of the most wonderful time of my life.

At the party, I met Chad Sanders, he owned a large construction company near Miami. We talked about the issues he was having at one of his projects, an old factory which had lay empty for some time. He had bought the plant with the intention of renovating and splitting the building into several bespoke units to suit smaller businesses, ready to let or buy. The minute renovations started all hell had broken loose. Contractors were reporting what had been described as a dark shadow at the back of the building, electrics going off, tools going missing and metal objects being thrown across the factory floor. Each time Chad brought in men to start the renovations, they worked a few days and never came back. The project was now behind schedule and running way over budget. Contractors said the building was haunted resulting in tradesmen walking off site too frightened to go back. The work stopped. Chad had sought the advice of a local psychic and had requested she got rid of whatever was haunting the building. He had approved her fee and instructed her to do whatever it took to cleanse the factory so renovation work could resume. The medium was called Dolores, she was well known in the area and came recommended. She had guaranteed to get rid of whatever was haunting the building. Three weeks later the psychic was still struggling to remove the stranded spirit. Chad asked if I would come along and meet her, I agreed, I asked Chad not to divulge who I was. I met Dolores Mayer at the factory, she recognised me right away and made no big deal about who I was and why I was here. She had the cliché look, exactly how you would imagine a psychic to appear. She reminded me of the gypsy fortune teller at the fair, scarf around her head and large hooped earrings, black hair, and thick black eyeliner. My first impression of her was not good.

Chad, Dolores, Chad's business associate, Michael and I met and walked through the building. His dog a large Rottweiler called Monster who tentatively, and after much persuasion, entered the building with us. It was daylight when Chad unlocked the huge doors and walked inside this massive factory. Once inside, Monster the dog, ran ahead and started sniffing and randomly barking, the noise echoed in the empty building. Dolores almost immediately began talking to someone who she claimed was the previous owner. She said he was upset with the renovation work being done to his factory. He was refusing to leave and demanded the work be stopped. I was fascinated how she was able to communicate with this spirit and yet she was unable to name the man. Considering what Chad was paying her I found her advice and investigation process both weak and unconvincing. Her acting was equally mediocre. This was such a large place, and the stakes were so high, Chad needed answers along with a solution to his predicament and not some charlatan fleecing him for money.

'No one can guarantee the removal of a spirit, you can't make something leave if you can't prove 100%, they exist in the first place, she's a fake!' I told Chad.

Ten minutes after being in the building Dolores claimed to

sense the spirit. She dramatically informed us it was a man, and he was standing beside Chad. Dolores claimed the 'man' was angry and wanted them out of the building. I certainly couldn't see anyone beside Chad. I mentally questioned where she was going with this charade as Dolores was not capable of any kind of psychic ability, a lot of her answers were purely hypothetical, she believed she was gifted and could communicate with spirits but as far as I was concerned, she was out of her depth. I could tell she disliked me, but I was not here for her approval. Her observation was little more than guess work and her conclusion as to the haunting was little more than obvious. A male, angry spirit in a factory, he was unhappy with the renovations taking place! It was hardly a radical theory. Dolores was a committed illusionist, she used dishonest methods to trick people out of their money, Chad was just her latest target.

Without warning I was being mentally dragged to the inner sanctum of the factory. My body was not moving, just my mind. I began to drift away, it was lovely, it felt like I was floating just a few inches off the factory floor. I could hear Dolores and Chad talk but it was in the distance. My body felt like it had no weigh to it. I could see a man working the machinery, he was loading and unloading what looked like large metal parts. He was just going about his job, despite there being no machinery on the factory floor, the man went about his actions of cutting the metal blades one by one. He dropped his steel blade and the noise resonated around the empty factory.

The clatter of metal startled Chad 'What was that noise?' He asked with a tinge of fear in his voice.

I was in a different head space, I had to communicate with the man in front of me.

'What's your name?' I asked. He turned towards me.

'I'm George, what's your name missy?' 'It's Catherine,

pleased to meet you.'

'That was my wife's name.' George replied.

'Why are you here George, did you work in the factory when it was open ?' I was looking for answers.

'It's a fine job, worked here all my days.' George started to walk away.

I followed him. I never turn my back on a spirit until I know what I am dealing with. 'Do you want me to follow you, George?' I asked.

There was a loud metallic bang. 'Did you throw something George?' I knew he was playing with me and trying to keep my attention.

George looked content moving around his workstation as he would have done when he worked at the factory. Moving machine parts around as if he were still doing his job. Monster the dog came over beside me and began to bark furiously. George shooed it away and it ran off whimpering with his non-existent tail between his legs.

'George, I need to know why you are here ?' he did not respond.

'George, you are dead, you know this right?' It was a crazy thing to say but some spirits do not know they are dead. He stopped what he was doing and looked right through me.

'Ofcourse, I know!' he replied, with a slight tinge of anger in his voice.

'You need to leave, you can't stay here, you need to move on and rest in peace.' I awaited his reply.

'I don't want to go anywhere.' George was determined to stay, I explained if he did not leave others would come back and try to chase him out of the building.

Despite years of paranormal investigation no one knows why the dead continue to haunt us but one thing for certain George was trapped. Had he some unfinished business and was not prepared to go without a fight or had George been refused entry to the afterlife and was he now being forced to walk the earth for eternity.

'George! George! Stop for a minute and tell me, why are you here?' I had to raise my voice to get his attention.

'I need to know what is going on, I want to help you?' I continued.

'I want to stay and finish my job, I like the company of the workers, once my job is done, I can move on, I mean no harm to anyone.' confessed George.

Delores and Chad watched as I spoke to an unseen entity. Chad's business partner had long since fled along with Monster the dog, it was all too bizarre for him.

George's haunting was a classic one, he had decided to remain in this world to protect or watch over a person or place. In this case it was a place, the factory. George told me he had worked in the building for over fifty years, man, and boy. It had been his life; he had been so committed to his role in the company he saw little of his wife or children, who subsequently left him. His job was his love and his life. A downturn in business and the factory doors closed. His world was shattered, the familiar faces he saw everyday were now gone. He considered his work colleagues as his family. George was unable to adjust to his lonely existence at home, he returned to the place he loved and threw a thick hemp rope over the steel roof support and hung himself.

The sounds George was making were simply to let others know he was there. It was attention seeking. He had touched a few of the workers on the shoulder not realising the fear he was creating amongst the men. Those who heard and saw him in the factory were terrified. The building now had a reputation as being 'haunted'. Exaggerated claims and unseen entities kept the construction workers away. I communicated with George, I asked him how we could co-exist and work together. It had to work, for everyone's sake. George agreed he would stay until the building work was complete. We agreed there was to be no throwing or moving of any objects whilst the construction workers were on site. I said he could remain in the building, but he could not distract the others. I took his silence as a 'yes' and the mood in the building started to feel less heavy and more positive.Dolores had begun to wave bundles of lit sage around the corners of the building, along the windows and doors. Chanting all sorts of hocus pocus.

'There is a male malevolent spirit in this building, the sage will cleanse and purify the area and get rid of this evil spirit.' Dolores wafted the sage smoke with outstretched arms as she walked around the inside of the building.

I looked at Chad. 'George this is Chad, he owns the building and says you are welcome to stay but there needs to be some changes.' George said nothing he just gave a slight nod.

I turned to Chad. 'Please inform the men to come back to work, you have my word they will not be disturbed, there are no evil spirits, no malevolent spirits, just a lost soul, an old man, harmless and alone. Once the construction work is complete, he will move on.' George smiled a toothless smile. "Yes missy" he said.

I asked Dolores to stop waving her sage bundles in the air, the gathering was over. We had come together to connect with the spirit of the dead, we did that, and we had closure. George was going nowhere, not just yet. I watched him return to his workbench and continue with his work. He meant no harm. This misunderstood lonely spirit simply needed some friends to keep him company. I said goodbye to George and left the building. I watched Chad from the front seat of his car, hand a stack of dollar notes to Dolores. She turned to look at me but did not wave goodbye. I never met her again, why would I.

Over the coming weeks, the men returned to work. Chad and his construction workers reported less paranormal activity. Chad explained to the men who George was and why he was in the building. With the renovations well underway the guys chose to embrace the reality of the situation; George was just part of the team, and they were no longer frightened or feeling threatened. It became common practice to greet George in the morning and evening as they packed up. It would seem George enjoyed the company of the other men and their banter as he went about his working day. It was a beautiful example of the living and dead working together every day. In the main, the dead don't mean us any harm, we can co-exist and when it works, it's a good feeling.

It had been a successful investigation. My aim to stop the haunting was accomplished and although I felt sad for George and all the lost souls out there, I knew I could not save them all.

January 1982

America was everything I had ever dreamed about, and I was starting to have doubts about returning to London. The closer my return date got the more I wanted to stay. I extended my break and had Jemima cancel my upcoming appointments in the UK. She moved out to America to be with me on a temporary basis. Jody was left in charge of the London office located at my house. I had every faith in her. Jody would fax over important documents for me to sign and between her and Jemima they worked well together despite the time difference. Jody organised our green cards, American bank accounts, a driving license, health insurance, the red tape involved was all too much for me to be bothered with.

In February 1982, Jemima and I signed a short-term lease on a large apartment in the upper east side of Manhattan, New York. It had an incredible vibe, a slower pace, museums, and superb eateries were all in the neighbourhood. I adored the location especially when the leasing agent reliably informed me Robert De Niro had an apartment in the same building. I never saw him; I think the realtor lied! New York welcomed me and I felt it was an ideal launchpad for my American career.

New York was nothing like London, everything was extreme, the people, the fashion, the attitude, if you woke up at 6am there was a diner open serving food and coffee on most street corners. You could sit all day and night just watching endless television, with dozens of cable channels to enjoy , back home in the UK we only had three. (Channel 4 did not launch until November 1982.) I loved to people watch in Times Square with its dazzling lights and enormous advertising boards which dwarfed anything you saw in London. New York was flamboyant and I had fallen in love with her. Peter and Irina supported my decision to stay and live there, it was the perfect base. I already had a few American clients but now I was based in New York I was accessible to anyone who had the money and the inclination for a private consultation with me. Jemima quickly set up meetings with NBC and ABC networks. I was offered a weekly slot on the number one breakfast show which was recorded live in New York each weekday morning. It was hosted by Americas golden couple. My 8-minute slot on prime-time morning television would allow me access to millions of homes across America. For me, breaking America seemed to be so easy. Jemima was turning down offers as new opportunities came in every day. She was making huge decisions on my future and setting out clear objectives, and they didn't include signing off every deal that came across her desk. Requests I would have said yes to, Jemima put on the back burner whilst she negotiated other, more lucrative options. She possessed exceptional sales skills and never took her eye off the ball. The clients loved her eloquent and quintessential English accent. Her vocabulary and perfect articulation of words made her a big hit with agents and their representatives. From a business perspective I could not imagine my life without her at the helm.

'We need to be selective; as your Manager I have *my* reputation to think of!' Jemima stressed the word 'my' every time she said it. It was one of her statement words.

Jemima had a very sensual tone. She made reading out a shopping list sound sexy. I missed the whole sexy chapter; I am not sexy. When I stood beside Jemima, I never felt comfortable, she was a gorgeous looking woman with a fabulous figure and extraordinary long legs. She towered over me in height and even more so when she wore her heels. Men just adored her, when she accompanied me to meetings and events, all the male eyes would be on her and not me. The power of being beautiful, and intelligent, Jemima possessed it all. Invariably, Jemima would have a date on her nights off, but not me. My date was normally with a pizza or a large tub of ice cream. The longer I stayed in New York the more weight I was putting on. The Big Apple was a constant reminder of food, the city smelt of food, every street housed a wonderful delicatessen or a family-owned diner with a fabulous reputation. It was impossible to avoid take away food and it became my own personal battle to limit the amount of food I was consuming. My diet consisted of take away food and TV dinners. I became obsessed with fresh coffee in the morning and a Danish pastry.

It was my daily ritual. The morning buffet which was set out at the television station was laden with an array of yoghurts and pastries along with fresh donuts which I could not resist. Jemima was furious and demanded I went on a strict diet. She monitored everything I was eating and weighed me once a week. The Americans are extremely body conscious especially if you work in front of a television camera, you had to be slim and well-groomed and extremely attractive on the eye, it was a major requirement on morning television. From the female news readers to the weather girls each person was groomed to perfection, and no one seemed to have a hair out of place. Every detail was combed, sprayed, coached, manicured, and fixed into position. The make-up was heavy with clever hi-lighting and blending. Hair was stacked high and rigid with hairspray. The need to look flawless and perfect was a require-ment of being in front of the camera. I relied on some very clever and creative make up being applied by a team of pro-fessionals before I was permitted to faced their early morning viewers. The last straw came one morning when one of the le-gendary male presenters whispered in my ear off camera.

'You need to lose some weight if you want to be taken seriously in this game!' Cheeky bastard! I thought.

I answered him back. 'So says the man with an Elvis Presley wig on his head!'

I later learned you never talk to show business royalty in such a manner if you want to stay in the industry. Working on TV not only changed my career but my life. I don't court publicity, but it goes hand in hand with being famous. They say fame changes you, but it doesn't really, it changes how other people react to you. The people of New York are used to celebrities walking about the city and often don't bat an eye. They tend to keep you down to earth by reminding you that, 'You're not all that!' This was refreshing as I could go about my daily business without much disruption.

Jemima had organised several newspaper and magazine interviews. She wanted to work on my image and how the public perceived me. Jemima had decided, the little girl who grew up talking to dead people was to be overhauled into a new character. She wanted me to come across as a strong, driven, independent woman, the type of woman who commands respect and authority the minute she comes into a room. I thought I already was that! I could probably pull this character off, but I was not as fast as Jemima, she was the queen of the rebuke with a single, brutal one liner response.

I once heard her answer a journalist who asked the question.

'What was her favourite position?' And without a second thought she answered, 'CEO of course!' That's my girl!

August 1982

The temperature in New York city was searing hot. The heat outside during the summer months made it almost impossible to live without air conditioning. Bizarrely, I had taken to jogging in Central Park with a small group of runners and had lost over two stone in weight. I felt and looked great. One of the gossip magazines had reported my dramatic weight loss was due to 'A failed relationship which had left me broken hearted and refusing to eat.'

I was fascinated to know who this mystery man was as I had not dated since Jim died. The newspaper article made me laugh and at the same time made me feel desperately unhappy. There was no special man in my life, I had no admirers, nor had I been asked out on a date. I was starting to ask what the hell was wrong with me! I wanted what all women want, to be loved, put on a pedestal and be part of a happy, loving couple. Jemima went on dates as often as I went food shopping. I do appreciate she was beautiful, tall, and intelligent. But I had a lot to give, I wasn't unattractive, and my long curly red hair always got me noticed.

Jemima was a hard task master and made it her business to keep my diary full of appointments. I would often do ten straight days before I got a break. If I was not being interviewed, I was writing for a newspaper, attending social events, mainly charity lunches or dinners, which I hated. The women who ran these charity gatherings had no idea about what was going on in the real world. They were married to wealthy prominent businessmen and thought it was important to be seen raising funds for various charities located in New York. If truth be told, they didn't really give two hoots about the charity. I decided, very quickly, mingling at these mundane events was not for me, I had no respect for these pretentious, two faced, women, most of whom had never encountered hardship in their lives. A major incident to them would be a broken fingernail or losing a button off their Chanel suit. I asked Jemima to decline all charity invitations. All invitations received the same reply.

'RSVP, Regrettably I am unable to attend your event due to another commitment. An anonymous donation will be made to your worthy cause.'

We rarely donated, but Jemima would appear incredibly humble if asked if it was us who 'Made a large cash donation to the charity anonymously ' She was magnificent in passing the donation off as one of ours. She would say, 'It's crass to discuss what charities we donate to; we prefer to remain nameless and discreet thank you! It wasn't me, hell no, I was much too tight, but I liked people to think it was.

Apart from the television appearances, still, most of my earnings came from private consultations, these were highly lucrative and took me into the homes of the rich and famous. I was rarely star struck but I was often left disappointed by some of celebrities I met, especially those that I admired.

One such person was an America singer who had made her fortune in the last two years by plagiarising up and coming artists, stealing their compositions, and masquerading them as her own by changing a few bars or cords here or there, just enough to keep a judge sweet and keep her out of the courts. Miss Bloom was a phenomenal artiste, a dancer, a singer, a musician. She had a cult following of females who dressed and looked exactly like their pop star idol. She had requested a meeting with me while she was visiting her exclusive residence in New York. Both Jemima and I were happy to oblige. We both loved her music and admired her work. As I sat in her penthouse apartment, I waited and waited for her to show. If the view over the Hudson River had not been so fabulous, I would have left sooner. When she did finally decide to show up, I was furious! She swanned into the room without an apology or explanation as to why she was late, followed by her entourage of hangers on and yes men. After a bit of small talk and introductions I was feeling extremely uncomfortable. Miss Bloom was more than a Diva, she was a twisted bitch! She demanded from me more than I was willing to give. Jemima could see in my face I was not embracing Miss Blooms comments.

'So, you're the one who can see the dead, well let's see if you're any good then honey.' She goaded me. Her entourage had a giggle at my expense. Note to self –'never be in this woman's presence again as I am liable to punch her!'

Her questions were demeaning, and her attitude was disrespectful. She was holding court and today I was her preferred game of amusement, but not for long. I allowed no-one to treat me like this. I was unable to communicate with any spirits she claimed she 'could feel around her.' Miss Right Now was an attention seeking narcissist and I no longer wanted to stay in her company.

'I'm sorry, this session is over !'" I said as I got up off the sofa ready to leave.

'What the fuck! You better sit down right now missy!' Miss Bloom protested but I had heard and seen enough. She was a spoilt, vile individual.

'I am unable to feel any positive energy around you and I no longer wish to continue!' I tried to defuse the situation.

Unexpectedly, I was overcome by a strong presence which made me feel nauseous. I sunk back into the sofa. A forceful energy came rushing into the room. It was a sensation I had never experienced before and never wanted too again. I became anxious and wanted out of the apartment. I didn't care who she was, I wanted out – fast! Miss Right Now was not having any of it and certainly was not happy with my stance, she demanded I sat down and 'got on with it'. Bloom was clearly a woman who was used to getting her own way, I can't imagine people who disagreed with her, kept their job! The room was oppressive, something was draining my energy and my head was throbbing. I could hear something running around the room, at speed, but I could not see anything, suddenly, it jumped onto the sofa where I was sitting and ran round the back of me. It moved around the room again, this time as it jumped on the sofa it punched at my chest, I flinched in pain. I was unable to see anything, but one thing was for sure, this persistent presence was not going to let up. It jumped onto the sofa one more time and I got up. A rip appeared on the arm of the couch on which I was sitting. We all saw it being ripped by an unseen force. The tension was tangible, I was dealing with an entity I could not see but knew it was evil. Bloom remained calm, watching me fight off the unseen force. It felt like I was swotting an angry, persistent fly that had the better of me.

'There is something here which is negative and trying to dominate everyone in this apartment.' I cried out striking the air with my open hands.

I couldn't see anyone, but I could feel the room was charged up. There were energy balls darting all around me. I stood up and threw my hands out as if I were stopping traffic. I screamed and the whole room fell silent.

"SHOW YOURSELF NOW !" I yelled and to my surprise, it did!

A male apparition appeared right up at my face, He was a small man, small in stature, small in mind, small in body. He was hideous, his face was contorted and intimidating. I was truly frightened from him. I could feel his breath on my face, it was cold and smelt foul. I closed my eyes; I was unsure if I was the only person to see him, judging by the reaction of everyone in the room, they were aware something paranormal was taking place and they were witness to it. I was uncertain as to what they could see.

Cautiously, I stood my ground and faced the apparition, it was my first demonic entity. Its foul language was almost as vile as the smell that came from it. Who or why he was here was not known nor did I care to know? I felt out of my depth and for the first time in a long time – I was frightened. I began to recite a verse I had learned many years before as I feared this day would eventually come. With all my strength and courage, I commanded the evil entity to leave. I began.

'I want to exorcise the negative spirits that are in this apartment , I cancel all demonic assignments on any of the people who live here, I command all demons who are here, you must be removed from this place, you do not have permission to ever be here again.'

The room became bitter cold and there was a rotting smell in the air. I fought to keep the entity at bay, it was overpowering and trying to invade my body. I was experiencing extreme head pains and began shaking uncontrollably.

'You have no power over me, and I command you to leave this home!'

I repeated the verse but there was no response.

'I am going to bless this place with holy water and blessed salts.'

I was prepared. I had these items with me as I wanted to protect myself and those around me. I continued.

'Evil spirits I command you leave now; you have no business in this home!" I was terrified. Jemima was on her feet, hugging her bag and coat.

'Those spirits who do decide to stay must protect this home and the people that live here, so this property and those that remain here flourish in peace and happiness.'

I said prayers from an old torn bible as I nervously dosed the holy water and salts around the room.

The pain in my head was blinding me. A shocked Jemima came to my aid. She insisted we got out.

'You're not an exorcist, this is not our concern, let's get out of here and they can contact a priest!' She grabbed my arm and pulled me towards the door. The singer's manager hastily came over to me.

'You're going nowhere, you better finish what you started.' she demanded.

'Let her go !' Bloom yelled; she smiled the most horrific smile.

I looked at the singer and asked, 'I think you are evil - yes?' She looked me straight in the eyes and I swore her eyes turned black in colour! Bloom grabbed my arm and I quickly pulled away from her. Her strength was more like a strong man than a petite woman.

'No Miss Catherine, seeing is believing, and I never saw anything, no one did, I don't think you expected to meet me today, did you?'

Who had I just met? Was she suggesting I had just met a

demon!

Her tone was hostile and aggressive. She threw tea and cake at me and around the room. Her erratic and violent behaviour frightened Jemima and me. The whole situation was crazy, her entourage stood like soldiers around the room unaffected by what had just happened.

'Our paths will cross again, sooner than you think, we have unfinished business Catherine!' Blooms tone was dark and threatening. I wanted the hell out of there. NOW! Her parting words alarmed me as this woman had so much influence over millions of teenage boys and girls all over the world. My head was throbbing, and I was no longer willing to stay in the apartment. Jemima joined me and we left the situation. We got up and rushed out without saying goodbye as I didn't want to turn around. I was terrified I might see something I didn't want to see. Jemima and I fled the apartment, the elevator ride took forever, but once on the ground floor, and the elevator doors opened, we were off. The concierge screamed at both of us to stop running, we didn't listen, instead we continued to run and never stopped for three blocks. I could never look or listen to Miss Bloom after our strange encounter. I could never quite work out what happened that day and Jemima and I didn't want to speak about it, she simply gave us the creeps. I destroyed her singles and albums and forbid the girls to play any of her music whilst I was around.

December 1982 - Thursday 23rd December

The money was coming in and I was enjoying all the trappings of my success. Earning excessive amounts of money is a powerful feeling. It's addictive, it makes you even more ambitious, it gives you security and independence. My desire every day was to make more money because I never wanted to go back to where I originally came from. Money is the best invention of all time, it is the instrument that allows me to interact with influential people and decision makers, who in turn allow me to make even more money. Money goes to money. The more time I spent with my wealthy clients I aspired to be like them. I was now speaking the language of money. It was written on my clothing, on my handbags and in my address, only those that understood my wealth recognized the designer logos that adorned me. Chanel, LV, Hermes, YSL. Christian Dior. I craved expensive things and I adored my fabulous lifestyle in America, I was living the dream. I was no longer that wee girl from Paisley, if the truth be told, it was just a distant memory. I loved it when someone recognised me on the street or asked for my autograph, it made me feel important and loved. I courted the press and gave interviews at the drop of a hat. I knew I had made it when I let Manhattan Elite, a New York socialite magazine into my Manhattan home, they took incredible images of me in my apartment. Draped over the chaise lounge, pretending to cook a meal in the kitchen area and looking forlornly out of my magnificent floor to ceiling windows. I had the apartment professionally cleaned before the magazine arrived and spent hundreds of dollars on flowers which were strategically placed throughout each room. The magazines discerning readers had requested a look inside my beautiful home and an insight into my life, I obliged, I also accepted the $3,000 cheque that went with the invasion of my privacy. The flowers cost me $250! It was a good day at the office.

New York was fabulous but my contract for the breakfast show had come to an end and Jemima was unable to negotiate a deal I was happy with, so I was shown the door. I think my co-host had a lot to do with that decision, we never got on after my Elvis Presley wig comment. My Friday morning 8-minute slot had served its purpose, it had allowed me access to the great American public. It was time to move on, those in the know had advised me to get a good agent who knew the American marketplace and move to California. Hollywood was to be my next stop.

No longer content with living in a rented apartment in Manhattan, I wanted more, I wanted to be in the sunshine with a house that had a pool and overlooked the Hollywood Hills. I wanted to be surrounded by all the pretentious and insincere characters I recognised from television and the big screen. I wanted to say to the British public, look at me, the Americans have taken me to their heart and just adore me and its likely I will not be coming back to the UK. I had reinvented myself and now it was time to move onto the next phase of my life. I became quite ruthless regarding my career and was in the envious position of being able to pick and choose who I would and would not work with. I asked Jemima to scale down my client base and increase my fees. I told Jemima I was moving to Los Angeles, California. Tinseltown was calling my name and I wanted to hit the town running. The night before Christmas Eve I told Jemima of my plans. Her response was not what I expected.

'Actually Cat, I was hoping to speak to you about my

career, I want to go home for a while, I want to be with my family.' Jemima had kept that one quiet.

'Are you thinking about leaving me?' I asked selfishly thinking more about my needs than hers. I was shocked and wanted answers, but Jemima was ever the diplomat, she remained calm and simply asked for some time out to think about her future. I never for a moment thought she would have considered not working with me. Jemima would be hard to replace, and she knew it. I was a good judge of character, but Jemima was a mystery to me, she kept her private life private and only told you what you needed to know about her personal life. I adored her; I had grown to trust her. She was more than just my right-hand woman; Jemima understood me and often knew what I needed before I did myself. I was paranormal sensitive, I sensed things and I felt things, I often wore my heart on my sleeve, but Jemima was an enigma, she never really revealed her true feelings, and she kept her cards close to her chest. Her private education in one the UK's most elite schools for young ladies had shaped her for life with a very British stiff upper lip. I don't think I ever saw her cry. Jemima was a self-confessed elitist; the description 'snob' just didn't cut it when defining Jemima.

She and I were at opposite ends of the social class hierarchy , I was born into a working-class family and had moved up the social rankings, I considered myself upper middle class, the only thing I believed that stopped me achieving upper class status was my education. Jemima argued I was from a working-class background and as far as she was concerned I could never be middle class, I could only be wealthy.

'If you are born working class, you will always be working class. Much like your place of birth, you were born in Scotland, you will always be Scottish.' Jemima was certain I did not have the etiquette or the breeding to be upper class. I did not fit the criteria.

Knowing there was a possibility of losing Jemima presented me with a unique set of challenges, none of which I wanted to face. We flew back to London on Christmas Eve, business class on British Airways. Jemima wanted to spend the festive season with her family and the new man in her life. I invited Gran to my house in Notting Hill and Jody had arranged for private caterers to come and prepare Christmas Lunch for Gran and me. I knew she would hate it as she liked to be in control when it came to cooking Christmas dinner. I had a case full of Christmas gifts, all beautifully wrapped. I loved Gran's face when she opened them, if I told her how much they cost, she would have collapsed. She had no comprehension about brands or value. I loved this about her, it was so innocent. I considered her the only family I had left, the only person who wanted to spend quality time with me. I was looking forward to spending Christmas in London with Gran, catching up on all the gossip from back home.

London Heathrow Airport was quiet, it was Christmas Eve, and everyone was desperate to get home. Jemima and I collected our cases and made our way out of the baggage hall to our waiting car. It took me a few minutes to register Jody was standing in international arrivals waiting for us. I knew by her expression something was wrong.

'Jody. Why are you here? Is something wrong,' I asked.

'Yes. I'm sorry, it's not good news!' she replied.

CHAPTER 22

The end of an era

Gran died peacefully in her sleep; 75 years young. She had travelled down from Glasgow on the overnight sleeper train to be with me for Christmas, a journey she absolutely loved. She enjoyed the motion of the train as it left the station and the clackety-clack noise it made going over the bolted metal bars that held the tracks together. She loved the screaming of the train as it raced through the sleeping stations along with the continual rocking of the carriage that guaranteed she would sleep like a baby throughout the night, arriving refreshed at Euston Station in the morning. It was a journey she had made many times as she feared flying, who knew this would be her final time. The train inspector found her dead in her cot bed. He contacted the police, and her body was taken to St Thomas's hospital morgue for a postmortem. The thought of Gran being found by strangers and taken away in a body bag distressed me. Jody had been contacted whilst Jemima and I headed back from America. I was asked to identify the body before it was transported back to Glasgow on the request of Bill and Maureen. I arranged for my grans body to be driven back to Glasgow in a private hearse along with two drivers. I didn't want her to be alone as she travelled home. I bought cassette tapes of Matt Monroe and Patsy Cline and asked for these to be played on the journey back to Glasgow. I knew she would have liked that.

It took me some time to come to term with gran's death. I was overwhelmed with sadness and became depressed. I didn't realise it at the time, but I should have got professional support to help me deal with not only gran's death but the death of Jim and my mother Margaret. Gran had such a strong personality, she was a caregiver of all things good, she was a decent person, a good friend and played such a huge part in my life. Gran may have been in her twilight years, but she had a young soul and heart. After her death, I tried to contact her, but it wasn't to be. She came to me in a recurring vivid dream along with Margaret. They both looked so much younger and were smiling, I tried calling out to them, but they could not hear me. I believe it was their way of telling me they were together.

Christmas 1982 and New Year's was the worse imaginable time for me, I had never felt more alone. The days that followed grans death, I heard nothing from the family. No one called from back home to ask how I was or what the funeral arrangements were. I asked Jody to get the details from the undertaker about the funeral so I could plan to attend. On the 6th of January 1983 I flew up to Glasgow in Peter Malones private plane with Jody and Jemima to attend the funeral. I knew my attendance would be of interest with the press, but an invasion of my family's privacy for the day by a few photographers was not going to stop me attending my gran's memorial service. There were many people at the church service simply to see me, so I wore a large brim black hat and kept my head down determined not to be photographed crying. The girls stood either side of me to shield me from the cameramens lens. It was all about Gran and not me. Bill requested I did not attend he told Jemima 'It would be a media show if I was there.' There was no way I was not going. As expected, someone alerted the press, and I was photographed at Glasgow Airport. Jemima managed to get all three of us into a chauffeur driven car which had been allowed access right up to the plane on the runway, something normally reserved for royalty or dignitaries. Once in the limousine we made our way to the church to pay our respects for the last time.

Bill met me at the entrance to the church and asked me not to go to the cemetery. He kissed me on the cheek, but I felt no love. He had aged considerably since I had seen him last, his face showed no emotion, reluctantly I agreed to his wishes and stayed away from the graveside. There was no warmth or hugs just a cold instruction. I was fragile and needed my family today, but it wasn't to be. There was to be a small purvey at the local golf club and again it was suggested I did not attend.

I was shocked at Maureen's appearance, this was the woman I thought was my mother, the woman who had held me and tucked me into bed, she looked gaunt and skinny and had aged rapidly, she looked ill. Billy came over to me and gave me the biggest hug.

'Our mums an alcoholic, it's killing her.' he said very matter of fact.

Billy smelt strongly of alcohol and cigarette smoke. I felt emotional when he referred to her as 'our mum'. Had the drugs affected him so much he had forgotten she was not my mother! Mary did not attend and sent an enormous and tasteless display of flowers which would have looked more fitting inside a hotel reception area. Maureen never looked at me or acknowledged my presence at any point during the service. I wanted so much to go over and hold her, but I knew this would not be welcomed. As we left the service, I knew I would never return to my hometown, nor would I reach out to the family again. I wanted to say goodbye to Bill and Maureen, but they jumped into a car immediately after the service, I was not prepared to chase after them. A piece of me died that day. Thankfully, I had the girls beside me. A few press photographers hung about outside the church and some fans had come to support me. I thanked them as I went into my car and headed back to the airport. My time here was over. I wanted to head back home, to London.

Diary Entry - Tuesday March 22nd, 1983

'I don't need to live a lifestyle I need to live my life' I would love to meet someone and be showered with affection and love. Must attend a gallery launch tonight, could see it far enough! Boring!!!

I wasn't looking forward to the gallery launch that night, but they say the best nights out are always the ones you don't want to go to. It was a private art gallery in Mayfair, and I just knew the room would be filled with pretentious art critics and wealthy undesirables with too much money and bad taste in clothes. The original prints which were on display could not be described as 'fine art' it was rubbish, you do have to admire these so-called artists, they were having a laugh at our expense. What I can only describe as different coloured lines of paint on white canvas sold for a serious amount of money and a half-finished landscape that looked like a three-year-old had painted it at nursery had everyone talking. Apparently, the gallery specialised in what was called abstract art. I was an awful critic, Jemima said I was a 'barbarian' and was 'devoid of any artistic taste', but why lie when the truth will do. It was a shocking waste of paint and canvas. Jemima was in her element, but I was bored senseless. The buffet and champagne made up for what had started as a boring evening. The gallery was a who's who of the rich and famous. We all recognised and acknowledge each other, even when you didn't know someone, it was considered good manners to give a knowing nod of the head or a two-finger wave on passing. It was the international sign language between us showbiz types. A makeshift bar had been erected at the back wall and I made my way to it. It was like the bar from Star Wars, I was surrounded by the weird and wonderful of the socialite scene in London.

I ordered a gin and tonic and was handed a flute of champagne! It was a complimentary champagne bar for the evening. Perhaps they didn't want people getting drunk and mouthing off about all the shite paintings that hung on the walls!

I was approached by a rather attractive looking man, he leaned into me and whispered.

'Paul Newman said this about poker players, if you can't spot the sucker at the table within the first five minutes it's you!' We both laughed.

His name was Paul Leighton and he brought sexy to the room; within forty minutes I was smitten. With his Caesar style brown hair and hazel eyes, he was rough and unrefined, nonchalant, and aloof. I adored his complete revulsion of all things conceited. He was just my kind of man. We chatted for hours and exchanged telephone numbers.

Paul and I started a relationship which became serious very quickly. I absolutely adored him; he was a portfolio manager for one of the biggest banking institutes in the world. I found it captivating how he managed his clients, making informed decision on how his wealthy clients should invest their money, researching the markets, company earnings and stock market prices. Like me, he was a commoner who had made a career out of obtaining money from our wealthy clients.

Paul and I met up several times a week. I looked forward to him coming to my house in Notting Hill. I had put America on hold, for the moment, the thought of not seeing Paul was enough for me to remain in London. This suited Jemima, she wanted to spend more time with her fiancé and had no intention of going back to America with me for the moment. I was destroyed by her decision; our working relationship was perfect. Every executive we met in America loved Jemima's accent and business expertise. I just loved her!

Paul moved into my home in July 1983, and I couldn't have been happier. Like all relationships it was amazing at first. We became quite the celebrity couple, invited to most of the key parties and social events in London. Life was good. I was in love and all I wanted was to be around Paul. He would tell me, he wanted to spend every second with me, take care of me, it was everything I needed to hear. He set me up with one of his clients, a well know concert promoter and together we arranged a tour of the UK. Paul invested in me and created a theatrical event that was sure to draw the crowds. It was a new concept to come to the stage and it received rave reviews. The full show commenced with two mediums in the first half of the performance, interacting with the audience, answering ad hoc unrehearsed questions. The male and female couple were basically my warm-up support act. It was all, part of the buildup for me coming onto the stage, creating tension, and anticipation.

After the interval I would take to the stage for the last two hours. Normally I started the show by talking about my life. I chatted about how I knew I was different and how those around me recognised I wasn't like them;

I questioned the verbal abuse I received because I was 'different and weird.' I explained, how as a child and a teenager, I lived in my own wee world, my own vacuum because no one wanted to talk about what I was. I would share stories with the audience about my past experiences communicating with the dead, describing individual occasions and snippets from my childhood until the present. My conversations were full of emotion. When I took to the stage, my performance became a one woman show which largely was unscripted as I would often go off on a tangent. I would confront the elephant in the room and allowed myself time to talk to the audience, they became the show, they had the opportunity to ask me questions, a new concept at the time, an audience led production, the participants became the actors.

I had a runner in the theatre who would dash about handing

the microphone to the audience member I had chosen to talk to. I would pick up on lost souls and spirits who had a message for that audience member. Afterall that is why most of the people had come, in the hope of hearing from a loved one close to their heart who could offer them closure from their loss. I had no filter, I had no desire to dress up any direct communications I had for the audience, I simply would deliver the message in the same way it was conveyed to me. This approach would often offend, frighten, or even shock the audience, especially if the person was taken under horrible circumstances.

The newspaper reviews were sensational, and theaters would sell out within hours of the dates being announced. The demand for tickets was overwhelming and additional shows had to be added. The audience were entering a production where my performance was unrehearsed and raw. The controversial content and delivery filled theatre seats, the public couldn't get enough of my direct approach, and shocking revelations aimed at the unsuspecting audience members.

During one performance I picked up on the lost spirit of a teenage girl who had taken her own life, hung herself whilst her parents were at work. She had been bullied at school for years, there had been no let up, day after day mentally and physically bullied by the same three girls. She had become so depressed she started self-harming, cutting, and slicing at her arms and legs with scissors, pulling out her own hair, strand by strand till the point she had to wear it in a high ponytail to conceal the bald patches on her scalp. Bullying never leads to good things, when you can no longer run and hide, it leads to isolation, shutting down and avoiding everything you know, people, places, feelings. Her mother was aware of the bullying and did little to stop it. The bullying stopped the morning she placed the rope around her neck and jumped off the hall banister. Her spirit wanted her mother to know she could have helped, she could have stopped the persistent abuse, she could have cared. Her hatred for her mother shocked everyone in the theatre, I had a full conversation with the dead girl whilst on the stage, my microphone was not turned off, I repeated what the teenage girl said word for word so the theatregoers could be part of the communication. The audience was deadly silent as I conversed with the unseen spirit of this young lady on the stage. Her name was Rebecca, she was 16 years old, she came to me with only one message, simply to let her mother know she was constantly let down by her. Rebecca had been angry and profoundly depressed the day she took her own life. She blamed her mother who never kept her promise to protect her, she would fail to turn up at the school gate to pick her up, missed meetings with the head teacher about the bullying and probably worse of all blamed Rebecca for being bullied. Rebecca spoke from the heart, she was angry and resented her mother, she had felt ignored despite pleading for help. As expected, her parents were upset and angry with my comments and were even booed by some audience members as they got up to leave the theatre. I called out to them to come backstage and meet with me after the show, but they never showed up, choosing instead to talk to a national newspaper. Their story merely increased my notoriety and boosted ticket sales.

I will never apologise for telling the truth no matter how hard it is to hear. I will say it as it is, this is who I am, and I am unapologetic. What I had to say might not always have been politically correct, but it was the truth, and the truth can be powerful stuff. If you cannot handle the truth do not come to one of my performances. I was a bridge between the dead and the living, I was not prepared to compromise my position when a spirit wanted to connect with someone in the theatre. My advertising campaign was updated, and we had a disclaimer added which I made everyone sign as they entered the theatre, it added to the drama and the curiosity of my performance.

'By entering this theatre and buying a ticket for this performance you give myself and my production team permission to include you in my performance. Should I contact a spirit who wishes to communicate with you or a member of your family you will be receptive and considerate. This is a live show and I make no apologies for what you are about to hear. You have been warned !'

Paul used this disclaimer and had it printed on the reverse of every ticket. Initially, it was a stunt and was picked up by the newspapers however, it legally protected me from anyone trying to sue me after a show. Additionally, the statement increased my notoriety, venues were selling out and the publicity and subsequent demand for tickets. It was genius.

My theatre shows propelled me from star to icon in the United Kingdom. In the early 80's I was performing in theatres by the mid 80's I could sell out stadiums. In the mid 80's only rock stars and the evangelistic brigade sold more tickets than me for a live performance.

Paul introduced the additional concept of a Meet and Greet after the show. For an additional cash fee, the audience got to meet me in person. I would sign autographs and smile for photographs with members of the public. It was all additional revenue. By the end of each performance, I would be mentally and physically exhausted, the Meet and Greets became tiresome and predictable but Paul insisted they had to be done, the tax-free revenue they generated was astonishing. I left all the financial aspects of the tour to Paul and his business partner Michael Morrison. My only concern after a show was to be rushed back to my hotel room just before the headaches would start.

I had sold out concerts in London, Manchester, and Birmingham, In Scotland, I performed in Edinburgh and Aberdeen but refused to perform in Glasgow. Additional dates were added to what was initially an eight-date whistle stop tour, it turned into a sixteen night sell out British tour. The hours were long, but the money was pouring in. The nights I was not on stage, or giving private consultations, I was giving interviews or appearing on talk shows. Paul came to all my performances and dealt with the cash that was being collected from the Meet and Greet. He told me to trust no one, he gave up his job in the city to be my manager much to Jemima's dismay. Paul was ruthless and bulldozed through every situation without any thought to anyone's feelings. He announced his commitment to me, and our future, I believed him. I was so besotted and in love with the man. He was a sociopath, workaholic; he felt no guilt for the harm his decisions caused. However, he was my rock and I simply adored him. In my eyes, he could do no wrong. He said all the rights things to me when he talked about love, our success, the future, our money, and he was making it all happen. He believed I was destined to be a worldwide phenomenon and I believed every word he said. My relationship with the girls was dwindling as Paul took control of the decision-making reigns. I wanted everything he predicted and hung on his every word. We became insular and lived in our own little bubble where he called the shots, I did everything he said. I trusted him and felt protected around him. I believed he only wanted the best for me, for us. I no longer wanted to be a big fish in a small pond, I wanted to cross the pond again, and dominate America. I had already tested the market once and knew with Paul by my side, I could be an even bigger success.

**

Diary Entry - Friday 23rd September 1983

Today, I am marrying my rock, business partner and lover Paul Leighton. I cannot tell you how happy I am. I have everything and more. I am a woman in love as Barbra Streisand would say. He has promised to love and take care of me forever, a promise is forever, isn't it?

It was a whirlwind romance, Paul and I were a formidable couple, we made the merger official on 23rd September 1983. We didn't tell anyone about our plans to get married at Lambeth registrar office, Paul thought it was for the best. I wore an outfit from a little-known design student called John Galliano. There was no flowers or confetti, no reception, and no photographers. We got married, came home to Notting Hill, grabbed our suitcase and passport, and flew to Paris for the weekend. On my return to Notting Hill, my cleaner, June, a genuine East Ender, looked like a duchess and spoke like a fishwife, was the first person to congratulate us on our good news. She was delighted. Jemima and Jody were less thrilled. Jemima and Paul did not see eye to eye and were often at loggerheads. She claimed Paul would try to undermine her in front of business executives or other members of the team. Their bickering and arguments were becoming intolerable. Paul suggested Jemima and Jody should go as they no longer fitted the dynamics of the new business. I was against it from the start as both girls had been loyal to me and I trusted them both. I considered them friends and not just employees, but Paul insisted. I didn't have the guts to attend the meeting where Jemima was dismissed, and I didn't have the courage to contact her afterwards. I was a coward, I never really got over the loss, Jemima had been a trustworthy and reliable influence in my life, and I did her wrong. No number of apologies would ever change that. I was brutally wounded when Jody went to the press with a story about how badly she had been treated whilst working for me, she had described Paul as misogynistic and controlling. She claimed Paul had taken her aside and accused her of theft. Money had gone missing from the cash box in the office, the police were brought in to investigate the theft and a bag search found the exact amount, £320, in Jody's possession. She was dismissed on the spot; any charges were dropped. She proclaimed her innocence to anyone who would listen as the whole sacking was played out in front of other people. Paul took her office keys and escorted her off the premises. I was told she left the building crying uncontrollably. Paul demanded I had no contact with Jody, he said our lawyer had insisted on this. I later found out this was a lie. Many months passed before Jody agreed to meet me, I had pestered and hounded her to join me for lunch to talk over what had happened, she refused every time. After further attempts I managed to get her to agree to join me on the Portobello Road for a coffee, I arranged the meeting behind Paul's back as I really wanted to put things right. I had prepared a speech and wanted to say how sorry I was for everything, but Jody never showed up. I learned later that evening she had been killed in a freak accident. A van had mounted the pavement and hit her. She died on the way to hospital. Jody was only 24 years old. If it were not for me, she would have been at home safe and sound. I never forgave myself for her untimely death, months later during an office clean out, an envelope was found behind a filing cabinet containing the missing £320.00. It had all been a massive misunderstanding which had resulted in such a horrendous outcome. I never went to her funeral as I was away on business. On reflection, it was not an excuse. I should have cancelled my meeting and gone; it would have been the right thing to do.

Paul looked after all my financial affairs. He had been assessing my funds and had suggested some long-term stocks and share investments which offered a better return than the interest rate I was getting with my bank. He arranged for offshore accounts to be opened so I could avoid paying crippling tax whilst still living in the UK. Paul arranged for the mortgage on my office and home in Notting Hill to be paid off in full, saving thousands of pounds in interest. Following my husbands, advise we created PK Concerts Limited, Paul created the company and managed the new business set up. Share allocation and director responsibilities were prepared by our company accountant. I left it all to Paul and Michael to arrange the financial side of the business. Paul and I were partners in every sense, the more he committed to me the more I felt secure. As my business partner and husband, we trusted each other when it came to making the business a success. I knew I was wealthy, but I had no idea how much I was worth. Paul had appointed a Financial Director, Tony Heron, to the business. I knew little about him apart from what Paul told me, he came recommended and I went along with the decision. I signed the official paperwork to agree his position within the company and left it at that. I rarely spoke to him or saw him at the Notting Hill office. He produced balance sheets and other financial statements which I never understood, it was all just numbers to me.

I had all the attention that comes with fame and no longer lacked the means to protect myself from it. Paul organised a bodyguard, a minder, his name was Bobby, he was an ex-marine who soon became my silent shadow. I was working hard, week after week without a break. Paul was keeping my diary jammed packed. As far as he was concerned, a day with no bookings in the diary was not permitted, blank pages indicated no money was being generated. I was under so much pressure and after a few months I seriously needed a break.

Paul said, 'I was a commodity and the demand for me was high.'

People were always all around me, telling me how wonderful I was and how much they loved me. Most of the time, I didn't believe them. It wasn't a normal position to be in, being told how fabulous you are. It grated me and I started to disbelieve the people who lavished me with this verbal bullshit. I was unable to leave the house without being heckled or stopped for autographs. And there were the crazies, the disbelievers, the brigade of haters who chose to make my life miserable by calling out obscene names at me on the street, writing about me in the press and discussing others similar to myself on the television. The skeptics were frightening, I could feel their hatred and you could never anticipate their actions. The abuse was mostly verbal but sometimes it was physical, I once had a woman throw a cup of milk on me, eagle eye Bobby saw it coming and pushed me aside.

For the best part, when I had time off, I wanted to be left alone, away from the prying eyes and endless questions, I didn't want to be with anyone except my husband. Paul was often in a different world to me, he enjoyed company and routinely invited people to the house, many of them I didn't know, hangers on, friends of friends, most of them were superficial. I was becoming insecure; I didn't like strangers in the house. I especially didn't like Paul's assistant. She was like a drum, small but made a lot of noise. Her name was Penny. I never liked her, there was just something about her !

By November 1984, Paul and I had been married over fourteen months. We hadn't celebrated our first wedding anniversary simply due to my work schedule. I had been invited to join Peter and Irina in Majorca to celebrate my 24th birthday. I had no relationship with the family back in Scotland, but Mary had been in touch, and I decided the time was right to meet up again. I wanted her to meet Paul, plus it was time we met Pierre. We arranged to meet when I arrived in Majorca.

Diary Entry – Majorca. Monday 12th November 1984

Happy Birthday to me. My birthday morning started off with an argument, Paul, says we must move to America for a year due to tax reasons. It was always part of the plans, but it has come sooner than I expected. I need a few months break as I am exhausted both mentally and physically. I want to rent a house by the beach in Malibu and just enjoy long walks along the sand, drink wine, look out at the sea in the evening and recharge my batteries. Paul has said this is not possible. I need to hit the ground running and make my mark on the USA. I just don't know if I have the strength!

The spirits of Gran and Margaret rarely came to visit but I sensed them around me today. Margaret put her arms around me, and it felt like a warm invisible hug. When I am alone, I feel this warm sensation wrap itself around me, the feeling of love and warmth can be extraordinary. I know Gran and Margaret are together, knowing they are still around me, looking after me brings me a great deal of contentment.

I had caught Paul reading my diary, so I was wary on what I reported. The last thing I wanted was to start another argument as he took things to the extreme and I ended up feeling I was the one in the wrong. His ability to deflect a situation was incredible. I was going to discuss with Peter and Irina about my move back to America, but I wanted to do this on my own. I had to find the time, away from Paul. I loved the company of Peter and Irina; they were like parents to me. Peter had met Paul once before, but this was the first time we had stayed as guests at their exquisite new villa. Majorca was stifling hot; it was wonderful to feel the sun on my body and the sea breeze in my hair. Bobby my bodyguard was not required as the Malone's had their own security and Irina's Russian bodyguard was available if I needed him. Igor was like a James Bond baddie, he was terrifying.

I left Peter and Paul to discuss business on the golf course whilst Irina accompanied me to meet my sister Mary at a local restaurant. Mary was extremely excited when I introduced her to Irina, and it didn't take long for her to invite herself and Pierre back to the villa for that evening's annual White Party (all guests were required to dress in white.) On arrival at the restaurant, Mary air kissed both my cheeks and handed me a beautifully wrapped diary. Her Scottish accent had all but disappeared and was replaced by the most convincing French tone of voice. She complimented Irina and made a fuss over me, and how I looked all grown up, well I had turned twenty-four. In her best fake French accent, she exuded.

'Oh! Happy Birthday dahling, you look fabulous.'

Mary wasn't interested in celebrating my birthday, it was all about social climbing, who she could meet and add to her portfolio of wealthy friends. She namedropped some 'C' list celebrities who frequented Pierre's restaurants, many of whom Irina or I did not know.

'Do you know our dear friend, Prince Rainier of Monaco?' asked Irina, naturally she didn't!

The Malones social standing afforded them connections with some of the most famous and affluent people on the planet, some of which were going to be at 'The White Party' Mary seemed desperately excited. I thought I had better have Igor on duty just in case he had to deal with my sister!

As expected, the dinner party was elegant and tasteful, giant lilies with candles floated on the pool and guests were treated to glasses of champagne and blinis with Russian caviar. Enrique Lopez, a close friend of The Malones, a man described as the undisputed King of Latin pop, Spain's biggest export, sang for the dinner guests. He slowly swayed in and around the dinner tables oozing sex and testosterone, the ladies loved him. The walking groin was Spain's version of Barry White.

The Malones White Party guest list was like a Forbes Who's Who. Famous actors, two world renowned singers a super model or two, football players, a fashion designer from Dior, Majorca socialites and many well know business magnates along with their wives or was it their mistresses. Who knows? It was one of those nights you looked at someone and said, ' I know their face, just can't place the name!' As ever Peter and Irina epitomised old world glamour and etiquette and were the most gracious and generous hosts.

Mary's restaurateur husband Pierre was charismatic and much older than I anticipated. He was courteous and well mannered. He clearly was a man of means with several successful restaurants and nightclubs in Cannes, Nice and Monaco. Unlike Mary he was discreet and restrained. As I watched

Mary interrupt conversations and work the room, I could not see what Pierre found appealing about her. Granted she was beautiful, but she lacked any substance, she was arrogant and self-indulged. Mary always brought the conversation back to talking about ....Mary! I once thought she possessed an air of style and sophistication, but that was when I lived back in Scotland and a battered sausage dripping in lard was classed as sophisticated.

Back then, when I lived with my family, I was inexperienced and naïve; I never knew anything about how the other half lived or how to conduct myself at social events and dinner parties. We never had dinner parties! The nearest we got to a dinner party was at New Year when the neighbours came in after the bells and Maureen made cheese sandwiches with margarine and salad cream.

I had a lot to thank Jemima for, she taught me so much about decorum and good manners. More than just table etiquette and what knife and fork to use, she taught me how to interact and start conversations, how to ask engaging questions, bring a gift for the host, thoughtfully plan for the event. Her finishing school teachings were never lost on me. She shared her cultural status and secrets, normally held for the wealthiest members of the upper-class society. Jemima taught me well and I missed her.

I was suddenly interrupted by a gentle whisper in my ear. I turned quickly and there was Max. We both smiled at each other. Peter and Irina's son would be forever young, he accepted he was dead and wanted to live on in harmony with his parents. Irina had commented that she knew when Max was about as things would move, the music sheets on the piano would blow over or the pages would be turned to his favourite recitals. His scent would be in the air and his laughter could be heard in the distance. Knowing Max was around brought the Malones a great deal of comfort. I previously asked Max to show himself to his parents. In confidence Peter and Irina had confirmed they had seen their boy, not once but twice. He did not speak, he simply smiled and then disappeared.

Peter and Irina took me aside and presented me with a beautiful birthday gift, an exquisite pair of Tiffany diamond stud earrings. I was overwhelmed by their generosity and kindness. Paul said he had left my gift at home.

'It was much too big to bring to Majorca.' Paul deflected beautifully as usual.

CHAPTER 23

Living in a loveless marriage.

January 1985

Sometimes I don't enjoy, I just endure and that is how I felt about the pending move to America. I realised I had to live outside the UK for a period because of tax implications but I had no idea Paul had no intentions of joining me. Working and living together had been torture over the last few months, we had been going through a tough time. Our marriage was at breaking point and there were rumours of his infidelity, which he denied.

Paul expected me to work to an impossible schedule, which he controlled. There was little or no breaks for weeks on end, the extreme work pace was taking its toll on my mental health; it was no surprise I became ill and unable to sleep. The doctor advised bed rest for a week, but my diary was jammed packed, I was unable to schedule bed rest for another few months!

My relationship with Paul was more important than his relationship with me. I had become a commodity to him, nothing more. He would have me stand like a child while he reprimanded me for the most ridiculous things, I was walking eggshells around him. Our marriage was a mirage, it just wasn't real.

'Who do you think you are, you are insufferable, intolerable, only focused on yourself, everyday day, every second is about you!' His verbal accusations came from nowhere and left me battle scarred. My success had gone to his head and rather than protecting and loving me he chose to humiliate and abuse me, not physically at first but mentally. In company he was a perfect gentleman, witty and gregarious. As a couple, we communicated very little, and I sensed he was being unfaithful. He denied this. I didn't have to listen to stories, a wife just knows these things. He would stay out all night and showed me little or no affection. It was a loveless marriage and I felt like a failure. I longed to have Jim back as I missed him so much, he would know what to do and what to say.

The showbusiness facade was cracking especially after a rival Sunday magazine ran a kiss and tell story about Paul and an extremely attractive model, is there any other? They had been photographed coming out of Stringfellow's nightclub. The most humiliating part of the newspaper feature was, this girl's ability to describe the inside of our home in Notting Hill, she had taken pictures of inside my wardrobe and private possessions. Paul laughed the newspaper allegations off and insisted she had taken the images whilst at one of the many house-parties Paul had given while I was away on business. He rehearsed a very convincing explanation and referred to the girl as 'a fame seeking attention seeker.' The girl had taken her story to Joey King the number one public

relations guru who fed the tabloids with all the juicy fodder that sold Sunday papers. Paul brushed the story aside and insisted it was nonsense, I secretly believe he enjoyed the attention it brought, it put him in the spotlight for once. He detested being known as Cat Jamieson's husband!

Paul's extra marital existence was taking its toll on me. He had a doctor prescribe me medication, sleeping pills. I was hesitant about taking them at first, but I loved the sensation it had on me as I sunk into my pillow and drifted off to sleep without a care in the world. I wanted him to stay home and work at our marriage, I didn't want to leave, I wanted to delay America and was happy to pay the extra tax to save our relationship, but Paul was insistent, he was on the telephone at all hours, sending faxes, booking projects, arranging interviews, and meetings with agents in Hollywood.

'I will arrange the appointments and schedule the meetings from our base here in London. I've organised an agent to oversee the day to day running of your diary and make sure you are where you need to be.' He made it sound so cold and calculated. I liked my lifestyle in London, I liked my security, and I liked my comforts. America on my own frightened me, my husband on his own in London, terrified me!

I never asked for much in our marriage, I was just asking the wrong person. All the things I initially loved about Paul were now all the things I hated. He was controlling, it was his way or the highway. He managed every aspect of my life, my money, our business, he even controlled what I said. The only time I had freedom to speak was when I was performing. Paul was the master of deflection, if I raised an issue and wanted answers, he would turn the allegation right back at me. He lived a privileged life at my expense, wearing the best clothes, he drove an expensive Jaguar car, if he bought jewellery for me, he bought the matching piece for himself. He had a drawer with a watch for every day of the week: Patek Philippe, Rolex and Breitling. Tiffany curb link ID bracelets and diamond cufflinks. Despite my fame and fortune, I never really escaped my working-class roots and sometimes when I felt naughty, I would treat myself to a kebab and four bottles of coca cola at the weekend, but Paul never expected to eat or drink anything but the best. He would cringe with embarrassment if I drank from a can and would insult my working class, Scottish background. My gran would have been furious at his treatment towards me, but sadly she was not here to defend me. What was once heaven had now become hell.

Every detail of my move to America was planned out by Paul and there was nothing I could change. There was no room for movement or compromise. My flight had been booked for the 1st of April 1985.

***

I had come into the office one morning and I overheard Paul's assistant, Penny on the telephone screaming at someone who was obviously looking for payment. She was putting them off and insisted,

'Let me just stop you sir, debt recovery agents will not help recoup the payment as there is no money to pay the account! Have a good day. Goodbye!'

I immediately asked what she was talking about, Penny suggested I speak with Paul regarding the company and its current financial dilemma. I had no idea about what she was talking about. As I left the house to go to the bank, I was stopped outside by a newspaper reporter.

'Cat, do you have a comment on the collapse of your company PK Concerts Limited ?'

Shell-shocked and confused I made my way back to the house where I asked Penny to give me Paul's diary. I had to find him and get answers. An hour later, he could not be located. Penny never returned after lunch, she emptied the petty cash box and left a handwritten message inside it:-

'Money due as I have not been paid. PS your husband was shit in bed . Good luck!'

Paul came home late in the evening. 'What's going on Paul, what's happened to our business, I've had reporters banging on my door all day ?'

He began to talk. 'You *have* to go to America; the business is not making a profit!' he hesitantly admitted.

'What do you mean – NOT IN PROFIT!' I was livid, how could it not be making money, I was working my ass off. Where was the money!

'The 1984 Tour didn't make any money, the sales we forecast were not achieved, outlays were too high, you wanted a tour bus, overspending, the mortgage on this place ....' he went on and on 'merchandise and ticket sales did not cover the overall cost of the tour and associated costs, commissions, theater costs, overheads.......' He rambled on with pitiful excuses. He talked in accounting jargon in the hope I would just accept the explanation for our failing company.

'Commission! who the hell got commission, where's my money Paul?'

'It's too late, it's gone!' he screamed

Paul threw his dummy out the pram and went into deflection mode. I had had enough.

'I want to call a directors meeting, I want to speak to the bank, I want to see the financial statements, the cheque book stubs, I was to see paid for invoices and any outstanding invoices, I want answers Paul!'

His face said it all, he was a liar, he picked up his Jaguar car keys and stormed out the house. I never even mentioned Penny's note, he would only have denied it.

'I want a divorce! It's over!' he screamed as he slammed the door.

I sat in the silence of the house and thought about my situation, I was having to move out of my home, away from people I loved, leave the country I was born in because I was unable to afford to live there. I had a husband who saw me as his personal possession, a product which supplied his primary income. It was a light bulb moment and I felt sick deep to my stomach. He was right, our marriage was over, and I was totally alone. For a moment I wanted to run after him and drag him back, beg him to stay, but sometimes you must accept when something is over. I poured myself a gin, removed my huge diamond ring and expensive Cartier watch. I unclipped the

Chanel necklace and Tiffany stud earrings the Malones had gifted me and placed them all in an empty ashtray on the table.

None of it meant anything to me. I looked at it as it lay in the glass ashtray and thought how insignificant it looked, if you didn't know it's value you would have thought it was a stack of costume jewellery. It was just stuff and really meant nothing to me, it did not define me. It did not make me happy, but it made Paul happy. I no longer made Paul happy. I poured another glass of mother's ruin and wished Gran and Margaret would come to me, but they didn't.

Paul never came home that night. I took two sleeping pills and crashed on the sofa. Eight hours later I was on the telephone, there was only one thing to do. There was only one person who would know what to do.

***

I picked up the telephone and dialed the number. The phone rang five times before it was answered.

'Hello, it's me, please, please don't hang up, I need to talk, I've been such a bloody fool!'

I got in a taxi and travelled to Chelsea in West London, arriving just before 7pm, it was dark outside the stunning townhouse. I rang the doorbell and waited.

'Come in.' I walked into the lounge and broke down, crying uncontrollably.

'I have been a bloody fool; I have never felt so lonely. Jemima can you forgive me!' I begged, hoping she would say yes.

Jemima stood in the lounge doorway; her face was expressionless. She rolled up her sleeves.

'I'm going to let you cry, I want to hear you from the kitchen, I will make us some Chamomile tea, you're going to drink it and I am going to tell you a few home truths about your narcissist of a husband!'

Jemima talked as she walked into the kitchen. I was prepared for a tongue lashing. If this is what it took to get our friendship back on track, I was prepared to listen to anything she had to say. Good or bad. Jemima was keeping her cards close to her chest as usual and me at a distance.

I cried out to her. 'I think I'm having a nervous breakdown!'

'NO! you're not!'

Devoid of any emotion or sensitivity I was shut down. 'Right, Miss Jamieson, remove your selfish earmuffs and listen to a few home truths!' Jemima placed the tray of hot tea on the table and prepared to hold court. Jemima had waited a long time for this opportunity and was prepared to put me well and truly in my place. I listened; I agreed. I had been blinkered and blinded by what I thought was a husband's love. Jemima had no sympathy.

'Karma – cause and effect, karma is the effect of your actions, it effects your future happiness. You can't have it all ways Cat.'

Jemima summed up my crime like a high court judge.

'Only self-preservation was on your mind when you joined forces with that man. Both you and Paul's actions had terrible effects on myself and others around you.' I wanted to shout out 'Guilty as charged-judge' but felt Jemima would think it was inappropriate.

'You don't ask for very much in life Cat, but you have been asking the wrong person!' She was right. Jemima warned me, my marriage to Paul was going to be a costly mistake! I feared it already was. We drank more tea and talked for hours, never having girl friends in my life to confide in I opened my heart and feelings with Jemima.

'Do you think he still loves me?' Jemima didn't even think about her reply. ' No, I don't think he ever loved you, he loved the idea of you! Love doesn't come back again, when it's packed its bags and gone you've got to go to.' Science and reason may not have all the answers, but Jemima did.

March 1985 - 'It's all about the money! Honey!

I requested an extraordinary Board Meeting with the other directors. I asked the Financial Director, Tony Heron to bring to the meeting the current Financial Statements. I wanted to know exactly what was going on in the business. In the short-term Jemima, took me aside and we spent the day fast tracking me through the mind-numbing art of understanding financial accounts. She took me through each line on the company year-end accounts and the profit and loss statement. I picked it up rather well.

'Call Tony and ask him to fax over the Year End Financial Statements.'

Jemima was on a roll, and I was impressed with her tenacious approach to defend my lack of business acumen.

After spending the day together, I was armed with a newfound confidence. I was ready to enter the male dominated board room composed and ready for an extraordinary battle. It was Jemima who suggested she dealt with taking the Minutes of the Meeting. I agreed.

Eventually some of the paperwork arrived. The stack of pages took forever to print. Jemima patted the paper together and began reading the details.

'Cat, what is your understanding of your position in the company ?'

Jemima's tone was worrying. I shook my head. 'What do you mean, I'm a director, it's my company !' I felt humiliated at my lack of knowledge regarding my own business. 'I think its 50/50, half Paul's and half mine.' I presumed.

"You're not the majority shareholder, Paul is!" Jemima was as shocked as I was. Paul was the majority shareholder with 65% of the shareholding, I had a ludicrous 20%, the rest was split between Tony Heron and one other.

Over the next few weeks, I wasn't quite prepared for what was about to happen in my life. It was about to take a twisted turn of events. Paul had been incredibly cunning. He had set up the business in such a way the Articles of Association did not allow for a 'minority shareholder' to call a general meeting. All meetings had to be approved by the majority shareholder and this could take up to 21 days to be held. The directors had also vetoed Jemima being at the meeting to take minutes.

And so, the battle commenced. Paul raised the divorce action, and I was served papers at the Notting Hill property, as this was both the matrimonial home and the registered business address. Notting Hill had been my happy place; I adored the house; I immediately fell in love with the property at my first viewing. Latest information verified that the Notting Hill property was an asset of the company. It was my understanding that cash deposits I made had been set against the mortgage and the property was mortgage free. Where had this cash gone? Notting Hill had been pulled from under my nose, having been tricked and cajoled, into signing the property over to Paul and the business.

'Sign this Cat, it's for the house, we need to make some ownership changes purely for tax reasons, it's still your home.' I remembered him saying as I signed an abundance of documents, not knowing what I was putting my name to, just trusting the man who was asking me to sign on the dotted line. After all he had my best interests at heart – didn't he ?

Paul had put the house up as collateral for the business after he lured me into a false sense of security and lied. It was all a mess and flawed with deception.

My Notting Hill residence was an asset of the business and as such was held by the bank to pay off any debts which were owed. There was no money in the business account and Paul had emptied our joint account of any funds. All I had was my jewellery and clothes.

Paul changed the locks on the Notting Hill house and refused me entry, homeless and humiliated I moved in with Jemima. I had £400.00 to my name, a case of clothes and the jewellery I had put in the ashtray. Paul removed anything else of value from the house. I was left homeless and penniless. All I had was Jemima, the Malone's, and my name.

April 1985

Peter Malone appointed his personal barrister based in London, to represent me. Charles Turlington was a barrister, of such high standing, solicitors and lawyers chose him to represent them in court. He spoke at you and not to you and was an expert in court room advocacy and litigation. Charles specialised in both commercial and family law. He excelled in giving skillful legal advice and once in the courtroom he overpowered the opposition into submission simply by his ability to recite the law and put forward an unquestionable legal argument for the client. I rarely understood much of what he said, as he never put anything into layman's terms, he just gave me a look of total disdain each time I was in his company.

'Do not answer any questions you have not been well versed in answering by my team, do you understand Ms. Jamieson ?' I had been programmed to answer a multitude of questions with specific responses. I was terrified to open my mouth.

Turlington's paralegals set about gaining all the documentation and information they required to come to an amicable settlement, but Turlington advised from the start. 'This *will* go to court, there is no doubt. You have been implicated in several fraudulent transactions. This could result in a custodial sentence, unlikely but we need to contest your innocence and fight to clear your name.'

Based on my current financial situation, I could never had

afforded such elite representation, but I gave my word to Peter, I would pay him back, somehow.

My story was highlighted in his newspapers, the public were interested and because of our friendship I was never portrayed as anything more than a woman who had been scammed and conned by the man, she loved and trusted. The public were on my side.

Peter and his advisers took control of my legal predicament. If this was to go to court, they thought it was in my best interests to leave the country as soon as possible after the trial, mainly because the tax man was now aware I was living in the UK. The last thing I needed was a massive income tax bill on top of all my other outlays I was struggling to pay.

With a newly single Jemima back managing me, Jemima booked one-way tickets to LAX Airport, for the 5th of May. I had one week to raise as much cash as possible. Paul had already emptied the joint saving account which had tens of thousands of pounds in it and the business bank account had been frozen. I was reliably informed the expensive Jaguar car, which Paul had as a company vehicle was repossessed. Charles removed me as a director from PK Concerts Limited and a letter from Companies House confirmed this. He said I had to distance myself from the disgraced company. The only money I had coming in was from prominent clients who were flying in from around the world for private consultations. For these clients, I requested payment in cash or direct bank transfer into my private bank account. The bank that looked after the royal family's money no longer thought it was appropriate, I continued to bank with them. They cited 'insufficient funds' as the reason my account was closed. I was an embarrassment to them. The small amount of interest I accrued was transferred to a high street building society and my account was closed. How the mighty had fallen.

I would never have considered bankruptcy as I had

worked too hard to fall at the first hurdle in life's tempestuous journey, it was a glitch, I had been knocked down, but I was slowly getting back up, onto my feet. Paul had left me and that had set me free, our end was the beginning of me. I had the one thing that defined me. My name. Cat Jamieson and like the proverbial phoenix I was about to rise again.

We needed to raise money quickly, so Jemima suggested an upmarket pawn broker in Mayfair. I knew my jewellery had been valued at £50,000 for insurance purposes, my diamond ring alone was worth £10,000. Jemima brought the pawn shop owner to her flat where he inspected and valued the haul. He made me an offer to sell him the lot. It was way below the estimated value, but it was second hand, and I needed the money. Mr. Wiseman was a hunchbacked Jewish man who smelt of mothballs. He was devoid of any personality and little conversation.

'It's used and not new jewellery, being bespoke it will be difficult to sell, there is no call for a diamond of this carat size, remember that's what it's worth new, it's not worth that now. It's a fair offer, Ms. Jamieson, take it or leave it , you won't get a better deal ?'

Jemima did the negotiating, and we shook hands on a cash deal of £15,000. He pulled the cash out of his battered attaché case which he had handcuffed to his wrist and the deal was done. It was to be our set up money for America.

Paul had made no contact with me except via his lawyer. He had every intention of getting as much money as possible from our divorce despite already draining me financially and swindling me out of my life savings and home. I was being contacted by companies looking for money, Paul was still illegally writing company cheques knowing they would bounce. He was also fraudulently signing my name on company cheques and other company documents. Debt recovery letters were being forwarded from the Notting Hill address to

Jemima's flat where I was staying. Bills were mounting up and the pressure of living out of a suitcase was making me feel depressed. I was drinking heavily and looked gaunt and haggard. Pictures of me appeared in a national newspaper, I hardly recognised myself. I was on the verge of a nervous breakdown. London was the last place I wanted to be, but I had stay for now, it was going to be a hostile place to live during my bitter divorce. I had to stay healthy and strong to see me through the court case.

Diary Entry - Sunday 28th of April 1985

Journalists were banging on Jemima's door early this morning looking for me to give a statement! Peter's (Malones) Sunday tabloid has run an expose on Paul, he was caught and filmed selling over a quarter of a million pounds worth of drugs! Karma!

The four-page feature pictured Paul with several fake cartel gang members in a hotel suite in London. He can be heard discussing the 'guaranteed supply of cocaine' as he was 'personally behind the importation and distribution of much of the drugs in the city'. The grainy footage showed him taking the money from the undercover representative and incriminating himself in other illegal ventures, including money laundering and the supply of prostitutes. The footage finished with the room being raided by a barrage of police, shouting, wielding guns and badges. Leighton had been caught, hook, line, and sinker. He couldn't claw his way out of this, the evidence was overwhelming. He was on his way to prison, but our legal battle was still not over. I still had to face the divorce.

The Malones kept a discreet distance for a short while, I believed the entire thing was set up by Peter, maybe not directly but I knew he was involved. He was on his yacht in Ibiza when the news broke. I was eternally grateful for everything he had done for me, I tried to call him, but his personal assistant said he was out of range and would call me back when he became available. Perhaps, he was frightened I may say the wrong thing on the telephone. It was over a month before I heard from either him or Irina. The Malones friendship went above and beyond what I could ever have imagined. They were my very own earth-bound Guardian Angels.

Sunday 5th May 1985

As Jemima and I sat in our British Airways Economy seats on the 5.25pm flight to Los Angeles, California, we both faced an uncertain future.

The purser suddenly appeared beside us on the aisle.

'Good evening, ladies, would you be kind enough to follow me into Business Class, we have two seats available for you beyond the curtain.' Just before we took off, I turned to my friend and declared.

'Our bond is stronger than our fear, America is calling us Jemima.' 'I will drink to that Cat.' Jemima and I clinked our champagne flutes together and toasted our future. Things were starting to look up already.

CHAPTER 24

A new life in America 1985

By the late Summer of 1985, Jemima and I were settling into our new life in California. She was managing my destiny, negotiating, and representing me with a brutal enthusiasm. The American dream team had hit the ground running. The diary was busy, and I was prepared to work harder than I had ever done before.

I rented a house on Malibu beach, it was more than I expected to pay each month, but I fell instantly in love with the location, the beach, and the sound of the ocean. I loved the seclusion and respite the beach house offered. Living beside the ocean allowed me to distance myself from the madness of my divorce and the rapid pace of the city. I didn't mind the long drive along the Pacific Coast Highway into the various television Studios in or around Hollywood. Knowing I was travelling back to my beautiful home after a day's work was the perfect reward.

Jemima, as expected was a star with the agents, she was able to open doors and talk to all the right people. By January 1986, I had accepted and signed a contract to appear in a weekly 'ghost hunters' show. I liked the concept and set up. There was to be just four of us, featuring in the show. Myself, another two hugely different psychic mediums, a sceptic, and a four-man film crew. The brief was simple. Members of the public would invite us into their homes to investigate reported hauntings and paranormal activity. We would go into investigations blind, with little knowledge about the alleged disturbances. As a four-man team we complimented each other, working together to identify the source of the haunting and move the lost soul on to their final resting place. The pilot show was an amazing hit. The ratings for the first series were impressive and the studio executives were already talking about series two and three. Massive billboards promoting the show were erected all around Hollywood, California and one was featured in Times Square, New York. The show was called 'Ghosts, Psychics and Skeptics' One of the reasons the show was a success was due to the chaotic relationship I had with the other two psychic mediums who featured in each episode. I was unscripted and unpredictable. I could see and interact with the spirits; I was able to transfix the viewer and hold their attention during my communications with the dead. The other mediums on the show were more theatrical, pretending to be possessed and feigning being touched. My co presenters had to put on a show as they were less gifted than I was. I knew they could not see any apparitions and had to rely on myself to reveal who the lost souls and spirits were that inhabited the various properties we visited. According to the daily network rankings our show was taking audience figures from the other networks. Each sixty-minute episode was a massive hit. Advertisers were on a waiting list to book commercials during our show and were paying premium rate for the privilege. Returning viewers and new viewers just kept growing every day. I credited myself with the show's success. It was pure commercial entertainment and was ridiculously cheap to create. Each show took as little as two days to shoot, and production took another three days to edit. America had welcomed me into their homes. I had become a celebrity in the most bizarre manner, and I wasn't overly happy at the way I was being portrayed. I valued my psychic skill far more seriously than I was being portrayed on the show.

Despite the success of the show, I was still tied to a strict contract which didn't allow me much movement in my career. I was having to turn other lucrative television work down as the fine print in my agreement didn't allow for me to work for any other network or production company. My salary had been fixed for the first series of twelve shows and I had to rely on private consultations to make up my additional earnings. I was making a good living which was just as well as I had some major debts which had to be paid off. My divorce legal team were costing a small fortune back in the UK and I was trying to contribute as much as possible towards them. I had a huge rental to pay on the Malibu home along with all the household bills associated with it. We take the National Health Service in the UK for granted, in America health insurance is a huge chunk of your earnings and I was paying for both myself and Jemima. Jemima had given up so much to be with me, she had followed me to the states and left her family back in the UK, so I paid her a good salary and a percentage of each booking she made. It was only a matter of time before she would be my business partner but for now, I had to rebuild my confidence and develop my American portfolio of clients. I wanted to break America and my dream was being realised. I was proud of my working-class background as it had instilled in me a strong work ethic, or maybe I worked so hard because I owed so much money and didn't want to reach rock bottom again! There was no going back to being on the breadline, I had found my perfect home, I wanted a life on the beach far away from the bleakness of London and I was prepared to work extremely hard to maintain this.

When I wasn't away filming, I had private consultations to attend. As my celebrity status escalated, I commanded a higher fee from clients. The price doubled almost overnight and still they came. My schedule was stringent and allowed for little or no leisure time. When I had any downtime, I would walk along the beach with my feet in the ocean, the sun on my face and the gentle wind in my hair. It was the most wonderful sensation, life in Malibu was effortless and soothing but it took money.

***

The legal situation back home was gaining momentum, Charles Turlington's office updated me on a regular basis mainly by fax. I had been warned the outcome would not be good and to be prepared. Mr. Right had done me wrong, but Paul, despite being in remand for drug trafficking charges, was still dragging his feet with the divorce. Turlington, was the only man I knew who could stab you with a jagged one liner and rip you between the ribs before you were even aware you had been hit, was having no more stalling by Paul or his lawyers and brought the legal action to an end. It was all over, after a lengthy battle, there was nothing left. There were no winners, except the lawyers. What was once a thriving company, PK Concerts Limited, faced crippling debts and was placed in the hands of a receiver. My beautiful home in Notting Hill which was a company asset, was sold to pay off the bank and other debtors. I was left with next to nothing. Many debtors received nothing as the bank and the lawyers took most of the money. What was left, legally had to be split equally between Paul and me. I had been well and truly shafted. Across the pond it was headline news, in America it scarcely made page three.

PK Concerts booked venues, promoted concerts, and sold live show tickets not just for my stage shows but for other clients across various genres. It was insane to say the business was losing money and place the blame on me. The company had been poorly managed. Paul Leighton used the companies bank account to fund his own lavish lifestyle. In the end, jobs were lost, lives were ruined and smaller business owners who relied on our company lost thousands of pounds. It was a heartbreaking situation. I had been removed as a director so was unable to prevent a lot of the devastation taking place. Despite no longer having a connection to the business I was the person the nation linked with its collapse, the British public hated me for this. I promised myself once I was stronger and mentally stable, I would return to the UK and via one of Peter Malones newspapers I would tell the real story, the truth. I would have my say when the time was right. The public needed time for the dust to settle. For now, the land I didn't want to leave no longer wanted me there.

Paul Leighton served three years of a five-year sentence, ridiculous when you think of the devastation he caused. I was told on his release, Leighton like any snake slid under the radar, the last anyone heard of him, he was with some young socialite in France, whose father owned an English premier league football club. He was probably still living off some of my missing millions which no doubt he siphoned from the business account before it went tits up. The thought made me sick to my stomach, but I vowed it would never happen again. I also vowed to repay some of the smaller clients who lost out. It would be the right thing to do.

Summer, August 1986

I loved all the things America had to offer, but I did miss a sense of community living in Los Angeles, Hollywood was fast with a selfish facade, no one had the time or inclination to stop and talk, in comparison my home life was all about the beach and centered on solitude and privacy.

I went to a meditation class and dabbled in a bit of yoga. I got use to asking for tea and the waitress bringing me iced tea (which I detested). I would flag down a cab instead of a taxi. I was starting to sound American, I wanted to honour my Scottish heritage but found I was slipping into a phony America accent. A cross between Sheena Easton and Lulu.

I despised the morning traffic yet loved the long drive home at night along the Pacific Coast Highway with the car windows down smelling the scent of the ocean and watching the sun go down over the horizon. I had travelled a long way, both emotionally and from my homeland. My unique ability had taken me away from my family and friends, I had lost my mother, discovered my father was not my father, the man I loved, Jim, died long before his time and broke my heart, I married a man who took everything I ever earned and left me in the gutter to start again, I was a self-made millionaire one day and had lost it all a few months later. My good friend Jody and beloved Gran had died. I was now part of a television show which was making the all-male creators behind the show millions of dollars and my life was being controlled by a contract I could not renege on. My blueprint of male relationships was they either died, lied to me, left me, or cheated on me. It was time I took back some control in my life.

Millions of people watched me every day and yet I had only one person in my life I trusted and called my friend. Her name was Jemima.

***

It was a beautiful Friday on an August evening; we had finished filming for the day, and I arrived at my Malibu home about 9pm . Jemima came out to meet me at the car.

'What's up?' I asked, 'You never come out to the car when I arrive!'

'Cat, there is someone here to see you, he says he is your father!'

Diary entry - Friday 5th September 1986

It was one hell of a day filming, we captured on film overwhelming evidence there is life after death. The critics can say what they like, but I now have tangible evidence on film with eyewitnesses. Life is good and I haven't said that for a while ! Malibu has brought me so much happiness. Today, I feel free, I think I am starting to mend my broken heart.

What we filmed today shocked everyone. If I ever wanted to dominate America, this was the one piece of film that would jolt the nation.

'Ghosts, Psychics and Skeptics' was filming in a family home in the Hollywood Hills, this property had impressive views panning downtown LA to the Pacific Ocean. A retractable wall of glass brought the outdoors, indoors. The property was private, modern, and extremely expensive. On first site you would have said it was perfect. The young executive couple who had bought the property, contacted the producers in the hope we could shine some light on the strange goings on at their home. Something had 'infiltrated their home recently'. Manifestations, black masses, and strange noises had been reported and not just by the couple, staff members had seen and heard odd things. Our team and the cameras had been invited along to investigate the claims about suspected paranormal activity. The couple were initially not frightened but recently the activity had become more aggressive and was starting to frighten the couple and affect their relationship.

The team working on our show consisted of a parapsychologist called Chris Forsyth, a sceptic, he was English and lacked any signs of charisma. He was there to disprove everything we found. Chris would put forward a scientific or rational answer to all our findings, he was the type of person who would have argued a Jaffa Cake was a biscuit. He was possibly the most boring man I had ever met. After each investigation as we closed the show, he would utter the same lines.

'It was exciting, it was different, all four of us had very different , unusual experiences, whether its haunted or not, I remain skeptical, but I am open minded to the possibility.'

Mariah Beaumont had big hair to go with her big mouth and big head and spoke with a strong southern drawl. She claimed to be a 'world renowned' psychic medium and would randomly name drop well known personalities she had worked alongside. She was totally believable and completely over the top whilst filming on location. She would go into a trance or become 'possessed,' it was all for the camera ofcourse. Mariah was cunning, during breaks in filming she would come to my trailer and asked questions about the entity. Once filming commenced, she would simply repeat what I had told her. I learned to keep my mouth shut or simply feed her the incorrect information which would cause no end of drama. Cindy Carter, a New Yorker, was more credible and could communicate with the spirits, but she was the first to admit she could not see them. I was impressed with her ability to lead the team during the initial part of our investigations, by identifying the spirits and energies in the locations we visited. Cindy was one of the most credible psychic mediums I had ever met. I liked her a lot.

The format of the show would be as follows, Cindy would initially sense the spirit, and I would then see and speak to them. Mariah would jump on the bandwagon and use our information to create drama and bring tension to the show. Chris was forever the sceptic, throwing doubt and questioning our experiences. He dismissed conspiracy theories and claims of the paranormal and sought answers from science and subjective analysis. I was not a doctor, but I think he lived life on the spectrum, possibly suffering from some form of autism or Asperger's syndrome.

Mariah, I believe, had no psychic ability but had an incredible talent to take the audience on a journey, she pulled at your senses and played with your imagination, she taunted you, she questioned your logic and judgment about a situation. Is it fact? Is it fiction? Did I really see that? Did I really hear that?

You questioned your own intelligence on what you were seeing and hearing. Whatever it was Mariah said or did, you were willing to believe it, no matter how far-fetched the story was, you believed what was happening because you were enjoying it. Writers called it suspension of disbelief. Mariah performed it beautifully.

My obvious communication with the spirits would be the major focus of the show. I was becoming the star and taking center stage, much to the resentment of the rest of the team.

The Hollywood location we attended was active from the moment we arrived. Our first day of filming at this palatial house produced a significant amount of spiritual activity. Mark the owner had described, energy orbs which were a nightly occurrence inside the house.

'It was just the norm, lights going on and off, things moving of their own accord.' He was very casual about the goings on in his home. I thought to myself, how can this be normal!

Our initial task was to find out why the hauntings had shifted into something more negative terrifying the owners.

I encountered the entity almost immediately but chose to say nothing. I went from room to room and said my piece to camera.

Spirits can be trapped in places often because they do not know where to go. They are caught in limbo, or they need their story to be told, they are seeking justice of some kind by remaining earth bound.' The viewer and the producer loved my delivery and simple explanations. I rarely needed any prompting, normally I could say what I needed to say in one take. For the American audience, I toned down my Scottish accent and spoke much slower than I normally would.

The energy changed in the house. Cindy was in the dining room; she had picked up on a negative spirit.

'It's not diabolical but it doesn't want to be here.' She spoke whilst wandering around the room. Mariah joined us.

Cindy resumed her questioning. 'Are you an energy we should be frightened from?' A bottle slide along the bar and smashed on the tile floor. The cameraman was ecstatic as he captured it on film.

'Thank you, thank you. Can you do that again?' an approving Cindy asked.

'You're here with us, put a show on for us, show yourself to us?' Cindy was focused on having the spirit manifest.

Less than a minute later a vase of flowers flew off the table and smashed on the floor. Something intelligent was trying to communicate with us.

Cindy continued. 'This spirit has been invited into this home by someone who was provoking it!' Cindy was correct, I knew it was a tormented spirit looking for a way out and not being able to find it, it had no intention of leaving as it was gorging on its host, using her to perform its evil activities. Cindy was unable to see the entity, but she could feel it. I could see him, and I did not like what I saw! This malevolent spirit was intimidating and threatening, coming into my space, up to my face and provoking me. It's contorted features and malodorous stench made me gag. Its language was vile and there was no reasoning behind his depraved behavior. I didn't want to spend any more time in the property, I wanted to get out. I was aware the cameras were rolling so I had to stop myself from throwing up on the spot, it was the darkest, most menacing thing I had ever dealt with. Not only were we filming a television programme, but we had a duty to help this family get rid of the negative energy haunting their home. Spirits can sense when you're frightened and I was terrified, but the job had to be done. There was going to be a fight and it wasn't going to be over quickly, it was going to be a long night. The spirit was moving about the house, waiting for us to make the wrong move. I was in a state of fear. It was powerful and I had no idea how we were going to contain this evil force. We had to work together.

It had attached itself to someone in the home. I felt a weight on my chest and a heaviness in my heart, I was beginning to feel anxious as I learned more about this vile entity. Sage and holy water was not going to remove this evil spirit! One of the most dangerous things we do during an investigation is conduct a ritual because it can put us in harm's way. You have no idea what you are conjuring up, and the damage it can do. Cindy was making me nervous as she was taunting the spirit, she may have sensed him and been aware of his disapproval, but I could see him, dart, and move about the rooms. He would mutter and shapeshift. In between his hateful ramblings I discovered he was a murderer, he boasted about killing several men and women in the downtown part of Hollywood, mainly down and outs with no family, the weak and vulnerable of society who would never be reported missing. He chose different methods of execution to avoid detection and slip under the nose of police investigation. Searching out prostitutes, who serviced the needs of the twisted and warped in humanity. His own death was sudden and merciless. Stabbed in the neck by possibly his next victim and left to die. He wasn't ready to leave this earth and wanted to experience his addiction through another living person. Jennifer, Mark's wife!

I was extremely uncomfortable in the location, and I was concerned for everyone involved in the filming. I didn't have a good feeling about this investigation and was struggling with extreme headaches.

I spoke with the producers off camera. My communication with the malevolent spirit was not suitable for the format of the show. Its use of words and gestures was shocking and disturbing, I was unable to repeat them. My purpose in the show was to honour the dead and give them a voice, but its words were not suitable for anyone to hear.

Despite the soaring temperatures outside, the atmosphere and temperature in the house was cold and unnerving. The building was active with all sorts of noises, they came out randomly from various rooms. Recording equipment was failing and batteries were losing their charge. The production team were nervous after one of the girls who was violently sick had to be escorted off the property.

'Don't anger it!' said Cindy 'It's an extremely aggressive male spirit, it's not a demon. This entity is capable of doing a lot of serious damage' Candy was concerned, and Mariah was confused, this was not our typical investigation. I was uneasy. I spoke to camera.

'This is not a typical investigation, and I don't think we should continue; something evil has infiltrated this home. We are hunting a killer and not just a rogue spirit. It needs an exorcist and not a cleansing!'

I asked for the filming to stop and took Cindy and Mariah aside. We all gathered off the grounds of the house, the film crew, and the production team. I told the girls I was not willing to continue as I feared this was a dangerous spirit who could cause a great deal of damage. We were out of our depth, and I demanded we called in a professional from the church. I believed, a priest was required to perform an exorcism on Jennifer and the house. We were dealing with a force so diabolical I refused to stay on the property and walked off. I declined to go back into the house until my demands were met. As I left the property, I could taste the foul smell of the entity in my mouth. I asked for a glass of water and rinsed my mouth out onto the street. I accidently swallowed some of the water.

Normally, between filming I sat in my trailer and listened to music, Simple Minds, Erasure or Sade. It helped me relax and cleared my mind. I had severe head pains all afternoon, normally, I found listening to music helped but not this time. During the break in filming, I grabbed my car keys and promptly left the property. It was about four p.m. as I drove along the Pacific Highway. I realised I was not alone when a disgusting smell overpowered the inside of the car and a vile taste appeared in my mouth. I opened the window and fresh air came flooding in. I knew immediately, I was not alone. My worst fears were happening, it had followed me, it was in my car, trying to attach itself to me. I could sense it. I slammed on the brakes and turned the car around and drove at speed back to the property in the Hollywood Hills.

Back at the house, the production team were waiting on Father Delaney, he was a well know exorcist who lived thirty miles away in Anaheim. The catholic church requires that each diocese has at least one specially trained exorcist, a priest who knows how to distinguish the signs of demonic possession from those of mental and physical illness. I demanded Delaney got here as soon as possible and joined me in my trailer. I was tense and frightened. I had Cindy perform one of her ritual cleansings on me. She burned sage in my trailer and in my car whilst chanting and warning the spirit to leave. I had holy water brought from the local church and splashed it over my face. I even drank some of it from the bottle. I fought hard to keep it off me and out of my body. Father Delaney arrived on site and immediately came to my trailer. I instructed him to re-move the spirit that was trying to attach itself to me. I believe my strength and ability to communicate and recognise spirits saved me from possession. The breakthrough came after I was violently sick and I saw him back off, walk away, head down. I felt I had confronted the beast and won; I was obviously not the weak host he wanted. He left me because he was not getting the addiction it wanted. It was an evil lost soul that had a strong attachment to this world and had become earth-bound. The team and the crew went back into the property where Mark and Jennifer were waiting in the kitchen. The cameras were rolling as Father Delaney and his assistant prepared themselves for the cleansing. They went from room to room driving out the evil spirits which had infested the homeowner and the property. The cameras captured the black mass as it moved around the room. Shifting in shape and size.

'Show yourself!' I called out. The air felt musty, rotten, and unpleasant.

'I can see you and I am not frightened from you, show yourself one last time?'

The apparition appeared long enough for everyone in the room to see it. The footage that was captured was shown all around the world and my celebrity status unexpectedly shot through the roof. Father Delaney and his assistant performed the exorcism on the malevolent spirit and Jennifer, it was performed off camera as Delaney refused to be filmed. Before Delaney left, I shook his hand and he blessed me. I could feel his fear in his handshake. The house and Jennifer were both cleansed and no further incidents were recorded. This episode became the most watch show of the season breaking audience ratings across the network.

The Hollywood Hills house was my last investigation, I left the show, my contract was up. Once I left the show it was never the same, the ratings tumbled, and the show was finally pulled. Cindy and Mariah despised me for leaving and never spoke to me again. Sadly, Cindy died from a blood clot in the brain just after she turned thirty. Chris went back to England and a life of obscurity and Mariah married some studio executive and lived the life she always wanted.

Additional Diary entry - Friday 5th September 1986

I was terrified today. I hide away from demonic spirits as they terrified me, these spirits can attach themselves to you, follow you home and penetrate your life causing personal desolation, damaging relationships, and tearing families apart. Most demonic attachments end badly, either the possessed person takes their own life, or they are diagnosed as psychotic as most doctors are unable to tell the difference between possession and psychosis. Both portrayed similar characteristics, paranoia, inability to concentrate, depression and suicidal thoughts, inability to sleep, anxiety, losing their family bond. It would be extremely rare for any doctor to diagnose demonic possession. Far easier to prescribe antipsychotic drugs to reduce the hallucinations and delusions. I have no desire to conjure up evil spirits and have no idea how to perform rituals. I leave the demons to those who know what they are dealing with as you never know what might come through. Good or bad! Today I faced my ultimate fear, God only knows what would have happened if it had entered my body!

CHAPTER 25

Expect the unexpected

August 1986

"What do you mean my father is here?" I looked at Jemima in total bewilderment .

I sat in my car for a moment thinking about why Bill Jamieson was here at my Malibu home, had Maureen died, was Billy dead, had he come to apologise, how did he know where I lived? I was frightened to go indoors.

As I walked into the lounge, I was expecting Bill Jamieson, it was not Bill, I knew right away it was Jon-Jon O'Malley my biological father. His striking red hair and sparkling eyes looked exactly like mine. I was speechless. He introduced himself as Jon-Jon O'Malley in his thick Irish accent.

'I thought it was time we met.' he said. We shook hands formally and I asked him to sit down. We talked a little, just general chit chat building up to the real reason he was here. He was charismatic and handsome; I could see why my mother fell in love with him. He thanked Jemima who unbeknown to me had taken a call from Jon-Jon asking to meet up with me when he arrived in California on business. Jemima had been trying to find my father for some time with little joy. Notoriously secret, the showmen community was unable or unwilling to help her locate Jon-Jon. They were a close-knit community and wary of outsiders. She had not expected him to turn up at our Malibu house unannounced, but Jemima was comfortable enough to let him wait in the outdoor porch overlooking the beach, knowing I was on my way home.

He sat on the sofa across from me looking tanned and fit, his curly red hair hung just above his shoulders in a wild unkept style. It looked like his hair had not had a cut in a while. He wore a biker's style leather jacket, a white t-shirt and jeans which had faded from wear and tear. He did not look like a wealthy man, but it was clear he was a man of means with a successful family business back home.

We studied each other as we spoke. I had his colouring and features. We had the same smile and almond shape eyes. He talked fondly about my mother Margaret, and he stressed how their relationship was doomed to fail from the start. Age and cultural family differences stood in the way of them every being together.

'It was just a non-starter.' said Jon-Jon in his fabulous Irish accent.

Bill Jamieson and Jon-Jon senior had made it perfectly plain, they could not and would not be together. Jon-Jon was destined to marry another showman's daughter and that is exactly what happened. Jon-Jon said he never forgot Margaret and produced a tattered black and white photograph from his wallet. It showed Jon-Jon and Margaret hugging and smiling into the camera, both looking so young and in love. Jon-Jon said he knew right away I was his daughter when he saw me on the television. Everything fell together, the date, the location, my name, when he saw me in the newspapers and heard me speak on the radio, he was convinced I was his child. The resemblance was uncanny, we even had the same mannerisms.

He was proud of his heritage and culture; he loved Margaret, but he accepted his father's decision and had no intention of disrespecting him. He risked losing his place in the family hierarchy if he were to disobey his father's rules. The O'Malley's traveling fairground had passed from father to son for generations, one day Jon-Jon's own sons would inherit the business as he and his brothers did from his father.

I listened to him talk for hours. He spoke about his role in the family and the close bond showmen have with their extended family.

'We all travel together, grandparents, parents, and children, living, and working together, sharing everything we own.' He made it sound so loving, one big traveling household. It was all they knew, being together. I was envious, I had missed a lot of real family love. I wanted to meet them.

When Bill and Maureen Jamieson discovered Margaret was pregnant, Bill Jamieson was livid, he wanted to find the boy responsible. Margaret had no hesitation in telling them it was Jon-Jon junior O'Malley's baby she was carrying. Bill's secretary was put to work with finding the whereabouts of O'Malley's Fairground. They were on a new site 40-minutes' drive away. Bill got in his car and drove to Hamilton, he was going to give Jon-Jon junior a good kicking, instead he met with Jon-Jon senior. They spoke in his trailer, Bill told him his daughter was pregnant by his son. They decided Jon-Jon would have nothing to do with the pregnancy and the child would be brought up by the Jamieson's as their own. Jon-Jon senior gave Bill Jamieson a one-off payment for the infant and asked him never to be contacted again. Bill stuffed the cash in the inside pockets of his jacket and trousers. Jon-Jon senior would see to it his son had nothing to do with Margaret and Jon-Jon junior would never be back in the Paisley location. Jon-Jon junior married soon after Catherine was born, to a girl from another showmen family. He put Margaret to the back of his mind but never forgotten her.

'You are just like my grandmother, Jinty Malone she was born with the same gift' said Jon-Jon. 'She is no longer with us, but Jinty was highly respected by all the showmen and their families, she was quite a character. Spoke to the dead, she did.' I loved him being here. I could feel Margaret's spirit around us.

He changed the subject. 'Jemima called my office, I recognised the surname, the location and I just put the dates together and it all added up. I knew you were my child.' He spoke with such passion.

I was elated he had come to meet me; I was excited, my mind was racing ahead of myself, I wanted to meet the family, my stepbrothers, and the massive showmen community. Why else would he be here, he obviously wanted to introduce me to the family. The meeting was going so well, and I felt a connection with the man who was my biological father. I wanted so badly to be part of a family unit.

'When can I meet my family?' I asked but the answer came back too quickly, it was a firm 'No!'

'It's not possible!' replied Jon-Jon.

He tried to explain why it was impossible. No one knew about me in the family apart from Jon-Jon senior. Introducing me as his daughter would only cause problems between him and his wife. I would bring shame on his community having had a child out of wedlock with a woman who was not part of his social upbringing. The culture he was born into would not tolerate the dishonesty and he risked losing his prominent position with his peers. He was Jon-Jon O'Malley, patriarch of the family, a respected man held in high regard by everyone who knew him. The community described him as an honest and honorable man, their opinion of him would change if they learned he was my father!

'So why are you here ?' I asked, tears building in my eyes and my temper starting to flare.

'I just wanted to meet you and tell you I never knew the truth about you Catherine'

Yet again I felt duped, why had he come here? He never made any contribution to my upbringing and now he was standing in front of me, bragging about his loving family. His successful family business and his wonderful children. At no point did I hear him say sorry or ask me to be part of his life, even if we had to keep it a secret from the family, I would have gone along with that, but no. It was the same old pattern. I let people into my life, and they break my heart, when was I ever going to learn.

I called out for Jemima. 'Can you show Mr. O'Malley out please, he is leaving!'

He reached out to shake my hand, but I turn my back on him. This is not how I had imagined our first meeting would be. I felt cold and dejected. He had broken my mothers' heart and now he was about to do the same thing with me. My head was pounding as the energy in the room had risen and out of the corner of my eye, I saw Margaret, crying, she walked towards Jon-Jon. She lovingly clasped her hands around her lover's face, Jon-Jon touched his face as if he knew someone was there and for a moment, it looked like they both made a connection, I told him.

'My mother is here; she is beside you.' He turned and looked towards me and said,

'Tell Margaret, she was the love of my life and I loved her with all my heart.' For one moment he placed his hand on his heart, where Margaret had already placed hers. Could he feel her? Did he sense she was in the room?

'I always loved you Jon-Jon.' Margaret whispered.

'And I will always love you my dear Margaret.' he replied!

The only noise in the room was from the waves as they crashed onto the shoreline. Margaret wrapped her arms around Jon-Jon's neck, and I watch him wrap his arms around her waist and kiss her on the lips. What I witnessed never left me, I wanted to ask more questions, I wanted to know how he knew Margaret was dead. Did he have the same gift as me ? On reflection he understood my power better than I did, I needed to know more about my history, especially The O'Malley family, but I knew this would not be forthcoming. Jon-Jon had come to deliver a clear message. Yes, he was my father and no, I would never be part of his family.

Jemima came into the room as Jon-Jon walked towards the door to leave, he turned to say goodbye before he left but did not wait for my reply. There was no mention of another meeting. He came into my life as quickly as he left it. Everything I had ever rehearsed about meeting my father for the first time was forgotten about, I didn't know if I felt sad or numb. I had more questions than answers but let him go. My biological father was alive. He walked unannounced into my life and for a few short hours I was in love, excited, looking forward to the future and meeting the family I never knew and as quickly as he walked in, he walked back out again. Gone. Exactly as he had done with my mother. I never heard from him again.

Jon-Jon junior died several years later and left his fortune and successful theme park business to his three sons. I read about his death in the newspaper. He died in his sleep at the age of forty-nine. All his children were named in his obituary. I was never mentioned in his will or anywhere else. I was the great secret. I did wonder what happened to the old tattered black and white photograph of him and Margaret?

Diary Entry – Saturday 14th February 1987

Another Valentine Day with no beau in tow! Jemima brought home flowers and valentine cards which have been sent to the office by fans, I do not possess enough glass vase containers, so I went down onto the beach and handed out bunches of flowers to everyone I met. Back at my beach house I cracked open a bottle of champagne and sat on my porch and read my book with the noise of the ocean in the background. It was one of the few days Jemima had closed off my diary. Today I enjoyed reading, watching Miami Vice and The Golden Girls on NBC. I had no debilitating headaches today; perhaps, the champagne keeps the pain away! Happy Valentine's Day.

Romance eluded me. I envied Jemima who chopped and changed her lovers as often as her clothes. She was a free spirit and loved being in love, meeting someone for the first time and falling in love, getting to know all the wonderful new things about the men in your life and feeling the adrenalin rush around your body when they called you on the telephone. Once that started to deplete for Jemima, so did the guy.

I was never asked out, I thought being famous made you more appealing, it had the opposite effect for me. At home, I was very much alone most of the time. The never-ending array of functions, and events that I was invited to, I found boring and pretentious. I only attended if I absolutely had to. Going outdoors had started to get more difficult and a lot scarier. You cannot become as famous as I was and not be recognised, you can't have that career with that level of fame without taking all the abuse that comes with it. Not everyone likes you. I was not emotionally wired to be famous. I was never able to deal with the intrusion into my personal life. Because of my past issues with individuals, I was not willing to let just anyone into my private space, so I put up imaginary barriers.

Often, I felt like I was trapped in a gilded cage simply by the nature of my work. I was a workaholic and found it difficult to switch off. It was hard to trust anyone, so I kept my distance when it came to meeting members of the other sex, Jemima told me I frightened them off. I understood I was the subject of much press speculation and interest but most of the material written or said about me was incorrect, it was pointless trying to rectify it, so I didn't. Everyone wanted to analyse me, stick probes onto my head and record brain waves. The sceptics wanted to catch me out and prove I was an imposter, the more evidence I gave them the more they hounded me. It took a long time, but I finally learned to ignore much of the outside pressures.

Dating opened me up to being misquoted by the dishonest element that tries to befriend you, so I chose my friends carefully. My moto was, 'Never stop being a good person because of bad people' I was unwilling to be any man's badge of honor and perhaps I gave off a vibe that said stay away! My trust issues made me paranoid, and I sought solitude at my beach house. It would have been so easy to fall into a reclusive lifestyle, but I had Jemima forever filling my diary with work and managing all the madness that was my life. She truly was my rock and I relied on her much too much.

I was driven by fear, the fear of losing it all, losing the fine things in life I had grown to enjoy. My beautiful home welcomed me like a big hug each time I came home, I loved the property so much I bought it for well over the asking price. I had regained financial security and felt so blessed. I never tired of the adulation but being famous was overrated. Being famous is like a sickness, you love all the attention but it's the confinement that makes you ill. One poll put me in the top twenty of the world's most influential women. Influence them to do what? Fame comes at a great cost, your sanity, your privacy, and your soul. It's emotionally and spiritually exhausting, everyone wants a piece of you, managers, fans, the media. I could never have imagined in my wildest dreams I would have so much wealth and power in my lifetime. I could never have imagined the loneliness and suspicion that came with success. Some people love you and others absolutely hate you and neither are uninhibited in telling you how they feel. It takes a certain type of person to tolerate the continual interruptions in your private day to day life. I grew tiresome of it all. At times I was exhausted and often thought about pulling the plug on my career. I had evolved from girl next door to global phenomenon. Critics had such a challenging time deciding on why I had been so successful, what was my talent ? I could talk and see people who were dead, it may not have been a talent in the conventional sense, but it was a gift none the less. Some days it felt like a disability. I had all the fame, and all the wealth, but this was not where happiness was. I was sick and tired of everything I did being under a microscope and analysed. There was no relief from it all, it was relentless. The continual intrusion into my life was making me more of a recluse. To sustain such a crazy existence was no longer tolerable. I had made enough money for everyone, agents, accountants, Jemima, and myself. It was time to get out of the media spotlight and think about the future before I was ravaged by depression.

***

Jemima closed off my diary indefinitely from 1st April 1987 and I made my way to Peter and Irina's palatial home in Majorca. Jemima returned to London to be with her family. As usual the Malones welcomed me with open arms. I wanted for nothing, and I spent the next eight weeks concentrating on my inner self. I had always struggled with my weight, so I focused on getting into shape, both physically and spiritually.

I did a yoga class every day at the villa along with Irina. I drank little alcohol and swapped my high calorie American burgers for lean chicken and a mediterranean diet of tuna salads, olive oil and fresh fruit. I was allowed access to Irina's personal trainer who put me through my paces, he put a training plan together for me which made working out fun. I soon learned to really enjoy exercise, especially when I could see the change in my body shape. Peter would laugh at the various detox concoctions we created in the kitchen.

'Irina doesn't eat any more she refuels.' laughed Peter.

I had long conversations with Peter and Irina about my career, they cared for me unconditionally and never asked for anything from me. A huge part of the best part of my life was when I was with them. Max joined us most evenings, he remained forever young and full of energy playing with the lights and the baby grand piano. Peter and Irina would spend the evening rejoicing in his presence.

Majorca saved my sanity. I fell in love with the island, I fell in love with me, and I fell in love with life. I had stopped the noises in my head and the pain in my heart. I felt ready to return to America and resume my career, at a slower pace.

Dairy entry – Friday 5th June 1987

Flying home today to America. I had the most horrific nightmare on the flight back home. I dreamt I was pregnant and had lost the baby in the most traumatic circumstances, it just goes to show even flying first class doesn't always allow for a great sleep! All the way back I was uneasy and feeling sick. I hate flying, especially on my own.

I felt and looked fabulous. I had lost a lot of weight and the yoga had toned up my body, my skin was lightly tanned, and I had blond highlights put through my thick red hair which had been cut into a short bob that sat just above my shoulders. I not only looked physically different, but I also felt different. I was ready to face the world. In Majorca I had started to jog along the beach, nothing too strenuous just a few kilometers each morning with Peter's dog and one of Irina's Russian bodyguards. I was looking forward to jogging on the beach in Malibu.

When I arrived at my Malibu beach house, Jemima was already there. She had prepared lunch and lost no time in telling me all the gossip from back home.

'I have some wonderful news for you.' said Jemima 'Guess who is three months pregnant ?'

'I have no idea, tell me who?' I asked with little enthusiasm due to jet-lag.

'Me!' screamed Jemima.

I was delighted for her. My best friend was having a baby. Whilst we hugged, I had the most horrendous feeling about this pregnancy. I instinctively knew this child was going to be born dead!

Diary entry - Thursday 12 November 1987, My 27th Birthday.

Happy Birthday to me! I've lived such a full life and yet I am only 27 years old, I've learned to lower my expectations if I want to be happy with myself and life. I have everything but love. If I had one wish it would be to have Jim in my life. I have never recovered from the emotional trauma of losing him.

I am a traditionalist ; I am affected by tradition. I am just a page in its book, and I want it to be a good page. It was traditional for me to write my diary page every day, recording my feelings and emotions, documenting my deepest thoughts and experiences. My diaries were free from judgment and criticism, initially they were written as a pastime as I enjoyed recording my day-to-day activities. As I grew older, they became records of my moods and feelings. My diaries were personal and intimate thoughts laid out on paper, laced with honesty and sentiments. They were not for public consumption. Not yet. In my mind, I had preserved my life in words. They were part of my legacy, I envisaged my journals being passed onto my children who would read them and have a greater understanding into how their mother lived, my likes and loves, how my mind worked and how I independently flattened a path through the madness that was my life. I had fed on problems and obstacles and grown from them. I wanted my children to know no matter what situation or conflict I had to endure I never gave up. I never threw in the towel, I simply used it to wipe my tears away and got up and got on with it. I wanted to choose who saw and read them.

You can't imagine my utter shock when some of my personal entries from my diaries were published in a trashy American magazine. I hired an attorney to get the diaries returned but the damage was done. The culprit was the cleaner, a woman who Jemima and I had trusted to come into our home, clean, shop and go, turns out she had been helping herself to money, food, clothes, and anything else she thought would go unnoticed. We had become complacent, leaving things about the house as we felt our home was a secure place. The diaries would have gone unnoticed until the whole of America started reading them standing at the supermarket checkout. I felt violated, my personal life invaded and most of all let down by yet another human being. I made a conscious decision that no strangers would be welcome into my home or in my life.

Jemima often had people telephone her at home, when they called, I would leave the beach house to give her some privacy, descending the twenty wooden steps down onto the beach where I would jog along the sand. I never received telephone calls from my family back in Scotland. They no longer wished to have anything to do with me. Whilst I ran along the edge of the ocean, I decided to reach out one last time to Maureen, Bill, Billy, and Mary. I was going back to the UK in a few months on business and decided I wanted to meet them, iron out our issues, for the last time.

Dairy Entry – Tuesday, 1st December 1987

To sell out not one show but three back-to-back performances in New York has blown me away. Tickets sold out in 24 hours. For those that have paid good money, stood in a queue to buy tickets, supported, and welcomed me back to New York, I promise to put on the performance of a lifetime. I am truly blessed.

I was treated like royalty whilst staying at the Plaza Hotel. My suite overlooked Central Park where I walked each morning with my cup of coffee and a minder. One morning I was convinced I saw John Lennon, sitting on a bench smoking a cigarette. He lived in the Dakota building one hundred yards from where I saw him, and he loved to walk in the park with Yoko Ono. I said to the minder. 'We just passed John Lennon sitting on a bench.'

My minder smiled and asked me, 'For a cup of what I was drinking!' We both giggled and continued with our walk.

Diary Entry - Tuesday, December 15th, 1987

I was being interviewed on a radio show by controversial rock radio DJ Randy Fools and his madcap studio team. The show was fast paced and full of wise cracks. Randy had a wicked sense of humour and a massive following of listeners. Even the ones who hated him listened in to his daily show just to hear what he had to say. Controversial and loud. His show had the highest audience figures in the lucrative ratings war and Randy and his posse took the station right to the cusp of the radio authority regulations, pushing the boundaries in the interest of gaining more listeners and being even more controversial. The production was slick, fast, and even the most serious guests were subjected to ridicule and humiliation. Today, a couple from Hollywood who organised ghost tours had taken photographs of spirits at a 'haunted' cemetery in California. She claimed to be a psychic medium, but she was a fake. They both took their jobs extremely seriously and were on the show to promote their business and the afterlife! Her faced dropped when I walked into the studio. Randy was in his usual high spirits, his posse hanging on his every word. The studio was loud, laughter, clapping, cheering. The odd couple were dead pan serious talking about their graveyard sessions and passing round photographs that Randy painstakingly mocked as he described them to the audience. I listened and enjoyed the banter in the studio, it was well rehearsed and yet came across as spontaneous. Randy orchestrated the team like an expert conductor, when to laugh, when to clap, when to cheer. He brought me into the conversation by asking.

'Surely all graveyards are haunted, goes with the territory, right Cat?' He was deadpan and yet clearly ridiculing the odd couple.

My reply was straight to the point. 'Most graveyards are not haunted, think about it, why would a spirit linger in a grave-yard a place where they never spent time in life, so why stay in death, it's just a place for the resting body and nothing more.'

The odd couple gave me a look of total disdain. I was dissing their claim to the existence of haunted cemeteries. The studio phone lines all lit up.

Randy, no stranger to controversy was enjoying rocking the boat. The studio descended into chaos as he answered tele-phone calls from listeners, putting them live on air. Callers were screaming at the couple and calling them fakes. One lis-tener went as far as to say they had cheated her mother out of money after they claimed to have contacted her deceased father. The couple may well have come into the studio with the hope of advertising their business, they certainly got the publi-city they wanted but it wasn't the positive feedback they were expecting.

During all this madness I got summoned to take a telephone call, it was urgent. Jemima had gone into labor and was on her way to hospital. I made my excuse and left the show. By the time I reached the hospital Jemima had given birth, the little girl was stillborn. Jemima was inconsolable with grief, the father of the child sent flowers but never visited her. He couldn't, he was a married man who chose to stay with his wife and not his lover.

Thankfully, her mother and sister were already on route from London. It was a tough time for everyone, especially Jemima.

The following day we were back at the Malibu house, Jemima sunk into a major depression. Her mother and sister stayed longer than originally planned as we took care of Je-mima's needs. She was hearing and feeling things she could not explain, she told me she could hear a baby crying and felt her baby kicking inside her. She cocooned herself in her bed-room and asked to be left alone. Once or twice Jemima saw me leave the house to walk along the beach and she joined me. We said nothing and just walked and listened to the sound of the waves. Slowly the grief lifted, and the crying stopped. The pain had been absorbed and her smile came back to her face. One afternoon as Jemima sat in the sunshine, I saw the child snuggle into the side of Jemima as she lay on the deck chair. I said nothing as I did not want to upset the moment. I never saw the child again or heard her but knew she was at peace. Jemima said she would never come to terms with not being a mother, I knew in time she would heal but for now we all had to help mend her broken heart and lift her spirits. She called the little girl Angel. It was truly a fitting name, a little human being of such extraordinary beauty who would always be remembered and loved.

CHAPTER 26

We reap what we sew

Tuesday, 1st March 1988

I brought home two twelve-week-old mongrel dogs from the animal shelter. They were going to be put to sleep as the shelter was full and the puppies needed urgent medical attention which the shelter could ill afford. I paid for the veterinary work, and the dogs joined our family. I called them Bill and Ben after a children's television cartoon I loved to watch when I was a little girl back home in Scotland. Bill and Ben, the Flowerpot Men. The puppies were a wonderful distraction in the house. They brought a great deal of fun and mischief to our home and were adored and pampered by Jemima. They gave her a much-needed outlet for all her love. Inevitably the puppies became her substitute babies.

I tried yet again to send some love to my family in Scotland, but they ignored my request to fly over and restore our broken relationship. Mary responded almost immediately by fax. She was thrilled and looked forward to introducing me to Vanessa, her two-year-old daughter, the news came as a welcome surprise and despite our previous run-ins I was excited to see them. Both Mary and Vanessa would be flying out to join us in a few weeks.

Diary entry – Monday, 4th April 1988

We reap what we sew. If you start something good, you get something good but if you start something evil, well, you tend to get something evil in return. This is what I love about my life, I try to do something good passing on the love from the spirit world to the living. I am fascinated by the mystical activity I witness daily. I am invited into a stranger's home, and you never know what is going to happen when you get there. Not everything is as it seems and never are two consultations the same.

A black Mercedes came to pick me up prompt at 8am, I was travelling to Beverly Hills for a private meeting with a wealthy business woman who had flown in from New York to meet me. I knew little about her and that is exactly how I liked it. She introduced herself as Carol Weller. She was recently widowed, inheriting millions of dollars from her husband's estate. Despite her wealth her life had been overshadowed by her dominating husband, in death as in life he continued to control her. Carol radiated wealth; her home was magnificent. She purposely took me through the enormous living area and out into the garden. We sat beside her swimming pool as her housekeeper served English tea and finger sandwiches. It was all very refined. I didn't feel the need to get involved in any small talk and got right into the session. I watched Carol intently, she came across as calm and professional. As I listened to her talk about the 'dangerous male entity within the house' I could hear recurring words in my head, they were repeated over and over.

'Failure is not an option; failure is out of the question' she grimaced when I said the words aloud. Turns out, this was the line her ex-husband would yell at her over and over. He was a successful businessman, who was not renowned for the way he treated his employees. If monthly sales targets were not achieved, heads would roll. You were only as good as your last sale and if you couldn't run with his rules, you were shown the door.

Her magnificent house was heavy with bad energy, and I could feel something wasn't quite right. There was a female and a male presence in and around Carol. Just like my public performances, during my private sessions I have no filter. I would say what came into my mind or reveal whatever the spirit wanted to say.

'Your mother is beside you.' Carol flinched, her face went pale, and she almost knocked over her China teacup. Her mother had grey hair and was petite in size. She looked like old money and was dressed in a Chanel style suit. She had so much to say, it was easier for me just to repeat everything she said rather than summarise what she was saying. I switched on my cassette recorder and began to talk.

'Your mother says you looked after her all her life now, she wants to look after you. She wants you to be strong and follow your feelings, she is telling me you learned from her. Now this is her way of warning you, don't fall into the same trap she did.' I stopped to sip my tea and listened to what she wanted me to say next.

'Do you understand what I am saying ?' I stopped for a moment to get Carol's approval.

'Yes.' She replied. Her façade had dropped as I dug deeper into her mind and private thoughts. She confided in me that her mother suffered from severe depression and took to her bed for days on end, Carol and her father took turns to look after her. Her mother and father were not a good match, her mother confessed she married for money and not love. I began to speak.

'You have married for money, and you will pay the rest of your life just like your mother did.'

Carol threw me a look of contempt; I was revealing too much of the truth and she wasn't at all happy. Marrying for money, a common component in a lot of Beverly Hills marriages. It didn't start with Carol; she merely inherited this trait from her mother who married for the same reason.

Life isn't about being rich, well-liked, or perfect. It's about being real, modest, and kind. I knew this from experience but so many people especially in this town only ever chased the former, it was all about the money, who had more, who had the best, the biggest, the most expensive. Wives were replaced faster than their cars and women turned a blind eye to their husbands' infidelities. Everything was disposable and replaceable. Women in this town either put up or shut up. Most Beverly Hills middle-aged women I had encountered, lived a lie, pretending to be content but merely existing within a miserable marriage waiting for their shelf lifetime to come to an end. Living in Beverly Hills was like watching a beautiful swan move on the river. Above the water it was elegant and controlled but underneath they were paddling like crazy.

'Your mother is always about, supporting you, she wants you to know this man might be stronger than her, but he has something he needs to communicate before he moves on.' I had Carol's full attention.

Carol claimed she was being terrorized by what she believed was the spirit of her late husband, she wanted to know why he was here and why he would not leave. It made sense that he was the one causing all the disturbances in the house. Carol admitted her personality and mental health had declined since the hauntings started. Whatever was affecting her behaviour was inside the house. Despite looking strong and in control she confessed to being deeply depressed. There was no love in her voice when she spoke of her deceased husband, Howard. I could sense Carol felt uncomfortable when I questioned her about him. Something wasn't quite right, so I asked her permission to summon him. I had to know why he was angry and unable to move on. Carol claimed she was the victim of a horrific marriage. I had to hear Howard's version as often things were not all what they appeared and there were always two sides to a haunting! Carol said she never got to carry out her husband's final wish after his death, she insisted he asked to be cremated and his ashes scattered out at sea. Mysteriously, his ashes went 'missing' from the funeral home, she reported them as stolen but, they were never found.

During our conversation, at no point did she show any emotion about her deceased husband. Back in New York, Howards family wanted a traditional burial in the

Hamptons and were furious at Carol's decision to go ahead with a cremation. Could this be the cause for Howard's unrest and his anger towards his wife or was there something more sinister at play.

Howard didn't take long to show himself. As I walked back into the house, I was drawn to a large room that was being renovated. Inside what was once Howard's office there was an unnatural shift in the energy. Howard was here, he was standing by the huge fire; he appeared as a large foreboding figure with no hands or feet. The area around him was ice cold despite the scorching heat outside. This dark menacing figure was angry and troubled. I asked Howard to talk to me, he asked for help! I could feel his sadness as he began to speak, what he told me was distressing!

Depending on how we die our souls can remain in limbo for a period of time or they can be trapped in a location. If they are not ready to cross over their spirit remains earthbound. There are many varied reasons the dead do not move on. Sprits may be trying to get something done which they were unable to do before they died, or they may have an important message they want the living to know about. Howard blamed his wife for his death, she left the property whilst he was having a life-threatening asthma attack. As she left the house Carol removed his inhalers from around the home. Those that remained had been drained rendering them useless in an asthma crisis. Howard panicked and tried to crawl to his car to retrieve another inhaler but collapsed and died before he got there. He was found by his distressed housekeeper.

Howard in death was unwilling to forgive his wife for having him cremated. Carol had omitted to tell me Howard was Jewish; it had been some time since he had seen the inside of a synagogue but a Jew none the less. Howard was outraged at being cremated on the Jewish Sabbath, the Saturday, it commemorates the original seventh day when God rested after completing his creation. Howards immediate family expected their son to be buried and not cremated. Generally, the destruction of the body is forbidden in Jewish law.

'It's against my beliefs to be cremated and she was aware of this, my body was destroyed, my physical body belonged to God.' Howard was enraged.

'It's in gods' hands now I said. 'He is the one who loves us, God knows you were wrongly cremated.' I sympathised and had empathy for the dilemma he faced upon death. I knew enough about Judaism to know millions of Jews had been killed and cremated during the Holocaust, under these and other circumstances rabbis agree that Jewish law does not apply. This offered no real consolation to Howard. He had pledged to make his wife's life 'one of a living hell' whilst he remained in the earthly realm. Howard was so traumatised by his death he missed his opportunity to see the light and cross-over. He had now become stuck in the physical environment.

As is the Jewish custom Carol had Howard's funeral within 24 hours. The only people to be contacted were work colleagues and out of town friends. Many of whom were unable to attend the service. Carol was extremely careful to inform non-Jewish acquaintances. His family were contacted after the cremation.

It was a truly appalling mess which could not be rectified. Carol had put the error down to her personal assistant not sending out the announcement until it was too late. A heinous and unconvincing lie.

Howard told me his wife had his two loyal Doberman Pinchers put to sleep after his death. She always hated the dogs in and around the house, they reminded her of Howard. There can never be a reason to have two healthy dogs put to sleep. It should never have been allowed. Howards Persian cat was found in the swimming pool around the same time.

'She drowned her!' he yelled. 'That bitch kill her, my cat would never go near the pool!'

Carol's calculated coldness infuriated me. I had arrived at her home expecting to find a woman terrified by an unknown entity which she claimed was haunting her and her home. Instead, I was faced with a cruel and vindictive woman who believed with her husband dead she could enjoy her life without any remorse for her actions. Carol had been unable to evict the tormented entity she correctly identified as her late husband and instead resorted to assigning me to cleanse this emotionally charged property, but I decided I was not going to do her dirty work. Howard had no intention of moving on whilst his wife was still alive. Instead, he projected anger and negativity towards her, it was exactly what she deserved.

Howard Weller in life, had been a domineering harsh task master, a cantankerous and unhappy individual who spent a great deal of time either working or enjoying time with his loyal dogs and cat.

He was protective of his wife despite her loathing of him. He shared his life with a woman who felt nothing for him, she had no respect for him in life and even less in death so maybe he had every reason to delay his final departure from this world. Carol had intentionally calculated the humiliating desecration of his body and Howard was determined to seek revenge in death. He told me his truth and for the first time I supported his energy manifesting in the home. I was unwilling and unable to guide his spirit to the other side until he had accepted his death, his presence was going to be here for some time yet.

Carol Weller had well and truly made her bed and now she had to lie in it, no matter how uncomfortable it was going to be. She was destined to be haunted for much of her life, no matter how many homes she purchased, Howard would follow her. Carol Weller got what she deserved. We reap what we sew!

I ended my communication with Howard before heading back outside. I found Carol Weller sitting in the shade by the pool. I made my apologies and explained there was nothing I could do as the spirit had refused to leave the property and I wished to have no more to do with the haunting. There was nothing else to say.

She branded me a fake, a time waster and demanded I return her fee. Her change in personality resembled that of a socio-path. She maintained eye contact with me as she defended her compelling and believable lies. This woman was a cold-hearted murderer, she had gotten away with killing her husband.

'I know what you did Mrs. Weller. I heard it from your husband's mouth. I know about the asthma attack, leaving him to die, the inhalers, the dogs, the cat.' Carol dropped her fake smile and sat back in her chair, possibly thinking about how she would get rid of me.

'Have you heard the expression; we reap what we sew Mrs. Weller? You married your husband till death you do part, did you not?'

Carol gave a slight nod and said nothing. Her look of total disdain was enough to convince me she was a cold-hearted killer.

'How well do you know the works of William Shakespeare Mrs. Weller?' Carol looked baffled.

'Read Hamlet's soliloquy. To be or not to be. I fear you will carry this burden until you shuffle off this mortal coil'

'What the hell are you talking about you are making no sense, I am starting to wish I never invited you here, you are quite deranged!' I looked at Carols revealing face, there was guilt written all over it. 'Mrs. Weller, in short, Howard will be here by your side until you die and join him!' I inflicted the final blow. I lifted my bag, the tape recorder and left the premises. When I looked back Howard was standing by the library window. I waved him goodbye accompanied by a wry smile. I listened to the cassette recording in my car on the drive home. I heard Howard say thank you before the tape became mangled inside the cassette player and snapped.

I suggested to Jemima we deposit Mrs. Wellers fee into a charity box for a local Doberman Pinscher dog rescue. Whilst there, our attention was drawn to a puppy with the most amazing story. He had been named Howard by the center. It seemed like an omen, he was found in a dumpster, starving and near to death, he had lost an eye during a beating but fought to survive despite the odds. A few days later, I took him back to Malibu with me, he deserved a forever home full of love. I renamed him Mr. Thor; little did I know how much love he would bring into my life.

Diary Entry - Friday 15th April 1988

Let the madness commence, we have a toddler and three puppies at our home, all fighting for our attention, but the biggest diva is Mary, she demands more attention than the others combined!

Mary and Vanessa had arrived, and the house was turned upside down. A toddler and three puppies make for an extremely noisy house. It was wonderful. Mary was like a tornado hitting your home, she was a force of nature, rushing about, causing a mess and a trail of destruction behind her, bringing a mansion size personality to a beach hut size house. She was never going to be mother of the year, it simply wasn't possible, what mother sleeps through her own child crying? Her priority and first love in life was herself, it always had been. She loved Vanessa, which was abundantly clear, she just didn't know how to love her. It reminded me of Gran, she found it extremely difficult to show any affection, but I knew she loved me. Mary had developed a sense of entitlement and simply expected to have whatever she wanted, whenever she wanted it. Vanessa was a beautiful looking child with an adorable personality, sweet and sharing. She must have taken after her father as I recognised none of these qualities in her mother. Jemima was in her element looking after Vanessa, preparing her outfits, changing her nappy, and feeding the child. Mary was happy to let her get on with it, back in Monaco she had two nannies to look after the child. Mary was smart enough to know, having Pierre's child made her financially secure for the next eighteen years.

Mary updated me with all the news from home, as she stayed in touch with Billy from time to time. Maureen and Bill were back together, they had become drinking buddies both enabling each other on their need for alcohol. They were both alcoholics. The need for a drink was greater than the desire to eat. They both placed alcohol above all other obligations including work and family. It was a sad situation.

Bill retired after Thomson Pumps was bought over by an American company and a new Managing Director was put in place. He lost his sense of purpose and his lover who moved away to be with her sister. He had no hobbies and struggled to find a pastime that entertained him enough to make it enjoyable. Playing golf simply led to drinking sessions in the club house, followed by more alcohol with Maureen back at their home. Mary said Maureen was an alcoholic with little time for anything else, living on vodka and a slice of toast per day was only going to lead to an early grave. Our brother Billy had lost his job and had settled on a life of drugs and petty crime. He tried several times to sell a story about me to the newspapers, but they no longer found his material credible and refused to interview him. Mary said he was old before his time. He hung about bars in the hope his reputation and relationship to me would earn him a pint or two. He was an embarrassment to the family and was known to the police having been caught shoplifting, stealing alcohol and other petty theft crimes. It all seemed a million miles from my extravagant lifestyle. I no longer recognised or connected with anything from my up-bringing back in Scotland. I had worked hard; I was like a phoe-nix who had risen from the ashes, having reached rock bottom I had started out again, working hard, and focused. I was proud to be Scottish but had no desire to return and live there. Now I was a success, on my own terms. I did not need the humiliation my family brought with them, I was not embarrassed about my past, but I could not condone their lifestyle of petty crime and alcoholism. I had reached out too many times. As I sat in my Malibu home, I recalled growing up in our dysfunctional family, moving out of our rat-infested tenement into our new build council house, it all seemed like a distant memory. Back then we were content with our lot because we knew nothing else. Now, when I reflect on my childhood, I struggle to remem-ber anything beautiful, it flatlined for me some time ago. I was extremely lucky to have broken the cycle and got out, moved on, made a good life for myself in America. I had everything I could ever want, money, success, and fame, I lived in a fabu-lous home in Malibu, I had everything except a family. What I wanted could not be bought. I craved a partner and a child of my own. It hadn't transpired yet but there was still time. In-stinctively, I knew it wasn't going to happen.

Success - I put it all down to Maureen and Bill and I thanked them for that, if they hadn't pushed me out of their lives, I might never have taken the path I did. I thanked Jim, he urged me to achieve all I could from my life, he was my soul mate, and he would never be replaced. He believed in me and never asked for anything in return except love. I missed his love every day.

I was enjoying Mary's company; I had forgotten what a wonderful sense of humour she possessed. During our long conversations sitting out on the decking, I guessed there was more to come from Mary, and I was right. She and Pierre had separated. Mary said the marriage was over a long time ago, but never said if there was anyone else involved. Pierre agreed he would support her and their daughter but only if Mary stayed clear of any controversy and kept his name out of the press. A private man, he didn't want the world to know anything about his personal life. Mary had agreed so long as he kept her in the lifestyle to which she had become accustomed. This wasn't possible as Mary's demands changed from month to month, her spending knew no bounds. Mary was unable to keep to a budget and spent her husband's money at an incredible rate. When he had his lawyers chastise her on her overspending, she threatened to expose her husband's personal life through the newspapers. She fabricated stories and Pierre was forced to use the courts to control and silence her, it was the only way, otherwise he could be extorted by her for the rest of his life. I listened to her go on and on, pleading poverty and being a victim. I knew Pierre had had a rough ride with Mary, she was high maintenance and self-indulgent. There was no reason for her bitterness, the marriage was doomed to fail from the outset, like everything in her life, Mary's love had to be bought. I have no doubt little Vanessa had been brought into this world as a bargaining tool. As she raced around the decking being chased by the puppies and Jemima, I felt sad for the little girl. Her multi layered mother was just waiting on Pierre negotiating on the child's future. All Mary wanted was for the child to go back to her father, Mary to move back into the family home, and for her monthly allowance to be reinstated. Everything had its price, even little Vanessa.

When Jemima retired to bed along with the child and dogs, Mary and I sat on the decking listening to some music. Belinda Carlisle sang, Heaven is a Place on Earth on the radio before we put George Michael's 'Faith' album on the turntable. It was a beautiful evening, the full moon reflected off the ocean and the waves crashed onto the shore. I was enjoying every moment; I had no difficulty bonding with Mary as she opened-up to me about her life. For a moment, she dropped the egotistic pretense and the fake accent, it felt just like it did when we were little, when Margaret, Mary and I snuggled up together in bed on those long chilly winter nights in our damp bedroom, with the ice on the inside of the windows, tucked into bed with the army blankets which made your skin itch.

As I cleared up, Mary ventured down to the beach, she wanted to stroll along the coastline before bed. We had been drinking so I asked her not to go into the sea. After an hour I became increasingly worried, there was no sign of her. Mr. Thor was barking at the house, I signaled for him to follow me, down onto the beach. I picked up my flashlight and shone it down the beach and over the water. I couldn't see anyone in the distance. I began to panic. Mary had drank too much alcohol and I shouldn't have let her go off on her own. I ran along the beach calling her name. My worst fears were realised when Mr. Thor came across her shoes and dress on the sand!

I called the police; the following morning the police confirmed the body of a female had been found a hundred yards along the beach from my home. A postmortem confirmed she had drowned. I identified her body and broke the news to Pierre. He was broken and asked for his daughter to be flown back to France. I duly obliged. He sent the nanny ahead to accompany the young child on the long flight back home, I knew I would never see Vanessa again. She gave me the biggest smile as she was carried from the beach house by the nanny. Pierre had requested for Mary's body to be flown back to Monaco where he would conduct a private burial. Pierre was discreet and dignified, he conducted himself in the most professional manner to protect Vanessa. Mary's untimely death affected me deeply, I blamed myself as I should have gone with her down onto the beach, I would have stopped her going into the water for a swim. Despite being a strong swimmer, the mix of cold water and alcohol was a deadly cocktail.

I did not attend Mary's funeral; my attendance would have sent the paparazzi into meltdown, and I wanted the funeral to be respectful and private. I said my goodbyes to Mary before her body was sent back to Monaco and her final resting place. I heard through the media grapevine, Bill and Maureen did not attend their daughter's funeral.

Peter and Irina sent me and Jemima flowers, they asked me to come and stay for a few weeks at their Florida home, but I declined, I wanted to spend some time alone at the beach with Mr. Thor who seemed to sense I was broken and needed mended. It took a few weeks for the media to stop printing articles about the drowning, some of the copy that was written was so offensive and slanderous it shocked me to my very core. Being in the public eye can often be destructive. It has a bright and dark side. One minute they adore you and the very next they are ripping you to shreds. Thankfully, none of Peter's publications followed the story out of respect for me and my sister. For days, a helicopter circled above the house as we hid inside away from the cameras glare. The public are obsessed by celebrity and my privacy was ignored by paparazzi in their quest to get a photograph for their editors. It was a challenging time for everyone. I was thankful dear Vanessa was so young, she would have no memories of her mother as she grew up. I could only hope they would say good things about Mary as deep-down she was a good person. I knew Pierre would provide all the love the little girl would require. It was the perfect outcome for him. Pierre said he would 'keep in touch' but we both knew he wouldn't. Vanessa would be protected and hidden from the public glare, and that included the association with me. Staying in her life would only create publicity around her and draw attention to my niece as she grew up. I understood Pierre's concern and thought best not to pursue any visiting rights to the child, after all Mary was not my biological sister.

***

By the summer of 1988 I was heavily involved in producing my own television shows and selling them to various television networks. 'The Catherine Jamieson Experience' proved extremely popular very quickly, bringing in huge ratings and popular with advertisers. The thirty-minute show featured me, going into the homes of the famous and speaking to deceased family or friends who had a message they wanted to pass onto the living. The format was ridiculously simple and cost so little to produce and edit. The interest in the show was way off the scale. For me it did three things:- It gave me the power to create unique and entertaining content which viewers wanted to watch and in turn generated a lot of money for my business, it showcased me to the American audiences and raised my celebrity profile by keeping me in the public domain and finally, and more importantly I was steering the ship, I was in complete control of my business, both financially and creatively. With so much at my fingertips why wasn't I happy?

Jemima had returned to England to be with her family for a few months and I missed her dreadfully. I was taking the next step in my career on my own and I was terrified. The stress resulted in painful headaches. When these came, I would take to my bed with the dogs and close the blinds.

Despite attending private clinics and paying for the best consultants in the country there was no concrete diagnosis on what was causing the head pain. Prescription painkillers made me feel queasy and dazed but it was the only treatment that had any success in lowering the pain. Over time I learned to live with the discomfort which increased during and after communicating with the spirits.

CHAPTER 27

Meet Chad

I met Chad of all places on the beach. I passed him each day whilst I was out jogging along the shoreline with Mr. Thor. I said hello and he said hello back. One day, he turned up at my beach house with some flowers and a verbal invitation to attend a party further along the beach. I was thrilled, he was lovely, very down to earth and his intentions seemed genuine.

'Hello, I'm Chad,' his teeth and tan were perfect, very Malibu.

'We pass each other every day, I wave at you, and you smile, so I thought, I'd ask you to join me and meet the neighbours at a house party a few houses along the beach, no catches, just some laughs and some good company, what do you think?' He waited for my response. How could I say no.

I loved his approach, straight to the point, it was refreshing. Chad became a terrific addition to my summer. Having Chad in my life reduced my stress levels, he was so laid back and never seemed to be fazed by anything. He no longer needed to work, and had sold his travel company a few years before, he now spent his day's hanging about the beach, kayaking, enjoying healthy food and good company in the evening. He was a free spirit, carefree and in charge of his emotions. Chad had no interest in designer clothes or fancy cars, he never discussed money and by all accounts came across as unassuming and down to earth. He owned one of the most expensive houses on the beach and drove a beat-up old car. He was a maverick and lived by his own rules, he did as he pleased when he pleased. My headaches were less frequent when I was around him simply because he was so relaxed. His attitude was 'life was too short' I liked this. I think he was good for me despite the age difference, he was fifteen years older than me. He never asked anything of me and was completely oblivious of my celebrity status. Chad had no desire to be seen in any media pictures with me or partner me to any high-profile events. I understood his reasoning behind this, not everyone wants to be the partner of someone who is in the public eye, especially if you have chosen to escape the rat race and opted for a quieter life by the beach. I could see a future with him, my biological clock was ticking so loudly I was convinced you could hear it. I desperately wanted to have a child but Chad, much to my surprise absolutely forbid it. It was gut wrenching; he was happy with the relationship as it was, but I wanted to start a family so badly. The thought of going through life and not being a mother was not something I had ever considered.

Chad was great fun and I adored spending quality time with him, but I was not the only love interest in his life.

He was not into commitment and used the term 'hopeless romantic' as an excuse to date other women behind my back. He might have been a man who didn't follow the rules, but I did. I was a one-man woman and was not willing to share my man.

One afternoon I was jogging along the beach with Mr. Thor, and he started to run towards Chad's house, I called him back, normally his recall was excellent, but he continued to run up to the property and onto the front decking. Mr. Thor sat by the patio doors and waited for me. I sensed something wasn't quite right as I bent down to put on his lead, I peered through the glass door. What I saw almost made me swallow my tongue. I fell backwards and tripped over Mr. Thor, he let out a yelp and so did I!

Chad was shagging the brains out of a leggy blonde who was

on all fours on the sofa. He was going at it like a Grand National jockey, I was mortified and stunned into what to do next. Another naked leggy blonde appeared and started to snort cocaine off the coffee table! She looked up and pointed at me outside on the decking and without a word of a lie she screamed.

'This coke is incredible; I can see that psychic bitch Catherine Jamieson looking at me guys!'

I made a hasty retreat and what turned out to be a relaxing jog became a four-hundred-yard sprint back to the safety of my house. I was out of there. I was in shock. Confusion reigned and I stayed off the beach for a few days simply to avoid seeing Chad.

A week passed and he never called me, no explanation no apology. A week before Christmas my status was back to being single, by Boxing Day I was officially over him.

CHAPTER 28

A new decade

Diary entry – Wednesday, 15th November 1989

As I was driving along the Pacific Highway, Neneh Cherry was playing on the radio, 'Buffalo Stance', I love it , it's an amazing song about strong women. Strong women like me! I went from an enormous high to a tearful wreck as Kate Bush sang 'This Woman's Work', one of the most emotional songs I have ever heard. Absolutely awesome! The world seems to be filled with so many wonderful female singers, Annie Lennox, Lisa Stansfield, Stevie Nicks, Madonna, and the all-girl band The Bangles. Us ladies are taking over the world!

By November 1989, I was celebrating my television production company having a top five ranked evening show in the Los Angeles Metropolitan area. After New York, Los Angeles was the second largest media market in North America. My company, CJJ Broadcasting was the region's largest independently owned television corporation. Our rise had been phenomenal, and I put our success down to our creativity and honesty. I was never constrained by what our studio executives expected of me. I just did what I did, and no one questioned it, if it didn't work, we pulled the plug on the filming. It was that simple. Our paranormal shows were authentic and unmissable. We produced two of the highest rated tv programmes in the region. I was in negotiations to syndicate the shows across America in a deal which would have made millions of dollars. It was an exciting time in my life.

I was 29 years of age with a business acumen which would

have put a Harvard business professor to shame. I had vision, I surrounded myself with good people who had the same vision as myself. My team and I produced incredible content which in turn created dynamic programming. There was an insatiable demand for the work we were producing but more importantly, Jemima was back.

The television executives loved Jemima. Her quintessential English accent, public school etiquette and her masterful use of vocabulary, opened all the right doors around Hollywood. Jemima was a true English rose, she never went to the beach or sat in the sunshine. Her pale skin was flawless, always basted in a high factor sun protection lotion and her face was always shielded by a large floppy hat. She was the only person in my life I trusted, and we made a formidable team, a power couple, two powerful women in Hollywood, it was a unique situation. Jemima prepared a three-year business strategy which focused on our commitment to make innovative television shows and pilots. All my private appointments were halted unless the clients were prepared to pay a four-figure fee for a one-to-one private consultation. Jemima was building our brand, an exclusive brand, she had set up a price which only allowed the wealthy access to my diary. Basic economics, supply and demand, the demand for my service was exceptionally high, and this was reflected in the cost. I had no competition; I was the only genuine psychic in the world, no one came near me. The back lash to this was from the media, they slammed me for 'selling out' and 'snubbing those who had supported me in my rise to fame.' Just like the cynics and disbelievers I completely ignored them. I had every right to reward myself with as much money and power as I could create. Touring was out of the question; a one-off show was approved, but that was a year down the line, this would be televised as part of a pay per view deal. Peter Malone and I were in discussions over this event, but the time and venue had to be right. I wanted to broadcast from Madison Square Garden, but the venue was booked on the dates we submitted, Peter wanted to broadcast from Las Vegas. Pay per view viewers would be guaranteed a premium seat at this one-off monumental event. It had proven successful for boxing events generating millions of dollars. It would give the world access to a live performance and not just the wealthy. Everyone would pay the same ten dollars; everyone would have the best seat in the house, and everyone was welcome, there would be no travelling expenses and we could never sell out. I wanted the world to join me. It would be one of a kind, it was to be called - Cat Jamieson World Arena Show.

Twenty dedicated team members were focused on one thing, creating high demand television shows, pilots, and one-off specials. Jemima stepped up to the mark and created a production team of young, dynamic, new starts who had little or no experience of television production but were enthused with original and creative ideas. We met at our newly acquired downtown Hollywood office and brainstormed ideas, the people, and places we wanted to investigate and interview. Within our team, ideas and enthusiasm were abundant, we often ran over the allocated time for our brainstorm meetings as the team were obsessed with creating new and original formats. There was a creative buzz in the building. We were all contributing to programming which was changing the way people thought about the paranormal. Was there such a thing as a haunted building? Was there life after death? Only the dead and myself knew the answer to that question.

I had an account set up with a local pizza company and anyone who needed to eat could call them and they would send a delivery to the office. It was a staff incentive long before its time, but I wanted to show my appreciation for all their arduous work and commitment. Those who stayed behind to work late had dinner on me. I allowed the team to come to work dressed in a relaxed casual fashion, I believed, if you felt relaxed it allowed your creative energy to flow more easily. I took the dogs into the office whenever I made an appearance, I also allowed the team to bring their dogs into the office on a Friday. It made for a nice vibe, chilled and tranquil.

Ideas were for sharing and that's what we encouraged the team to do, to put forward their suggestions, no matter how bizarre or crazy. In return, the team member was paid and credited for the idea if it was used. Ideas are evolution, they are open to anyone once they are out there, so it was important we were first to get them out there to our millions of loyal viewers. The crew became pioneers in the field of paranormal television shows and our young team members were credited for their input. The 1980's was the decade of greed, we wanted to make the 1990's a decade of trust and reward.

In June 1991 we recorded a new episode for our number one television show 'You won't be Alone', the format was like our other award-winning shows, after all I had no other talent, and it was what the viewers wanted.

I surprised members of the public who wrote to me concerned about their home or their place of work being haunted. I literally turned up with a film crew on their doorstep un-announced. As always, I investigated and documented my findings. I would communicate with the spirit or entity and pass the message to the living person being affected. I then would try to resolve the situation or help the spirit move on. Not every visit was a success and I introduced new 'psychic mediums' into each episode. They helped me determine if there was an actual haunting to be investigated prior to me being involved. This allowed the production team to eliminate time wasters who fabricated stories in the hope of appearing on the show. It also created visibility and publicity for new up and coming psychic mediums.

Based on my troubled upbringing I was keen to find apprentices who had the 'gift' of talking to lost souls on the other side. It's important people recognised that mediums are just ordinary people who have the unique ability to fill the void between the living and the dead, some mediums communicate their messages well and others choose not to divulge their power for fear of attack and intimidation. Suppressing your psychic gift can lead to depression and a solitary existence. Either way, one should not be ashamed or try to hide their spiritual talent.

When I advertised for psychic apprentices to apply for several positions within the company the production team were inundated with letters from all over the world. Telephone interviews were conducted, and the candidates were shortlisted. Those selected would be offered a position with my company and a base to stay with other team members at our West Hollywood apartments. Under my guidance I wanted to eliminate their concerns and offer encouragement, develop their talent and ability to communicate effectively and efficiently. I understood the complexities of having a spiritual gift and I took it upon myself to educate and inform my apprentices how to safely communicate with the spirits. I would give them the means and the tools to embrace their gift. It's one thing having a gift, it's another thing using that power to communicate a message from the dead to the living. A psychic medium must possess some basic core skills, they should understand grief and be sympathetic about the loss of a loved one whilst providing accurate information, their name, description and specific characteristics of the person who is dead. So many mediums have no idea how to pass on a message that makes sense. I was here to nurture their natural ability and incorporate a little of my teachings into each episode. I was the teacher, and the apprentices were my students. The format was another success for our company.

Carl Steinbeck – big shot movie producer

Whilst on location, and the cameras were running, things took a turn for the worse on one episode. Carl Steinbeck was a bit shot movie producer, his home in Bel Air was magnificent. The haunting was reported by Mr. and Mrs. Waites, the husband-and-wife team, who worked as housekeeper and chef at Steinbeck's house. The Waites had both seen shadows and witnessed things moving in and around the house, they were a middle-aged English couple and came across as dependable witnesses. The security cameras had recorded the garden chairs moving by themselves beside the swimming pool and a football and tennis balls rolling about of their own accord beside the tennis court. Some investigation was conducted to ensure things were not being moved intentionally and by all reports everything would appear to have been legitimate. The Waites didn't look like the type of people who would make up stories about a haunting.

The culprit of their haunting was identified within minutes of me entering the house. It was Misty the Golden Retriever, a fifteen-year-old dog who loved the couple so much she refused to leave after dying. The atmosphere changed the minute Misty was mentioned, she was a much-loved dog and was sadly missed. Misty had not crossed over rainbow bridge but stayed with her owners. Once we established it was man's best friend, Misty, simply playing with a ball at night, some of the stress began to dissipate. Misty was a gentle, playful, blond Golden Retriever who was adored and sadly missed by everyone. She sat by Mr. Waites leg, looking up adoringly at her master. 'Go ahead and throw the ball' I suggested to Mr. Waite. He looked at me as if I were mad. I handed him a tennis ball. 'Go on, throw the ball.' He threw the ball and Misty chased after it. The ball could clearly be seen moving along the side of the pool before it rolled into the water.

'I see Misty isn't keen on going into the water, how odd for a Golden Retriever not to do this as they love the water so much!' I said as I watched Misty pace along the side of the pool eyeing the ball.

'She won't go in the pool. She had an accident as a puppy and almost drowned, she has been terrified from the pool ever since!' Mr. Waite was delighted to hear his loyal dog, Misty, was still about, in spirit form.

'Misty will only pass over once you join her Mr.Waites'

Over the years, I had seen many loyal pets who have died but remained with their owners. They wait for us and walk with us in the afterlife, their love never dies.

Carl asked to be included in the filming as he mentioned the tale of Misty haunting the house would make a great theme for a movie. We all went into the house, and I asked the new apprentice, Sarah, to concentrate and tell me what she was picking up on. The minute I started filming with Carl, I was overwhelmed with a great sadness. I looked at Carl.

'He's here. He's in this room, I need for you to show yourself?'

The colour drained from Carl's face.

'Who is it?' asked Carl. 'Who am I speaking to?' I asked.

The spirit answered my question. 'It's your father.' I replied. Carl displayed genuine fear.

'My biggest fear was you would make connect with my father; I was terrified of him.' Carl's fear was genuine, the cameras kept rolling. I had my apprentice beside me.

'We all did everything to keep him happy as he had a terrible temper.' Carl continued to speak oblivious to the cameras in the room, he eyes darted from corner to corner, they were full of panic. Why was he so frightened of his father?

'Show yourself!' I demanded.

This was his father's chance to come through and speak out. Jonathan Steinbeck appeared to me, he stood behind his son. He was a powerful energy who commanded your attention. He had the look of a man who was prepared to fight and had the scars on his face to prove it. He wished to communicate; he had a lot to say before he was willing to move on.

I asked everyone to clear the room as the camera continued to roll. It was just me, Carl, and Jonathan. I gave him the opportunity to speak with his son through me. Almost immediately I could feel there was a lot of emotion in the room. I repeated what Jonathan said.

'I had a gambling addiction that ruined an important financial situation, I gambled the money we saved for a deposit on a house. I neglected my family, I left them without while I spent my money at the racetrack or playing cards.' he confessed.

I felt the need to pinpoint things that were accurate to gains Carl's trust, so I repeated what Jonathan said word for word. I continued.

'Your father died alone but he was accepting of this, he has no idea what killed him, he went to sleep and never woke up. There was no pain no suffering' Carl's father was a functioning addict; he gambled any money that came his way and even with a considerable win, he found it hard to quit and would inevitably gamble his winnings. It was a repetitive cycle.

Jonathan's mood was determined on whether he had scored a few winners or had lost money. A tough day at the racetrack resulted in his wife being subjected to violence and beatings. The family lived in fear as to what state he would be in when he came through the front door.

Carl's mother couldn't cope with the violence and the gambling and moved back to stay with her mother. Alone with a child to raise was no easy task in 1960's America. Struggling to manage Carl alone, his mother was unable to cope. Through no fault of his own, Carl ended up being raised in numerous foster homes.

'I loved my horses more than my family.' Jonathan confessed. Carl was eleven years old before he was allowed to go back home to his mother.

Carl became emotional as he reflected on his difficult childhood, despite everything, he loved his father and missed him terribly as a child.

'My father would sometimes be allowed weekends with me; I would wait all day for him to turn up and sometimes he never showed up. As the cars went by the house, I would pray the next car would be his, it rarely was' Carl admitted with tears in his eyes.

'I was that little boy who was left on the doorstep' he was visibly upset as he recalled his painful childhood memories.

'If he *did* turn up, he would head to the bookmakers, and I would sit in the car with some lemonade and a bag of crisps whilst he gambled any money he had.'

Carl forever put his father's addictions down to himself, blamed himself for the fighting between his father and mother. His father had once told him he should never have been born, he never forgot this. Carl carried a lot of secrets that had been lost in history. Recollecting old memories was only digging up the past, Carl was prepared to face his demons but less willing to face his father. I was validating my communication with the spirit of Jonathan Steinbeck and Carl was terrified.

'Am I in any danger being here?' Carl asked. I told him 'No' – I lied!

Jonathan Steinbeck was not only a compulsive gambler but a violent and abusive man who wreaked havoc on his families lives. His mother said it was an illness and everyone should understand his outbursts, the family were expected to tolerate his irritability and walked eggshells around his bouts of depression and guilt. He would steal and beg for money, if pleading failed, he would resort to violence. It was a mother's rage and a father's burden. Jonathan Steinbeck was not a man who apologised.

I told Carl his father was so sorry and apologised profusely for all the pain he had caused him, his mother, and the family. To have Jonathan apologise was a shock to Carl. When he was alive, he had never heard his father say sorry to anyone. He was too conceited. In life Jonathan Steinbeck was not a loving, diligent, conscientious parent. Like all addicts he was a liar and a thief.

Jonathan was always a distant father, fierce and intimidating. Carl could never get passed the superficial side of him.

' I always understood why he did what he did on an intellectual level but emotionally I could not understand!" said Carl, as he searched for meaning in what was happening. Old wounds were not going to be healed just because Jonathan had come through to regret his earlier actions.

'Your father says he loves you very much, his fondest memory is of you and your new bike on Christmas Day.' Carl confirmed his father's memory and added, the bike was later sold by his father to a neighbour, the money was instantly lost on a horse race. Carl had to watch the lad next door ride about on the bike, another horrible image burnt into his memory.

'Carl, you must let go of this burden, you did not cause his addictions and your father is here to tell you he regrets all the damage he has caused. He says he is proud of you.' I could only pass on the message, but I feared the words fell on deaf ears. Carl acknowledged he was stunned and was struggling to understand what was happening, his father's regret would help him on his road to recovery, but healing would take a long time. Carl may never fully recover from his father's actions.

Jonathan Steinbeck came across as sympathetic and repentant, however, his powerful presence said something else. He filled the area with negative energy, the environment felt oppressive and upsetting. In death as in life Jonathan Steinbeck brought mixed messages into the room. Was he compassionate or just malicious? Carl never had the support of his father growing up but, in time he would let go of his burden. With therapy he would slowly start to feel loved and inspired.

The hurt caused by his father would need to be accepted by Carl before he could finally feel free from his control.

There was no plausible explanation for what happened next. A recording device picked up a man crying and then asking to be forgiven. It was an intelligent Class A recording, caught crystal clear on the tape recorder. Carl recognised the voice immediately; it was his fathers!

EVP, also known as, Electronic Voice Phenomena, is the recording of spirit voices. Sometimes they can sound very mechanical but on this recording the voices had a human tone and sounded natural. EVP was open to conjecture and ridiculed by many skeptics but there was no doubt the male voice on the recording appeared to be answering directly to our questions. Only I could see Jonathan. I asked him to show himself and appear to his son. Suddenly the lounge was full of energy orbs, shooting around the room, beautiful little balls of pure energy. Many people claim these orbs are the manifestation of ghosts, other claim they are simply dust, pollen, or insects in the air, like all matters associated with the paranormal, there existence may never be proven. Jonathan came forward and wrapped his unseen arms around his son. Carl looked at me, his eyes wide open.

'I can feel him!' he was startled. The cameras were still rolling as Carl broke down and sobbed.

'I love and forgive you father!' he cried out.

'I can rest easy now, knowing you love and forgive me son,' said Jonathan.

The room began to shake, I thought for a moment it was an earth tremor but quickly realised it was Jonathan's energy leaving the room and moving on. Such was his sheer presence and power; we all felt the forceful energy exit the room, even those outside the building witnessed the shaking. A frightened Sarah came in and stood beside me. What we then witnessed next was not captured by the camera as it was just out of shot, it was however evident by Carl's stunned response he could see something that terrified him. It was Jonathan, he made one sudden appearance before he vanished and was gone, forever. Both Carl, Sarah and I saw him. It was the end of a troubling haunting and a classic case of a spirit unable to rest until it had passed on a message to a loved one. What had once been residual energy full of suffering, pain and aggression had now moved on to rest in peace.

Because of my sensitivity to the spirits, they can completely drain me of all my energy. I have such a strong connection to them as their channel for communication I have a duty to pass on their messages to their family and friends. Carl was able to validate Jonathan's presence, he saw and heard his father speak. It was the greatest proof I could have asked for. Once the room settled and Carl's anxiety eased, both he and I held each other tight as we reflected on what had just happened. The sun's rays defused through the window blinds and cast shadows across the carpet, the spirit had gone and the energy in the room lightened.

I told Carl I was looking forward to seeing the edited highlights of the live film footage as it would make great viewing. Carl's face immediately changed. He refused point blank to approve the use of any of the recordings taken in the lounge. His whole persona changed, he became abrupt and asked me to leave. He asked for the cameras to be removed and for us to 'get out' the house. It was a strange and ominous change of demeanour. Before we left Carl asked for the Kodak film from the recordings, I refused to part with it and left the house distraught and flustered. On the roadside one of the cameramen recorded my disappointment as I said my piece to camera about what had just taken place. I wanted to capture the moment and the emotions into which I was tapping. As expected, my head pains were horrendous, and I ended up being driven back to my home in Malibu with a cover over my head to keep the light out. The evidence we had captured was groundbreaking and I am certain the episode would have been a massive hit, but Steinbeck had no intention for any of it to be aired. He certainly preferred being behind the camera and not in front of it!

Within days I was served legal papers by the biggest law firm in Los Angeles. Carl wanted all the film to be sent to his office. If I divulged or aired any of the footage that was captured within Mr. Steinbeck's property, I would be sued no doubt for millions of dollars.

Carl and I know what really happened that afternoon, so I left it like that. He had too much power and influence over Hollywood to pick a fight with. He knew everyone and was well respected by all the major studios and television networks and I didn't need the grief, so I sent him the tape and moved on. Not before I had it copied ofcourse!

Science has a long way to go to proving the existence of the afterlife, but what Carl Steinbeck saw that afternoon proved beyond all reasonable doubt, ghosts do exist!

CHAPTER 29
Travelling Back Home

Diary entry – Sunday, 10th November 1991

Travelling back to Scotland to film a documentary about my childhood. Travelling light, myself , Jemima and four of the crew. There's a lot of excitement as none of the team have been to the UK. Jemima has put together a spreadsheet scheduling all aspects of the filming. I've bought everyone sweatshirts, walking boots and padded jackets as they have no idea how cold it's going to be. Four days in Scotland and three days in London.

It was odd booking first class flights for me and Jemima whilst the rest of the crew were in economy or 'steerage' as Jemima referred to it. I wasn't comfortable with the idea, so I had Jemima negotiate flight prices with the airline for the crew to travel in Business Class.

I knew the moment we were flying over Scotland as we descended into the dark foreboding grey clouds. I have never landed at Glasgow airport and not come through thick rain filled clouds, it was a sign of what was to come. I predicted, rain, wind, sunshine, and sleet all the seasons, often in the one day. Zip up everyone, we had arrived.

When you're Scottish you carry it with you everywhere you go. I don't miss my home, but I am proud of my heritage. The America audiences loved my Scottish accent. It was bittersweet being home. As we departed from the plane the icy North Sea wind hit me square on the face, I welcomed the familiar cold damp air, it tasted fresh and clean in my lungs compared to the oppressive orange smog of Los Angeles. On a hot sunny day, the orange smog is one of the few air pollutants you can see. Malibu offered a cleaner natural environment compliments of the Pacific Ocean.

The filming schedule was full on. We visited Paisley, the town I was born in, I was surprised to see the original tenement we lived in as a child was still standing. The camera captured my reaction as I stood outside the familiar building, I once called home, it had been destined for demolition and only escaped the wrecking ball by a whisper when a private developer bought the building and converted each apartment into modern refurbished one and two-bedroom flats. The sandstone bricks which use to be black with soot had been sandblasted clean and were now a wholesome blond colour. New double-glazed windows replaced the bulky sash windows and a door entry system for security had been installed. Originally, three flats occupied a landing now it was just two. Where there had once been twelve homes there was now only eight. Each with their brand-new bathrooms, central heating and fitted kitchens. I was excited to see inside our old flat. The professional couple who owned it had agreed to let me film inside for a small fee and some photographs with them. It was barely recognisable and yet strangely familiar. I stood in what was once our old bedroom and closed my eyes. I could hear Margaret and Maureen reading aloud from the Jackie magazine, problem page and Billy play his Subbuteo soccer table game. We were happy despite the building being overrun with rats and seriously overcrowded. The house may have been modernised and updated but my memories remained the same. I wasn't surprised to see Billy, the little boy who died, still sitting on the landing steps. He was bouncing a ball and looked blue in colour. He glanced at me, smiled, raised his thumb, and then disappeared; it was almost like he was acknowledging my success. I could hear cantankerous, old Mr. Robertson coughing from his emphysema, the noise resonated around the stairwell. I remember a neighbour saying to my mother, he smoked over one hundred roll up's a day. God knows what his lungs must have looked like when he died. The building was still alive with the spirits of the dead. Perhaps they had come out to welcome me back.

Filming was easy, it was so natural to talk about what you know and love. I was used to working in front of a television camera, I could normally do my piece to camera in one take. The sun stayed out and the sky was blue whilst we were filming in Seedhill Road. We managed to finish recording ahead of plan with minimal interruptions. The minute we finished filming the sky soon clouded over and we had our first major downpour of rain. It was as if the heavens were crying, we were leaving. We filmed at my first primary school and then at the fashion shop I had work at when I was a teenager. Jemima had done her research and I was joined by an old friend from secondary school. We had tea in a cafe in Paisley, the owner's son was a rock and roll star and most of the time the café was full of fans who lived in hope their idol would suddenly walk through the door and start waiting tables. Gillian was a girl I knew from school, we had been friends for a while then she met Jim, they became inseparable and soon after school they married and moved away. Gillian was back home now staying with her parents. Jim had died, he dropped dead at home in front of the children from a heart attack whilst she had been out shopping. She sat in front of me dressed like a woman in her fifties, drab and grey like most of the people of the town. As I looked around everyone looked like they were just existing and not living. There was no colour to their soul. I was sad to see Gillian had let herself go and looked older than her years, the once attractive and fashion-conscious young girl I knew had gone.

The cameras were rolling when Jim joined me, he sat beside Gillian in the alcove seat by the window. He looked just like he did in high school.

'Jim is here, he says to tell you, he's not happy about you

giving up the flat?'

I had no filter and started to repeat what Jim was saying. Gillian was stunned, she continually glanced at the cameraman and the production team looking for an answer to what was going on.

'Jim says enough of the dwelling about the past, it's time to pick yourself up and make a life for you and the wean.' (Scottish term for child) He had so much to say, it made great television. I asked Jim to verify who he was, and he came up trumps. He told me several private messages that Gillian confessed were correct. He described their home and spoke about their last holiday together with the baby to a caravan park in Ayr by the sea. I was not a medium and could not predict the future, but I could sense Gillian would leave today knowing I had genuinely communicated with her deceased husband. Jim said he wanted her to enjoy her life to the fullest and he would wait for her. Gillian said her husband, Jim, was her hero. It was during times like this I craved my own hero, someone who would love and wait for me. As time progressed, I feared I would never find a forever partner. There was no Mr. Right in my life and there hadn't been for some time. I would even have settled for a Mr. right now if truth be known.

Gillian signed her agreement to let the company use our film footage. I enjoyed the time I spent with her, we use to be such good friends, one of the few I had. I asked Jemima to pay Gillian double our agreed fee. We promised to stay in touch, but you never do. My lifestyle had changed so much I could no longer relate to the people or places I knew from my childhood. What would our telephone conversations sound like?

'Eh, hello, I had dinner with Elizabeth Taylor and Michael Jackson tonight at a gala ball, how was your day? How was your cleaning job and did the social security sort out your family allowance money?'

Jemima had contacted Maureen and Bill and they agreed to

meet me whilst I was in Scotland. A corporate suite was organised at a prestigious hotel in Glasgow and a chauffeur was
booked to pick them up and bring them to the meeting. As part
of the agreement Bill had requested a fee to appear on camera.
Jemima had organised the £3000 to be deposited in his bank
account on the day of the meeting. I was extremely nervous
and suffered a terrible headache which threatened to stop the
filming and the meeting going ahead.

I bought gifts and booked a private table for dinner. Thinking
ahead, I wanted to invite them to my Malibu home, they would
love it there. My intention was to hold out an olive branch and
put behind us any issues they had with me, start afresh. They
were due to arrive at 3pm. I watched as a chauffeur driven
Mercedes drove up to the grand reception entrance. I rehearsed
in my mind what I would say as they came into the room, my
heart was pounding. I checked myself in the mirror and took
several deep breaths. Jemima went downstairs to the reception
to meet them as I paced the room. She came back five minutes
later to tell me they had not shown up. The Mercedes was for
someone else. I was upset but not surprised. I rarely could predict the future!

The crew had the day off and travelled to Edinburgh for some
well-deserved sightseeing. I was delighted they were having so
much fun. For me, there really was no point in staying another
night in Scotland so I had Jemima organise a private jet to take
her and I back to London. A driver took me straight to The
Savoy where I was welcomed by the butlers as if I owned the
hotel. I called Peter Malone and broke down on the telephone,
he and Irina were at their London residence, and we met up for
dinner and drinks. They treated me like family and that was
enough for me. I was angry at myself for being so gullible and
sensitive, I had let my guard down. I enjoyed a few days alone
in London while Jemima spent the time with her family. As far
as I was concerned I with spending time with my real family,
The Malones.

Summer 1992

I think many people would sell their souls to be wealthy. Its human nature to continually wish our lives away, hoping for money, success, keeping up with the jones and having bigger this and better that. There are so few people happy with their lot. The saying, 'money doesn't make you happy' must have been penned by someone who had little money because let me tell you, I could not be without my wealth.

'You can't buy happiness' sure you can, the thought of how much money I have certainly brings me a great deal of happiness. However, the thought of losing my wealth is a persistent worry.

I live a very privileged lifestyle and have no intention of spoiling it. Losing my capital and social status doesn't bare thinking about. For me, there is no going back, I don't think I could survive.

Monetary loss can increase the risk of suicide. I have encountered many spirits from all walks of life, who chose suicide to deal with the pain and depression of losing their livelihood. It's never the right answer and those left behind are left to pick up the pieces. When I communicate with these spirits, they tell me they ended their lives because they couldn't face the embarrassment, it was too much to live with. Losing their job and security had left them in such a depressive state they were unable to face the disappointed from family and friends. Losing respect from their peers was just too much and they are unable to face the world after being judged a failure. Stop! Think about those you are leaving behind. Suicide doesn't stop the pain; it hands it to someone else. It's a permanent solution to a temporary problem. All suicide souls have a sad story, happy people do not take their own life. One such earthbound spirit I faced was a young lady who committed suicide after losing her West End career.

Chloe was a dancer and a beautiful singer, well on her way to becoming the darling of the West End in London. Theatreland had been calling her name for many years, her career had been arduous and challenging but hard work had finally paid off. Now, she was a success and enjoyed her status within the theatre community with celebrity friends and acquaintances. A viral infection soon put an end to this. Her vocal cords became inflamed and damaged. She ignored doctor's advice. Desperate to return to work, she never took enough time to recover before heading back to the stage. Having lost her voice and with no signs of recovery her career collapsed, and her mental health was severely affected. The show must go on and cast members are replaced without a second thought, in time, when you are out of the public domain audiences soon forget who you are, there is always someone waiting in the wings to take your place. If a celebrity is out of sight, they are out of mind. Sadly, we are all replaceable.

After months of depression, Chloe threw herself in front of a train. Her dental records were her only means of identification. Ironically, her final act of taking her own life put her name back out into the public domain, she was front page news and her suicide featured on the evening news bulletin on the BBC. Her tragic demise was the subject of several television talk shows and radio phone in's. Chloe was gone, she had struggled emotionally and thought she was alone. Chloe believed no one cared but so many people loved her, but you don't know this when you feel so low. Suicide is so final; we all want to say 'Stop! Come back, you have proved your point!' But it's too late.

Family and friends had all taken their eyes off the ball and now she was gone. Her friends listened but they never heard her cries for help which were hidden deep in her conversation. They didn't listen enough when she was alive, now it was too late, she was dead. Suicide spirits often come to me with a sense of regret, the aftermath of their death profoundly affects everyone around them. It was like throwing a pebble in the lake, this single act is followed by a series of ripples and there is no way of telling where or when these ripples will end. The feeling I got from Chloe was that of extreme grief and sorrow, it was a spur of the moment act, a cry for help gone wrong, if she had only waited another few days her life would have taken such a dramatic turn for the better. But surely someone who wants to die from suicide just wants to die ? No. Chloe didn't want to end her life, she simply wanted to end the pain in her life, she didn't know what else to do. She roamed the earth, sad and alone, afraid to go into the light. Like a fragile little bird, you would never have guessed this was a woman who had filled west end theatres, enthralling audiences with operatic arias and popular hit songs. Chloe had not accepted her death and had delayed moving on, despite my attempts to persuade her. Unable to use her own body she was desperate to undo her error and eager to enter another body which would allow her to use their energy to stay connected to this world. After many hours, our war of attrition was over when I was finally able to summon Chloe's deceased mother who came forward and guided her daughter into the afterlife. Only then could Chloe rest in peace, free from any shame, guilt, or fear.

Diary entry – Thursday, 12th November 1992

I used to be an optimist, that's one of the most pessimist things I can say, I use to be an optimist! It's my birthday, yet another one without a man in my life. Still, forever the optimist! Jemima gave me the most beautiful diary and a box of Scottish fudge and tablet made on the island of North Uist in Scotland. Jemima told me, she explained to the lady the fudge and tablet was a gift and the order was required as quickly as possible. Jemima said the lady was called Agnes MacDonald and she did not do anything in haste! In fact, on the island she said there was no word for 'quickly' as they were so laid back. How wonderful. Just like the fudge and tablet.

Jemima was dating Tom Truman, an executive producer for a large television network in Los Angeles. He was handsome, intelligent, courteous, and wealthy and I hated him, I knew he was going to take Jemima from me, and he did. They announced their engagement at my birthday lunch, odd timing I thought as he produced a massive diamond solitaire ring and slid it on her finger. Jemima had everything I wanted, she had sex appeal, every man I knew thought she was attractive and flirted with her outrageously. She had incredible style and good manners. Beautiful inside and out, Jemima could interact with anyone. Everyone fawned over her, she was everything I wished I could have been and wasn't.

She had been a loyal friend and business associate; I was exceptionally lucky to have her by my side. I knew what was coming but didn't want to hear it. I wasn't her mother, and she wasn't my sister, but I relied on her so much I could not tolerate her leaving me, but I knew the day had come. I could see the fear behind Jemima's eyes as she began to talk.

'We've decided to move in together, we want to set up a home, try before you buy if you like!' I liked her approach, a bit of comedy to soften the blow. Ever the gentlemen, Tom had his arm around her waist the whole time. I lifted my Baccarat champagne flute and congratulated them.

Diary entry - Saturday 5th December 1992

Whitney Houston was belting out 'I will Always Love You' on the radio. It was number one in the American charts. I turned the volume down as I was fed up hearing it. I bet Dolly Parton isn't ! Wow! how much money has that unexpected hit made her. It has just gone 8am and I am in my perfect place. Sitting on my patio, overlooking the beach, coffee in hand, watching the waves crash on the shoreline with my dogs by my side. This is my go-to place and I just love it. Its Saturday and I am enjoying a well-deserved day off, reading the newspapers, TIME magazine had Princess Diana on the cover.

Living on my own wasn't so bad, I have got the dogs and a stray cat that visited ever now and again when it wanted fed. I got myself a housekeeper but only after a vigorous search, references, and recommendations from friends. I was so guarded about my home and personal life I wasn't willing to just let anyone into it. Dottie was a fifty-year-old Irish woman who came recommended by a friend of Peter Malone. She was everything I could have asked for and was completely oblivious to my fame. Dottie was a feeder. She would load me up with lots of carbohydrates in the shape of delicious pasta dishes and stews with dumplings. I ended up putting a lot of the weight I had lost back on as I could not resist her food. I would immediately go to the fridge after I had been away all day on set or in meetings just to see what she had prepared for me. Good comfort food always satisfies. Dottie was just what I needed at the right time in my life. She had a fabulous sense of humour and I adored her Irish accent, the American accent begins to pull at your ears when you continually hear it.

Dottie kept her cards close to her chest when it came to talking about her family, but I never thought much of it. I was starting to trust people again and the vibes I got from her were of honesty and loyalty. Two components money could not buy. Fate had brought Dottie to me, and I was soon to learn our paths were strangely linked.

Diary entry – Sunday, 7th February 1993

Charity event at The Beverly Hills Hotel. I cannot be bothered going but Jemima has called in sick, and I need to host the table we have booked. My anxiety has brought on a dreadful headache, do you think I would get away with not turning up? Would anyone notice? Ofcourse, they would!

I met Tony Valance at The Beverly Hills Hotel; he had an intellectual dry wit, and I did nothing but laugh all evening in his company. I was so pleased I went; he was the best thing about the evening. He was a guest at my table and the minute we were introduced I was hooked! Everything about him intrigued me. He was typically, tall, dark, and handsome, old enough to be my dad and had a tan to challenge George Hamilton. He owned a real estate company with offices all over California. His company only represented the extremely affluent. I was over the moon when he invited me to a cocktail party in Calabasas. Tony and I met several times, each time at events he had been specifically invited to. Restaurant openings, a jewellery launch on Rodeo Drive, a rock star's housewarming, new club opening on Sunset Boulevard. He certainly had a hectic social life. I was falling in love; he was saying the rights things and I was enjoying his company. He would come over to my Malibu home and stay overnight and I visited his magnificent house off Mullholland Drive. I even met his daughters and son.

We had been going out a little over two months, it had been a real whirlwind romance and I was enjoying the excitement of being in love. One evening, we went to dinner at The Beverly Hills Hotel, the place where we first met. A car came to pick us up at his house. When we arrived at the hotel, he asked me to tip the driver which I thought was odd, so I gave the driver fifty dollars and went inside to the ever-discreet restaurant. After a romantic meal Tony asked for the bill.

'How do you want to split this, down the middle?' I was absolutely mortified and at first thought he was joking. This man was a multi-millionaire and was asking me to split the cost of a dinner.

I looked at him totally aghast. He dug a bigger hole by saying,

'You asked me out for dinner so technically I should be asking you to pay for the meal!' He laughed out loud, and I desperately wanted him to jump up and scream 'Joke!' but no. Tony was deadly serious. I made my feelings known about his lack of manners and when I opposed and declined his *kind* offer to split the bill, his personality changed. It wasn't the cost of the meal it was the approach and the mentality of the man; this was supposed to be a romantic dinner for two. He excused himself to go to the washroom, I waited twenty minutes and he never came back. I settled the bill, and the General Manager organised a driver to take me back to Malibu.

I never met Tony Valance again socially. I think I had a lucky escape. On reflection, every event we went to was invitation only, with a free bar, buffet, or dinner. I never once seen him put his hand in his pocket for money. He was the strangest character I ever met, and they say the Scottish are tight fisted!

Diary entry – Tuesday, 23rd March 1993

Bombshell has been dropped! I feel physically sick! The chances of this happening must be a million to one!

It took me a few days to comprehend what just happened. Dottie had accidentally dropped her guard and discussed personal details about her family back in Ireland. It started out as an innocent conversation over a cup of coffee. I listened as she spoke about her strict upbringing and how she had been rejected by her family after meeting a young man. She fell pregnant at 18 and decided to marry the baby's father, his name was Justin Basa and as far as her family were concerned, he was the wrong religion and the wrong colour. Their violent marriage lasted a little over two years. Justin and Dottie left Ireland and set up home in the London Borough of Tower Hamlets in his mother Pearls, council flat. Dottie hated everything about the family, the house and the area and made plans to escape from the minute her son, James was born. It took six months, two black eyes and several broken ribs before she could escape from her living hell, but she stayed strong, silent, and focused. The day was coming, and she had set the wheels in motion. Once she made the move, she would have to leave the country, if Justin found her, he would slash her throat.

It was only a matter of time before he would kill her if she stayed as the beatings were getting worse!

'Make no mistake womun, you're mine and you'll do as yer told!' He would spit in her face and remind her of her place every day in his thick Jamaican accent. 'Once we have the money, I'm taking James to Jamaica for a while to meet his family.' Dottie knew if Justin took the child, he would never bring him back. Time was precious and she would have to work quickly to make her escape. She could trust no one, she learned to be obedient around Justin and his family. Despite being a dutiful wife, she was subjected to daily abuse. Dottie bit her tongue and focused on the goal, to escape with her son - alive!

A black child and a white mother moved to America in 1963. She arrived in New York with six hundred dollars in her pocket and the promise of a job as a housekeeper with a wealthy family in Manhattan. She promised herself anything would be better than living with a violent partner in a loveless marriage in a deprived part of London.

New York was tough, she worked a seven-day week, cleaning, cooking, and playing with the children. She lived in with the family and their three children in a lavish apartment that overlooked Central Park. Her tasks were not exclusive to housekeeping, she went way beyond what was expected of her, Dottie brought all the children up single handedly, and saw to their needs as their parents travelled the country and attended political events. Dottie was hired by Senator Johnston, close friends to New York royalty and the husband of socialite Carolina Johnston. The children saw Dottie more often than their own parents and a special bond was created. Dottie lived for her son, and he in return adored his mother.

Her son, James, fitted in well and became great friends with the Johnstons children.

There was no going back to Ireland or England. The money she took wasn't hers, it was stolen in an act of utter desperation. She stole the money from Justin, from right under his nose as he slept. He worked with a thug called Danny Ronson, they collected protection money from shops and bars for a gang based in the East End of London. After they had been collecting, they brought their haul of cash back to Justin's flat on a Saturday night and someone came on the Sunday to collect the cash and drop off their commission. The money sat in the lounge in a black mail bag, no one dared to touch it. Justin left a switchblade razor beside the bag of money as a warning. Dottie knew there was only a short window of opportunity to steal the money once it was in the house. She had been planning her escape for over six months, every detail of her getaway had been considered. Mentally she had taken notes as a paper trail would only have endangered her life if Justin had found it. She had packed a small case and hid it outside at the back of the house and planned to buy what she needed when she got to New York.

A long-term pen pal had found her a job, she burnt every letter that arrived from America for fear of anyone seeing them. Dottie arranged passports for her and James and hid them beneath a floorboard in the bedroom. The night of the escape she was shaking with fear. Everything was laid out, the small case was left behind the outside bin, jackets and shoes were in position, her handbag was beside the front door and the passports were hidden beneath the outside door mat. She waited till Justin came to bed. After midnight she slipped out from beneath the covers and tip-toed over to the child, she had to move quickly! She lifted James from his cot and quietly went into the other room. She worked to her plan, gathering everything that had been left in place. She tied James across her chest and pulled on her coat and placed her bag across her body. Her hands were now free to pick up the small case. Heart pounding and adrenaline rushing around her body she lifted the money and crept out the front door. She worked fast and descended the outside stairs as she had rehearsed. Once she had the small case she walked out into the street, petrified she was about to be caught she raced to the main road and flagged down a taxi. Once inside she took several deep breaths as she contemplated what she had just done. She reached into the mail bag to look at the money and smiled. It wasn't over yet, but she could sense freedom, she had crushed three of his mother's sleeping pills into Justin's tea, it would buy her some extra time.

'Heathrow Airport as quickly as possible please!' Dottie sank back into the seat; James was oblivious as he burrowed into his mother's breast.

She had done it, she had bloody gone and done it!

She left with little from her old life, mainly the clothes on their backs and an outfit for arrival. At the airport she stuffed as much of the money into her bra as possible and stepped onto the aircraft and never looked back. It was only when the plane took off from the runway and climbed into the early morning sky, she heaved a sigh of relief.

The day Dottie landed in New York; President John F Kennedy was assassinated in Dallas. It was 22nd November 1963. Doris O'Malley Basa became Dottie O'Neill, New York was the perfect place to disappear into the crowds of people. She erased all signs of her past life. If she stayed in England, she would have died, she had branded herself a thief, it was a desperate act by a desperate woman. She promised herself once she got back on her feet she would pay the money back, but for now, no one was going to find her in New York. It took a while for her to stop looking over her shoulder. Dottie kept her head down and worked hard, within five years, she had established herself as one of the most sought-after housekeepers in Manhattan. When the children grew up and left for university, she left New York for pastures new. James attended Columbia University, a private ivy league university in New York City and was funded by Dottie and the Johnstons. Every cent of Dottie's salary had gone towards her son's education. She was going to see to it that he wouldn't live the life she had lived, she wanted him to follow the American dream and excel in his chosen career. A BA in Economic and Political science, James wanted to follow Senator Johnston into politics and Senator Johnston was willing to support him. Dottie moved to California as the New York winters became too cold and depressing. She headed for the sunshine in California and worked for one of Peter Malones associates. Her reputation for honesty and discretion fitted the bill for the perfect housekeeper.

Dottie had worked for me less than six months when I

discovered the astonishing truth as to why she had come to America. She was discretion personified and revealed nothing about her background. She protected her identity with ferocious intent. I confronted her one morning as we had coffee.

'Dottie what does the name Doris O'Malley mean to you? Your sister Christina wants you to know she loves and forgives you.'

Dottie dropped her teacup and sat stunned across the dinner table from me. She was unable to speak.

Dottie O'Neill was the sister of Christina O'Malley, Jon-Jon seniors' sister. Dottie was my father's aunt! It was a million to one chance she would end up as my housekeeper! We both had no idea of the connection, but it changed everything between us. I told her nothing about Jon-Jon junior being my father but suggested she took a few weeks paid holiday while I decided how best to deal with this astonishing turn of events.

'Your secret is safe with me, we all have skeletons in our cupboards, even me.' I said in the hope of softening the blow. She had kept her anonymity for over twenty years and now I had presented her with the truth. We both had to think about where we would go with it.

Dottie had been raised by a strong , powerful family in Ireland, The O'Malley's. I believe she had been sent to me but a far greater force than I could communicate with. It was meant to be, and I accepted this. What else was she hiding, I had to know why she had left the security and community of the O'Malley family.

When Dottie left, I took to my bed, the chronic head pains were intolerable. I took the prescribed pain killers the doctor had given me, but they only subdued the pain for a short period. I would black out the sunlight from coming into my bedroom and pull the cover way over my head. The dogs would all accompany me in bed.

Over the years I had been examined by many doctors at great expense and no one could pinpoint the precise reason for the extreme pain. Over time, I had learned to live with the excruciating discomfort.

I worried, as the pain was recurring more often than before. I never mentioned to Jemima as I knew she would be concerned, she suspected something was wrong as I was taking more and more time off work due to illness. When she questioned me about it, I would push it aside and simply say I wanted to work less and live a little more. Afterall, how much money does one person really need in a lifetime. I was at the top of my game; my company had such an impact with audiences we were being nominated for and winning television awards. The recognition was wonderful and winning credibility from the public was so important. It proved we were doing something right.

Jemima and I had more money than we could ever have imagined. For the first time in my life, I was content. I acquired two more abandoned dogs from the kill shelter and adored watching them settle into their new home. One was a rottweiler who had been terribly mistreated and never lived beyond the reach of his chain. He followed me everywhere and enjoyed a life filled with love and freedom at my beach house. The other was a boxer who was completely mad.

I finally felt at peace with life and had come to terms giving and receiving love from my dogs. Maybe Mr. Right wasn't out there. Maybe I was looking for another Jim knowing full well he could not be replaced. For the moment I was happy being an island on my own.

***

When Dottie returned to work, she asked to talk with me. 'It's a difficult subject but I want to you to know the truth' she said.

We sat down at the dinner table and poured some tea, Dottie talked about bringing up her son, alone without the help of a family.

'I met and fell in love with the wrong man, he was the wrong colour and the wrong religion. I fell pregnant out of wedlock and my father; a strict guardian of the family ran me out of Ireland.' Dottie gazed into her tea as she recalled her upbringing in the strict Irish showman family.

'My father said I had brought shame on the O'Malley family and wanted nothing more to do with me.' I could feel her pain.

'It had just gone 1961 and I was a white girl with a Jamaican partner, we struggled to find a church to marry us and ended up getting married in a register office, I wanted my child to be born in wedlock.' Dottie removed a faded photograph from her purse. 'This is James, my boy'

'I ended up in London after being chased out of Ireland by my brothers, they threatened to kill me if I returned.' Tears began to well up in Dottie's eyes.

I said nothing, I just listened.

'He wasn't much of a husband or a father; he beat me black and blue in front of his family. I hated him for it, I ended up in hospital once with broken ribs.'

Dottie was saying so much more than I had expected, it was time she let it all out. She had suppressed her feelings for years, now it was time to talk. I topped up our cups with more hot tea and listened intently.

'I had to get away, or I was sure he would kill me, despite being petrified with fear I had to escape. I would rather die trying to get away than exist day to day in hell.'

I reach out to the woman opposite and placed my hands on hers and listened. She was a captivating and proud woman, a true survivor.

'I stole his money and ran in fear of my life. I changed my name from Doris O'Malley to Dottie O'Neill. I regret nothing and thank God I am here today to tell the tale.'

I wanted to tell Dottie Jon-Jon junior O'Malley was my father, but I still had trust issues, despite this good woman confessing her deepest darkest secrets to me, I declined to tell her mine!

Diary entry – Saturday 27th March 1993

My beloved Doberman and loyal companion Mr. Thor passed away. He crossed Rainbow Bridge this morning. He was on his favourite spot, on the decking enjoying the sunshine, when I went out to sit by his side he was gone. As the vet took him away for a private cremation I broke down and cried. He was a wonderful companion and I loved him so very much. He wasn't just a dog; he was part of the family; he was a piece of my heart. A dog shows you so much unconditional love, they don't care, how much money you have, how expensive your home is and what kind of car you drive. I allowed the other dogs to see him before he was taken away, they all sat around him in silence, they knew he was dead. The loss is massive, and my heart is broken. Till we meet again my beautiful boy xxx

I cried for two weeks solid. I stopped the day I collected his ashes and brought him back home where he belonged. I was convinced I heard him wander around the house in the evening and once or twice I felt him brush pass my leg. It brought me a great deal of comfort knowing he was about.

Diary entry – Thursday, 1st April 1993

My mother as I knew her, is dead. I received the sad news today. I loved her but sometimes people do not want to be loved. Maureen Jamieson, I want to thank you. I never got the chance to tell you in life, just how much I appreciated your love. I'm sorry it turned out so badly for us. I never stopped loving you. Till we meet again, may your soul rest in peace. x

All morning, there was something gnawing away at me. I felt a powerful jolt on my side just after lunch time which almost floored me, I instinctively knew something awful had happened. My overwhelming desire to telephone Bill and Maureen could not be suppressed. I had Jemima call them for me, but their telephone rang out. I had no idea how to contact Billy, I don't think anyone did! I called out for Margaret and Gran to help me, but they never appeared.

Bill called Jemima and not me. He delivered the worse possible news and if I am honest, it didn't come unexpected. Maureen had died, cirrhosis of the liver.

Over the years she had become an alcoholic; her health had suffered considerably when she began to substitute vodka for food. Like all addicts she was consumed by her addiction, Bill was her drinking partner, instead of curtailing her addiction he merely added to it, it was like the blind leading the blind. It was a tragic end to her life and yet it was inevitable.

Despite my 'father's' years of philandering, he had always returned to Maureen. They fed off each other and I suppose they deserved each other. Maureen used Bill as her crutch when she became depressed or menacing and Bill used Maureen to hide his own alcohol demons or to recover from his disastrous affair. They were not my biological parents, none the less, they brought me up as their own and I considered them my parents. It was their decision to isolate me from the family and not mine, I had no control over this. It was painful and unforgivable, but they had their reasons and I had to respect this. Over the years we lost touch and became distant. Never a day went by when I didn't think about them. I reached out many times in the hope they would invite me back into their lives, but it fell on deaf ears. After being rejected so many times, I simply gave up trying. If things had been different maybe I could have saved them, the guilt was awful, here I was, with all this money and power but was unable to save the life of the women who brought me up as her own. My God, the newspapers were going to rip right through me!

By late afternoon, I was sitting on the decking, it was a beautiful spring day, and I was feeling sad, being melancholy is underrated. I was listening to Dire Straits, Brothers in Arms. The title track 'Brothers in Arms' pulled at my emotions with its beautifully sad guitar riffs, the unmistakable sound of the genius named Mark Knopfler. He seduces you and pulls you into this ballad with such epic magnetism, I shut my eyes during the guitar solos simply to soak up every note. The mood changed when 'Tunnel of Love' blasted form the Bang and Olufsen stereo. The production and quality were exquisite. I wanted the music to take my mind off Maureen's death, but it only reminded me of the many times we put on the record player, turned up the volume and we all danced around the lounge to the likes of Elvis Presley, Dusty Springfield and The Drifters. I cried tears of joy and sadness.

The dogs were unsettled and paced about the decking, the evening sky was full of stars, and I could see distant lights. The lights became brighter and clearer as they approached me on the decking. Several balls of light hovered beside the edge of the decking and the stairs that led to the beach, without warning they merged. An image began to appear, I could make out the outline of a woman. It was Margaret, my biological mother. She smiled at me, and I cried.

'I love and miss you so much.' I sobbed.

'She has gone, Maureen has gone! Is she with you?' I asked.

'Yes.' came Margaret's reply.

Margaret stayed for a while; her white dress swayed in the

gentle evening breeze as she floated at the top of the stairs that lead to the beach. She looked at peace and vanished as quickly as she appeared but not before she blew me a kiss and told me she loved me. The dogs howled and barked for some time after she left. They sounded like they were in pain. Perhaps they were crying.

It was the end of an era. I wanted Maureen to rest in peace with a respectful and reunited family send off. I decided to travel to Scotland and asked Jemima to contact Bill, I wanted to oversee the funeral arrangements. I wanted to pay my respects to the woman who cuddled me when I was a child, and tucked me into bed at night, placing a kiss on my cheek. And to Bill, the man who carried me on his shoulders and taught me how to tie my shoelaces and play chess. The first man I looked up to, it felt so important to reach out and make my peace with him.

The following day, Jemima assisted Bill in making all the funeral arrangements, she organised flights back to Scotland and Dottie stayed to look after the dogs and the house. Jemima finally got a hold of Billy and they discussed me coming over for the funeral. Despite leaving several messages Bill was difficult to contact. Why was I so terrified to meet him face to face, or was it him who was frightened from me?

Thursday - 8th April 1993.

As usual the heavy grey rain clouds welcomed us as we descended into Glasgow Airport.

It was a horrible day, everything looked like a negative, shades of grey and white. I hated being home it was so cold and unwelcoming. I realised today; my home was California and no longer the UK and certainly not Scotland.

I was nervous when we landed as I didn't know what to expect. Jemima warned me there were photographers waiting in the terminal. Someone had leaked to the press I was flying in for the funeral. I couldn't bare going back to the family home in New Weston, so I stayed away in a hotel suite in Glasgow.

Jemima had managed to trace Billy and met him at the lawyer's office along with Bill for the reading of Maureen's final will and testament. I did not attend. As expected, everything had been left to Bill, Billy, and Vanessa. I was not mentioned.

Jemima arranged separate suites at the hotel for Bill and Billy so we could talk in private away from the prying eyes of the press. Billy was the only one to show. He appeared late in the night and caused a drunken scene in the reception area. Jemima and a security guard managed to control the situation but not before a photographer had taken some pictures and a story had been leaked to the press.

I refused to see Billy in that state, I wanted to meet him when he was sober and lucid. No doubt Bill blamed me for the article in the press despite staying well away in my bedroom.

Maureen had an open coffin the night before the funeral, she was placed inside the chapel so family could go along and pay their final respects. I did not go to see her body as I wanted to remember her as she was when I was a child. Maureen was always impeccably dressed, her face was always made up, her scarlet lips and fingernails suggested she was a woman who took pride in the way she looked. I didn't want to think of Maureen any other way.

I prepared myself for the funeral and hoped that the newspapers and media would not spoil our privacy, but ofcourse they did.

The Day of Maureen Jamieson's Funeral
Monday, 12th April 1993

As expected, the chapel was full. Bill had taken the decision to embrace everyone as they came into the church and took the time to accept their condolences, he simply shook my hand and said nothing!

He obviously wanted to make a fast getaway after the service to the cemetery. As I walked into the chapel, the atmosphere changed, and I sensed all eyes were on me. I wore a wide brimmed hat which shielded most of my face. It was impossible to remain incognito, everyone wanted to see the world-famous celebrity who had flown in from Hollywood; was she smiling, was she crying, did she look upset, what designers coat what she wearing? Today, was about Maureen and not about me.

Inside the church was marked by a rare coming together of what was left of the family. Bill, and a sober Billy and other distant family members I had not seen in years. Any personal animosity was put to the one side as a mark of respect for Maureen. Bill was distraught, he was heartbroken over the loss of his wife and looked visibly upset as he sat in the pew. He was shaking and scuffling with himself, I was worried watching him. He looked gaunt and old, ravaged by the cigarettes and the alcohol.

Bill and Maureen had been married for 50 years and knew each other for many years before then. They had been friends, lovers and then a married couple, parents, and grandparents and now one had died, how was the other to survive. So many memories, so much love. No parent should survive their children, but Maureen and Bill had buried two of them. Over the years this church had been the host to so many family deaths. Bill stood up and leaned over the coffin, he was crying loudly, as Billy reached for his father Bill fell backwards and fainted at the foot of the coffin. The congregation gasped. It had all been too much for him. The incredible heat in the church, his lack of food, Bill had not eaten in two days, it was obvious he was undernourished and dehydrated. I rushed to his aid and along with my brother we sat Bill up against the pew and removed his jacket and loosened his tie. Overcome with grief, his face was ashen white, there was no consoling him. We stood Bill up and Billy and I slowly led him to the back of the church.

'Best not crowd him, let him get some air, thanks every-one' requested Billy.

Perhaps he let me help to keep face, maybe Bill didn't want the congregation to see him push me away.

This was not a drama to be carried out in front of an audience, it was a time for dignity and privacy.

Once seated and out of sight of the mourners, I asked him how he was feeling.

'Should I call an ambulance for you?' I asked whilst wiping the perspiration from his forehead with my tissue.

This request was met with condemnation. Bill had no intention of leaving, he simply wanted to stay for his beloved wife's service.

A small window had been left open allowing a gentle breeze into the back of the church. I held Bill's hand whilst Billy, my brother went in search of a glass of cold water. As Bill and I sat alone, he squeezed my hand tightly, nothing was said but we both knew this was his way of saying he cared. I looked at him and whispered.

'I am so, so, sorry Daddy!' he squeezed my hand even tighter as tears rolled down his cheeks.

'Please forgive me Catherine, I always loved you?' he whispered.

Suddenly, out of the corner of my eye I saw the brightest light appear in the church, it exploded through the church doors and moved towards the alter where it settled. Through it emerged an apparition, a young couple, a bride and a groom, the way they were dressed suggested it was the late 1940's, he wore a double-breasted black suit, his hair was greased back, and she was in a white simple lace dress and veil with a small posy of flowers. They were smiling, linking arms as they stood at the altar. Both were so incredibly young and happy. I looked around the church, no one seemed to have noticed the couple. I turned to Billy.

'Did you see that?' he looked at me, 'See what?'

His expression confirmed he could not see the young bride and groom that I could see. No one could, it was only me. The adrenalin was running around my stomach, today of all days I did not want to be challenged by any spirits. I could feel the trickle of perspiration running down the side of my face and I wiped it away with the back of my hand. My head was aching, and emotions were high, I began to shake, my senses were heightened, and I knew this was not going to end well. I began to fan my face with the Order of Service. On its front page there was a sepia picture of Bill and Maureen on their wedding day. This was the couple I could see at the altar. Bill's hand went limp.

'I want to be with my bride, let me go to her Catherine' he whispered. I saw his spirit rise from his body as it sometimes does just before death. I knew he was dying. I held on tight to his hand as his breathing became croaky and hoarse.

'Go to her daddy, go to Maureen and be together for eternity!'

Bill released his hand, and I knew he was gone.

He joined his bride. The newlyweds, Bill and Maureen Jamieson kissed, embraced, they turned to wave to me and then walked into the brightest light together, they looked celestial and youthful, destined to be as one forever in the afterlife. I was overcome with euphoria knowing they were together; it eased the pain of Bills death knowing he was with the woman he loved.

Bill died holding my hand, I felt his forgiveness shift into the palm of my hand and for one moment I was gripped by an overwhelming feeling of love. No words were required, we were finally reunited in his death.

We moved Bill into a side room, and I cradled his body as Billy discreetly waited for the paramedics. Whilst I held Bill, I reverted to that little child who loved and looked up to her daddy, I had an overwhelming sense of sorrow, maybe if I had reached out to Maureen at the end of her life, we could have restored our relationship and forgiven each other for the pain we had created, but we cannot change the past. Death is so final for others to comprehend but I know love keeps us together, in life and in death. Bill and Maureen were together and would be forever in their eternal happy place.

Maureen's funeral went ahead, and one-week later Bill was buried beside his beloved wife. I was not in attendance, I made my peace with the family and made my way back home with Jemima, to Malibu, knowing Bill and Maureen were both together, resting in peace.

CHAPTER 30

The Final Days Of Summer

Late summer 1994

Life was sweet, I was successful, wealthy, and content. There was nothing I couldn't buy. There was no man in my life, so I had fallen in love with myself and enjoyed every day to the full. What I lacked in my love life was more than made up for by the unconditional love I received from my dogs. Over time I learned not to search for a lover, if he was out there, he would find me but so far romance had eluded me. Not everyone was destined to meet Mr Right and no man I met ever came anywhere close to Jim. Jemima said I compared all men to him; I probably did judge all men by his standards, and I wasn't prepared to settle for anything less. Even after all these years I still missed him, no man could hold a candle to my Jim.

I was determined to be someone who did good in their life and had used my psychic ability to make something of myself. The paradoxes of a woman with multiple roles, businesswoman, charity ambassador, TV personality, international celebrity, property investor.

I was radiant and passionate in each role, but now I was happy to hand over the reins. I no longer coveted celebrity or money. It would have taken me ten lifetimes to have spent the money I had earned.

Jemima was happily married and expecting their first child. She and Tom had purchased a second home further along the beach in Malibu, which surprised me as Tom was very much a conservative, Beverly Hills type of character. They spent most weekends there and Jemima and I would often meet up. Jemima had taken a back seat role in the business as she prepared for parenthood. She was nesting, enjoying many hours shopping for baby clothes off Rodeo Drive and dropping by my home to show me what she had purchased. I absolutely loved sharing our free time together. Like me, Jemima had no delusions of grandeur and never flaunted her wealth. She was discreet to the point of being inconspicuous, even the ten-carat diamond engagement ring Tom had given her was often left in the safe as she preferred to attract as little attention as possible when she was out and about. Jemima's life now revolved around her husband and preparing for their first child. She lived in a bubble of happiness, and I hoped it would never burst. Strangely, I was never jealous, simply proud, appreciative, and fiercely protective of our friendship.

Jemima came from old school money, private schooling, and a famous barrister for a father. In contrast, I was a rough diamond, a working-class girl from Scotland. I wasn't born with a silver spoon in my mouth, I was new money as Jemima referred to it. I behaved like I had been brought up surrounded by wealth because of all Jemima had taught me. She had impeccable manners and never spoke about money, she taught me everything I knew regarding good manners and etiquette. No matter what she did she always looked graceful. Jemima made eating spaghetti look elegant, bringing the food directly to her mouth, keeping her back straight, unlike me she never slouched over the dinner table. Watching Jemima eat was like watching a chess player. Every move on her plate was calculated.

Beverly Hills was full of pretentious and fake people, and it was important you recognised this if you wanted to survive there. Jemima was an English Rose in a garden of artificial sunflowers. She was my best and most loyal friend and I felt blessed she was part of my life. I had lots of acquaintances and celebrity 'friends' but Jemima was my one real friend.

We discussed everything, there was nothing I kept from her such was the trust we had in each other, however, for months, I have been having visions, dreams, and feelings about my life coming to an end. I was not afraid to die, I was at peace with the thought of moving on, resting, and not being continually bombarded by the spirits of dead strangers who saw me as their only way to communicate with their loved ones.

My headaches had intensified, no doctor or specialist was able to offer a definitive diagnosis about the root cause or why I was in such intense pain. I was told, trauma from my childhood or adolescence probably contributed to my chronic headaches. I was prescribed medication which did little or nothing to reduce the discomfort.

My quality of life was becoming so bad I no longer could endure the pain; I was taking prescription medication to sleep and pain relief medication throughout the day. I became a bit of a recluse and began to dread coming face to face with the living or the dead; I stayed home to try and avoid any lost souls trying to communicate with me and immediately stopped any private consultations, instead I practised meditation in a quiet area of the house. The day job was the last place I wanted to be, so I no longer took part in any new television productions or attended any business meetings. Instead, I observed from afar and agreed or vetoed any plans which were risen at board level. As company founder and Chief Executive I had overall control of the business. My company now concentrated on syndicating and selling our shows throughout the world. The demand was phenomenal and generated revenue beyond our expectations. I became a global success. The 'Spiritual Encounter's show 'and 'Catherine Jamieson Talks with the Dead' were massive hits in over 20 countries.

My extraordinary gift had now become my mental burden, mentally and physically the pain was taking its toll on my whole body. I would shy away from the world and found solace living like a hermit in my Malibu home. I had little or no contact with the outside world. Jemima and Dottie were the only two people I allowed into my home. I had always been the freak in the room, the girl who speaks to the dead. The only way I could control the number of spirits who tried to communicate through me was if I stayed at home and kept the outside world away from me. I had security cameras and patrolmen on site twenty-four hours a day keeping people away from the house. Depression became my new companion, and my mental health began to suffer. I was overeating and drinking much too much simply because I was bored and who could resist Dottie's wonderful concoctions she would leave in the fridge for me to dine on. I was merely existing and not living. Days morphed into nights, nights became excruciatingly long, and I feared going out of the house. For the first time in my life, I feared the dead. I refused to visit with Peter and Irina Malone as I was worried Max would manifest and drain me of my energy. I was one of the biggest names in America and people were starting to ask questions about where I was and what I was doing trapped in my home all day, blinds and doors closed to the outside world.

Apart from Jemima and Dottie, and the dogs, no one could connect with me; despite all the followers and all the thousands of fans around the world I was essentially alone. I was having irrational thoughts and took to staying in bed for long periods of time during the day. Dottie would serve me food and walk the dogs along the beach. I would stand and watch her from the decking, unable to venture down to the sand as the sunshine made my headaches even more painful. I took more medication to help with the pain, this only dulled my senses and made me sleepy. I had a new house mate; depression, she stopped calling on me and decided to move in. We comforted each other.

I never felt special, and I never felt pretty, I only knew

I was very, very, sad, and alone. I had everything but nothing. I found it difficult to get over the death of Mr. Thor, my loyal Doberman Pinscher who was sadly taken from me. Despite it being almost a year since his death I still missed him. He simply went to sleep and never woke up. How many of us would like to think this is how our life would end, pain free and with dignity, falling asleep and never wakening up. Everything I had ever truly loved had been taken from me. Had I sold my soul to the devil and craved the celebrity and money more than happiness? Would I have been happier at home back in Scotland, a mother, a wife to Jim, leading an ordinary existence. Jim may still be alive, and we would be together. My life had been a journey littered with headaches and hauntings and now I wanted to get off. I could no longer live my life for others.

I was trapped in a gilded cage, and I wanted out. I had come to a decision, I wanted to end my life, I no longer wanted to suffer. I wrote letters to those I cared about and acknowledge those who tried to protect me. I asked them to forgive me. I felt a sense of relief and calm reaching the decision to end my life. Those close to me will know, it wasn't a case of why but when I would do it, as they saw me slip deeper and deeper into a terrible depression. There are two certainties in life, your birth, and your death. The Dalai Lama describes death as a natural process, a reality that must be accepted if you remain in this earthly existence, there is no escaping death so why worry about it. I have accepted death and welcomed it. Death for me could not come soon enough. I simply wanted to rest in peace. I had made my peace with Bill, the man I have always thought of as my father. I had returned to my roots and reconciled with other family members I had little contact with over the years. When I left Scotland, I knew I would never return and was at peace with that decision.

I had lost touch and became distant from people and reality. My gift for communicating with the dead was the one thing about my complicated identity that seemed positive. It was my shield and it protected me from real life situations, now the dead were killing me, the pain they brought with them was no longer tolerable. I thought about dying everyday but never had the courage to take my own life. I could feel my body shutting down as the war of attrition between body and mind slowly diminished. Everything I loved I started to hate, the crashing of the waves, the sounds from the beach, the wind, and the birds. It magnified in my head and increased the pain. I was unable to shut it out, or turn down the sound. It went on and on and on.......

Diary entry – Thursday 18th August 1994

I listened to Kate Bush, her incredible album 'The Sensual World' and watched the sun go down from behind the glass doors. Its natural beauty is phenomenal and overwhelms my soul each time I look at it. I missed Mr Thor, he was such a big part of my life and I adored him. The dogs have been guarding me all day, hanging about me, and looking at me forlornly. They have been whining and burying their heads into my side. I wonder what they are sensing. I have been a mess of emotions today and my dogs have picked up on it. There is a belief that dogs have a sixth sense and can sense death....

At night I would kick back on my sofa and watch the sun go down beyond the windowed wall.

I lay down on the sofa and placed the headphones over my ears just as Kate Bush began to sing, 'This Woman's Work'. Having lost myself in Kate's lyrics and haunting music, I closed my eyes and sank into the cushions on the sofa. I felt myself drift off, it felt peaceful and soothing. Tonight, there has been no pain, no anxiety, no self-doubts. It's been a good night. There was a feeling of expectation in the air, it was focused all over me, much like the dogs I can sense the dead. I could feel someone was in the room with me but I kept my eyes closed as I feared it would be a lost spirit who would drain my energy looking for my guidance. It was difficult to resist opening my eyes but when I did, I was presented by an overwhelming feeling of love in the room. For one crazy second, I thought I was dreaming or Jemima had organised a surprise party and invited everyone I loved and missed, if I was dreaming, I didn't want to waken up!

My mother Margaret was standing beside me with my father Jon Jon. They looked so young and happy. Jon-Jon had his arm around Margaret's waist, and they were smiling down at me. Maureen and Bill stood across the room, smiling. They were as I remembered them when I was young. Maureen wore her bright red lipstick, they both appeared to me like angels. A hidden light seemed to radiate from everyone. Granny was nagging the Grandad I never met but I recognised him from his photographs. Gran looked over and smiled at me. To her side was Jody, she was glowing, appearing in great splendour, she looked beautiful. Mr Thor was by my side, he appeared majestic and magnificent. I pulled him to me, and he excitedly licked my hand and face, the way he did when I had returned home having been away. He was so pleased to see me! Mary, looked beautiful, she walked towards me and knelt down by my side.

'He has sent his Angels to surround and protect you' I heard her whisper.

There are lots of souls here, some I recognise some I don't. There was no heaviness, I was feeling entirely serene, surrounded by all the people I loved.

Have they come to join me, or have I come to join them? There is no pain, I look around the room and I want to greet and talk to everyone. But there was one person missing!

Over the years I have been asked so many times,

'Where do we go when we die?' There is only one group of people who can answer this question accurately, the dead.

From the moment we are conceived we have a soul. The armour we wear as we walk the earth disintegrates on death and the soul lives on forever. In most circumstances the soul moves from this earthly plain to the afterlife. It is here we are finally reunited with the ones we love; this can be a man, woman, or animal. They wait for us. I cannot describe the afterlife, nor can I say if there is a heaven or a hell. I just know the dead walk amongst us looking for ways to communicate their message.

I always believed when I died, I would be with the one's I loved. I looked around the room and walked amongst the people I loved. There was someone missing, someone I had to see. Where was he? The room was bright as the rising sun light permeated through the window blinds. The space was busy and there was lots of chatter, but I could not make out any of the conversations, it was simply a morphed muffle of words. My head pain had completely disappeared, and I felt truly wonderful. The words, 'No more bitterness, no more resentment' continually ran through my mind.

I breathed in joy and extreme excitement as I looked around me. I moved through the crowded room; my eyes darted around searching. I glanced into the corner, and there he was!

Jim, my beautiful Jim with the stunning smile and wonderful kind heart. My kindred spirit. He appeared heavenly, handsome, and exactly as I remembered him. In an instant our eyes locked, and he beckoned me over to him with outstretched arms. Everything I ever wanted was standing in front of me. I threw my arms around him and held on tight. The feeling of love was irresistible, I was safe, I was fulfilled. I was loved. All I ever wanted was here in my arms.

'Take me with you, Jim, I don't want to live this life anymore without you.' I sobbed.

'Come with me wee girlie, I'm never going to let you go again!' he said.

I glanced over at the sofa and saw my limp body, I looked like I was sleeping. I was dead, but my journey into the afterlife was just beginning.

Jim held my hand as we went out into the night air. We kissed under the stars with the sound of the waves crashing on the beach. Mr Thor followed us out onto the decking. The gruelling head pain had disappeared and was replaced by a feeling of joy and contentment.

Ironically, I felt alive, more than I ever did when I was living.

I was asked many, many, times in my career,

> *'When we die, do we join the ones we love on the other side?'*

> *'Yes, we certainly do. We join the ones we love when we die'*

The End or is it just the beginning?

Catherine Morag Jamieson's Legacy

Catherine Jamieson was just 33 years old when she died. Cause of death, Glioblastoma, an aggressive type of cancer that growths within the brain. Even if it had been detected sooner, the prognosis was terminal. Dottie discovered Cats body in the morning, within an hour it was headline news, within a week the front of the beach house was swathed in flowers placed by devoted fans and well-wishers.

In accordance with Cats Last Will and Testament, she was cremated, and her ashes were scattered over the sand in front of her Malibu home.

A self-made multi-millionaire, Cat's estate was valued at over $60 million, with no children or partner, she had carefully chosen organisations where her wealth would make a massive difference to those in need. As an animal lover many charities benefitted from her estate, donations were received by over 100 dog and cat shelters all over America.

The Catherine Jamieson Foundation was created. The organisation supported young adults who were raised in care homes who had no or little funding available to attend college. The foundation also supported teenagers who were being brought up by grandparents and other family members. Scholarships once awarded did not have to be repaid.

Mary's daughter inherited $100,000 dollars and a fund was set up for Vanessa which she could only access from the age of 21.

Billy was included in the will, but there was one requirement. Cats' estate would fund him to attend a residential programme at The Priority Clinic in Scotland. There he would receive the best possible treatment and support for his drug addiction. If he could survive the three-month residential course and remain drug free for a further year, he too would also inherit $100,000. If he failed the drugs test, he would not receive the inheritance. The idea reeked of failure. Billy attended the world class treatment centre for three weeks before climbing over a side wall one afternoon. He was later found dead with a syringe in his arm in a well-known drugs den in the outskirts of Glasgow.

Dottie was rewarded for her loyalty; she bought a car and a small condo with her legacy. She was financially secure for the rest of her life. Jemima hired her as her housekeeper and between them they looked after Cat's dogs.

Dottie invested in her son who, after graduating university forfeited a career in politics and became one of Americas biggest psychic mediums.

As a descendant of the O'Malley family, he was born with the gift of second sight. He used his exceptional gift to help and guide people from all walks of life.

Dottie, discovered her estranged husband was still alive, living in the same flat in Tower Hamlets, she sent back the money she had stolen all those years ago.

She added interest. Dottie wrote on the thank you letter.

'Thank you for the loan, please find attached a cheque for £3,000. The money I took saved my life and that of my son. I have never forgotten and have lived every day hating myself for stealing the money. I always vowed to repay it and today is that day. I have made the cheque out to Battersea Dog and Cat Home Payee only. Best wishes. Your estranged wife'

Cat left Peter and Irina Malone $300,000 dollars as a thank you for all the support and encouragement they had given her. She asked them to donate the money to a charity of their choice. The Malones continue to have Max visit them. Sometimes he has the energy to appear beside his beloved piano bringing great joy to his parents.

The bulk of the estate was left to Jemima, Cat's most loyal friend, she inherited Cat's shares in the company and millions of dollars in real estate. Jemima decided to sell the business to a television mogul for an undisclosed amount of money. Jemima sits on the board of several charities and donates hundreds of thousands of pounds to various charities around the world each year.

As the main beneficiary of Cat's estate, she never disclosed how much inheritance she received. As Jemima said

'It is obnoxious and vulgar to discuss one's wealth!'

Cat's diaries are kept under lock and key in the vaults of a Los Angeles bank. They are now the property of Jemima and not for public consumption.

Two months after Cat died, Jemima gave birth to a baby girl. Cat, if she had survived would have been the child's god mother. Jemima named the little girl, Catherine Jamieson Truman after her extraordinary best friend.

Catherine Jamieson, an ordinary woman who lived an extraordinary life.

Acknowledgements

Thanks to Kyle my son and my close friends, Julie and Aileen who had to listen to me go on for over a year about writing this book.

Much love to Mr Thor, a loyal Doberman who sat beside me

on the sofa as I wrote most of the copy for my first novel. He crossed over Rainbow Bridge in June 2021 and broke our hearts.

About the Author

Chrissie Heron was born in Paisley in 1964. She spent most of her life working in the advertising departments of several Scottish commercial radio stations before climbing the ladder to take on the role as Managing Director. Disillusioned with the media she waved goodbye to the corporate world and set up her own marketing company. She lives with her son in Lanarkshire and dabbles in writing books, travelling, and spending time with good friends.

Follow Chrissie Heron on social media:

Facebook and Instagram chrissie.heron

Email Chrissie at chrissieheronauthor@aol.com

Website www.chrissieheron.com

First published in Great Britain in 2021 by Amazon kindle. Copyright Chrissie Heron, 2021

Cover photography: reproduced by kind permission of Ronnie Bales, Photographer from Paisley.

The moral right of Chrissie Heron to be identified as the author of this work has been asserted in accordance with the Copyright, Designs and Patents Act 1988. All rights reserved. No part of this book may be reproduced in any form or by any electronic or mechanical means, including information storage and retrieval systems, without written permission from the author, except for the use of brief quotations in a book review. This book is the work of fiction and, except in the case of historical fact, any resemblance to actual person, living or dead, is purely coincidental. Every effort has been made to obtain the necessary permissions with reference to copyright material, both illustrative and quoted. We apologise for any omissions in this respect and will be pleased to make appropriate acknowledgements in any future edition.

A CIP catalogue record for this book is available from the British Library.

Numbers TBC Hardback ISBN TBC Ebook ISBN TBC

Kindle ISBN and Audio CD ISBN and MP3 ISBN TBC

Printed in Great Britain
by Amazon

77278509R00246